CW01560544

LOST CITY

ALI MITCHELL

Book Cover by Milbart Arts

First edition 2024

This novel is dedicated to:
Jordan, Joe, Indigo, Mirella, Annie, Chloe, Skye, Ash, Alex, Tobei, Reba, Abi, Ruru, Mya, Paige, Vic, Gab, Lark, and Zoe.

To my favourite author, Marcus Alexander, who started this dream and passion of mine when I was just eleven years old (Thanks for all the support too!)
To my parents, whom I would not survive this world without.
And to my sisters, my lights in this world.

And finally,
This novel is dedicated to those who read as an escape from reality. I hope you fall in love with these characters just as much as I did whilst writing. They've been a part of me since I was just 12 years old.
I hope they'll forever be a part of you too.

Welcome to Lost City.

Though this book is marketed as Young Adult, this is for the OLDER part of Young Adult. 15+ since there are depictions of violence, death, and gore that can be uncomfortable for younger audiences.

Prologue

Achillea and Ambrosia had never seen the stars.

Not because they spent so much time inside their ruined house, or because they never went out late, or because they never left their shelter in general. It was because they couldn't see the sky altogether.

Their life was mundane. They had a plan for the following day. There were rules to be followed, so why would anyone break them to risk standing out from a dulled crowd?

It wasn't enough to be trapped without light. Nothing was ever enough for Achillea. Unlike the rest of her kind, she *yearned* for a reason to venture out into the unknown, to experience an adventure outside of the norm. The places she read about, the legends she grew up with, and the myths that were sung to her always seemed so exciting. Much more so than the life handed to her on a platter.

Legendary folklore were bedtime stories while she was growing up – it included this fantasy-like place. This *supra terram*. Where the creatures were different from them. With blunt teeth. Curved ears. Without a lust for blood like many of Achillea's kind owned. *Supra,* they didn't have powers to protect them. They had nothing to defend themselves with. What kind of world was that to live in? They seemed to need catching up. The people above knew nothing of the inventions in Achillea's home. Simple things: different fabrics for clothes, electronic devices, and lights.

However, not all these stories were as wonderland-like as the last. Achillea could never deny or ignore the nightmares that plagued her mind as well.

They were raised with the knowledge that the creatures above the earth's surface (those not crushed beneath) were preferred over them. *The chosen ones*. Well, that's one twisted truth. All the cousins knew of the species above the ground was that they were favoured over their own kind. According to these legends, Mother Nature was the one to choose. Therefore, they were named the 'chosen ones'.

Pluto, God of the Underworld who goes by many names in many mythologies, was said to have sworn to protect the people down below. So He separated the inferior. However, Jupiter, God of the Sky, is said to have twisted it into a more forbidding story that eventually would've been passed to the Royals underground. The people hidden under the surface were the mistakes. They were never to have existed in the first place. As a result, He did the righteous thing, and pushed the imperfections deep into the earth's core. Never to be seen again, which meant that His puppets above were safe from harm. That was how the story went.

Despite this, Achillea kept scavenging. Kept listening to her folk songs, reading the novels, and dreaming of what it was truly like in the place she wanted to be most. But most of all, and most importantly, she wished to see the bright lights that illuminated the darkness of the night sky once the sun had disappeared.

The spectacles named *the stars*.

One late night, Achillea snuck up to the rooftops, climbing on the ruined frames of her shelter, and pulled herself up onto the broken tiles, careful not to fall through. She laid down, facing up to the stone dome caging the place she was forced to call home, taking in a deeper breath.

I wonder what it feels like to have the wind blow bitter cold against my skin.

Ambrosia joined her. Gradually, it became a small tradition of theirs to sit and stare, wasting their time picturing a life in a different reality, a world entirely removed from their own. "One day, we'll make it up there. We'll find a way, I'm sure of it." Ambrosia gripped her cousin's hand tightly beside her. Achillea brushed it off, denying her words. *She's young and hopeful.*

However, that fantasy became something to hold onto with all their hearts. They would make up stories in the dark, their own version of a delusional source of comfort.

Their families, on the other hand, had a different idea of what they considered to be fun. They would steal and commit treason for giggles and dares. They wanted to take over the monarchy for themselves. Wanting to have complete control over the city, but what happens when one accomplishes this goal, and the others are isolated, handcuffed in a cell? The Royals hurt them, so why shouldn't they hurt them in return?

The cousins were viewed merely as children to everyone, but there was an advantage to this. If they were children, no one would suspect anything should they suddenly disappear for a few days, right? And if their families held all these fairytales about the creatures up above, someone must have seen them. So that meant there was a way out.

Achillea wanted to see, once and for all, what the constellations looked like dotted across their heads.

"Ambrosia, we should go," she said.

"Huh?"

"Up there, supra, we should go." Achillea pointed her finger above their heads. "Just think, if we make it up, we could actually see the stars instead of just imagining. With our own eyes!"

"How exactly do we do that, Achillea? I want to, I really do, but how? We can't go without a plan, Lea."

She simply shrugged her shoulders, turning her head to Ambrosia. "I don't know just yet, but I could find a way. I'm sick and tired of waiting."

She could find some way up above, Achillea knew it, but not without Ambrosia. They imagined what those chosen creatures looked like, dreamed of what the weather was like, wished to see that galaxy. Together. It was never an individual thing, and so if she saw the stars, she would see them with her favourite person. Not anyone else. Not even on her own.

Ambrosia's lips stretched across her cheeks, showing off her two deep dimples.

"I'm surprised you haven't suggested it sooner, hun." Then the next thing they knew, they were walking through deserted streets, roads and pathways towards the library.

Days turned into weeks. Weeks turned into months. Months turned into years.

Achillea and Ambrosia always searched for something more. Every so often, they'd grow distracted by books of different constellations and tales tying to them. Achillea thought she had found everything linked to the stars, but apparently not. In fact, there were hundreds and hundreds of books on the matter.

A year passed when they found something that fed them hope in escaping. A few friends decided to join their mission, sick of the patriarchal society they were trapped in, of how everything worked in accordance with each other—how the Royals led everyone with Nobles by their side to oversee the mission. How sections of the city would help provide for all. How, according to all, everyone was happy. *They ignored the poor peasants.*

In the group of friends, there was Marina, the eldest who begged to oversee this mission. Peri, who just wanted to be included—whatever Marina, her sister, did she wanted to do too. Marcose and Celeste were best friends and wanted to see what the fuss was about. And finally, Draven. Both

Ambrosia and Achillea's close partner in crime. Perhaps some would become bored eventually in the new world, if so then they'd simply return. But they refused to fail without even trying.

The last time someone recorded going above ground level was approximately 200 years ago. They returned with scrapes and bruises, and decided to hide the simple button that allowed the platform to rise. It's said some of the greatest *intelligent vampires* created it, but didn't do a good job concealing it. According to resources, when the platform hit the top of the cavern, the rocks opened up completely, crumbling to the bottom.

"Easy. There's seven of us here. Between us, finding a button embedded inside a brick on a tiny castle tower will be easy!" Marcose said, trying to speed the whole process up, becoming more impatient with every passing moment.

"Who says it's definitely on that tower?" Draven muttered. "The books could be lying. They're ancient afterall."

"No way. It has to be real, there's nowhere else." Ambrosia replied. Draven's eyes narrowed on her.

"Okay, then, even considering that, how do we get in?" For once, she was speechless, and without a plan. The castle perimeter would be heavily guarded.

"Fire?" Ambrosia shrugged her shoulders up and down, and looked to her cousin for an answer. "A distraction?"

Vincent Cinus loved fire.

And because he loved fire, Draven Cinus found the perfect opportunity for his little brother to be involved in this grand scheme, even if he was too young to join them *supra*.

Vincent created a distraction for them by setting a local building alight. He was mesmerised by the flames, the way they danced in front of him and his fingertips. But one thing led to another, and it began spreading. So once the screams began, fear seized his mind and he ran to his raven haired brother as fast as he could, despite the warning of staying behind.

While the Knights were distracted by the fire close by, the small group of friends snuck inside the castle grounds with a small child toddling after them.

Achillea, having revised the blueprint plan of the castle several hundred times beforehand, led everyone directly to the tower. With her chest heaving, she raced up the spiral staircase, eager for what would happen next. *It's happening.* She was going to see the stars with her favourite person in the whole universe. Her hope was as pure as could be, adrenaline filling her veins.

Sneaking in was the easy part and the distraction was the precursor to breaking and entering; everything up to this moment had been child's play. But now they had to find the button embedded in dulled graphite bricks.

They didn't wait to begin the search, hastily rushing from side to side atop the castle tower. *We must look ridiculous,* Draven thought to himself for what felt like the hundredth time over, as he caught a glance at Ambrosia inspecting a pile of bricks on the floor corner.

He went over, ushering Achillea towards her cousin. Through the shared look between them all, they seemed to have a similar thought: *Rubble like this had no place on top of the castle tower.*

Achillea bent down and began pressing her thumbs into the ruins before, finally, the brick at the bottom of the pile moved inwards with little pressure. A jerking sound below immediately rang in their ears, shaking the tower as if a tremor had struck. Achillea clinged onto Ambrosia as a short Vincent was heard squeaking from the side, "They're coming!"

Knights were sprinting up the staircase in an attempt to stop the group from their next move; not even Achillea knew what she was doing now, though. Draven whipped his head back to the boy hanging onto the door frame just in time to watch Vincent launching himself closer, behind his brother for protection.

"What the—"

The ground shot into the air, as if the landing they were searching had detached from the tower itself. Draven toppled over and landed in front of Vincent who looked ecstatic at the surroundings moving below in a thick blur. Stepping towards the edge to see the home they were leaving down below, he screamed over the noise in awe, "Whoa!"

The cousins held each other's hand, grip tight, and stared up at the cavern roof, watching a crack form above. Achillea held her breath – the realisation her dream may become true suddenly too overwhelming. Ambrosia held her even tighter, as if she would never get another chance to.

The ceiling crumbled. Pieces of earth falling onto smooth, and spotless stone. All until a hole formed in the dome, a gateway into a new world. To explore the unknown.

Achillea saw a glint of the stars.

And, *oh,* how beautiful they were.

Her eyes instantly glued to the starry sky dotted above their heads. At first, she tried counting them. She didn't expect to see so many span such a small glimpse of sky, but they seemed to be endless. Too beautiful. So breathtaking. She kept losing track, and had to restart, over and over again. *20, 27, 49, 52, 63...*it never ended! Suddenly all those sleepless nights, all those hopeful days spent in the library, and all the tears shed over a broken desire—suddenly they all seemed worth this tiny moment. She smiled until her cheeks ached with fresh pain. Her heart calmed to a more reasonable speed, comforted at the sight unfolding before her. Tears glistened in her eyes before sliding down her cheeks in pure happiness and relief. Her fantasy became her reality. And every moment she stared, speechless at the world hiding away, something was telling her, *It was worth the wait. It was worth it all.* The stars were real. And if stars were real, then what else was?

Ambrosia quickly drew Achillea from her daze, drawing her attention to the new world surrounding them. Grass, flowers, nettles, things they'd only ever fantasise about seeing all around them. Nudging her side, they're eyes land on a small family walking out of a dimly lit village, with a tiny baby in woman's arms.

"Those must be the creatures. *Hominies,*" Achillea muttered in amazement. She didn't expect them to be so similar to herself.

The clothes were the biggest difference; they truly were behind in the grand scheme of *time.* They wore rags, thin ones at that, and their hairs were tangled messes. Achillea herself was dressed in many layers of black clothes with millions of pockets to carry everything she needed and, of course, her weapons were strapped to her waist with a cape over the top. She was like a shadow, easily slipping into darkness. Her hair had been straightened, and extensions had been put in just that morning, so the brief change was still fresh in her mind. But as they got closer, the family began staring directly at the odd group. Achillea stepped toward them, a friendly, warm smile plastered on her lips, fangs on show, because she thought nothing of it. Surely they had heard of their kind before, like how the *Nosferatu* were aware of the *hominies'* existence too.

Then the father stopped his partner and child, continuing to stare at them. They started mumbling under their breaths about the small group, Achillea able to catch some familiar *anglicus* in some places but not enough to form a coherent sentence in her mind.

How odd to hear it in person.

Achillea was particularly focused on the fact she didn't know many *anglicus* words. She was the strongest speaker of the group, but not the best by far. Everyone below spoke Latin, however, the books she read said the main language up top was english. At least, in this specific region anyway.

So she learned a few basic *anglicus* words, but not enough to insist they came in peace.

So instead, Achillea raised her hands up in a sign of no harm intended. And she said in broken *anglicus*, "It well." She narrowed her eyes on the family edging back as the man looked to his home village not so far away. Their eyes were smaller, with rounder pupils instead of slits and their teeth completely flat. No fangs in sight. Her eyes dropped to the toddler in the woman's arms, with short, black hair that was thin and wispy, and a smile lighting up the sky. She laughed a little, pointing at Achillea, gurgling some more.

"Why did you follow? I told you to stay behind," Draven questioned Vincent behind the cousins.

"I'm not a kid! I'm sick of you going off on your own and never involving me!"

"You created a distraction for us! Isn't that enough?! Besides, you *are* a kid, and it might be dangerous up here!"

"It's your fault I'm up here! It's your fault I wanted to come join you! It's your fault—"

"Just shut up!" Draven yelled at the top of his voice, and immediately regretted it, guilt washing over him in an instant as Vincent's face broke for a split second. "Vince, I—"

"I'm just a baby to you, aren't I?" He paused. "A baby would do this," he stamped his foot, "a baby would do this," he started to cry dramatically, hiding the fact that he was truly weeping slightly, "a baby would do this—"

Vincent marched past Draven and towards the baby. The family took steps back in alarm and he stared at her for a short while.

"Vincent?" Achillea asked softly. He raised his boney hands up and pointed them at the baby like claws, and snarled, shouting for a cruel, cruel joke. "Vincent!" Achillea grabbed his arm harshly, and pulled him back as he spat at the small toddler just as she opened her mouth to scream.

However, the creatures from the dark didn't spit saliva, they spit blood. Pure vampire blood. In that moment the woman cried out, leaping back whilst holding her baby girl closer to her chest. Her thin hair – once black – faded into an unnatural white.

The woman pointed at Achillea, screaming in a shrill voice.

"Demon! Witch!" she sobbed, and Achillea took a step back, letting Vincent go as her heart hammered inside her chest once again. This time, out of fear.

"No, no, no."

But that was the only word she knew well enough to say in objectification. She had heard those words before. Read them in books. Demon and witch. *Daemonium. Maga.*

The family ran back to the village with tears staining their cheeks and their little girl screaming in pain.

Achillea looked up to the stars, as if seeking comfort from them, her limbs freezing. *Don't take it away from me,* she thought to herself, but who was she begging?

This scene changed everything. The story was altered for the rest of history. They had changed their own fate. Their destiny unclear from that moment forward. Perhaps for the better, perhaps for the worse, that's up to you to decide.

Guards came forward to detain the group of strangers. Too quick for the creatures to fight back. The humans were violent.

One of Achillea's friends was stabbed in the back for retaliating as a threat to never defend themselves. To never beg for freedom again.

So, they were all dragged into cells with weak bars, through wooden huts, and stone shelters. Whilst imprisoned, the guards never put them on trial. Only gave them food and water on occasion. The humans didn't know what demons were held in their cells. And the *nosferatu* never knew how to kill the humans back then either. They thought over it too hard, and assumed it would have a catch instead of plain and easy.

It turned out to be very simple. Let them bleed.

In the books they had read, these *hominies* were depicted as the perfect ones. But they didn't seem so flawless up close. *They murdered innocents.*

Time passed, yet never moved at all. The remaining vampires were imprisoned for over 300 years. And even then, they weren't able to find a way back underground straight away. The place they tried so hard to escape from was the place they craved for the most.

Was it all worth it, though?

Achillea pondered for years, decades, and even centuries. She never found an answer for it, because she didn't want to face the complete truth. No, it wasn't worth it. Because she lost four of her friends to her fantasy. She grew up in a prison cell. After that first night of escape and freedom, she didn't see the stars for over 200 years.

It seems Achillea's kind were trapped below because of how different they were. How flawed. And just for that, they were to be kept away, trapped for eternity in their city.

But they had that city. They had that home. And they still wanted to escape anyway. How ungrateful.

Little did Achillea, Ambrosia, Draven, and Vincent know, it would be around 400 years until they would get to pay back the village that held them hostage.

Little did they know that approximately 400 years later, they still wouldn't have seen their lost city.

But they were close again. They could hope.

This story begins on Thursday the 8th of October, 2037. In that exact same town, named Hillark. This time, Achillea's ready to take back what's rightfully hers.

~*Impetus*~

Savannah

8th October

Everything is as it was meant to be. For once.

Zack and Oskar are in a tree, racing to the top to see who's the fastest. Whilst Luka and I stand to watch at the bottom. There wasn't enough room for all four of us to jump in and join the competition, but I didn't exactly leap at the opportunity to get back in a tree, not when I broke my arm from falling from one a few years back.

Luka turns his head to look at me, and when I catch him, he smiles and reverts his attention back to the idiots. My lips tug into a smile too, despite him already looking away. Even a simple glance causes goosebumps to prick up all along my arms.

"Ha! I win, once again!" Zack cheers, his head bobbing above the wilting autumn leaves at the very top. He punches the air, and exclaims proudly at the top of his lungs, "I am victorious!"

"Such a cheat—you got the easy side. More branches there, and stronger!" Oskar points out. "I want a rematch!" He makes it to the top, perching himself comfortably beside Zack on a branch of his own.

"You're such a sore loser. It's hilarious."

"Will they *ever* stop bickering?" Luka laughs beside me, looking up at the two.

"I don't think that's possible. I thought you, of all people, would know that," I comment. He glances back at me, and my nerves freeze up.

"There's hope, isn't there?" I return his smirk and a moment passes between us, shared in time, and all is peaceful again.

Until a blood curdling scream erupts from the background of the streets.

I flinch violently, shivers freezing through my spine. The hairs everywhere on my body – my arms, necks, legs – stand up, and I stop breathing completely. Then suddenly, Zack cries out from above us. When we whip our heads up to him, he's falling down and fast from the top of the tree, scraping his clothes against the twigs and branches, cutting his skin.

"Zack!" Luka exclaims breathlessly, and quickly steps below, ready to catch him with open arms, but instead, Zack grabs the edge of Oskar's clothes as he tumbles. Oskar bends down, and reaches for his wrist, clasping his fingers around his skin and heaves him upright, bearing his teeth until his cheeks go red from the weight.

"I got ya, I got ya—" He lowers him onto a stronger, steadier branch below his feet, and once his footing's secured, Oskar lets him go, and only then does he release his breath into the crisp, cold air.

"You okay?" I call up to Zack. He nods a few times, not daring to look down at us below, especially when another quieter scream echoes in the distance, towards the centre of town. I keep my eyes on Zack a moment more to make sure he doesn't fall again, whilst Oskar reaches over to him and through the branches to loosely hold onto his arm, offering him support. He then looks out towards the sound's origin, as if he could find the source from this far away. Only then do I turn my head towards the houses. We're in the woods right now, which is south from the town we live in: Hillark. Never have I ever heard a scream like that.

"Is...everyone alright?" Luka breaks the silence first. His eyes dart around the area, scanning our surroundings, searching for danger. I look at him, edging closer towards me, eyebrows raised, looking for an answer. His eyes are wider than usual, and I can't help but notice the shaking of his hands as he hides them behind his back.

"Maybe it was a couple kids playing stupid pranks on each other," Oskar mutters, staring at Zack again, who's taking deep breaths. In through his nose, out through his mouth.

"Is everyone okay though?" Luka repeats. I merely nod, pursing my lips together. He narrows his eyes on me, glancing up and down, watching my own shaking hands. "Are you sure?" I give him a shrug of my shoulders and drag my attention back onto the path leading to our houses, a sense of dread filling my veins.

Zack exhales heavily above us, and finally speaks out, "Let's just go. I don't want to stay here any longer."

"And you'd rather go into the town where we just heard that freaky shit come from?" Oskar exclaims, almost laughing. "That's how horror movies start!"

"Where else would we go?" Whilst them two make their way down the tree, carefully and gradually, Luka steps beside me, gazing into my eyes.

"Savannah," he speaks softly, plain and simple, yet his tone always manages to catch my heart off guard. Which I have a love-hate relationship with, I've discovered. "Like Zack said, I'm sure—"

"Yeah, yeah," I brush it off, and roll my shoulders back until they give a satisfying *pop*. "It's probably nothing." And yet I appear exasperated. I meet his eyes with my own, and give him a small smile. He gives me a wider one in return. One with false confidence.

"Exactly! So try not to think about it much." He nudges his shoulder into mine, and I'm grateful he's here as Zack and Oskar leap down and land on the ground. Luka looks away in time so I can hide my cheeks burning a ghastly crimson.

'Try not to think about it.'

But there's a voice at the back of my head, repeating over and over and over again, *what if, what if, what if.*

Because *what if* someone's in trouble? *What if* someone's in danger? *What if* that scream was a cry for help?

MATTHEW: Anyone wanna go to the shops with me? I'm bored and I have money so I'm going to spend it recklessly and impulsively.

PIPER: I would if I could, but sleep is more important! And I'm tired. Therefore, goodnight people.

ME: It's the middle of the day...

PIPER: And?

ME: Nvm.

OSKAR: me, Zack, Luka and Savannah are out now anyway. We can meet you there if you want?

MATTHEW: Okie! See ya soon :))

PIPER: OH! Did anyone hear that scream btw?

ME: We did, yeah.

ME: Are you okay?

PIPER: Of course I'm okay! I'm in my bed, safe and comfy. You people are in the wilderness, are YOU okay??

ME: What do you think?

PIPER: whatever. Don't die anyway :)

ME: Same goes for you too. Goodnight. Ttyl.

PIPER: MWHA <3

Originally, I planned to leave as soon as we got out of the creepy woods, but then Matthew said he wanted to go to the shops with us. I want to see him, despite seeing him five days a week. He's like a brother to me, after all. Any chance I get to see him, I seize it.

The air is tight and suffocating in Hillark. I notice Luka watching everything around us, just in case.

A few streets in, I catch his eyes, and I simply smile his way, but he barely smiles back. I know him well – but the whole comfort thing I'm still working on, so considering saying something to him sets a flame in my stomach. But I won't let it stop me from at least trying to help him relax and keep calm, like he's done for me so many times. So despite the anxiety twisting and churning at the bottom of my stomach, I go over in my head once more what I'll say, and then...

"Luka." I step closer to him, shoulder to shoulder, and he turns his head. "You're the one who told me not to think about it." He immediately looks away.

"I know."

"So, why are you an exception?"

"I'm only looking out for you guys. Is that such a crime?"

"If I'm not allowed to worry, surely that means you're not allowed to."

He rolls his eyes, and for a split second, he brushes the back of his hand against mine. My breath catches in my throat – like an electric shock between our hands, and I almost look down to see if there was an actual spark.

"Again." He holds his hands up, facing me with a smile on his lips that makes my heart skip a beat or two. "Only looking out for you."

"Well." I take a silent breath in as deeply as I can, attempting to settle my nerves. "I appreciate it." He drops his hands. "But there's no need."

From that moment onwards, he seems less on edge, more talkative, and more present.

"Why, hello. I thought you'd be around here!"

Oskar's the first to look up from the path at an approaching Jess.

Oskar's face quite literally lights up. Big beaming smile, eyes brightening, his two shallow dimples on show. He even wears a thin coating of blush covering his cheeks and nose. It's been a while since we've seen Jess. He attends a different school – a private one at that. And we miss him dearly. It's never been the same since he left.

He's as short as a 12-year-old, despite being the oldest of us all. He has big almond doe eyes, his hair a soft golden shade, like an early autumn sunset. I know he wants to dye it all black someday, despite his unique cross between blond and brown. He has a split in his left bushy eyebrow, which Matthew and Zack encouraged him to do because he was too scared to do it on his own. He wanted to do that for years before *actually* shaving it, and he hasn't complained about it since, and on top of all that, he has the thinnest lips that Oskar can't help staring at every now and then.

"Jess, oh my god!" Oskar throws his arms out, bursting with excitement, and speeds up to be the first to steal a hug from the smaller boy. He wraps his arms around his shoulders, squeezes tight, and Jess laughs, the sound echoing around us. He happily returns the gesture, his head peeping over Oskar's shoulder to stare at us. He waves, catching my eyes. I smile and wave in return.

"You're alive!" Zack exclaims, patting his head. He's smiling, looking up at us as he and Oskar let each other go.

"Of course I am! That school won't be the one to finish me off. At least not just yet," he remarks.

"What will be then?" Luka questions, tilting his head towards him with a playful smile that catches me off guard. "Life, and all its glory? Parents? Sierra?"

"Ha, Sierra? She's the one keeping me sane in my house." He smiles and glances at Oskar when he mutters, "University will be the death of me, and I'm not even starting it yet, I'm just applying." He lists off each reasoning with each of his fingers, keeping count. "There's eczema too, external family—"

"Eczema? Is your eczema... alright at the moment?" Oskar asks carefully, yet eagerly, as they lock their eyes onto each other. I'm just as relieved when Jess nods happily.

"Still a struggle, but not as bad as it was a month ago or so."

"That's progress!" Oskar claps his hands together, and slaps Jess on his back and he chokes out a laugh.

"Congrats, Jess, we're happy for you," I say, but no one's prouder than Oskar. After all, he's the one who's helped Jess the most with his skin. And now Jess is glowing again.

"Thank you," he says, flustered.

He joins us to meet Matthew, his best friend. His smile is bright as he lays eyes on Matthew as if it's been years – a big toothy type of grin, laughing out loud when Zack points it out. "Look at this little face!" But he doesn't care how silly he looks, which is as it's meant to be.

Oskar watches Jess' eyes beam with joy, he blushes a bright red again, covering his cheeks with one of his palms, unable to look away from him it seems. Sometimes they're unbearable to watch, living so oblivious to the other's feelings.

Matthew's face lights up, matching Jess'. He rushes to us, trapping him in an almighty tight hug, maybe to make sure he doesn't disappear from his arms. Matthew isn't much of a hugger really, but whenever Jess is around, that's thrown out the window.

"You're here!" Matthew exclaims. "You're actually here? It's been too long!"

"Matthew," Jess muffles his speech against his best friend's clothes. "You're strangling me!" He pokes his side and is set free, engulfing a ton of air for his lungs dramatically.

"Sorry!" he laughs. "I'm just excited, it's been a week or two, hasn't it?"

"It's been too long," Luka points out. "We need to hang out together more."

I nod towards him, relieved we have this moment before he's swept away again into the abyss of school work he has.

"We should kidnap you," Zack jokes, but I swear he might half heartedly mean it.

"Oh my god, yes!" Oskar exclaims, and edges closer to Jess.

"We are *not* kidnapping Jess from his sister!" Matthew warns them, pointing his index finger, flicking between Oskar and Zack, but his playful smile gives him away. "That might be your worst idea yet."

Zack rolls his eyes, and Oskar stares down at Jess, now beside him again.

"Well, if Jess says it's okay then surely—"

"I don't want to leave Sierra," Jess interrupts Oskar.

"We could take her too—"

"*No!*" Matthew, Jess and Luka all say in unison while I watch the madness unfold, giggling.

"Anyway! Moving on!" Matthew stops them before it's taken too far. "Jess, join us. Catch up session?"

"What do you think I'm here for?"

"Oh, just to see our fabulous faces of course." Zack leans into Jess' face. "Why else?"

Jess merely rolls his eyes, pushing his face away from him, palm pressing against his forehead.

"You're unbelievable."

For that single moment of reunion between us all, I forgot about the deadly scream I heard beforehand. But soon enough, Oskar breaks the trance.

"Did you hear it?"

Jess looks up at him from his side. "Hear what?"

"The scream."

"Oh." He looks down, at his feet more specifically. "Yes, I did. I was in my room." Then it must've happened between his room, the woods, and possibly Piper's house if she heard it too. In the middle of all those – or worse, there were a few screams, but we're all thinking it was just one that all of us heard. "In fact," Jess continues, "Sierra ran in, panicking. Our parents couldn't care less, blaming it on the 'kids these days'. They thought it was all a prank so they didn't care if Sierra was worried or not. Told her to simply calm down."

"Is she okay?"

He nods and adds, "A little shook up afterwards, but nothing pokemon couldn't solve." Suddenly, I'm hyper aware of everything. What I could lose if this scream was deadly.

I notice the way Jess stands between Matthew and Oskar, who look like bodyguards with them being so tall and him so tiny. And I notice the way Zack and Luka always walk beside each other, Luka in the middle to be beside me as well, and I even notice the way Luka glances at me every so often. When his skin brushes over my hand once or twice. The way Oskar's scraggly, long, and extremely frizzy black hair bounces with every step in front of me.

Our laughter fills the air. It's familiar. It's safe. It's home. I don't know what I'd do if I lost it.

"We need to leave, Julia! Now! We're running out of time, so please, let's—"All of our attention is drawn to a man shouting by the counter.

"Honey, you can't seriously think what you've seen is real, do you hear yourself? I have to finish my shift, okay? Why don't you go relax until I'm off? If it's something you want to show me then—"

She's being so reasonable about it, but the man raises his voice even higher, sending shivers down my spine, listening intently.

"I'm not showing you anything! We're heading out of town, together. I swear, it's not safe here anymore! Please, baby, believe me."

It's not *safe*? I widen my eyes, breath catching in my chest. What did he see? What did he hear? And what does he know? My stomach folds into itself. I swallow hard, forcing a lump down my throat, but it doesn't make it any easier to breathe. What does all this mean? My chest is getting tight. *Suffocating*. Safe?

A soft hand brushes over mine, and everything freezes in time. It's enough for me to grab my bearings and get out of my mind, grounding me to the floor. I exhale sharply, too scared to bring my eyes up to see the guy who's helping me. I know who it is, and if I look into those clear ocean eyes, I won't be able to look away again. I gulp down a few deep breaths, in and out, best I can, averting my eyes to my feet. In for four seconds, hold for four seconds, and out for four seconds.

"I can't just leave."

"Please."

Luka wraps his hand around mine as gently as he can, as if he's trying not to alert me, shake me from my daze, not trying to bring any more attention to him trying to help, but every nerve is tingling in time with my heartbeat. I bring my eyes up to catch him looking towards me at the same time, joining eyes in sync.

The couple lower their voices and I hear them walk away from the till completely.

Luka breaks the trance we've found ourselves in first, sighing heavily, shaking his shoulders around, loosening them. He drifts his eyes around the shop, and at the others before landing them back on me.

"Jesus." He shakes his head. "They couldn't talk in private, could they?" he mutters, and flinches when someone bursts out of the shop. I turn my head to see the man storming out, swiftly followed by Julia, calling after.

"Agreed," Matthew says, "that didn't need to happen in public."

"That's worrying," Jess mutters nervously. I nod, staring at my feet, before noticing Luka still holding my hand. My cheeks flush. "Really worrying."

"You okay?" Luka asks beside me, and he nudges my hand, and once again, I merely nod, unable to find the right words to answer. And that's when he squeezes my hand goodbye and let's go completely.

"I think I'm gonna go," I announce, lifting my eyes to see them all, looking anxious.

Oskar murmurs to Jess, "Yeah, I think that's best for everyone right now. Some weird shit is going on." He then nudges Jess' shoulder. "I'll walk you home."

Jess' cheeks go bright red and he smiles.

"I'd like that."

"I'll facetime you later, Jess!" Matthew exclaims. "See you tomorrow?"

"Hopefully!"

"Mum! Dad!" I shout once I've arrived at my house. "Did you hear a scream earlier today? I was wondering if you knew anything about it 'cause me and my friends are worried about it." I kick off my shoes and I drop my bag onto the sofa. Am I talking to a house of ghosts? I walk through the living room and into the kitchen, looking at the mess of the sides, splashed with water from the sink, knives on the floor and cupboard doors left open. My stomach plummets.

"Mum? Dad?"

I frantically begin searching the house. Every single room. Under beds, and in closets. In the bathrooms, and behind doors, but *there's no one in the house*. I'm alone. Completely and utterly alone in my own house.

I try calling both of their phones several times until realising my mum's is on the desk in the living room, and my dad's is on their bed upstairs.

"What the hell is going on?"

$\mathcal{S}$avannah

8th October

"Luka," I say, trying to hide the tremble in my voice. Piper's asleep. And other than her, Luka is the only one I want to go to for this. I try to catch my breath. But I only end up feeling more nauseous and light headed than before. "I can't find my parents."

"Oh, okay," his voice rings out in my ear. Am I overreacting? Maybe he thinks I'm pathetic. Maybe I *am* pathetic—

"Their phones are here, so I can't call them. The kitchen's a complete mess, which is *really* unlike them, and there's no note on the fridge. And the back door's unlocked!" The words pour out of me. Maybe I want him to tell me it's nothing. That it's not something to worry about, because my mind is a tornado flying with different situations and *what ifs*. And it can't seem to stop.

"Have you locked the back door now?"

"Yeah."

Maybe I wanted advice.

"Are all the windows closed?" he asks.

"Yeah."

Maybe I needed him.

"Okay, I don't think there's anything more you can do. I can't think of anything."

"This doesn't feel like enough."

"I know it doesn't, but that's all you can do. Unless you wanna come to my house for a few hours," he says. I can feel my cheeks heat up at the idea, but I shake my head instead, and remember he can't see me. He adds, "But then they might come back and wonder where you are."

"I'd have my phone on me so they could text me," I murmur, but it doesn't sit right with me.

"Is the car still outside your house?"

"Yeah."

"It doesn't look good, Savannah."

"What do you mean?" My heart picks up the pace.

"What you've told me points to them leaving... and not exactly by choice."

Everything is still, all is quiet on both ends of the phone. I'm waiting for a 'however,' but nothing comes. I drift my eyes over my living room, and I fall onto the sofa cushions, running through my options, clouded by anxiety. *What if they're dead? What if they've gotten kidnapped? What if they just left to go somewhere without me?*

I'm home alone in a town where freaky things are beginning to happen. Just a couple of hours ago, we heard a blood curdling scream for what we hoped to be a child playing a prank. A man warned his partner that this place is no longer safe, that they should escape together whilst they still can. Everything must be linked. A small part of a larger play.

"Are your parents home?" I ask.

"No. But they weren't meant to be here anyway. It's my brothers that are worrying me."

"Your brothers?"

"Riley was meant to be taking care of Thomas, but no one's here." Dread fills my stomach. "Riley's phone is here and the PS4 was still on when I came in." I want to find them as well – surely they couldn't have gotten far – both Luka's family and my own parents.

I want to find Luka's brothers, because his voice trembles when he talks to me now. He shudders. His breathing turns shallow, like he can't quite get enough of it, and I want to fix that so desperately. Where to start the search, I have no idea. Leaving my house seems so daunting and overwhelming. But I'd rather have company than drive myself nuts.

"Can I come over then?"

"I thought you were going to stay there?"

"It sounds like neither of us should be alone in our houses right now," I say. I stand, heading towards my bedroom to find a thicker hoodie from my wardrobe.

"I can't argue with that," he says with relief drenching his words.

"We'll wait for your brothers to come back. Then I'll go, okay?"

"There's no rush." I smile a little before my phone vibrates. I look at it, turning Luka on speaker phone to see messages from the group chat.

MATTHEW: I don't want to alarm you guys, but I cannot find my mum and I am *slightly* worried?

"Oh no," I mutter.

"What?"

"Matthew's message."

He's silent for a moment, and then says, "Just seen it."

ZACK: my mum's at work but my dad should be home and he's not here.

OSKAR: Dad's at work and Mum's disappeared, but she usually randomly goes off on her own anyways sooooo.

OSKAR: What about the rest of you?

ME: Piper's asleep. I'm on call with Luka and my parents aren't home.

ZACK: Did we miss something whilst we were out in the forest, do you think?

LUKA: maybe. My brothers aren't here.

MATTHEW: Someone call Piper and Jess. I'm tryna get a hold of my mum.

ZACK: I'll call Piper.

OSKAR: And I'll call Jess.

Gasping, I leap out of my skin when I hear my back garden gate crash open and slam close.

"What? What is it?" Luka says urgently in my ear. "Savannah?"

"Give me a second." I edge closer to my window, peering outside to overlook my garden, all for tears to rush to my eyes instantly. Fear seizes my legs and I almost fall.

It's painful to breathe again, "People," I manage. "Luka, people in my garden. They've broken down my gate." I swallow, dryness filling my mouth with a disgusting aftertaste.

"I'm coming. Can you get out?"

I peer over the edge outside. I can't see them anymore.

Instead I hear the backdoor rattle.

"I don't think so," I say in a high pitched voice.

"Then I'm coming over." My mouth is ajar when he's slamming his front door shut. "Are you in your room?"

"Yeah."

"Is the door closed?" I look back at it sitting wide open. I rush towards it as silently as I can and shut it.

"Just done it."

"Is the front door unlocked?"

"I don't know," I whisper pathetically. "If it isn't, a key should be on top of the frame or—no, it's beneath a plant pot, maybe?" I hold my breath, straining my ears to hear rustling beneath my floor boards. They're trying to break in. I edge closer to the wall below my window, sinking to the ground without looking out, bending my knees to my chest.

"Almost there, just keep breathing, alright? It's gonna be fine." Luka is panting and out of breath.

"Are you running?"

"Couldn't you tell before?"

Muffled voices shout from below me, glass shatters to the floor. I hear them climb into my kitchen with a bang, feet clattering on the ground. I can't stop myself from breaking down completely.

"I'm gonna go, Luka." I rub my eyes with one of my palms. "I can't risk making much noise." I shiver with tears streaming down my cheeks.

"I'm almost there, Savannah. Just hold on."

"I'll see you in a minute." I hang up on him. I stuff the phone into my trouser pocket, hugging my knees closer to my chest, resting my chin on top. I'm not sure where they are now. I think they've made it to the living room, inspecting everything around them, a mess in their wake.

I'm trembling, shuddering violently. What should I do? What *can* I do, except wait for Luka to help me get out? We all know I'm not fast enough, or sneaky enough, or strong enough to get away from these burglars. Are they burglars? They're breaking and entering, so they must be. *What if they have a knife?*

The front door opens.

"Hey, who the hell are you?" The first man shouts in a shrill voice followed by a crash, clearly being knocked over. They continue, "Jack! Now's your time to show Vincent what you can do, and actually do your fucking job!"

I clasp my hands over my mouth tightly, heavy footsteps bounding up the stairs, my chest too tight to breathe.

I shut my eyes, bringing my feet closer into my body as my bedroom door whips open. Someone's running in, and rushing towards me. I don't know what shutting my eyes will do from the dangers in my house, but at least I won't see them. I won't know when it's coming, I won't know when my times up or where they take me. I can go in peace. I'll go without a hassle. They stand in front. They loom over me. They—

"Savannah, it's me!" I immediately look up at Luka offering his hand. "I'm here!"

He made it in time. *Again.* I grab his hand, and he pulls me up to my feet. Still trembling, still unsteady, still shallowly breathing, but now Luka's here. He's in front of me. He's staring at me. Luka's *here*.

"Run now, talk later," he says. "Keep up, and remember to breathe." He starts to rush out the door, squeezing my hand as tight as he can. I stay as close as I possibly can, so there's no chance I'll be left behind.

He abruptly stops, and steps forward like he's shielding me – no, he *is* shielding me from something. A man. *A burglar.*

"Go out the front door," they say calmly. I peer over Luka's shoulders. The man's in a black cloak of sorts, and below that cape is a uniform I've never seen before. Patterned purple shoulders, a gold outlining the many layers of fabric, black buttons in the middle, one side draped over the other. Lifting my eyes to his head, he has jet black hair, with a curtain-like parting, his eyes a bright piercing blue. He says, "The other guy will be waiting in the kitchen. Avoid him like the plague and hurry up. Zayne won't be happy if he sees you." His voice is deep and low, rumbling my ear drums, and his skin the palest of white, unnatural, almost sicklike. He's armed. He's glaring. *He's hesitating.*

Luka tugs me along, and past the intruder. I look back at him, glancing at my room, my teddies, my belongings. Will I ever see them again?

"Thank you," I barely whisper to the stranger, my eyes linger on his face a moment longer and he looks right through me. I turn to Luka, leaping down the stairs. He barges through the front door, and I slam it close after us, and we keep running, running, running.

I don't know what happens when we stop. If we ever do.

Are we safe? Or are we running from the inevitable? Maybe this is something we can never escape from.

"Savannah." Luka's panting, pulling my hand to a stop, his grip still warm and tight against my skin. "Slow down, we're out!"

I shiver when Luka lets go of my hand. He leans against a wall, trying to catch his own breath whilst the cold breeze pinches at my skin. I edge closer towards him. What if we're being watched? I search, unable to recognise where we are. I can't tell if we're somewhere I should know. I don't know if I've been here before. I don't know anything. My head's hazy.

I can't think straight, everything's a blur.

"Hey," Luka says beside me, voice still breathless. He knocks his hand against mine. Sparks set off again, but I don't look back at him, because I feel more tears at the back of my eyes. Then I realise there's no point hiding it and let go. "Savannah, we're okay, we got away, they're gone." Then he holds onto my sleeve, and I look up, locking onto his eyes immediately. He stares at me with such intensity, I might burst. He's seeing all the feelings

I've bottled up inside. Like he not only sees my fear, but feels it too. "Are you okay? Did they do anything or did I make it in time?"

Of course I'm not okay. I'm reliving something I'd much rather forget.

He sighs and steps away from the wall, walking towards me. "Anxious, then?"

I swallow, and nod.

And just like that, I'm caught in Luka's arms. So sudden, but I still wrap my own hands around him instantly—like it's second nature. I know where to rest my head on his shoulder, and I know how tight to hold him. He knows where to place his hands on my back. He knows when to squeeze me tighter, and he knows how to offer comfort when I start crying into his clothes. We know how to react, like this has been done before.

Hearing my heart beat outside of my chest instead of inside is like listening to a constant ticking time bomb, and just as I think he's about to let me go, he holds me even tighter, head falling next to mine.

"I'm here," he says softly. "I'm right here, and I always will be. Okay?"

"Okay," I mutter, feeling my face turn red. "Any ideas on what's going on?"

"I know as much as you." I loosen my grip on him first, because I want to breathe properly again and be free from the tightness of my chest. And yet, I don't take a single step away from him. I *do* take my hands back to rub the tears from my cheeks, whilst Luka holds my arms loosely. "Savannah, I—" Whatever he has to say has to wait for another agonising second. His phone starts ringing. He flinches, breaking his trance, digging his hand into his pocket. "Oh." He shows me Zack's name lighting his lock screen up. He accepts, playing it on speaker phone. "Hi—"

"I've tried Savannah's phone like five times, man. I'm really worried about her, is she okay? She said you guys were calling, and she stopped texting so suddenly—"

"She's here with me," Luka interrupts, glancing over at me.

"Sorry. I had a bit of a situation," I add.

"I assumed so." He sighs out of relief. "I'm glad you're alive. Oskar's called Jess, and he's okay. He's with his sister right now."

"And Piper?" I question.

"I couldn't get a hold of her." I take my own phone out, hoping to see some sort of message from her, a phone call, anything to indicate she's okay, but nothing pops up. "Listen, Oskar's coming over to mine now. Matthew too, come join us."

"Piper," I murmur. "No way am I going anywhere without knowing Piper's safe." It might be unreasonable, maybe I *should* just go join them, but I won't be able to calm down without knowing she and Jess are safe.

"Piper's close to your house, right?" he asks.

"Yeah, we're close. We'll stop by her house on the way to yours, Zack," Luka suggests. They said Jess was safe with his family still. I need to focus on finding Piper. One thing at a time, right? So I take a deep breath, looking around at the street lights flickering on, one by one.

"Sounds good, but promise me one thing..."

"Anything," Luka swears.

"Keep me updated, and keep texting." I want to ask who he thinks could do something like this, who would be prepared to, say, kill us? But after what just happened, I decide to keep my mouth shut, because something's going on and I don't want to be a part of it.

"Of course."

"Bye for now. Stay safe, I'll see you soon."

"You too. Bye," Luka and I say in sync, and he hangs up.

For a moment, neither of us do or say anything. Do we have to be sneaky in a town we call *safe*? This is the place we were raised. The place I met everyone I know. The familiarity—

"I suppose we should get moving before anything else happens," Luka breaks through the silence. He shoots Zack a text, then puts his phone in his pocket again. I can practically hear his hesitation before doing so, but then he offers me his hand to take.

And everything is still again. "Shall we?" he says softly. I shift my gaze up, and towards his eyes. "I don't want us to get separated. I figured if we're, erm." He scratches the back of his neck nervously. "Like, holding onto each other, we...won't suddenly disappear randomly. That's my train of thought, that's all." He gives me a stronger smile and I intertwine my fingers with his, and his cheeks burn a little red and he turns a little sheepish. I let him get a tight hold on my hand, warm and secure.

"You don't have to justify yourself." He nods, and looks away from my eyes.

And that just shatters my heart, just a little.

Luka checks every corner before letting us turn. He checks every alleyway, scanning houses to see if anyone's watching, all the time. Every so often he squeezes my hand as if to make sure I'm still here. It makes me feel less alone. The emptiness at the back of my mind from not seeing my parents is throbbing, and it probably will do so for weeks to come, but I won't rest until I see them again. I need to see their eyes light up, their smiles when they see me, and hear their soft voices when they speak. I need them like how Luka needs his brothers. I'll help him too. I'll help anyone I can in any way shape or form. As long as there's hope to see them on a brighter day, I will forever keep searching.

It doesn't take long until we're at Piper's door. Once we're in her street, I try to let go of Luka's hand to run, the suspense killing me, but instead, he just runs with me, tightening his grip on my skin, sending my nerves in a panic all over my body.

I don't call her name, I probably should. I rattle the door handle, but it's already unlocked. Dread sends shivers down my spine. I freeze.

"Savannah? Can I go first?" Luka asks when I'm just staring at the door for a few moments, letting my anxiety climb the height of Mount Everest.

"Sorry," I mutter and swing the door open.

"GET OUT!" A pillow's thrown at my face, and falls to the floor. "GET OUT, GET OUT—" She stops, and I watch her edge forward with wide eyes. "Savannah?"

"Piper." I gasp for air, a smile growing across my face.

"Oh my god." She chokes on her words, sprinting forward. My hands are set free, and this time, happy tears spring out of my eyes at the sight of a bedraggled Piper.

She leaps onto me, arms around my neck, and legs around my waist. I hold her up with all my strength as tightly as I can. So I can keep her safe from anything outside of this house. Anything outside the door that Luka's closing, anything in the streets, in the road, in anything. I bury my head into her messy short auburn hair, the jagged split ends rough against me, but I don't care.

"You're here," I mutter more to myself in reassurance. "You're actually here, oh thank god."

"Oh, hey. Sorry, Luka, didn't see ya there." Piper waves briefly at him, before reattaching herself to me, and I cannot describe the sense of relief I experience washing over my chest. Like someone feeding me air again after suffocating for days.

"I'm glad you're okay, Piper, and I *think* Savannah is too."

I don't let go. Her hair brushes over my cheeks when she leans back, to stare intensely into my eyes and I peer right back into her huge dark brown ones, and into her soul. She raises her eyebrows and smirks, letting out a sigh.

"If we were a couple, this would be a really romantic kiss scene, right now."

Luka chuckles behind us.

"Do we have to be a couple to kiss?" I ask.

"I want my first kiss to be with someone I love, romantically, Sav. Don't you even know me? No offence of course, you're quite sexy, but not my type."

I grin, letting her go so she can lean back whilst still holding onto my arms. She lands on her feet, flicking her hair out from her eyes, and clears her tear stained cheeks.

"So, what happened for you to be in such a rush?"

"Well, I'm sure you've heard some stories. But I was essentially attacked." I frown as her jaw drops. "Luka came and saved me—"

"A bit dramatic—" Luka interjects.

"It's true though. And I needed to know you were okay, Piper. But if you're now awake, why didn't you answer any of Zack's calls?"

"I had no idea this was happening and in my defence," she stares right back at me, "I woke up ten minutes ago to find my phone spammed with messages and calls. And my mum was gone." I take her hand, squeezing it tightly. She twitches, glancing at Luka and then at my hand. "They wrote me a note. I've got nothing else though. I've heard a few screams." She shrugs my shoulders and stares at me again. "I'll show you." She tugs me along and through the hallway and into the kitchen at the back of the house. I usher Luka along and he quickly follows. She leads us in and points at the fridge. A note beneath a magnet. In messy, and rushed handwriting, it reads:

Piper,
Don't leave the house. It's not safe anymore. Try calling family to come get you so you can be safe. They don't know you're here. Stay safe, darling. We love you more than anything in the world, and that will never change.
~ All our love, Mum and Dad

I wipe my tears from my face, lifting my head to watch Piper, who's just blankly staring at it. Lights are on, but no one's home.

"I'm sorry." I say.

"It's ominous," she states.

"It is."

"It hasn't hit me." She shifts her gaze to me, scrunching her nose up. "You know?" I nod at her, circling my fingertips on her skin.

"Are you okay?"

"It said, 'they don't know you're here.' What does that mean? Like what specifically, and who specifically? I just..." She shrugs her shoulders, up and down, an invisible weight bearing on them as she rubs the bridge of her nose. "Of course I had to be asleep."

"I'm surprised you didn't wake up," Luka says and glances his eyes over me. "They were quite loud —" Piper shoots her head up, and back to look at Luka.

"How do you know it's the same people?" she asks.

"We don't. We shouldn't assume," I add, shooting a look at Luka. But what if I'm wrong? I just don't want Piper to panic.

"How long *was* I asleep for?" Piper nudges my shoulder, reverting my attention back onto her.

"Everyone's missing someone," I tell her. "Not just me. Luka's brothers, Matthew's mum. People's families."

I stare back at the note, and so does Piper. Looking at the rushed handwriting, the jagged edges, a hole when the pen dug too hard into the paper. *They.*' It was more than one person. If Piper weren't asleep, then she'd be gone too. My stomach drops ten feet below at the thought. I look back up to her, and she meets my eyes.

"I'm glad you're here," I tell her. "Because as you already know, I—" Before I can even finish my sentence, she bursts in, rolls her eyes in a playful manner and continues my sentence with me instead of taking over.

"Love you more than words could tell." It cracks a smile out of her too. "Yeah, yeah, you say it all the time. It's kinda annoying, but I'll forgive you." But I know she knows I mean well. She looks at Luka, and punches his shoulder. "Goes for you too." He looks almost relieved, softening his expression when he glances between the two of us.

"More than words could tell," he echoes. I nod.

"Ever tell."

$\mathcal{S}$avannah⭐

8th October

"Zack wants us to meet him and Oskar outside Jess' house," Luka announces in the middle of the kitchen. He lifts his eyes to mine. "They've gone to get him, 'cause he's stopped answering his phone completely."

"What?" Piper interrupts before I get a chance to. He glances at her, and then at his phone.

"That's what it says." He begins typing again. Frantically.

"Have you told him that Piper's okay?" He nods, and sends off another message.

"And I added that we'll head over soon, but that we'll take our time, okay?"

Piper rolls her eyes, crossing her arms over her chest. "What more is there to do here anyway? It's wasted time if we stay here longer than we need to." I purse my lips together, staring out the window at the darkening sky.

"You could at least pack a bag. We didn't—" I glance at Luka. "I didn't get a chance to grab anything, and Luka was in a rush too," I tell her.

"What do we need?"

"I don't know, but—"

"Okay, well." She turns around, leans past me, and grabs the biggest knife from the breadboard. "Got what I need." I clench my hands into tight fists. "What is it?" She looks at me. "You're both looking at me like I've done something wrong."

"Do we really need a knife?" I say helplessly, feeling repulsed at the mere sight of it in her hand, despite knowing she'll use it for self defence.

"We don't know what's out there, Sav!" she exclaims, staring into my eyes, gesturing her free hand about in the air. "If they took our family, what do you think they'd do to us? I mean, you were attacked, right? What if they come back to take us all next? I'm not gonna go out defenceless." Her eyes are wide, and frantic, waiting for an agreement, but I say nothing.

"She has a point," Luka says softly. I glance at him, his lips pursed, a thousand meanings in his eyes.

"Do you guys want one? Plenty to go around."

"No," I answer immediately. "I'm fine, thanks." Luka shakes his head and she shrugs.

"Let me go check upstairs real quick," she says, giving me a smile and a wink, before quickly disappearing down the hallway. Knives to protect ourselves? It still feels wrong. Or will it always feel like that?

"Are you okay?" Luka asks me gently. My eyes find his immediately.

"I'm not sure. I don't know. You?" He purses his lips tighter, into a thinner line than before. He glances at the knife on the side.

"I don't know if I want to bring it. I don't think I need it," he says.

"But for self defence."

"I know self defence anyway. I took lessons, Savannah." He took lessons? He never mentioned it, not when he was coming to save me, *not that night*, not even in a fleeting thought in the middle of a conversation. "After what happened, I told mum to book me lessons, try and find a spot in a class or something." I flick my brows up, looking up to him, as my hand begins drifting away from his.

"Oh," I mumble quietly. Like it's the only thing I can say. He really went and did that?

"I know the basics. But I guess it'd help." He shrugs.

"You booked lessons afterwards," I say it like it's a question, but it's not, it's a statement. How else am I meant to react?

"It was one of those things, where..." His eyes drift around the room. "I felt I needed to know it beforehand. Like I was missing a crucial part. If I had known before, I could have helped more. And, well." He flaps his arms pathetically on either side of him. "I didn't know."

"And you still saved my life. You really are something." I crack a smile, and so does he half heartedly, "You gotta admit, that's pretty impressive. No prior experience and all."

Towards the end of year 11, I was being followed by someone dressed head to toe in black. I called Luka as soon as I noticed, and I made my way towards the shops where he said he was meeting me. We did it discreetly. I never blatantly said what was happening, instead, by me acting weird on the phone, he actually caught on. I kept asking where we were meant to meet, where he was until he said this,

"If you're being followed, tell me about your day."

"Oh, you know, my day's been stressful, as usual. School is something else."

When they grabbed my arm, and I looked back, I think I saw a knife on the inside pocket of his jumper. It was meant to shut me up, but instead I called for Luka. He turned up just in time. At first, Luka tried to reason with the stranger, posing as my boyfriend. He got me out of the guy's grasp by kicking him where it hurts most. His grip on me loosened and Luka pulled me free, and we ran away. He took me away, hand on my arm, tight in his grip.

"Yeah, well, it wasn't enough."

"I know. I can't believe you took lessons." He shrugs his shoulders, turning his head away to side glance at me.

"In case anything else happened again, I wanted to take them. It's come in handy, don't you think?" I lift my eyes to his, diving deep into his beautiful ocean eyes. Just like the waves, different shades interlock together inside.

I don't understand how he's acting as if it's not even a big deal to him.

The late, autumn sky is setting in a beautiful dark orange shade, blending with the early cyan of the night, not a sound to be heard. Not a person in sight.

It's peaceful, calm, and eerie. I wonder if we'll ever have those chaotic nights again when the town is lit up by houses, sounds of TVs, children laughing and shrieking. Yearning for this normal is not what I expected to be doing, I was never sure if I was content with that life. But it was familiar, it was without change. Sitting in the living room with hot chocolate, snuggled up to my mum whilst my dad did whatever he usually does at night. Curling up watching movies with them in the dead of winter or having barbeques in the summer.

I miss them already. Anxious thoughts swirl in my mind. Without mum and dad, how will I cope? I don't know how to be without them. An empty sensation fills a corner of my heart, or maybe it's being chipped away, slowly eating at my soul.

When will it hit me, well and truly, that I might not ever see my parents again?

"Hey." Piper nudges my arm whilst Luka leads the way in front of us. "I can read you like a book. What's going on up there in your head?" I smirk, and push her off.

"I'm just thinking," I say.

"About?"

"Parents." Piper, and Luka are the closest people I have. With them, I'm a song with simple lyrics, an open book, a nursery rhyme to be taught. They ask, and I answer. Well, most of the time anyway.

"Ah." She looks away from me, and nods. "Me too."

"Yeah?" I glance at her as she takes my hand.

"Yeah." She holds my hand.

"Even your mum's boyfriend?"

She chuckles, "For some odd reason, yes. He may not have been the best human being on this planet, but Mum liked him, and that was enough for what it was. He could never replace my dad, but he was good to her." Deep in thought, she flings her head back to admire the sky, swinging our arms as we walk down the path together. She's looking up as if searching for something, so I squeeze her hand even tighter, offering my support and safety. "He better take care of her, wherever those people took them."

"You think they're alive?"

"Duh. There's always some sort of hope, you just gotta find it." She flicks her eyes to me, and with her free hand, she gestures around her, and in a low voice she adds, "Amongst the darkness."

"You read that in a book somewhere. You did not just think of that." She laughs, then looks down at the floor ahead. She wears a sad sort of smile. One without the creases beside her eyes.

"I think my mum wrote it to me one time, I don't know. Even if it was from somewhere though, it's pretty meaningful, right?"

"I guess."

"I don't believe it." She looks at me with that same sad expression. Shrugging her shoulders, she says, "I just like the sound of it. Like something good will come out of something bad."

"Yeah, I like it. A life motto?"

"Okay, that's a little far," she chuckles. She picks out paper from her pocket, the note her mum wrote to her, and waves it in my face. "She always signed it from 'mum and dad' like she thought I saw him as a dad."

"Maybe she thought you did see him like that. You call them your parents."

"Only 'cause it's easier to say they're my parents than he's my mum's boyfriend." Valid point I guess. She turns away, and so do I, but I wish I held on tighter, I wish I never looked away, I wish I never let go.

She says, "I miss even him actually, but I'm glad I've still got you." She squeezes my hand tighter, "Because I really wouldn't know what to do if you hadn't come for me—"

It took *ten seconds* for her to say her final sentence, before she began to choke on her words, on her own laugh, coughing and spluttering. Gurgling and screaming. I turn my head to her to watch her teary eyes drift to mine, wide in trembling fear, before falling to her knees. Her jaw drops open to say something before collapsing, head smacking to the ground, leaving a nasty gash on her forehead, but that's the least of my fucking problems.

Her hand's limp in mine, but I refuse to let go, mind hazy and foggy, because she can't simply die on me, and this doesn't mean she's dead, maybe she's just injured, and maybe this is a joke and maybe – I register the sword in her lower back, dug through her clothes and into her flesh.

Sliced. Right. Through. Blood spurts out from the wound, tears spring to my eyes. It can't be, can't—just can't be—

"Hey! What are you- No, come on get up." I kneel down, and fall with her to my own knees, as if she can hear me, but she's turning paler by the moment. Her hand's still warm in my grip. I press it to my heart on instinct. "Piper, what are you doing on the floor…?" I squeeze her, tears exploding onto my cheeks. "Piper!" I move her, I even reach for the sword, maybe I can get it out, but before I can, my name is called from behind.

"Savannah!" I follow the sword with my eyes, all the way to its steel handle, gold intertwined with leaves, a white-gloved hand gripping it tightly, ripping the weapon from her now lifeless body, limp on the ground, but still in my grip. A man in black, with hair the shade of darkness and throbbing red eyes looks down on me with a gleaming smirk plastered on his lips. Sharp teeth. That glint in the light.

"I've found you." He points the blade at me, almost touching the edge of my nose, laughing hysterically as if this whole thing amuses him. He just killed my best friend. With sobs clogging my throat, I make a sort of wailing sound, almost choking on air when Luka pulls at my arm, before I truly am next. With my eyes blurry, tears streaming down my cheeks, I look back down at Piper, Luka pulling my hand free from hers.

As if she was holding on to me for dear life. *As if.*

"Come on." That's when I hear his voice, drenched in fear, and anxiety, and shock, and all those mixed emotions I'm feeling, but can't seem to express. "Come on," he barely whispers, yet I'm still looking at the man looming over my best friend with his blade at her neck.

He grins at us once again, grabbing her hair, lifting her up, slicing her neck in one smite, in one hit, in one moment.

I don't want to stop running, and I don't think I will. Not really.

"We should be safer down here." Luka hangs onto my hand, leading me down a deserted alleyway. We slow to a walk when we turn another corner to a dead end whilst the late evening draws closer.

I let go of him abruptly. He stares at me with wide eyes before I fall to the ground. All the energy sucked out of me. I can't even stand.

I lean on the wall, head on the cold bricks whilst I simply sob to myself. Shoulders shaking, breathing heavily, chest tightening. I curl myself up into a little pathetic ball, a lump on the ground, one hand on my head and fingers gripping messy, greasy hair. The other covering my eyes, as if it'd shield myself from whatever horror I just witnessed.

Take it back. Please take it back.

I glance through my fingertips at Luka sliding down the wall, facing his body forward to the opposite building, whilst mine's curved towards him. His head's on the wall too. Beside mine. Slowly, but surely, tears leak out of his eyes.

He stares at me. And I don't know if he's aware I can see him or not, but either way, he edges closer, lifting his closest hand to mine, the one hung loosely across my eyes. I lower my palm, simply staring through a blur of tears. He takes my hand, and rubs tiny circles on my skin. His gaze shifts to it, sniffing harshly.

And we stay like this, in this position—heads on the wall, eyes drifting everywhere and anywhere except each other, our breathing slowly returning to a more steady pace. Whilst he eventually stops crying, I feel as if my tears will never end. A waterfall without a start or a finish, built up so high inside, only ever bound to fall. Maybe this is where I stay to meet the light at the end of the tunnel. Because I can't picture myself moving. Where do I go next without my best friend beside me? Where do I run to? How? How do I- I don't—

"Take your time."

"We don't have time," I snap before I register what he said. I look up to him. "Wait, what?"

"Zack and Oskar are going to Matthew's first. Then Jess'."

"Isn't Matthew's close by?" He shrugs his shoulders, closing his eyes, head on the wall.

"I don't know where we are." He lost track. My heart aches. I gradually uncurl from my protective shield, shuffling closer, shoulders bumping into each other. He opens up his eyes a little, and turns his head towards mine. I sit on my knees. And without another word being shared, and without a dispute in my mind, I rest my head on his shoulder, before quickly falling into another sobbing fest. I don't have any control, I just want to feel...safe. And being closer to Luka will do that to you. He lifts his free hand over and across him to lay on my hair as he rests his forehead on mine.

"A few more minutes?" I suggest.

"A few more minutes," he echoes, but it sounds like he might be falling asleep. I don't blame him.

I'm lost. I'm tired. And I'm scared.

And I don't know how I'll make it as far as Jess' house. I don't know how I'll make it out as far as the next street.

"Just tell me when you're ready," Luka tells me softly against my ear.

"I'll never be ready," I mutter, "so just tell me when we *need* to go, and I'll go." I sniff, as he moves his hand on my head away from me.

"You sure?"

"Do we need to go now?"

"Preferably. We need to find out where we are." I lift my eyes to watch him look up to the sky turning a gloomy navy. "It'll be completely dark soon."

"Okay." But I don't move. I take a breath, and close my eyes.

"I'll be here. I swear." I sit up from his shoulder, keeping my eyes on him. I begin to let go of his hand, however, he just hangs on tighter as he stands to his feet. I follow his lead, stretching my legs a little, moving my neck more, and I hear a pop.

"Don't—" He locks me onto his eyes, and lifts our joined hands up in front of our gazes, and says, "Don't let go." I nod. I hadn't even considered it an option.

I'd like to believe Luka knows where we are once we step out into the street instead of hiding out in an alleyway. Luka peers his head round every corner to make sure no one is hiding, readying to pounce on us in the silent shadows. It feeds me a sense of security that I shouldn't be allowed, or *able* to feel right now.

"Did you tell him?" I ask, breaking the silence when Luka looks at his phone. "About what happened?"

"I had to."

"I didn't expect you to keep quiet or anything." He purses his lips together, glancing at me. "What did he say?"

"He hasn't said anything yet, look." And just like that, he passes me his phone. I quickly take it, gripping it tight to be sure I don't drop it, and begin scanning back his conversation with Zack from fifteen minutes ago.

ZACK: Going Matthew's first, then Jess'. It's just easier.

LUKA: We had a setback, we'll be on our way soon.

ZACK: Everything okay? Are Savannah and Piper okay?

LUKA: Savannah and I are fine, physically at least.

LUKA: Piper's... not.

ZACK: Well, is she gonna make it? Surely she'll be fine, I mean, what's the worst that could happen?

LUKA: Savannah and I had to leave her, it was too late. We're hiding now.

LUKA: I'm sorry. We'll be moving soon.

LUKA: On our way. Are you alright?

"I hope he's okay," he says as I pass his phone back. I know what it's like waiting anxiously on an important message, but not to this extreme.

"I trust him, you trust him. He'll be okay," I tell him, squeezing his hand. I don't want Luka to be in a far away mindset. I want him to be here so I know he's okay.

I suppose that's how he must feel with Zack. Hoping he's alright.

"I hope he is." He shrugs his shoulders and stuffs his phone into his pocket. I don't think I need to be holding onto his hand now, but I still do. I don't think he needs to be holding it back, but he still does.

"Look! That's them!" Luka exclaims, pointing in the distance at a small group turning a corner.

"Are you sure?"

"Yes!" Then he's dragging me down the path whilst he runs towards them. He's far too quick for my tired legs to keep up. But I push on for him, until I simply can't and I force him to slow down.

"I'm exhausted, keep going." I let his hand go, panting, when we get to the corner, leaning on my knees.

"Zack!" he calls, peering his head round the corner. His face lights up, and he waves at the group.

"Luka, thank god!" Zack's shrill voice yells.

"Where's Savannah?" Matthew questions anxiously. I pop my head round the corner too. Relief washes over my chest, and I allow myself to relax my muscles ever so slightly, slouching my shoulders forward. I walk out beside Luka as we make our way over to them. But they're already running over to us. Zack tackles Luka, Oskar hangs back, bearing a troubled expression whilst Matthew heads towards me.

"Everything okay with you two?" He brushes his hand over my arm, because Matthew's not a hugger, even at a time like this. "We were worried. You stopped texting the group chat, why?" He flicks his eyes between both of mine, searching for an answer to uncover. "You have your phone, don't you?"

"Well—I haven't had a chance to use it for several reasons." Despite having only just caught my breath, I feel breathless again. Like my lungs just aren't cooperating today.

"Can we get moving again please?" Oskar asks behind them, his eyes on the ground. "I'm glad you're okay, of course, it's just that we don't know if Jess is yet." He rubs his arm uncomfortably, kicking a stone on the ground.

"Of course, of course. Sorry." Zack breaks out of his conversation with Luka and ushers us along with them, his eye glueing on me for a moment. And something flashes between us. Something dark, something meaningful, something sentimental.

He knows. He saw the message. He just didn't know how to respond.

I look away first and at Matthew who's staring at Zack.

"To Jess," I say to break the silence. Luka nods, and we all slowly follow Oskar towards Jess' house. Anxiety settles in my stomach, making its way down and towards the bottom of my feet, legs turning numb. Again. When will this feeling go away?

"We're going to mine after Jess," Zack announces, solemnly. "Then we figure out what to do next."

Or we'll wake up from this godforsaken dream. Our parents will be here, we'll be safe...and Piper will be alive. I clench my hands into fists, holding back an ocean of tears behind my eyes. She never deserved any of this. I can barely believe this is happening to begin with, which is why a part of me believes it's all a hazy, foggy dream.

Just some wacky nightmare my mind is playing for a joke.

When we make it to Jess' house, I hold my breath. Zack knocks on his front door and Oskar stands silently beside him. The silence is more than just a *bit* unsettling, but I can't think of any words that could be said right now without disturbing anyones thoughts.

Oskar is the one that kept speeding us up, kept telling us about how excited he is to see Sierra again, about how he'll protect Jess. He's not said another word about anything but him.

The only thing on his mind is Jess.

I know Oskar refers to Jess as his home sometimes. I always thought mine was just with Piper, but then I began spending more time with these amazing people and discovered it can be more than one person. I truly hope he doesn't lose his home, his person, his source of comfort at the end of a long day.

They knock again. And again. The silence is suffocating.

"Jess!" Oskar yells, banging his fists against the door, yelling through the cracks. "It's only me, and Zack, Matthew, Luka and Savannah! No one dangerous, just please! Come out! I can keep you safe!" Safe...? I think to guarantee safety right now is an empty promise, nothing more nothing less.

No reply.

"Should we be shouting?" I question, looking back and around us, to see if that killer is close by. At the thought of him, his smile flashes in my mind and I shiver. Only Zack turns back to glance at me. Oskar's eyes are glued to the wooden door.

He takes a deep breath, and it's obvious to everyone what's racing through his mind. He looks at Zack.

"I'm going in."

"Oskar, wait, I don't think—"

"What else do you think we should do? I am *not* leaving this house without searching for him at the very least!" His voice cracks at the mention of Jess. Zack purses his lips together and looks at us behind him, searching for advice.

"I'm with Oskar. I don't plan on leaving without looking," Matthew agrees, trembling in the night breeze.

"I'm not going in, but I'll keep an eye out," Luka says.

"I'll stay with Luka," I say. Because that's what he said he wanted before.

"Fine. But how—" Luka's words are cut short, Oskar begins to kick the door. Thud, thud, thud. I've seen Oskar angry before. But he's never been as distraught as I'm witnessing right now. He's ruining himself – shattering into dozens of sharp glass pieces all around us. And no one can make him whole again.

"Oskar," Luka steps forward and grabs his arm but it's a useless attempt to stop him. He doesn't—not until the door breaks down completely, landing in the hallway of Jess' house, and it makes an all mighty noise, causing me to flinch.

All lights are off, and the furniture is completely ruined. My heart sinks in my chest. Not Jess too. Please not Jess. Oskar runs into the house, sprinting up the stairs and Zack swiftly follows, calling out his name. I don't dare speak or breathe a word. It's as if the walls shake and crumble when Oskar's upstairs. When he screams, "Jess!" my heart breaks in two.

I peer past Luka and at Matthew, just staring at the wall in silence. A second later, he's making his way inside, while Luka turns his back to it, scanning the surroundings for anyone else lurking close by.

"He was texting Zack, wasn't he?" I question. "I can't remember."

"He was on call to Oskar," Luka answers, taking a deep breath. Tears begin resurfacing my eyes, I close them tight. I want to go home, I don't want to be here. I want to wake up. "Jess is strong," he says. "And smart. He'll use his head. There's no way he saw them coming and didn't know what to do. No way he'd go down so easily." I purse my lips together, refusing to say, *'but what if...'*

There's a chance that perhaps we may never come across Jess again. And that small thought alone shakes me to my very bones. I loved him as I love everyone here. It's never the same without him. He's the one to keep everyone in check, without him...

Without him?

Oskar will crumble. Without him, Matthew will be in ruins.

"We should all be heading towards Zack's house," Luka mutters with a heavy chest. We look at each other, our eyes meet and the familiar shine is gone from his. I merely nod, as he gazes back at the house. "I'll go get them." He walks inside and up towards Zack and Oskar. I can very faintly hear their mumbling as Matthew walks back out of the house, and towards me.

"Where's Piper?" he asks. I simply stare at him. His expression softens once more. Tears glistening inside them, as he mutters, "I thought so."

"I'm sorry," I tell him.

"I'm sorry too." Silence surrounds us.

Zack, Luka and Oskar return to us. Oskar says nothing, walking straight past us all, Zack glances worryingly at me before following, and we all hurry behind them.

And with that, we all walk to Zack's house in complete silence, heads hanging low under a solemn midnight sky.

I head straight to the middle floor bathroom, locking myself in so I can get my head straight. But as soon as I close the door, I slide down, wrapping my hands inside my hoodie sleeves, resting them on my head, pathetically.

And I try, I try, I try to grasp an understanding of what just unfolded in the last two hours. No – longer than that? I don't know anymore, my whole concept of time is royally fucked up.

So, I wait, I don't know how long, for the tears to come and eventually, they fall at an alarming rate. I thought I was empty, but my body proves me wrong. My sleeves grow damp, and soggy. It's disgusting. But my heart is heavy. And it's aching for something. I don't know what. Comfort? A hug? Touch? I don't know, I don't understand. I don't understand at all.

"Savannah?" A soft knock is sent through the door. Matthew's kind voice echoes from the other side. "Can you open the door...please?"

"Why? Do you need to go to the toilet?" I don't bother masking my voice, I'm sure he already knows why I'm hiding away.

"No, that's not why." But he says no more, waiting for me to bounce back. But I don't. I don't have the energy to.

"Matthew?"

"Yeah?"

"I'm sorry," I manage to say before my voice trails off, cracking under the pressure.

"I'm sorry as well," he barely whispers. I clear my tears from my cheeks only to let more slide down, finally standing up. "But I'm here. I'm right here. Closer than you think."

"Your head's on the door, isn't it?"

"...No?" I chuckle lightly, glancing at my hand, and then at the white painted wood. I smile a little before laying my palm on the cool surface. "Please come down? It's not the same without you with us." It'll never be the same. Can't he see that? "You don't have to be alone." I unlock the door hesitantly, and he opens it on the other side, swinging it open.

He looks exhausted. And I suppose that's how I look too. His eyes are puffed, bloodshot, red, and teary. The bags under them have come out under the lights, his shoulders slouched, and low. He's been crying too. He doesn't bother smiling to conceal it.

"I..." Am speechless. I've never seen him cry before, or even seen the aftermath of anything like it. It's a little heart-wrenching to say the least. "Maybe he's still alive. Maybe we can save him." I don't say his name, he knows who I'm talking about. Saying it would only bring him more pain. He almost chuckles a little, rubbing at his eyes more, making him appear even more tired.

"Don't say that, you're giving me hope."

"Hey, stop rubbing." I step forward, tugging at his arms, feeling tiny and insignificant. He sighs, freezing for a moment, before dropping his arms completely. He stares at me, running his eyes over my dishevelled appearance as I did with him.

And then he hugs me closer to his chest. I wrap his arms around him in return, thankful for the sudden, but welcoming physical contact. His warmth floods my system, digging my face into his shoulder as a way of hiding.

Matthew isn't much of a hugger.

"We can look for Jess," I break through.

"Unlikely."

"Soon," I repeat, "I swear it."

Maybe it's an empty promise. Maybe I mean nothing by it. And maybe I have no control over what *really* happens. But even if it helps him feel even the tiniest bit better, a small piece of closure making its way into his heart, it might just be worth it. Because for all I know, he *is* still alive and well. Maybe he is still surviving.

I, however, have no hope of seeing my person again. She was my best friend through and through. And I watched her slaughtered beside me. I've lost my favourite person.

I end up crying on Matthew's shoulder, and he does the same to me.

Jack

8th October

Zayne hits me across the face with the hilt of his sword.

"You had one fucking job to do!" he spits. "You can't even do that!" He screams in the middle of a stranger's house we broke into, and ruined. "We got lucky with finding them, and we needed more hostages, you know this!" He and I are one of the sweeper teams. The aftermath of what the main Noble 'teams' have done. Finding them here was not *lucky*. I don't think he quite understands that his definition of the word and mine are two completely different things. Why can't he get that through his thick skull? Even after all these years.

"I knew damn well what I was doing, and I know we don't need them." And I stand for it.

"I don't know what you're talking about. People have been feeding you—"

"Oh, shut up. I can't be arsed to deal with you."

I shouldn't be talking to him like this. But he's not of a Noble rank, we're both Knights. Below them. There's no way he's gonna go blab that his 'subordinate' started talking down to him. It'd make him look weak.

"You are *impossible* to work with!" He throws his arms up in the air. "Impossible!" I roll my eyes, backing away from him.

"It's not like you don't say that every day. I get the idea. Go ahead and say it again. Rub it in."

"Don't talk to me that way. I have power over you." Because Noble Vincent likes him, yeah, I've heard the story several times before. I don't even know if that's true.

"We're the exact same rank. You have nothing you can hold over me. No orders because you *can't* deliver them."

"The point is, we lost probably the only two kids they sent us to scout for! Because of *you*!" He's getting too close for comfort.

"Well, you can go ahead and look for some more then, if it's so important to you. I don't want to be part of it." I turn my back on him, walking through the kitchen, and out the back door.

"Where do you think you're going?" he demands, catching up to me.

"Draven needs me."

"How would you know?" I trust Draven will vouch for me. He's my excuse. I look over my shoulder and back at Zayne. I'm sure the *kind* Noble would let me leave if he knew how Zayne treated me anyway.

"It's none of your business," I say, but a sinking feeling shakes my chest as he raises his sword handle again, and slams the pommel into my cheek, like he did a few moments ago. I grit my teeth, bite my tongue, stop myself from yelping in pain.

"You need to be more cooperative, Jack. You're lucky I'm here to be your partner in this stupid group or else you'd be with Vincent. You need to be reasonable when we're on missions like this." He looms over me when he talks, which only infuriates me more. Familiar metallic blood fills my mouth.

"I'll do that," I lock onto his eyes, flashing them in his direction, and continue, "when you stop beating me." And just like that, I sprout out bat-like wings, leaping into the air, before he can lay another hand on me.

I'm praying people don't notice the monster above as I fly ahead, although any traces left of humans in this town would be little to none. Better yet, they're concealing themselves underground, or perhaps they've escaped by some small miracle. Violet and I seem to be the only ones who think this is insane – taking over a town.

The wind is harsh today, so I stay close to the rooftops, sweeping past gutters and tiles that spread out for miles. I seem to interrupt a murder of crows on a satellite, happily tweeting to each other. As soon as they spot me from afar, they fly off in the opposite direction. When I pass them, they've already disappeared. Even the crows are fearful of the beast in the sky.

I arrive at the mansion, hidden in the woods by a thick forest. I disintegrate my wings as soon as I land in front of the double wooden doors. We use this mansion as the Ash and Raven clan bases. This is where Vincent and Draven, the Nobles, operate. Vincent's in charge of the Ashes and Draven's in charge of the Ravens. Sometimes, the Royals visit us. Those are the days I dread.

I sometimes don't understand why I haven't just left this place yet. Part of me stays for Draven, knowing he'd descend into madness alone. Part of me already knows that the outside world would reject us anyway. So what would the point really be?

So we always wait. For the right moment, when we've collected enough resources and we can run away for good.

I march into the main hall, past the guards, finding everyone rushing around. I don't know why; I don't care to know, so I ignore it. If it doesn't involve me to begin with, there's no need to stick my nose where it doesn't belong.

Violet's spotted me from across the hall, now headed in my direction with a confused expression plastered on her face. The closer she gets, the more concerned she seems, spotting the damage Zayne inflicted. I lift my fingers to my cheek briefly, feeling a bruise forming, tender to the touch, but she quickly grabs my arm before I can pass her, held at a sudden standstill, side by side in the centre of the room.

"What on earth happened?" she demands, her bright green eyes searching mine, refusing to let me look elsewhere even if I wanted to. But little does she know that when she's around, she's the only one who holds my absolute devoted attention, the only one I can think about, stealing the spark in my own eyes. She stops the world from turning when she walks in, beautiful and star-striking.

"What do you think?" I ask, softening my voice. She frowns, lifts her other hand across her body, tracing the new bruise on my cheek with the back of her index finger. "I'm fine," I insist.

"Quit the act." I purse my lips together into a tight and fine line. She lifts her eyebrows at me and tilts her head. "Jack."

"Violet."

"Are you okay?" I slip my hand into hers.

"I missed you."

"We were apart for little under a day." She smiles.

"And I spent it with Zayne," I comment.

"Fair enough. I missed you too." I lean in, landing my lips on hers, soft and slow. She's a familiar source of comfort in this forever messy and fucked up world. So when I kiss her for the first time in nearly a day, relief washes over me. A sense of relief only someone like her could ever give me.

I love her more than she could ever understand. More than words could ever explain.

"I have more to tell you later." Like why I'm in earlier than I should be. Why I left before the job was finished. About how I let two kids go.

She nods, and smiles more when I lean away from the third kiss. Letting my hand go, she walks away, keeping her eyes trained on me when she says, "I'll talk to you later."

"Stay safe," I tell her.

"Of course."

She's the only one keeping me from going insane. Well, her and maybe Draven. He's not a bad guy.

"Jack, Perfect!" Ah, yes, the voice that can ruin any day of mine. Even if it's complete bliss until I hear. His. Stupid. Voice. *One day, I'll escape. One day, he'll be out of my life. One day, I won't have to deal with him anymore.*

I turn around to face Vincent, walking over to me with a fiery smirk playing on his face.

"I need you!" He stops walking in this crowd of people and ushers me closer. "Come now!"

Perhaps he somehow found out about me letting those kids go, willingly. But they had no weapons, no nothing. One was in tears, and the other was only trying to help her. Like how I was with Violet on the night the man walking in front of me attacked us.

I follow him, reluctantly, into his office where he plans all his schemes and orders. But the next thing I realise, he's sliding wooden floorboards across the ground beside his desk to reveal basement stairs. My chest sinks even further as he walks down, because this cannot be good, whatever it is. I don't want to find out what he has planned for me down there. I'd much rather turn back, and run. I'd have a good chance while he's heading down deeper. But knowing my luck, if I did just walk away, he'd take it out on both me *and* Violet.

So instead, I follow him down, every step echoing against the cold stone walls. He sparks the lighter in his hands, throwing it between his fingers and twisting it around effortlessly, surprising how such a little light brightens the corridor ahead of us. The stone walls are damp and dark, a few torches scattered across the way, but never enough to let us see completely. Not without Vincent's lighter. Cells lead all the way down to our left, never a break from the steel bars, seeming to go on forever. My blood runs cold. I had no idea this was under our noses the entire time. *But I'm not surprised.*

What makes it worse, every single cell is full of people. Be it one or two teenagers, or six toddling children. I watch as I pass. They cower in corners of dimly lit jail cells. It's disgusting. Revolting. I keep my eyes forward, and at the back of Vincent's dark ginger hair. I don't want to make eye contact with anyone we've wrongly imprisoned. Guilt is already rocking the boat I sit in, a simple push overboard could send me drowning.

Then, someone small reaches through the bars of a cell and grabs my hand. Desperate and tight. I stop, looking back and down at a little girl, with teary eyes, curly hair, and dark, tanned skin.

"Mister?" she asks, trembling and shaking. "Where's my brother?" she croaks out, her throat rough and dry. My chest stings. *Brother*? I kneel down to her level, spotting these beautiful shining brown eyes, sparkling right back at me. They're mesmerising, even in this dirty state. "I thought he followed me here, he was right behind me!" I glance behind her to see if anyone was there to comfort her instead of I, but no. She's alone. Completely and utterly alone and she can't be any older than eight. "Please?"

"I don't know where he is," I tell her as softly as I can. Her brows curve and her expression breaks, eyes momentarily spotting two fangs of mine in my mouth, but instead of backing away, she holds on tighter and shakes her head low. Instead, her eyes tear up even more.

"What do you mean? I just got here, and he was following. I know he wouldn't leave, I know he wouldn't leave me alone here." Her tears spill over her cheeks, uncontrollably.

"Hey, calm down." On instinct, I squeeze her hand tighter. "What's your name?"

"Sierra," she sobs, rubbing one of her eyes with her palm.

"Sierra...?"

"Sierra Princeton." So presumably her brother will be a Princeton too. I could maybe check records, or I could find Draven, see if he knows anything. "Will you find him?"

"I will try my best—"

"Jack, if you just want a taste then perhaps I'd allow it. Just this once though! We don't usually let any old vampire have a snack from down here." Vincent smirks from afar, sending shivers down my spine as he walks to my side. I quickly let go of the girl, staring up at the Noble.

"She was merely asking a question." I stand up straight, avoiding both of their eyes.

"Come on!" Vincent puts his hand on the cell lock and begins turning the key he has in his grip, but I grab his wrist before thinking, pulling him from the cell and out of the way. He stumbles. I glance at the girl, who's backing away slowly, watching me in almost awe, wide-eyed, jaw ajar, brows raised. "Oh, come now, Jack." He edges closer to me, but I step towards the cell, unsure of whether I'm trying to save myself or protect the girl. The two seem to blend into each other. "Just one small drop!"

"No!" I yell. "I've told you once, I'll tell you again, I'm never gonna try it!" Blood, he means blood. He rolls his eyes, playing with the fire between his fingers, briefly mesmerised by the light, sighing dramatically so I quickly change the subject, "What did you bring me down here for?"

"To show you why we need as many people as we can get." How on earth did Zayne tell Vincent before I arrived? He grins at me, baring his teeth.

"Seems to me, you have plenty of people down here."

"But how many of these people will be able to feed the hunger of an army?" There's an army? A *vampire* army? "It's each clan's job and responsibility to feed their own people, but what about those who do not belong to a clan?" He pouts at me, his free hand on his heart like something is physically hurting him.

"Why is it our job? Why do we have to go and imprison defenceless humans who've done nothing wrong?" I raise my voice to him, testing the waters.

"Because we're doing the dirty work others don't need to do!" he cackles.

"But you enjoy it! It's not so 'dirty' if you enjoy ending people's lives."

"Most adults we showed no mercy to, of course, they're adults after all. They already lived a life." He finds this amusing and smirks. "But, the younger's blood is fresher, richer, thicker!"

"Shut up." It disgusts me.

"So, we keep the children to ourselves. When they're in their late teens, early twenties, that's when their prime time begins." I push down a gag to the pit of my stomach. "For the greater good, my dear Jack." He steps in front of me, patting my head patronisingly before I push him away. He walks past, laughing to himself.

"The greater good of what?" I mutter under my breath. I turn around, catching Sierra's eyes.

"Keep my brother safe. Please?"

"I'll try."

"Pinky promise?" She sticks her hand through the bars again, and without hesitation, I hook my pinky finger with hers, forcing the smallest smile.

"Pinky promise." I couldn't help my own brother. It's not possible I'll come across hers. I just want to let her hope. Even if it's just for a little longer.

I lie on my bed, staring at the ceiling when Violet finally returns from her errands. I sit up as she walks in, and she smiles at the sight of me.

"Welcome back, my love," I greet her. She walks in front of me, leaning down on my shoulders, pressing a kiss onto my lips.

"Thanks, darling," she giggles. "I would say, 'it's good to be back' but that's a great big stinkin' lie." She kisses me again, smiling into it, and I lay my hands on her waist. My hands always fit perfectly onto her body.

"How was it out there?" I ask.

"Messy."

"Messy?"

"We found *numerous* people, just in the streets, trying to find their friends. Florence caught them. I'm sure you know how the rest goes." She flicks her wrist and rolls her eyes.

"She didn't force you to help?"

"No, thankfully." She suddenly leans closer, her eyes narrowing to inspect the bruise forming under my eye. Like before, she traces her fingers over it, cupping my cheek, carefully and tenderly. "I hate him so much."

"So do I."

"One day, he won't be allowed, or even *able* to lay a hand on you."

"Oh, it wasn't a hand," I tell her. "It was the hilt of his sword." She rolls her eyes, stepping away from me to take her bow off her back, along with her quiver of arrows.

"Do you need ice or something?"

"Where are we gonna get that from?" She glances back at me. "I'm fine, honestly." I can't escape the sceptical look she gives me, glancing up and down, as if I'm lying.

"You said something happened, right? Tell me." She hangs up her weapons as I recall the events that unfolded, which now includes Vincent, and the little girl I made an empty promise to. How Zayne hid in the kitchen for those two kids. How I told them to run. About how the boy who held a knife struck Zayne when he arrived.

"I ended up promising to keep her brother safe. Or to at least try to," I finish. By this point, she's sitting beside me on the bed, hanging onto every word, murmuring replies as she holds onto my hands.

"Jack..." She shakes her head, looking away from me in disbelief.

"I couldn't say no to an eight year old!"

"But you could've walked away!" She itches her forehead nervously. "How are you meant to keep this promise? He might be dead for all we know. He probably is if he wasn't in the cells with her."

"I know." She looks at me again.

"You know?" She drops her hand back onto her lap. "You're too nice sometimes."

"But..." But she reminded me of myself. Of how desperate I wanted someone to tell me my brother was alive still, despite the fact I watched it all. How desperate I was for someone to protect him like how he'd protected me in the past. But nothing. I couldn't just leave her. She was desperate for some kind of hope. Even if it was delusional, empty hope.

"But?" she asks, turning to look at me.

"But she reminded me of me."

"Oh." She drops her expression. "Oh," she echos.

"I couldn't leave her without giving *something*. Maybe there *is* a chance that he's somewhere here. She seems to think he was following her, as any brother would."

"Hmm." She mulls it over her tongue, leaning back on the bed and against the wall. "I guess he might have. But then why wasn't he in the cell with her?"

"I don't know." She purses her lips together before springing herself off the bed, suddenly.

"What are you doing?"

"I thought we were gonna go nosey around?" She looks down at me, and I shake my head.

"I don't think we can risk it."

"Well, sir." She leans over me again, poking her index finger into my chest whilst one of her hands presses into my shoulder, setting my heart alight when she smiles down on me. "You have a promise to keep. And she's only a child, you can't break it."

"You were the one belittling me as to how stupid I was—"

"Shush! What's done is done, unfortunately. You gave her hope. We can't kill it, can we? Now, are we going to go poke around or—"

The door bursts open, and we turn both of our heads to see a young messenger boy scanning the room for someone other than us.

"Apologies, wrong room," he stutters helplessly, and leaves with a slam. Both Violet and I share a glance at each other, both the same question in mind.

"What in the world was that all about?"

"Or *who* in the world was he looking for?" I counter. Her eyes widen, but before I can say another word, she makes her way towards the door to investigate.

We walk down the narrow hallway towards the main area, close to the entrance of the mansion itself. The closer we get, the clearer we hear voices bickering, and interrupting each other. I can pick out Vincent's voice from a mile away, so if he's involved, it can't be good. We turn the corner, standing in the archway at the scene unfolding before us.

Vincent smiles devilishly on one of the staircases leading to the upper floor. Draven looks pissed standing beside him, head hung low. He glances at me, and then looks to Vincent, flicking some of his fringe out of his eyes. Draven's arms are crossed in front of his chest, his raven hair covering part of his face, looking down on everyone. He appears menacing and intimidating, but when you get down to it, he's one of the only people here who I'd argue is actually sane. Violet stares at me, then shifts her hand into mine.

"Something's wrong. I can feel it," I say softly. "They're waiting for something." Our questions have been answered. The double doors crash open, to have both Achillea and Ambrosia stroll through, so casually it's alarming.

"What the hell?" Violet exclaims, taking a step back while I just hold onto her tighter. "Why are Royals here?"

"I don't know, but whatever it is, it can't be good," I mutter under my breath so they can't hear, but despite this, Achillea glances directly at me. Maybe she has heightened hearing abilities I didn't know of. Whilst her head is held high and mighty, Ambrosia's head is low, staring at Draven with a wide grin, a greeting of sorts.

"Draven! Long time, no see," she exclaims, glancing back in her star-striking, blood red, glittering dress. I see what she's looking at only when both her and Achillea stop in front of the Nobles. A boy walks into the hall, looking around in a blend of fear and awe. A couple guards trail in after him as he stares at me.

It's almost like I recognise him.

When I step closer, I realise his eyes are identical to the girl's in the cell.

✦*Jack*✦

8th October

Sierra's brother.

He quickly looks away when he's jabbed in the side by a Knight to stay focused on what's in front of him. Tears break out onto his cheeks immediately. What are they doing to this poor kid? I step closer, unable to control myself, until Violet tugs my hand back.

"Jack, no."

I purse my lips together, glancing my eyes at the ground, then at the boy, stopping a few feet away from Achillea and Ambrosia. Draven's eyes are glued on me, and only me. He knows what's going through my mind, of course. This kid's in immense danger. What happened to Violet and I could happen to him right now, and I can't witness that and do nothing. Not again. Achillea glances at both Draven and Vincent on the higher levels. They make their way down silently, Vincent standing behind the boy, ushering the guards away. Meanwhile, Draven walks directly to us. Every time I spot him, I sometimes wonder if the whole reason we are still here in the clans instead of a cliffside somewhere is because I'd have to leave behind Draven. I don't plan on returning once I'm out. *Maybe I'm pushing it back so those goodbyes don't happen.*

"Who is he?" I ask.

"He came willingly. That's all I know. I think I've heard him talk about friends back in the town who survived but I couldn't be sure." Sierra told me he was following her, so that adds up. With everything that's happening in that town, they'll only have each other left. We can't split them up.

"I think his sister's in the prison below," I tell him as he stands beside me, raising an eyebrow, arms crossed over his chest.

"Oh?"

"Same eyes. I promised her I would keep him safe."

"Why on earth would you promise such a thing? And how did that come up in a conversation with her? Surely Vincent was there too."

"He was there to lecture me about why we need so many humans. Some sort of charity project." I roll my eyes at the memory, the echo of his words inside my head.

"That doesn't explain how you managed to promise something like that to her. It's impossible to guarantee anything to anyone in this world, Jack. I thought you, of all people, would know that." He glances at me for a moment, and then away at the boy. "Don't even think about doing anything to stop...whatever's going to happen."

"I don't want to know what you mean by that." He grimaces at my response.

"You already know."

"Stop squabbling. Jack's not going to do anything stupid so don't act like he will, Draven," Violet interrupts, looking at me and squeezing my hand in a warning. Draven is the only person here who we can talk to freely without worrying if he'll strike us or report us to the Royals. He's a Noble, like Vincent, but he's also the one who fed us when we were still getting used to vampire blood, gave us water instead of blood, and appointed us jobs to do when no one else would. He's the one who kept us alive from the very beginning.

That was before we got appointed to Vincent's clan, before the Royals found out who actually made us the way we are. We trust Draven, he trusts us. A mutual expression no one here could wrap their heads around.

"Jack's already involved by the sounds of it," Draven remarks with a sigh. "Vincent seems to be too."

"He's always involved with anything I do," I remark.

"You got that right," Violet snorts. "He's obsessed."

"Just don't give them more of a reason to dislike you, that's all." Draven murmurs. Vincent knows I hate it here, and I know he's aware that I hate him as well. But I'm not completely sure he *fully* hates me in return. He could do much worse things to me. He could force human blood down my throat. So what's stopping him? "Should you dig a hole deep enough to stumble into, I may not be able to get you back out of it this time."

"What do you mean?" Violet questions before I can, I focus on the way Vincent circles the helpless boy like prey.

"I need to be careful, that's what I'm saying." I break eye contact with the situation unfolding to stare at Draven. He glances between us.

"They can't take your Noble title away," I say. "Surely that's not how it works."

"They wouldn't. Others might."

"Ambrosia?" They're best friends, after all. Best friends don't ditch each other. If Draven's Noble rank was stripped from him, he'd have little to no conversations with Ambrosia afterwards. She wouldn't allow that. I know she wouldn't.

"She wants me by her side," he says. "And she's Achillea's cousin. Achillea would never do anything to hurt her. That includes being rid of my rank. They'll fight for me. But the other Royals may not be so forgiving." How many other Royals are there? I guess vampires are a much larger species than I had thought.

"You're saying you're in trouble?" Violet asks.

"Indirectly, yes. I'm a long way from that ever happening, however I don't want to speed up the process," he murmurs. "So you're on your own should you do anything stupid."

"I don't know what to do anyway," I mutter, looking away, guilt swarming my chest. I try to press it down, because I'm protecting my own skin right now. That isn't something I'm meant to feel guilty for. But do I deserve protecting? Do I matter that much?

Achillea stops talking to the boy. She stares straight back to me, like I'm her next target. Head held high, she looks so much mightier. Stronger. More regal.

"Jack," she commands, ushering me over and for a single moment, I don't move. My feet rooted to the ground, glancing at Violet longer than I should. "Quickly. I don't have time to dawdle." I rush along, letting go of my flower, biting down on my tongue. This can't be good. The boy looks at me with wide bloodshot eyes, his cheeks damp, irises shining like the girl's from below. *Mesmerising*. Definitely him. Now how do I keep a promise to keep him safe?

"You'll take responsibility for this child."

"What?" I blurt, flipping my head to Achillea.

"What?" even Vincent exclaims.

"What?" the boy whispers under his breath. Achillea merely rolls her eyes, her long, straightened black hair moving with her, tapping against her back.

"You heard what I said." She rolls her eyes. "I don't need to repeat everything I say, do I, Jack?"

"I thought only Nobles could—" I begin to speak against her thoughts before realising how bad of an idea that is. But for once, Vincent actually comes to my rescue, and says something worth noting.

"Does this mean the boy would be in my clan?" He claps his hands behind us. "Oh, goodie! A new edition to my big, happy family!"

I grimace at the word. *Family.*

"Yes, part of your clan," Achillea speaks impatiently, rushing through her words, and then glares directly at me. "Vincent informs me you and Violet have yet to try real human blood." I hear the boy start shaking, his breathing goes weird and unsteady. "Odd thing to find, especially in the Cinus clan." There's many clans under both of the Royals - but the main two they like to keep close are the Cinus clan (Vincent's clan) and the Ash clan (Draven's clan). The rest are deemed unimportant or simply too far away right now for them to care. She cocks her head to one side, staring at me patronisingly. "Won't you," she points an elegant finger at the kid beside me who whimpers on the spot, "perhaps take advantage of the moment—"

"No," I say plainly, and I can practically feel his eyes burning into my skull.

"No?" she questions, tilting her head back to centre, furrowing her perfectly shaped brows. "Why not? Honestly, it's a wonderful taste. You'll wish you'd tried it sooner. I know I was like that when I first tried it," she chuckles, glancing to her cousin for support, but in response, she merely shrugs her shoulders, crossing her arms over her chest, turning away from. "Ambrosia—"

"If he doesn't want to, he doesn't need to. He's not like others now is he, babes. What's the harm in letting him be?" Even *I'm* surprised by her sudden outburst, defending my word. She looks back at Achillea over her shoulder, flashing her dark black eyes at her, and then me, and then the boy. Perhaps I trick myself into believing it, but for a moment I see pity in her expression.

"Jack, you need to at some point in your existence. It's an experience. A wonderful one at that. You're not truly one of us without having tasted it at least once."

"No, no, no, no, no, please, no." The boy begins to shake his head over and over again, eyes darting from one face to another, but all I can do is simply stare at him. He has no idea how little control he has right now over what's about to happen.

He's been focusing too much on me, and not on the monster behind him. And so have I, I barely register Achillea marching closer, and closer to me. I turn too late. She's grabbing a hold of my neck, digging her nails into my skin like claws. Gasping for air, I force my eyes to meet her black engulfed ones.

Tales have told that she once bared beautiful hazel eyes, but with how corrupted she's become over her hundreds of years, and with the amount of blood she's drunk, her eyes turned to the darkest of black, and never reverted back.

I grab a hold of her wrist, trying to tug her off as blood slides down my neck. In a frantic panic, I even reach for my sword, holding the handle in case I need to draw in the next few moments.

"Why do you never listen to us? It's exhausting. Jack, we know what's best for you, I can promise," she says, patronisingly, a menacing smirk plastered across her lips. "Don't you want to become even more powerful? For both the army, and for yourself?" I grind my teeth, pressing my fingers harder into her veins, but I know I can't get away with acting against her, so I let go of my sword as well. She's a Royal, one of the most important people in our kind, I am two ranks below her. She's the founder of the vampire army. If I hurt her, I would find myself amongst the outcasts that Vincent mentioned earlier. And I so desperately don't want that. So I grin and bear it, staring right back at her. "Don't you want to be stronger than what you already are?" She grinds her teeth together, shaking her head. "You're lucky you're surviving as it is—"

"Achillea!" She's pulled off me abruptly. My hand flies up to my neck, covering two hole-like scratches in my skin, now bleeding a little, trickling down my skin as I watch Ambrosia pulling her back, away from me. "What the hell has gotten into you?" Achillea slaps her cousin's hands away from her, looking back at Vincent, nodding at him as a signal, and then she quickly walks off, and up the stairs. Ambrosia glances at me, shrugs her shoulders and follows, calling out her name.

"My turn for some fun," Vincent cackles. I turn my head, but I wish I never had.

He licks his lips, grabbing the boy roughly by his shoulders, spinning him around. He yelps, wide eyes, shaking in the Noble's grip, not even bothering to fight back. Then Vincent slams the kid onto the floor, pinning him to the ground.

He's sobbing, almost wailing, whispering something under his breath, shaking his head repeatedly, as if Vincent will change his mind. In the end, the boy shuts his eyes, as Vincent prepares to force his own dark shade of crimson blood into the innocent's mouth by forcing his mouth wide open. It drops from his tongue.

The kid screams as much as he can before he's drowning. My mind replays it all over again. The feeling of someone else's blood filling my mouth, forced to swallow before I choke to death. The warm liquid sliding down my throat, sinking into my stomach, the sudden sensation similar to if you were punched in the gut or worse, stabbed. His scream turns to blood curdling gurgles. He's desperately fighting the floor. Kicking and squirming. Wailing and sobbing. Trying to call for help that was never offered to him. His face flushed and red.

My stomach lurches for him. After this happened to me, after the pain had ceased to exist, and the aching was all I had left, I thought to myself, *'I never want anyone to experience what I just went through.'* Once I had woken up, searching for Violet who was shaking on the ground beside me, we both made a silent pact to never inflict that pain on anyone else. Never to become like them.

I fear I have no choice on whether people are placed in our shoes, and live the lives we lead. *They* are getting restless, *they* are getting tired, *they* are getting annoyed.

The worst of the process begins. The boy relaxes. His muscles growing limp, his legs giving up, looking as though his life is being drained from his very skin. His body's getting used to the new blood source, the new energy from within. The new...power. It's only natural that the old makes way for the new.

His once teary and paralysed eyes roll back into his head, but Vincent never pulls away. He won't even stop when he falls completely limp, hands falling from the vampire's neck and wrists.

"Vincent!" I take a step forward again, holding onto his uniform, but Draven is already grabbing the back of his shoulders, prying his hands from the helpless boy. Draven drags him towards the stairs before Vincent shoves him off. I hold my breath, watching the scene unfold. The ginger grimaces, wipes his mouth and glares at Draven.

"I wasn't going to do anything rash!" he claims, his arms out wide in a furious gesture, before delving into one of his pockets to fetch his trusty lighter to mess around with between his fingertips. "Overreaction much."

"You could've killed him. Excuse me for giving a shit," Draven remarks.

"Why would you care?"

"He's a kid!" I turn my gaze onto the boy and kneel down beside him. My responsibility. The golden-haired boy.

"I guess you're coming with me," I mutter under my breath, leaving Draven and Vincent to bicker. The first thing I do is wipe the blood from his face with my sleeve, knowing it's gonna be washed sooner or later. Then I turn around, eyes catching on Violet edging closer. I step over him, and grab his wrists from behind. I hoist him up and over my back, arms hanging over my shoulders. He's easy enough to carry on my own. I glance back at Vincent walking off, and Draven looking back at me.

I turn back and begin to head towards mine and Violet's room. She rushes towards me, shaking her head.

"Well..." She raises her eyebrows at me. "That was something I never want to witness again."

"Agreed."

"Do you need any help with that? Seems like you're struggling." I smirk, bumping her shoulder out of the way for me to make it into the corridor.

"I'm fine, flower." She rolls her eyes, biting back a laugh.

"I was just asking," she claims. "This kid – he's someone we have to take care of now?"

"Rather me than—"

"We."

I meet her eyes, slowing down in the hallway. She gives me a stern look.

"We," I repeat softly. "It's better *we* take care of him rather than Zayne or Vincent."

"That's true," she says, and I look forward once again, shifting the boy higher so he's more supported by my arms. "I hated every second of that," her words came out as a stifled breath, releasing tension in her shoulders.

"So did I," I mutter under my breath. "It wasn't pleasant." I stop in front of our door. "Would you do me the honours?" She walks forward, opens it up for me, giving me a concerned look in the meantime. I lower the boy onto my bed instead of hers, flat on his back as he stirs in his deep trance. I stand up straight, rolling my shoulders backwards until they pop freely.

"Hey." Violet turns me around, hiding a yawn, grabbing my arm. "Talk to me. Something's up."

"Love—" She wraps her arms around my waist.

"Jack, come on."

"It's just unpleasant memories resurfacing, that's it. I don't like remembering anything from back then." Like when she never stopped screaming and I didn't know how to help. Or when Zayne began beating me, and when we were separated. A time when Vincent ruined our lives. And everyone applauded him for it. I press my lips to hers, hands snaking around her back.

"You sure that's all?"

"Yeah," I say but then quickly add, "that and the fact I'm sick of everything here."

"We'll be out soon." She hangs onto me, leaning back with a smile. "Just think, soon enough," she yawns, "we'll be away from everyone here, all the vampires, all the monsters." But aren't we the same as them? "We'll run away together."

"I know, I know." I hold her tighter, staring deeply into her mesmerising emerald eyes. "It's been a while since you brought that up."

"Just because we don't talk about it everyday, it doesn't mean neither of us don't want it to happen." I watch her—just simply staring and smiling. "We'll make it out, Jack, I promise. When there's no excuse, and we know Draven will be okay. When we know of somewhere set in stone to flee to. When we have enough resources." I look away and at the boy, shivering in his sleep.

"Hopefully," I murmur.

"We will. Stop being so pessimistic. Wake me when he regains consciousness." She yawns again as I bring my eyes back onto hers.

"I swear, you are always tired." She leaves me be, and I watch her head fall to her pillow, closing her eyes tight. She flips me off, and I let out a deep chuckle.

My god is she adorable.

Perhaps an hour later, the boy stirs. His eyelids flutter open, then returns to squinting again, flying a hand up to his head. He grimaces, and he – incredibly slowly – opens his eyes.

Then all of a sudden, he sits bolt upright as if struck by lightning. His hand flings up to his chest, clawing at his clothes as instinct, and then simply stares at me with a creased forehead, drinking me all in. My blue eyes, the black hair, the mole beside my ear, my pointed ears, the fangs. Everything.

"What's your name?" I ask after a moment or two of complete and utter silence.

"Why would I tell you that?" I raise an eyebrow at him as he purses his lips together tightly.

"I'm Jack. Name for a name?" He hesitates, glancing around the room nervously. When he lays eyes on Violet, he pauses for another second, but I edge closer to him to get his eyes back on me. "I'm right here." He drops his hand to his lap.

"Jess." *Jess Princeton.* Matches his golden hair.

"See? That wasn't so hard—"

"Who's she?" he interrupts.

"Violet." If I'm going to win his trust I shouldn't keep meaningless things from him. "Under recent circumstances, this is your new... place of residence. The Ash clan for now."

"I—" He shakes his head, itching the back of his neck, eyes searching anywhere but me. "I'm here for my sister. That's all." He snaps his eyes back onto mine abruptly, glaring. "Give me her, and I'll leave. I'll be out of your hands—" He notices something abnormal in his mouth, and his hand flings to poke, but I grab his wrist before. He flinches, leaning away from me in a blind fear.

"They're sharp." The fangs.

"What have you done to me?" He pulls his wrist away from me and out of my grip, feeling his new teeth with his tongue. I don't think I imagine the tears springing to his eyes immediately either. "You've turned me into a monster!" he exclaims, jaw ajar, and my eyes shoot towards Violet stirring in her sleep but not waking. His voice cracked on 'monster'.

"Shut up! You'll wake her!" I hiss in a hushed voice. "She's not the one you're angry at and neither am I!"

"You fucking watched me become one of ... one of *you.*" He breaks a little more.

"Do you think I had a choice in watching such a disgusting show?" I retort. He tears his eyes away from me to stare at his shaking hands. "I'm meant to train you, according to the Royals. You're in the same clan as me, and you'll listen to my words or else it won't be pretty for either of us."

"I'm not staying!" he yells at the top of his voice. He wraps his palms into fists and slams them on the mattress. *Violet's sleeping.* I shush him, and I hesitantly reach for my sword to make him shut up. But it's an empty threat.

"Yes, you are. You have no choice."

"So you'll be controlling me for the rest of my life?" *Dramatic much.*

"No, I never said that. I'm going to keep both of us out of trouble best I can. At least with me, you have a chance of running away again, with your sister, all limbs attached," I tell.

"Is she okay?" he asks me, eagerly, leaning forward on the bed.

"Yes, I saw her. Said her name was Sierra. She made me promise to keep you safe actually." His eyes dart around the room, taking it all in again. I suppose he wasn't expecting me to say all that, let alone the fact I've seen her.

"You swear you aren't bluffing?"

"Have you told me your sister's name?" I question. He shakes his head.

"And why would I lie?"

"To blackmail me," he points it out as if it's happening right now.

"I never said 'you should stay or else I'll kill her.'"

He glances me up and down, calculating something inside his head. He hesitates when he says, "I apologise for jumping to that conclusion then." We've taken his home, now holding him hostage essentially, and *he's* the one apologising? Jess reverts back to fiddling with his fingers. Tapping them against his thumbs and counting the touches. "Why didn't you stop him though?" he asks in the quietest voice imaginable.

"Because it would have backfired. You're lucky Draven pulled him from you when he did. You could have died—"

"He should have let him," he quips instantly. My jaw drops just a little.

"And leave your sister all alone in a world full of monsters?!" I stand up, turning away from him, cheeks flushing from anger, and even more unpleasant memories. This time, *not* regarding Vincent. "Sleep there. I'll be expecting you to be ready to train tomorrow morning. You'll learn with me." And before he can respond, I head towards Violet without looking back at his reaction. *He'd rather leave?*

"Will you keep her safe? Will you keep your promise?" he says in a quiet and frail voice.

"I never break promises."

He would rather have died than stayed with his sister? How can he say that? *Is that what my brother thought?* I take it back, I don't want to know. Maybe Jess wasn't thinking straight, or maybe he truly believes she's dead and dusted. An idea of empty hope, hanging onto it before he drowns.

I lie beside Violet on her creaking bed, only just enough room for us both. I snuggle as close to her as I can get away with, trying my best not to wake her. I lay my head behind hers, brushing my hand lightly over her bare shoulder as gently as I can. I keep staring at her head. For a second, I think I imagine it when she looks back at me, straight faced, almost unimpressed. She looks exhausted. I must have woken her, or maybe he did, absentmindedly. Either way, she takes my hand harshly, giving me a small smile, moving it to be around her stomach. I edge even closer, resting my head in the crook of her neck, placing a kiss on her cheek. She smiles even more, holding onto me tightly. I revert back to resting my head on the pillow behind her, my breath against her hair.

I close my eyes.

She's here, right here, focus on that.

I do so, and with those thoughts, I drift into a dreamless sleep.

Jack

9th October

"Clan meeting! Get up!" Zayne very kindly shouts at the top of his voice at god knows what hour in the morning. I shake myself awake, finding Violet still in my arms as she sits up, rubbing her palms against her eyes. "Achillea and Ambrosia are gonna be there!" Suddenly, he's grabbing my shoulder, and throwing me off the bed away from Violet's warmth, rolling onto the ground with a harsh thud.

"Zayne, really?" she grumbles, swinging her feet off to land beside me. She offers me her hand and I take it, standing, brushing off any dust from my uniform that I never changed out of last night.

"Hurry up," he responds, looking down his nose at us. His glare drifting towards Jess who's huddling in the corner of the bed, looking in pure horror at us all. He's trembling violently and his eyes wide observing it all. "You too, newbie." He steps closer and closer towards the poor kid, unsheathing his sword, preparing to do what he's done to me so many times before. Jess flinches, his gaze glued to the sword as Zayne shows no sign of mercy on his first day in this monster infested prison.

Fear crushes my chest with its weight. I quickly stand, lunging forward, and I step between the two as Zayne throws his sword down at Jess, and it's too late for me to move when I notice him turning the blade towards my cheek. The kid shrieks when I take the hit for him. A moment of pure shock flashes across Zayne's face, but I grit my teeth and bare it as the sharped edge slices across my collarbone.

"What the—"

"Jack," Violet mutters, and stands, seemingly unfazed, set apart from the concern tainting her eyes as she approaches me. I glance back to Zayne, scowling as cool blood trickles down my skin and onto my uniform.

"That was meant to be a welcome to the boy, Jack. Learn to mind your own business and stop butting into mine," he spits at me. His teeth gleams with the smirk on his face, as Violet snakes her hand around mine.

"He's mine to train. Not yours."

"I can play with anyone I want to play with, brat." With those words still lingering, he turns and leaves along with his twin sister, Florence. She's the one who trained Violet to shoot. Flower's extremely talented – the best in the clan, even surpassing Florence, her own mentor.

"Jack, Jesus!" Violet turns to me and pulls down my collar to inspect the cut closely.

"It's nothing deep. I'm fine." I grab her wrists, letting her lock eyes onto me instead of drifting elsewhere. "We have to go to the meeting."

"We need to clean it up—"

"Get some tissues and I'll be fine." She rolls her eyes, but does as I suggest. She rushes off towards the bathroom, while I turn around to stare at Jess still curled up in the corner of the bed, with wide, bulging eyes. Staring directly at me.

"Wh-why did you—" He's a stuttering mess. Things are moving way too fast for him. His eyes have seen and heard too much in the past not even twelve hours. I'll be surprised if he lasts two weeks before he spins off the rails. Finding any means of escape.

"Get ready to go," I grunt, turning away from his pathetic gaze. "They haven't given you any uniform yet, so I suggest you use this to cover your normal clothes." I reach for my black cape from the floor, as Violet comes back in with a roll of tissue. I chuck the cape at Jess, but he merely glances at it. "The Royals will be there, so we need to go. Now." I turn, Violet immediately grabbing my shoulders and pressing the tissues to the blood still dripping down my skin.

"For a supposedly light injury, there's a lot of mess." She glares at me and I grip the back of her hand pressed to my collarbone.

"I can do it."

"No harm in helping." I shake my head and force her hand away to do it myself.

"We need to go." She rolls her eyes lightly, heading towards the door. I look back and Jess is fastening the cape around his neck, standing. He seems smaller than I remember. Or maybe that's his posture, trying to slip into the background and disappear. He looks up at me, fear plastered on his face. "Stay close to us." He nods and follows me out the door.

Jess keeps his head down low as soon as we leave the room. Seems he *does* have some sort of common sense after all.

"What do you think it's about?" Violet asks, low voice. as we join the mumbling crowd.

"Him," I speak honestly, glancing at Jess. "It has to be."

"Would make sense," she comments.

"The Royals were here yesterday because of it. Achillea was the one to tell me to take care of him. What else could it be about?"

"Could be about the town," Jess mumbles as he steps closer to us and I stare down at him.

"What do you remember?"

"All I did was run after my sister. That's all."

"Any friends?" I shatter his shield momentarily. His expression drops and momentarily looks at his hands. *What's going through his mind?*

"They're alive. They were texting me."

"Well, let's pray they're still alive now then." Violet nudges me and I look forward, reverting my attention back to Vincent, who's smirking to the crowd of his devoted followers from the stairs. Achillea and Ambrosia loom above him. But where's Draven?

"They will be, they have to be," Jess whispers to himself. Empty hope. It'll be the death of him.

"Silence!" Achillea cracks a rare, but stunning smile as the quiet echoes wash over us. "I've taught you well, that was quick." The crowd laughs in time, almost harmonising with each other, like it's a rehearsed routine. Violet, Jess, and I don't find this amusing.

"Now, now!" Vincent takes over once Achillea gives him a nod of approval. "The moment everyone has been waiting for has dawned upon us!" He throws his arms up in the air, hands stretched out in magnificent glory. "It is final!" His grin is wide, stretching across his cheeks until the wrinkles reach his eyes. "We have taken over Hillark!" A round of claps, cheers and applause ring out from all around us. But even past the noise, I still hear Jess gasp suddenly. "After decades and centuries of waiting! We can now, safely and quickly, move into our new home." He brings his hands to be over his heart, looking a little solemn. It's a terrifying sight to behold, knowing he's only pulling this move for acting purposes. "And so, on the 15th, the Ash and Raven clans will move in!"

Another round of applause erupts. I sneak a look at the kid. He's distraught in his own mind. He's not taking it in, he's not processing. This can't be good.

"Furthermore, the cells below are all full to its capacity!" That's disgusting. I look away at Violet for a moment and she looks back at me. She's just as creeped out as me.

"Therefore, we'll be holding a feast tonight as a celebration. All are invited. Afterall, the blood supply's overflowing, so we deserve to treat ourselves! The smell is ravishing."

"Gross," I mutter under my breath.

"Lastly, our lovely, lovely Royals, shall be joining us for the foreseeable future!"

My gut drops. Achillea will be watching my every move now. Every single move.

I snap my eyes back to the group on the stairs. A frightful sight. Ambrosia waving out to the crowd, a knife in her free hand, dancing across her finger tips. She's in her beautiful black star-embroidered dress that reaches the bottom of her heels. Even from here, her dark red eyeshadow ignites the room. Achillea in a tightly fitted cropped dress, a wrap of thin, sparkly material hung over her shoulders, falling behind, silver outlines across her chest. A crown sits on top of her straight black hair, which falls halfway down her back. Both Achillea's and Ambrosia's darkened skin glistens as if being oiled recently, but where on earth would they be able to find the materials for that? And then there's Vincent who holds his hands high, a lighter held in one of them, like he can never be parted from it. He wears black trousers, a white T-shirt, patchy with ash from gone-wrong experiments and tears at the cuffs of his long sleeves. Obviously he takes *much* care in his appearance.

A terrifying trio.

"I hope you all feel at home in our new town," Achillea says in a calm, eerie tone of voice before looking directly at me. She merely nods, and I refuse to turn away first. I clench my fists, nails digging into my skin. Why me? She lowers her head, shadows casting over her face, her attention frozen on me as Ambrosia exclaims:

"Dismissed," she says with a flick of her wrist.

A round of quick fire questions erupt from the crows, all for the two Royals – whilst Achillea rolls her eyes in annoyance, turns, and walks away, Ambrosia watches, shrugs her shoulders and simply joins the crowd. Vincent continues to play with his fire.

I disappear before he tries to offer me a human body or something revolting. Violet speaks to Jess, asking something before catching up to me in the corridor in a hurry.

"Jack," she says softly from behind. "Jess wants us to check the supply room to see if any of them are his friends." I roll my eyes, spinning on my heel to see them both simply staring at me.

"I'm not going in there and neither are you."

"Well, duh, I can't go in there with him because you're the one who's meant to be taking care of him. Not me," she tells me. That wasn't the whole reason, but we'll go with that.

"So, no?" Jess asks beside Violet, flicking his eyes between us with pleading eyes. Like a puppy begging for freedom. He clenches his hands into fists, sticking a stubborn chin out at me. His face suddenly turns desperate and an untold rage heats beneath his cheeks. "Why won't you help me?" *I'm trying.*

"Because Vincent will get the wrong idea and think I've changed my ways."

"You're not like him?"

"I thought he told you this already," Violet answers for me, as she shrugs her shoulders, walking closer to me. "So consider yourself lucky we were in the right place at the right time, or else you'd be stuck with probably Zayne." She glances at me.

"Like I was," I speak for her.

"Was he the one from this mor—"

"Yes, he was." I subconsciously, lift my hand to run my fingers over the new scab across my collarbone.

"And you're not bothered?" I walk towards our room again.

"It's not right by any means," Violet raises her voice, catching up to me.

"Of course not. I can't believe they allow him in your ranks," Jess exclaims from behind. "And I can't believe I'm here either. Or that this is happening. Aren't vampires meant to be... fiction?" He has no idea of the world he's a part of now. I barge through our door, planting myself on my own bed this time, embracing the fact Zayne won't be here for a while since he has errands to run.

"Will you let me look at that wound, Jack?" Violet complains as Jess trails in, closing the door behind him, looking very out of place.

"No, it's not deep I—" She interrupts me by pressing her lips to mine, quick and sharp, one hand on my shoulder, another on my cheek.

"Shut up. Unless you're using your mouth for good instead of nonsense." She sits beside me.

"What are you fighting for?" Jess suddenly asks through the silence. I stare at him. "I mean, the vampires?"

"They're searching for a city that's apparently beneath the ground," I exaggerate my tone in an attempt to show how impossible it really is, before rolling my eyes back to Violet.

"You don't believe there's such a place?"

"Would you believe them when they've fed you lies for over a decade? Then they come out and say it's all for a legendary city a few Nobles and Royals lived in 4oo and something years ago?"

"I suppose not."

"It's all a delusion," I mutter. "A fantasy that will get us all killed." He purses his lips, stepping forward to me again, I watch from the corner of my eye whilst Violet's still staring at that wound. After a few beats of silence and murmurs from her, Jess suddenly blurts,

"How did you... turn?"

"Whoa, okay," Violet laughs nervously, backing off from me to stare at Jess. "That's a step far—"

"I wasn't asking you. I was asking Jack," he says simply. His tone unamused and tired. Like he's *already* giving up. Surely not already. Not with his sister trapped. "Is that too far for you?" I glance my eyes over him, biting my tongue, desperation in his eyes. New space, new people, new blood. Perhaps he needs some sort of reassurance that he's not alone.

"Short and simple," I mutter reluctantly. "We were in the wrong place at the wrong time. Exploring an abandoned hall of sorts, a building on the outskirts of our home. Vincent was there and you know the rest. He wanted new Knights, and we were in his path—"

"Jack tried to protect me, but we were only, like, fourteen or fifteen."

"Seventeen," I answer for her. "Eleven years ago." Though it feels longer than that.

"Oh."

I turn to Jess. "How old are you?"

"Sixteen. Seventeen in December." And I'm turning twenty-nine then. He's almost half my age. And yet we're stuck in the same boat. Violet stares at me and I know we're thinking the same thing.

Poor kid.

Jess sits on the other bed close by. He takes the cape off and drops it onto the floor, and the way his shoulders slump in defeat is enough for guilt to twist in my stomach.

"I'm sorry. We can't be caught in the supply room, Jess," I tell him. He looks at me with slightly softer eyes.

"It's fine, I guess," Jess mutters. "Did any of your friends survive?"

"We never contacted them to keep them safe," I tell him how it is, Violet creeping her hand onto mine to hold close. "We never saw any of them again." His eyes widen momentarily, before breaking into an angry glare.

"You never tried?" He shakes his head. "I'm getting my sister at the first opportunity and then leaving to—"

"To what? Find a couple of corpses either on the table for tea, or laid on the ground of your beloved home?" Hurt flashes across his face in an instance. "Take your sister when you can, leave and go far, far away. Don't ever come back, don't ever risk your life again."

"I'd never abandon them."

"You abandoned them when you left for your sister. That was the price you paid. What you've become. Don't give yourself delusional hope." I turn away before I can watch his expression fall, but my attention quickly draws to the door, suddenly bursting open as Vincent walks through, stretching his arms out.

Great. What does *he* want?

"I thought I'd find you here!" He looks directly at Jess, whilst Violet squeezes my hand.

"What do you want?" Jess demands, lowering his voice a fraction.

"Oh, nothing really." He claps his hands together, wearing an annoying grin. "Just wanted to personally invite you to the feast later. I know Jack and Violet will never go." He rolls his eyes and grimaces at me before the playful smile appears back on his lips for Jess. "So—"

"No, thanks, I won't be going," he grimaces.

"Why ever not?"

"I'm not a monster."

"So, Jack's influenced you already?"

"What? No! This is my decision—"

"Like how it was yours to come here in the first place?" They're playing a dangerous game on a tricky slope. Vincent smirks triumphantly, and continues on, "Maybe when you smell it, you'll change your mind!" Excuse me? "Depending what *abnormality* you've inherited, will be whether you need blood to survive, afterall. But I'm sure Jack's gone through that with you!" I widen my eyes, I forgot about that part of his world.

"What?" Jess sits up, glancing at me, but I don't look at him.

"Oh? He hasn't mentioned?" *I didn't even think of it.* "Well, I'll leave it to him to explain. I have other places to be." He smiles, and with that, he skips out with a wave back at all of us, a wink at me and he slams the door close.

"What on earth did he mean?" I swallow hard, finally turning my head to look at Jess' dumbfounded expression.

"Different vampires have different abilities. If what he spoke of was true, you'd need to drink blood to survive, or you'll thirst to death. Then there's the intelligence thing, the flight, more and more. They say it's due to the evolution of our kind. There's some who can't bear to be in the sunlight due to decades beneath the surface, hidden in caves." His eyes widen, looking down at his hands.

"We're flighted. *Alatus* is the technical term. We've never tasted human blood before. We're not monsters," Violet finally speaks out. "At least, in that way we're not." I stare at her, clasping her hand with my free one.

"You're not a monster and you never were, nor will be, my love," I tell her. She smiles a little at me, and everything feels brighter again. But the moment is cut short as Jess storms out of the room. I quickly follow, leaping to my feet as anxiety grows in my mind, worried he might just try to leave. I call his name, but he continues to walk out and doesn't look back. Through the corridor, out the entrance and out into the early dawn wind. The sky's a beautiful shade of pink and fluffy clouds are dotted around our heads. So calm on such a mess of a morning.

"Jess!" He stops and looks back at me, clenching his fists.

"I could leave right now and no one would stop me. You would let me, and I'll never find out what kind of *monster* I am. I could just stay in the dark until I die." He looks away from me and at the forest surrounding us, the town in view down the path through the bushes. His eyes glued to it. The endless outcomes of escaping hasn't only plagued his mind. I know too. And maybe it's my fault I'm not out there already. But Jess looks at the opening longingly. His expression's soft. "I could go see my friends. Ask them for advice, what I should do." He looks down at his feet and then back at me. "But it'll never be the same." He lifts his hands to his lips.

"What about your sister?"

"It was just wishful thinking," he mutters and shakes his head with a heavy sigh. "Let me take a walk. Just around the forest, and I'll come back with a clearer mind."

"How can I trust you?"

"I will not leave her. It's not up to you what happens to me, and whose control I'm under. It's mine and mine alone."

I see my brother in him. Stubborn. Always fighting, but never sure who against. The thought strikes me, and I stay silent. He walks away.

I look to the sky. As if it'll give me hope.

Or am I searching for *him*?

I give up.

Savannah

12th October

Zack said everything would be fine. That we shouldn't talk about what happened on the 8th of October 2037. Luka told me he's only saying it because he's utterly terrified. But he pretends, just for us to feel better, to be able to sleep peacefully at night, to feel secure during the day. He told me Zack might be the most scared of us all.

So we pretend, not only for ourselves, but for Zack as well. Perhaps there was truly hope for a brighter sunrise. Even if I've never believed it.

It's been four days. But we haven't spoken of *her* or *him*. I never find the right words.

On the first evening, Zack let me take his bedroom and I stayed in there for the rest of the night, through to 2pm the next day. It was only when my stomach roared for food and water that I went downstairs. Minorly shocked at the sight of everyone simply watching TV. They told me good morning despite it being the afternoon. They never scolded me for being in bed for over twelve hours. Luka asked if I slept well. I said no. I got food and went back upstairs. To simply disappear.

Matthew followed and spent the next few hours with me, killing time by talking. I can't say I wasn't surprised when he said he did homework this morning whilst I was 'asleep'. It was so surreal. I was meant to be at school. But I just simply *wasn't*.

Last night, Luka came into Zack's room, carrying a sleeping bag in pjs. He slept in the same room as me. Admittedly, it was getting a little lonely.

We kept saying we were tired, but we still ended up talking deep into the night.

"I'm worried," he blurted out of nowhere, and cut right through the darkness. He looked up at me from across the bed, sitting cross legged. "About everyone. About you." I pursed my lips.

"I'm worried too. About you and everyone," I said, echoing him.

"I don't know how to help." He shrugged his shoulders – not in defeat exactly, but not in confusion either.

"We all need time." I thought that was the right thing to say—I couldn't think of anything else. But Luka replied with nothing and swung his legs off the bed and onto his sleeping bag, pausing a moment to stare at me.

"What if we don't have time?" Speechless. I was speechless. Because that was going through my mind too. Anxiety pooled in my stomach, digging into my veins, making its way through my body.

"I don't know." He gave me a small smile, glanced down at my hand and brushed his own against my skin. Very briefly. I wondered why he didn't hold on.

But now the 12th of October dawns, sunlight spilling into Zack's room. An early morning sky fills the crack in the curtain, a glimpse of the outside world. I make my way downstairs, where Luka, Oskar and Matthew are watching TV. Again. I wonder what stopped the attackers from turning off the electricity. I plant myself next to Oskar whilst Luka sits in the arm chair. We greet each other, talk, pretend to smile, until Oskar turns the TV off, and breaks the silence,

"We're gonna run out of food."

"We'll cross that bridge when we get to it," Luka says, frowning.

"We should cross it now." Oskar meets his gaze.

"Are we close to running out then?" Matthew mutters in a low voice, as if not to disturb Zack sleeping upstairs.

"I think so. Zack usually gets all his food shopping on the weekends, and oh, it's Friday." No need for the condescending tone.

"Maybe we can order—"

"Everywhere is out of commission for now," Matthew interrupts me. "Sorry." Unease creeps up my spine.

"If needs be, I'll go out and find shops that are open—"

"It's not safe," I tell Luka.

"Well." He shrugs his shoulders. "If it gets us food."

"If it gets you killed, it won't be worth it," I shoot back at him. He looks away from me, pursing his lips together.

I've lost *her*. Don't let me lose him too.

"So, what, we wait to starve?" Oskar questions.

"We wait as long as we can, and then we can go out together, as a group or in a pair," Zack announces behind us. I turn my head to watch him walk down the stairs, yawning. "Never alone." I wasn't alone. And one person in that trio got murdered. How is that going to help us if we always assume they'll have mercy on two people and not one?

"Oskar and I know self-defence. It should be us two," Luka adds, also staring at Zack.

"Makes sense to me," he agrees, and Oskar nods and turns the TV back on.

Noticing my hands begin to shake unconsciously, I take a deep breath, silently, in hopes no one notices my sudden uneasiness. But hell to that, these people know me better than anyone in the world. I dig my hands between my knees, squeezing them together to stop them, when a hand from the left edges beside my thigh. I look up at Matthew, staring at me.

"*You okay?*" he mouths in the silence. I just look away. It's not like anything can help me when I get like this.

"Zack, you should check the amount of food we have—"

"I thought we weren't going to talk about this for now," Matthew breaks through Oskar's demand, catching on quickly. They stare at each other, waiting a moment more for either of them to speak up again.

"We can't just ignore it right now, Matthew."

"Zack and Savannah have just woken up. Do we need to pester them like this so early?"

"It's 10am, it's not early."

"For some people it might be." Matthew's expression softens, and I drift my eyes onto Oskar, who's looking at the curtains guarding the sunlight breaking through.

With wide eyes, he asks, "Did you hear that?"

"Hear what?" Zack questions, walking closer. I strain my ears to listen. A woman. In the streets. Calling out.

I look to Luka first, who's leaning on the end of the armchair now, perking up.

"Helloo! Any survivors out there?"

My heart beats a thousand miles per hour. Hope swells in my chest for the first time in days. Hope for someone to help, instead of leaving us to our own devices.

I stand, following Zack to the window, and we both look out from the edges of the curtains. There's a woman who looks a little older than us walking through the street, calling out for anyone who's trapped or alive. Her voice is frantic and high pitched. She's tall, and her thick, long, raven hair falls halfway down her back, flowing behind her in the rough wind of October. She's searching the surroundings, a sour expression on her face; even from here I can see her bright and vibrant green eyes, especially when she looks in this direction. I hide.

"Oh my gosh," Zack mutters, stepping back. Before thinking it through, he rushes to the door, grips the handle and pulls. Matthew leaps up from his seat, while Luka runs to him, objecting.

But Zack's already opened the door for the first time in four days.

"Hey!" he yells and waves. Meanwhile, roots wrap around my feet, tangling between my toes, freezing me to the ground. *What if they're out to get us? What if they don't want to help us? What if they attack us?* We can't trust her. If Zack thinks otherwise, he's sorely mistaken. In this new dystopian-type world, we can't trust anyone not to kill us as soon as they get the chance. I watch Luka step back, wide eyes, shaking his head, cursing under his breath.

"Oh, thank god!" I hear her exclaim outside, running closer to us. "Someone else *is* alive!"

"Who are you?" Zack questions, and opens the door wider, practically welcoming her in to murder us. Luka quickly steps away, and out of view, chest heaving.

"Oh, was that another person I spy with my little eye!"

He gulps and looks back at me, finding my eyes almost immediately. He makes his way over, and whispers in my ear, *"Don't say a word."*

I nod, and he tells the same to Oskar and Matthew. Both agree, and Oskar stands, walking past me, standing beside the window. He peers into the unknown and spots the woman immediately. He doesn't budge as her voice carries into the house.

"How many people are in there with you? Any parents? Siblings?"

"Are you here to help us?" This isn't a very successful conversation. Both parties are avoiding the other's questions. It's getting nowhere quickly.

"Depends who's asking," she laughs. How can she laugh at a time like this? The world feels as though it's ending. And she's *laughing* it off? "There's a camp north of this town with food, weapons, people, tents, water, and more. I'm looking for people to come strengthen our numbers." That makes it sound like an army. *Is it?*

"Food?" Oh no.

I shake my head repeatedly over and over again, as if I have a choice of what happens right now. Anxiety twists my stomach, uncertainty fills my blood. I swallow hard. Surrounded by strangers, somewhere unfamiliar, it sounds like hell.

"Yes, why? Are you running out?"

"We have enough for now," Zack answers and glances inside at us.

"But...?" the stranger presses.

"But I don't know," he says.

"If you're not sure, then why did you come out so eagerly to greet me?" He snaps his attention back to her, whilst Oskar leans back sharply, looking at me, nudging my shoulder lightly. Letting me know he's there. He's here beside me. I flicker my eyes in his direction, and he just stares at me. Millions of unsaid words shared with just a glance of his eyes.

"Because I was surprised to see another living human that wasn't in a cloak or about to attack us."

"I'll take that. So, if you like, I can show you to the camp?"

Luka shakes his head, repeatedly, lunging towards Zack but—

"We'd like to accept then!"

"Great!" She claps her hands together, while Luka backs away, turning around, hands on his head in disbelief. Panic written in his eyes.

"What's your name by the way?"

"Thena Pires! Brazilian descendant, and you?"

"Zack."

"Nice to meet you, Zack." All of a sudden, her head pops around the corner of the door, gripping onto the edges, looking between us all. I instinctively stand back, bumping into Oskar. I mutter an apology to him, he says it's fine, whilst Luka refuses to turn around to face her. Rage washes over his face. "Hi everyone!" She waves.

"Okay, well." Zack gently pushes her shoulder back out the door. "We'll get ready, you can wait out here." She nods repeatedly, looking at him with a grin.

"Sounds like a plan!"

"See you in a moment—"

"With a crowd?"

"With a crowd." He closes the door and Luka whirls around, his arms over his chest.

"There is NO way in hell I'm going anywhere with her," he announces. "Zack, do you remember what happened to Piper?" He looks at me and I step beside him, wondering whether I should lay my hand on his shoulder or not. "What happened to us? To all of us?!" He looks at Oskar and then at Matthew. "You didn't ask if we were comfortable with anything you just agreed to. She invaded our privacy, just walked in! She avoided all your questions too, didn't you notice?"

"But she answered in the end, didn't she?" he fights back, just not as viciously. "She told us she could help us and—"

"Where?" Luka scoffs, putting his palms out in front of him. "Where is this proof?"

"She's alive, isn't she?" Silence settles. I can hear Luka's heavy breathing beside me. Zack looks at all of us, searching for his own version of the truth, but no one says anything to back him up. It breaks him, just a little. His face falls. "I just think- I just thought that we need help. Help to live. Help to survive." His voice, frail and weak.

"I thought your mum was safe," I point out. He shakes his head.

"She stopped texting me two days ago." And he never told us, just to keep up the facade. My shoulders slump.

"We just need more time," I mutter under my breath, unable to find the strength to say it louder. "We're still processing."

"We could get attacked again for round two. Don't you think going somewhere else would help us?" Zack suggests helplessly.

"And if she's one of the people who took Jess?" Oskar speaks up from behind me. "Eliza? Logan? Anyone?"

"We don't know if she can be trusted, Zack, that's all," Matthew adds, avoiding all of our eyes.

"Do we have another choice?" he shouts, clamping his hands tightly together in fists, voice breaking. I look at Luka, his brows curving in sympathy, sighing heavily.

"Zack, I don't know. If she means good, she could always come back to us. As Savannah said," Luka takes my hand in his. Maybe to make us both feel safer. "We need more time to process everything. We saw everything." He shakes, and I squeeze. "I don't think I'm ready to risk it all again."

"Then when will you be ready?" Zack asks softly.

"With our food situation, we need to go to this camp," Oskar breaks in, walking towards the kitchen, past us all. "We're all in this together so if we go, then we all go. No one," he looks back at Luka and I, "goes alone. No one stays behind. And no one is splitting up." He turns to us before going into the other room. "We get knives but don't tell her. We get our own source of water and food for now, so if need be, we can run. Should she turn on us, she won't have the element of surprise."

"You know a lot more than I had thought," Matthew comments.

"Considering applying to the army for years paid off – and all those fighting classes may be all for this moment, but I don't want to run anymore. If we stay, we might starve. If we go, we might get killed. Either one doesn't exactly seem promising."

"You've got that right."

"Are we doing this?" I cut in swiftly after Matthew.

"Maybe Jess is with them," Luka realises out loud. Oskar merely looks away at the floor, grabbing some clothes from the pile by the sofa.

"I don't count on it," Matthew says before he can. "Don't say it, you'll give me hope." He forces a dull smile at us, chest aching. Oskar leaves the room.

"Fine," Luka sighs, letting my hand go and flying his palms up in surrender. "We'll go." He walks off, past Zack and up the stairs. His shoulders slump, head hanging low, glancing back and then up at me.

"I'm sorry," Zack says. "For what it's worth. I thought this was best."

"And maybe it is," I tell him, walking closer, laying both of my hands on his shoulders, forcing him to lock onto my eyes. "But we won't know until we make a decision. So, we'll go with you, Zack. I'm sorry about your mum." His eyes swell up with tears so suddenly. He brings his palms up to wipe his eyes. I'm unsure whether I should offer him a hug – should I give him space or reassurance? He's been pretending for so long. These past four days have been exhausting. He doesn't deserve it all on his shoulders. That's not safe. "Let us help, it's not your job to take care of us. We should all care *for each other*. It's not all on you, Zack, but you've done a pretty damn good job of it."

"I hope it's the right choice to go, I never meant to upset Luka. It's just..."

"Hard?" I ask when he struggles to finish his sentence. He nods, dropping his hands to his sides. "You're not the only one that feels like that." I give him a small, but real smile. "We're all here for you."

"But Luka—"

"He is too! Do you really think he'd let this get between you two? You're best friends!" I laugh a little and it cracks a smile out of him too. I let his shoulders go, his eyes drifting to Matthew.

"I'm sure it'll be fine, we're just being paranoid," he echoes behind me. Panic settles in. I pass Zack, trailing up the stairs.

I knock on the bedroom door.

"Yeah?"

"It's Savannah."

"You don't have to knock," Luka replies gently. I open up the door, stepping in to see him sitting on the bed, peering out at the woman in the streets,Thena. "I think she's carrying knives with her."

"How do you know?" He looks at me, curled in a ball, holding his knees close to his chest.

"I saw a glimpse of one beneath her jacket."

"Is it definitely a weapon?" I gulp, uneasy. I shut the door, edging closer.

"I won't let her use it on you, Savannah," he says, and it's the most serious and honest thing I've heard escape his lips. I smile softly, sitting on the bed in front of him as he stretches his legs out again. "Okay?"

"I believe you."

He nods and looks back out the window. This time at the sky, the houses, the landscape. Of a place we once called safe and sound. Scanning his eyes over everything all at once. And I do too, the clear blue sky, the harsh wind blowing leaves across the pavement, the untouched houses without lights to ignite them with life. Let's never forget this place. "Are you okay?"

"I wish we could stay longer," he says. "We're always running out of time. I'm sick of it."

"So am I."

"It's unfair. But I guess we gotta survive, right?" It's happening too fast. "That's what Oskar said, didn't he?"

"He's changed."

"We all have."

"In just a few days." He looks back at me and then at the door. "Are they all waiting for me?"

"We can take our time." He leans his head on the wall behind him, closing his eyes.

"My second home," he mutters under his breath.

It dawns on me, in this moment, that Zack's house is where he spent most of his time. This is the place where we all met up on holidays and on Fridays occasionally; the place where we hung out the most since there was always so much space. We had a New Year's party here, where we passed out on top of each other around 2am, celebrating the new year, sleeping across the floor. This is where we exchanged secret santas, where we spent his birthdays, where we hung out on Valentine's Day.

Where Luka came to escape.

He suddenly sighs, standing up, looking around at everything. At the unread books stacked beside the bed, the crimson red walls we painted years ago, the black fluffy carpet that once was fluffier than my teddies, the rug in front of the door where many stains were settled, at the huge teddy on the end of the mattress (Zack's favourite), the curtains drawn close, ignoring the world outside.

At the pictures of us on Zack's notice board. Posing. Laughing. Smiling.

This is Luka's silent goodbye. The moment where he takes it all in, knowing that he might never return.

His silent farewell to the memories left behind.

He stares back at me, and mutters the words, "I suppose we should leave now, or else I'll end up staying here on my own." Never has such simple spoken words felt so heartbreaking. I glance back as we leave the room, remembering New Year's a couple years back.

We laughed until we couldn't breathe. It was the first time I ever felt like I was needed, loved, and important. Like if I weren't there, they'd miss me.

"Maybe my brothers escaped to this camp anyway. Maybe they made it."

Zack's waiting at the bottom of the stairs for us and his eyes meet Luka's immediately.

"I'm sorry," he says tightly. "I really am." Luka simply steps in front of him, engulfing him into a huge, fat hug. They rock back and forth, a small smile falters against my lips at the sight. I tear my eyes away toward Oskar and Matthew in the doorway to the kitchen, quarrelling over what to bring.

"We need to bring some sort of weapon, dude. We can't bring nothing," Oskar argues, holding a bread knife. "It's not much, but it's sharp enough to do some sort of damage for us to be able to escape. It can buy us time!"

"Fine, if you're so sure." Matthew rolls his eyes, looking away.

"I'm certain. Matthew, this is only to protect ourselves." Oskar playfully punches his shoulder with a forced smile to appear collected and calm. "I'm not doing anything else with it."

"I never suspected you would," he replies. Preparing to leave and never come back, huh. That's a step I never thought I'd be forced to take. Yet here we are.

As we stand in front of the door, preparing to leave, I glance back at what was once ours. Time to move along, I suppose. Although it breaks a piece of my heart, stepping outside into the brisk air, a small piece of hope resides within that I'll return someday.

But as of right now, with the sun blinding my vision, I know we're not planning on it. So I push that hope deep underground. Never to be felt and acknowledged again. I can't afford for that to affect my decisions from now on.

Luka bumps shoulders with me, as Zack squeezes past him to reach Thena. His lips pursed, thin and tight. Whilst Oskar and Matthew gather in front of us.

"You sure you're okay with it?" Luka mutters under his breath as Thena approaches us.

"Yes, I'm okay with it," I say softly, equally as quietly. He's carrying a knife too – he kept asking me if it was okay for him to bring one as well. He obviously doesn't understand the meaning of *yes*. I wasn't about to say no when it's the only sense of security we have at the moment.

"That didn't take too long, a small pack I see!" Thena announces, smiling to herself, hands on her hips as if she's accomplished something.

"Yeah, are you sure we can all go to this camp you're talking about?" Zack asks.

"Of course, of course! The more, the merrier! The more, the stronger." Wait, what did she say?

"We'll be safe...right?"

"As safe as you possibly can be," she answers Matthew, who edges forward a few paces. "Now, stop worrying, it's exhausting. Come on, keep up!" She turns and begins to walk the way she came from. "Oh, and be on guard please! Watch out and don't trust anyone in a weird cloak." I don't trust random knife ladies either.

This is the most exercise I've done in four days. I haven't had the strength to do anything except walk up and down the stairs every now and then. I stay as close to my friends as possible. Bumping shoulders with Luka occasionally, trodding on Oskar's heel at times, and almost tripping on Matthew's feet.

The camp can be seen from the outskirts of town. From a distance, all I make out are tents and a few people here and there. Then it starts expanding. More wooden stalls, more steel swords, the stringed bows, the pointed arrows, the silver armour, the *food*. There's a well near the farm, with people queuing up behind for a turn. It's as if we've travelled back in time. Since when was there a well close to Hillark?

A few people scatter around the outside of the little camp, nausea fills my stomach, so I look down and away from them, avoiding all eye contact.

"So!" Thena turns around suddenly, clapping her hands together. "There's two unused tents by my area that you guys can take, max is three to one tent. But before that, some of you should probably meet Selene, so she's aware of you living in her camp. I'm only the best friend." She exaggerates an eye roll, and Zack forces a laugh, quickly followed by Matthew and Oskar. "I'm also the captain. So I do run things here as well, growing numbers, training and all—"

"Training?" Oskar blurts. "What training?"

"Against the *nosferatu*, of course."

Is she talking about vampires?

"Any more questions?" she demands, glancing between our gobsmacked expressions. Matthew begins to raise his hand, but she whips her head round, pretending not to see it. "Good, you'll have a few days to 'settle in' before all that though. So, who's coming with me to Selene?"

"I suppose I will," Zack says and looks to us for someone else to join. I glance at Luka but his eyes are wide—like he's in shock. He doesn't seem to be listening, nor taking anything in right now. So I speak up, step between Matthew and Oskar, swallowing the gnawing anxiety, and I say, "I will too." Zack and I look at each other. He exhales in relief, a brief smile passing his lips.

"Fantastic! Let's go!" We glance back at everyone momentarily, whilst Thena leads us away from them. No one looks too thrilled about the whole concept of being split up, but Matthew still finds strength to force a reassuring grin and he waves to us.

"Bye, bye!"

We hear her before we can see her. A strong, feminine voice shrieks from behind a tent as we stumble closer. A tall woman with long paper-white hair stands, yelling at someone before they scamper off as quickly as they can. She shakes her head, catching Thena's gaze, then smiles through thin lips. Her skin as pale as can be, possibly a case of albino, her eyes bright and striking green, head held high. She seems to be around 5'11" in height, a little taller than Zack, her nose small and petite, eyelashes short and thin.

But, nevertheless, she's beautiful.

"Selene!"

"Thena, welcome back." Thena throws her arms up high, speeding up to greet her best friend.

"Did you miss me?"

"Always." The stranger smiles, but her attention's quickly brought to Zack and me. And I suddenly feel so much tinier beneath her silent gaze, as if I'm under some sort of inspection. "You found survivors."

"Yeah. Seems the source was right after all."

"Source?" Zack mutters under his breath before I can.

"They had no reason to lie." She brushes it off too quick for comfort, gliding towards us. Softly and slowly, like grace and elegance comes naturally for her. "Welcome to our refuge camp. Full of survivors and fighters from small villages that have been attacked previously," she speaks calmly, a friendly smile spreading across her face. "We're on a mission to find as many survivors as we can." And this 'source' told her that we survived? "Are there more of you?"

"Yes, actually, three others. Finding tents now," Zack answers.

"And what are your names?"

"I'm Zack, this is Savannah." She nods along.

"Well, Zack and Savannah, you'll be trained here, along with your friends. A weapon of your choice, of course, we provide everything including food and water." No clothes then, why didn't we think to bring some more then? I purse my lips, her eyes boring into me. Anxiety gnaws at my stomach. *Please stop looking at me.* I look to Zack, a cry for help in my eyes. His gaze moves seamlessly from me to Selene, quickly reading my expression.

"That sounds great! We'll leave you to find your tents." Selene nods at us, looking back at Thena, a silent understanding between the two.

"I know it sounds scary, but try to make yourselves at home." She looks at me and a pang of guilt twinges in my chest.

"Okay, thank you." Zack nods and smiles, so do I.

As trapped as I felt in his house, I want to be back in Zack's room again. Or better, *my house.* I should be in my own bedroom, maybe preparing for an upcoming exam, some music playing in the background and my black cat, Luna, sitting on my lap. But no. I'm lying on a lumpy fold-up bed that's not stable enough for me to even move an inch without the legs creaking obnoxiously loud.

Just staring at the ceiling. In silence. That's all there is to do in the dead of the night.

Zack and Luka are in this tent. Matthew and Oskar were invited to stay in the tent beside ours by someone named Annabeth—it seemed two tents weren't freed up, only one. We didn't talk much, but they seemed like a genuinely nice person, the opposite to how Thena appears. However, I still don't trust anyone here. Part of that reason is because I swear I saw tiny miniature fang-like teeth in the mouths of some people when they spoke. However, I pushed the sudden thought aside, believing it to be paranoia playing a part in my mind.

Zack snores. Luka's silent. With my mind speeding through millions of events happening all at once, I burst into a sudden round of tears. I cover my mouth, gasping deep for silent breaths into my lungs, careful to not wake a soul.

Nothing will ever be the same. I'll never be safe at home with mum and dad again. I'll never be able to visit the shops without wondering who I might meet. I'll never be able to go to school, or see Jess in the streets. I'm never visiting Piper's house again. I'm an orphan.

Breathing becomes difficult as my heart pours onto my cheeks and dampens my pillow. My chest becomes tight with worry and anxious thoughts revolving inside my head. I sob so hard, so uncontrollably that I beg myself to stop. *Just shut up*, because people are asleep in here with me. I could wake them. But the waves come and go, and I'm buried in an avalanche of grief. A part of me wants to convince myself that this is all a nightmare. Piper's alive and breathing, not covered in blood, not smelling of that disgusting metallic odour. But I push it back down, hope diminishing. Because I could be dead in a month. Zack could be dead. This camp could be ignited in flames. The future is no longer set in stone, nothing is planned, and oh how I hate the unknown. *Luka could be dead.*

I cry harder at the realisation. Because I've always thought I'd be the one to go before him, that way I'd never have to endure the pain of living a life without his light. But now, that's not certain. No Luka?

I don't know how long it's been since I broke down. Minutes blend into hours with alarming rapidity. But as I'm dozing off to sleep, drifting between consciousness and dreams, someone draws a blanket over me. Someone tucks me into this bed, to stop the cold from grazing my skin. A faint touch of someone's fingers through my hair. Only when my breathing returns back to normal, do they return to their own bed.

Zack was asleep. Luka was silent.

"If only I had the right words to comfort you." Luka was awake the whole time.

I fall asleep to his voice replaying in my head.

But I want my mum. I want my dad. I want to wake them up and tell them I had a nightmare. I want them to hold me whilst I sleep so I know both them and me are safe.

But I can't have that.

And can never again.

Savannah

14th October

We're given weapons. A variation of swords, bows, daggers, and guns, and we are expected to fight.

Savannah ✦

15th October

A week has passed since we were attacked.

Instead of waiting a few days for training, we were told to pick a weapon. I chose a bow. Unfortunately, Thena teaches this well, so she's the one who offers me guidance, tips and tricks. Oskar begins training with a long sword. Luka and Matthew, instructed by Annabeth, choose swords. Zack, on the other hand, chose a gun. The most lethal and powerful one of all. But there's something off about guns here. It's like they've been enchanted. Modified. They're harder to handle than 'normal' ones which is why not everyone has one. But one shot and it'll kill whatever Thena means by a *nosferatu*.

They began teaching us through simple defence moves. Blocking and advancements. It's all so exhausting. Overwhelming. I *just* lost my best friend, and I'm thrown into this?

"You need a close range weapon as well," Thena mentions this morning. "As you already know, I have two knives." My heart freezes. She turns around, showing me her two daggers. Embroidered with crystals. "Sylvie and Seth."

"You named them?"

"Yeah, well, I'm easily bored. Plus they're the only things I can rely on to protect me." She then kisses one of the blades, followed by laughter. "You look mortified. I'll teach you the ropes today, alright?"

"Do I need to?"

"Yes, yes you do. It goes hand in hand with wielding a bow and arrow. It's to help defend yourself up close. Nothing more to it." I swallow hard as she offers me her knives to grip and feel. I take a silent deeper breath. With my feet rooted to the ground, I take the handles tightly. "Not so hard now, is it?" Somewhere out there she'll have harmed someone with these. She'll have caused someone to panic, to run, to hurt, to fall, to scream. And I'm holding those weapons I so dearly wanted to avoid.

I will never wield knives against anyone. Not that I should ever need to. I never want to be around blood ever again. The smell. The crimson. The thickness. *Disgusting.*

She leaves after a lecture or two. I'm left gripping two daggers she's said are mine. Not her Sylvie and Seth. New ones. Glittering ones. Jewels embedded in the handles and the blades clean and new. As soon as I feel no one's watching me, I quickly toss them aside. My gaze drifts to Matthew and Oskar working through some sword exercises. Whilst Zack is targeting a dummy, I wander close by to him, surprised at how focused, how well he works around the trigger. How good his natural aim is.

"I see someone's enjoying themselves," I mutter. He jumps, looking at me with wide eyes.

"Oh." He shakes his head, looking at his pistol. "It's only a pistol. Noah would talk to me about them so I know a little more than I probably should."

"Ah, I see." He rarely mentions his big brother. He was in the army. Died protecting his best friend. I suppose it makes more sense why he chose the gun now.

"Practice makes perfect, right? I'm just trying to get better so I can help out more. Be useful."

"Fight their fight?"

"I mean, sure, as long as it's well backed up, and what they're doing is pure-hearted and actually good," he tells me, looking back at the dummy forty feet away. "There's nothing else for us to do. Doesn't seem like we're going back home anytime soon."

"How are you so chill about it?" I chuckle nervously.

"I'm not." Ah, yes, the 'pretend you're okay', but you're breaking inside. "I'm just stating facts at this point." That can't just be it. There has to be more they're not telling us. Maybe people are still alive in Hillark or even outside of this camp. We just might not ever know where.

A hand taps my shoulder. I turn around to find Luka gesturing to me to come with him, tugging at my clothes. My heart races a little faster, looking back at Zack.

"I'll leave you to it then, Zack." I turn around, following Luka.

"I thought you'd want to hear this. I came to find you as fast as I could."

"What is it?" Dread fills my gut, as he wraps his fingers around my wrist, leading me down a section between two tents. He faces me.

"Listen."

"—that's not why, Selene. You know that. I just want you to take a break. You've been working, and training, and travelling from one place to another for so long!"

"I don't have time," she grumbles in response. "But I appreciate the thought."

"You don't need to be doing this alone—"

"I'm not alone. I have you."

"That's not what I meant I—" A figure walks past the tents. I hold my breath, pursing my lips together, refusing to make a sound.

"Update?" Selene demands.

"The town is theirs," the messenger speaks. My stomach drops as Luka's grip tightens on my skin. The town...is whose?

"Good. They seem to be ahead of schedule then, which makes my life much more manageable."

"So, what now? You storm in posing as—" Thena's voice drifts closer and closer towards us. Too close for comfort. I pull Luka backwards, fight or flight mode kicking in. He quickly follows and we sprint back to the meadow, towards the front of the camp, his hand slipping into mine.

"What was that?" I exclaim once we slow down beside my bow and knives, lying on the grass.

"I don't know."

"Who's 'them'?"

"I don't know." He shakes his head. "But it can't be good." We lock eyes. "First they attack us, then take over the town?"

"Is it...I don't know, terrorists?" I suggest helplessly.

"I think we would be dead if it were." He slumps his shoulders, looking around us, alert. "Why is it all falling apart?" I sigh, squeezing his hand. "I was making progress."

"In what?"

"Family. School. Me. I even started to get closer to Riley and Thomas." *His brothers.* I frown, air tense around us as he lifts his head to mine, a sad smile fluttering across his expression. He means his mental state.

"I'm sorry, Luka, but I'm here for you, and as always, I'll help in any way I can."

"Same goes for you," he says quietly. I blush, glancing down at my feet, then drifting towards my weapons. His stare follows my gaze. I watch as his eyes widen a little.

"Are these yours?" he asks. Reluctantly, I nod and he looks back up.

"Not my choice," I say. "I guess it wouldn't hurt to—"

"But are you okay with it?" *No, I don't want those same old nightmares to creep back. I don't want to be scared to fall asleep. I can't—*

"I will be." I know I sound pathetic, even when it's leaving my mouth. "Let's not make a big deal about it." I grimace at my own words though. "I don't plan on using them, and hopefully I never have to."

"And even if it came down to it, I would step in for you." This guy right here, I don't deserve. He forces a playful grin, strands of brown hair falling above his eyes, as he puffs his chest out. "You know, with my sword and all."

"How's that going for you?" I smile fondly, up at him.

"I enjoy it for the most part. As long as I ignore everything else and trick myself into believing I'm in a fictional world. A knight in shining armour."

"For what it's worth, I'm glad you're real at least." He laughs.

"Back at you." A moment of silence settles in, procrastinating on what we really need to discuss. Unwilling to face the reality we've been given. "We should tell the others."

"And worry them?"

"They deserve to know." He squeezes my hand. I don't want to ever let him go, and maybe I won't have to. Maybe I'll just stay like this. This way he *can't* go. He *can't* leave and disappear like Jess. And I'd protect him like I should've with Piper. I could spare myself and the others the pain of losing Luka Vastia. Because let's be honest, if we lost our Luka, then it'd not only be a loss to our hearts, but it'd be a loss the world would have to pay for.

The warmth of his skin is still on my mind when we find Zack. He's in the same place I left him, which is no surprise. I sneak a glance down at our hands, our fingers intertwined. For a moment, I'm tricked into believing I'm safe.

I look up and Zack's looking at our hands too, a small smirk on his lips, arms crossed against his chest. Luka rushes up to him, letting my skin embrace the bitter air.

"So, it wasn't just a prank." His smile has completely faded now.

"I don't think that was ever a possibility, Zack," I mention gently.

"I was hoping it was." He glances at me, then at Luka. "What now?" He shrugs his shoulders in response.

"Are we in a hurry to make our next move?" I ask. "I mean, can't we just...process things?"

"If there's a chance Riley and Thomas are out there— I mean, if they got out alive, I should at least try and find them," Luka starts. My chest weighs heavier.

"But what can we do exactly?" Zack questions. "We can't go back to search. But we can't just stay here and do nothing." I gaze up at the puzzled and slightly terrified expression. He quickly recovers, looking away from both of us, his mind elsewhere. Luka steps forward and extends a hand out to comfort him, but Zack quickly bats it away reflexively. "I'm fine." *We can see through your lies.* Luka purses his lips and takes a step back.

"Sorry," he mutters under his breath.

"It's alright." The air is tense; I could suffocate under the weight of it all. Instead, I glance between my two friends.

"Let's sleep on it. Just for tonight," I say, cutting through. "Okay?"

"Yeah. Okay." Zack returns to his training with the gun that seems awfully familiar in his hands. The way his fingers run over the embedded silver, the way he brushes over the trigger, how he holds it, aiming perfectly. He's already used to it.

Before I can walk away, I turn to catch Thena waving and heading towards us.

"Luka," I mutter the words low enough, so she can't hear it. He perks up and sees her, stiffening beside me, forcing a smile in her direction. I don't bother. I'm tired.

"Hey! Is training going well?" There it is again—her teeth! They're sharper than the normal kind, sharper than mine, Luka's, Zack's, everyones! I clench my fists.

"Training's going fine, thanks." Luka nudges me ever so slightly, so I force a nod, eyes fixing on her teeth when she smiles. What if it's a tribe thing? What if it's a camp thing? It's the mark of her people, it means they're easy to pick out of a crowd?

I have to ask. I can't stand not knowing.

"Thena." I swallow the bile rising in my throat. "What's with your teeth?" It's something I've discussed with Luka in the evenings once or twice. He shouldn't be too surprised by my question, but still, he whips his head and turns his gaze to me, faster than I could blink.

"I thought you'd notice sooner or later." She draws her finger to her teeth and starts pressing, hard enough to draw blood, dripping down her skin. "I'm not human, if that's what you're asking."

"You're not?" Luka questions and my stomach drops.

"I'm a *nosfaratu* as well. Only, a good one who doesn't need blood. A vampire, if you don't know what that is—"

"Vampires?" I almost choke out some laughter. "You think we'll believe that?" Her face immediately drops, her eyes burning through me with a glare, expression blended to sourness.

"What else are you going to believe? I thought you wanted the truth, not something I made up on the spot."

"Vampires are fictional. They're not real."

"That's what everyone's been taught to believe." She smirks, cocking her head to one side.

"Because it's true. We've never seen one, so you can't exactly blame us for not believing you," Luka defends me, taking a step forward. "Don't get angry at us for what we've been brought up with."

"'Don't get angry," she scoffs with a roll of her eyes, "tell that to your girlfriend." Goosebumps spread up my arms and down my back, glancing at Luka and then back at her. Her hands edge towards her sheathed daggers. "Did you want me to tell you I made them sharp? Would that explain," she tucks her hair behind her ears, only now seeing their pointed edges, "these? Or the unnatural paleness of my skin?"

"How many of you are there?" Luka carries on despite my speechless appearance.

"Selene, Anna, a few more around here. Dozens in the town now. Infested, even."

"I don't believe it," I mutter more under my breath than anything, like I'm talking back to a parent. "I don't get it. If you've existed this entire time, how has no one made a report, or written an article or—"

"Shut up!" she snaps. "I'm getting tired of these questions." She turns away, and I step forward.

"Shouldn't we know more? If we're staying here under *your* supervision, then why can't we ask questions?"

"Savannah," Luka warns.

"We're here in your camp and we barely know anything about what you might be planning for us. I just want to know a little bit more than I already do, so I—" She turns back around glaring daggers in my direction. She strides directly to me and Luka pulls my hand back so I'm slightly behind him. Her lips are pursed and her hands are resting on her knives.

"You should watch your mouth, Savannah. I'm the one who brought you here. And I'm the one that can throw you out as quickly as you have arrived. Why should I give you more information when you don't believe the things I've already told you, hmm?" I shrink under her gaze, but don't back down. I stare right back into her deathly shallow eyes, despite the amount of nerves screaming for me to run. Luka is the one to keep me grounded and threads one of his hands through my fingers, the other palm he stretches between Thena and I, pushing her away.

"Give her some space! She was asking questions that we deserve to know the answers to!" He glares at her and she walks off in a tantrum.

But I'm no better. I look at Luka who stares back at me. I shake my head, let him go and walk away with my hands folded around me.

You can't knock on a tent's door, but I know if you were able to, Luka wouldn't be calling my name through the fabric right now.

"Savana?" He calls my name as if we were in year nine, and for a moment, I'm transported back in time to when he spelt my name wrong in text messages. It's as if we're thirteen again, to a time when it was much simpler and nothing had a lasting impact on anything we did. No idea for what was to come. "Savannah." I don't object when he pulls back the fabric and lets himself in. I think I called back to him to say that he could come in anyway, but I'm unsure. It all seems so distant. Like nothing's really happening. I no longer feel like I'm *here*. I'm simply existing, floating in and out of reality. Because how could any of this be real?

Luka's sitting on his bed, opposite mine, as I stare at the ground. Words are flying out of his mouth, but are they to reassure himself, or me?

"Savannah, are you listening?"

I break out of my thoughts best I can, shaking my head and gazing into those ocean eyes of his. He's frowning. "Look, what I'm saying is that I've saved you once, and I'll do it again." These words I hear, but I hear them without context. Tears spring to my eyes, or were they always there?

"If Thena really does kick you out, then I'll come too. I know you're not too keen on anything to do with fighting, but a little self-defence might help, just in case I'm not there. If we're separated, for whatever reason, and—"

"Do you believe her?" I croak out. He tilts his head to one side ever so slightly, expression softening. He shakes his head.

"No, no I don't. How can vampires be real? And how the heck have they been hiding all these years?"

"What if she's telling the truth?"

He presses his lips together. "Then I won't let her take it out on you."

"You're not listening." Hypercritical, coming from me. "What if I've blown up in her face for no reason? What if she really does kick me out—"

"I'll come with you."

"You can't leave Zack, and Matthew, and Oskar!"

"They'd follow." I don't want them in danger because of me. Never in a million years. Not for my stupid temper and mistakes. That's not fair.

"That's not what I want."

"I know it's not what you want, but it's what *I* want. I—" He inhales a shaking breath as a single tear slides down one of my cheeks. "I've already lost my brothers, Sav. Don't let me lose you too." His eyes stay focused on the ground, as he slides off his bed, shuffling closer to be at my feet. "Let me stay with you. I don't care where that might be, or where you might go, but if Thena does what she threatened, I want to stay beside you." He lifts his gaze to my eyes. A shine in them lights up my insides. "I don't care what anyone might do to break us, but you've got me. And you always will, as long as you need." His chest is heaving, as he flicks his gaze to my hands beside me, before leaning up, closer to my face, staring deep into my eyes again. "Savannah, I don't think I *can* lose you. So please." He lays his hands on my own, closing his fingers around my skin, gripping it tight. "Focus on that. Not her. I can't see a future for myself that's without you." And just like that, he leaves the tent, sniffling and wiping at his eyes.

As soon as the curtains fall, I burst out crying, hands glueing to my cheeks, shoulders shaking violently, breathing rough, sharp and shallow. How did we end up here?

I don't understand how I can let myself fall into some sort of slumber in circumstances like this. The wind roars outside the tent, snapping at its fabric. A few times, I close my eyes, almost wishing that the strength of it will whisk us away to somewhere else. But when it never does, I swing my legs out of bed. I stand, creeping past Luka and a snoring Zack, and out of the tent into the bitter chill of the night. I wrap my hoodie tighter around me, scanning my eyes over the surroundings, in case anyone's decided to take a midnight stroll like me. I don't want to run into anyone. I want to feel like I'm the only person in this universe.

My legs carry me away. I look up, but all the stars are hiding tonight.

Soon enough, low voices ring close to Selene and Thena's tent. I head towards them, light on my feet, careful not to make a sound.

"How do they know he'll be trouble? They have no proof—" Selene.

"They said he's different. I'm only a messenger, ma'am." I don't recognise this voice. It could be Anna? I turn my back against a wooden stall, peering past to see a woman with long, dark red hair, facing both Selene and Thena. She looks tiny in comparison.

"Where has he come from then that's such a threat?" Thena demands.

"It's not where he's from. It's what he's doing. He speaks up against Nobles. He walks off on his own outside their base, he doesn't seem all that entertained with the idea of holding a weapon and—"

"Then how is he a threat?"

"They said if he's already displaying this disobedience, then who knows how he'd act if he began training?"

"Then don't train him." I can practically hear Selene's eyes roll with that sentence.

"They'd have no use for him. But he refuses to leave without this other prisoner in the dungeons, ma'am. If he trains he'll be dangerous."

"I've heard enough. Dismissed." I hear faint footsteps walk away from the other two figures. Thena sighs pathetically.

"How can they be certain?" she asks.

"They're paranoid about a nobody."

"Should I keep an eye on him too?"

"No, or else you'll become paranoid as well. Your job is to stay here and build numbers."

"I wish we never got that message about those human kids in the town," she mumbles. Is she talking about us? "It was never worth the trouble."

"Numbers are numbers. They might still prove useful."

"I can't *stand* them!" I frown, leaning my head on the harsh wood behind me. I can't stand her either. But someone told them that we were…alive? Who would have known, unless…

Unless…

"Neither I, but you have to deal with them while I handle the Basedeke Royals." I'm getting more questions than answers at this rate. This is pointless. "Our time has almost arrived, Thena, don't let anyone ruin it."

"Of course. I'm starting to get impatient, that's all." I blink, raising my eyes up to the sky, where clouds are parted in a small gap. I spot three stars scattered up above. A small smile looms on my lips.

I quickly walk away before they catch me earwigging into their conversations.

Someone told them we were alive. Someone told this camp there were survivors.

Who?

I can only think of one person, but I think it's impossible that he's alive.

Almost impossible.

Not totally and completely. So can I hope?

Jack

15th October

A week has passed since we attacked.

They've told us we're making history today. A time to remember all those years of fighting and that the decades of neglect were slowly coming to an end.

Today is Moving Day, and it will be known as such until Vincent thinks of a fancier name. We head to Hillark, the place which isn't rightfully ours, and we pick a home and we settle. We claim it as our own, using torches and candles to light the place up since we're working on getting our own electricity and gas working again. Water is something we still have, fortunately. But no hot meals for a few weeks, maybe months. Not that any of us need it. It's just a luxury—to enjoy food without it being a detrimental part of our beings.

Vincent told me to pack early, because me, him, Violet, Zayne, Florence, and Jess will be the first people to go and pick a spot. So we can lay a mat down at the front door with the words, '*Home Sweet Home*' scrawled on to welcome any visitors we might have. We don't actually have anything of ours to pack, though. We left everything behind years ago, in our *real* home. So we bring nothing with us except spare clothes and weapons.

Early in the morning, Vincent wakes us and we head into town. Violet sticks beside me, our hands locked together the entire time. I tell her I know what house I'd like, and she says she'll stay with me wherever I go. But for Jess, I know this must seem horribly familiar. He scans houses, eyes drifting to one another. Sometimes his gaze lingers on certain buildings more than others. He stares at one block of flats in particular for a long time. The ones that Vincent disappears into to inspect. He comes out shortly whilst Jess glares up at him, as if the arsonist has trespassed on something dear to him.

"These buildings are severely disappointing." He waves his hand in dismissal and walks away. Jess looks about ready to use the sword Vincent gave him a few days ago against the Noble himself. A side of Jess I never want to see, to be completely honest.

We walk forward in silence. At some point, I bring Violet's hand closer to my chest, wanting her to follow me towards the lake, familiar from when I was last here, but she stands still. I look back to find her nodding towards Jess, wandering down a street like a mindless zombie.

He slows down, wide eyed, walking almost ghoulishly towards a specific house in particular. As if he's not in control of his own body. He stumbles up the curve, staring directly at a detached house in the middle of the row. I edge closer and closer with Violet, just so I'm in ear shot of him. I catch a glimpse of his lips pursing into a tight line, and his expression softens into something more sentimental and hopeful, before crumbling entirely. The house that's staring right back at him has beautiful plants all around the walls, embroidered into the bricks in a variety of different colours. Red, amber, yellow, brown, green. However, the front door's smashed open, the victim of being kicked down in a mad temper, lying in the entrance of the hall leading inside.

Violet pulls me back, shaking her head to give him a moment alone. But, *does he need help?* Does he need a source of comfort? Does he need me to do anything *for* him? Not that I could offer it.

His breathing shakes the world beneath our feet. Every step he takes is another he hesitates upon, and with each one, the more suffocating the air grows. The world is crumbling around him, yet he can do nothing, but stare at the broken rubble of it all.

He stands completely still a moment later, his lips parting, forming a mist in the breeze, sudden and sharp. He clenches his jaw as tears begin to drown his cheeks, bearing no sign of stopping. He lifts his hands up to look at them, then at the broken house of unpleasant memories. He seems yearning to enter, to see if anyone's alive. He wants to return home. But instead, he gives up.

He falls to his knees. Weeping. Crumbling. Sobbing to the sky. And whilst holding his head in trembling hands, he screams out a name.

"Oskar!"

His shoulders shake violently, breathing ragged and unsteady. I let Violet's hand go, sharing a glance with her as I edge closer and closer to him. He springs up to his feet, turning his head to stare at me with stern, deadly eyes.

"I'm sorry," I mutter, hands up in front of my chest. He simply straightens up, turns his back on us and starts walking away in the opposite direction to Violet and I, with his shoulders still shuddering.

"Why are *you* the one who's sorry? For all I know, you were the one to have murdered them."

"We're not killers," I say loud enough for him to hear. He looks at the house, remembers where he's going and looks away.

"Whatever. I can't trust your words."

"Where am I meant to find you?" I ask, shaking my head free from my thoughts. *I couldn't save them all.*

"Mountainside Street. 53. It's not far. Near shops," he answers before his voice gives out too. I make a mental note, and I turn my back to him, and stride to Violet.

"Poor thing," she mutters under her breath, eyes still glued to his figure getting smaller and smaller.

"Yeah, he hasn't got it easy."

"It's not like he even has anyone there for him."

"He has his sister."

"I meant by his side." She looks up at me, tilts her head and wraps her arms around my waist. "Like how I have you."

"Not everyone is so lucky," I comment, leaning down to meet her lips.

I know I shouldn't care. I don't even know him, but I hope Jess is okay. He's fighting for his sister, he's lost his friends, and he's been turned into a monster against his will. I can, at least, empathise with him in that sense. Even if I don't know the details of how he's feeling, I could sure as hell know by reading his face today.

The house I've chosen to make mine is the place I was in only a week ago, where I let those two teenagers go free. It's small, but Violet and I never needed a mansion. For the most part, we'll leave it untouched anyway. Just in case they return. Just in case they're alive.

Sleeping beside Violet in a king-sized bed makes me think back to the times we laid on the grass in my garden, planning and talking hopefully about anything and everything. Were we fifteen? Sixteen? At that time we were *only* best friends. We said we would get our own house, she would become a lawyer and I would become a teacher. Once we felt ready, we would move out of that house and start our own families, our kids would go to the same school and we would go on the school run with each other. We had it all planned out. Sleepovers and all, what presents we would get our kids, and what we would spend our money on.

I hold her hand beneath the sheets. I wonder what we would be doing now if none of this happened. If my brother was alive and if we still had our friends. If we still had our human blood. I kiss Violet, nuzzling into her neck, closing my eyes tight. I miss those days. And if we couldn't change what had happened, I'm glad we're here now. In a place where I can, at least, pretend we had our own way and our plan worked out in the end.

Her head rests on my chest. I kiss her hair, embracing the warmth of her skin on mine again. This is the one thing that's turned out right. Sleeping in our own bed. Knowing we've got each other and perhaps that can be enough again.

If I close my eyes for long enough, I can trick myself into believing that we're not *monsters*. But my reality is too heavy for me to dream of my fantasy tonight.

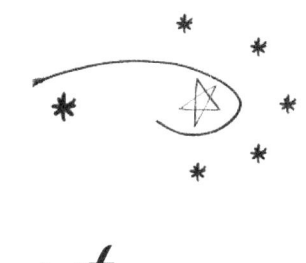

~Post Impetum~

✩*Jack*✩

29th October

Jess hasn't been seen for several days now. I've asked around, I've searched when on my travels, but I found no one's seen anything of a poor lost kid searching for a little bit of hope. I haven't gone to his address yet, this town is more of a maze than I had expected it to be.

Unfortunately, not all humans managed to escape before we arrived here two weeks ago. In the first few days, we'd randomly see people wandering the streets, calling out names I don't recognize. Vincent ordered certain Knights to search every morning and every evening for any survivors. That was the last time I saw Jess, on the 17th evening, I believe. All I remember was him refusing to take part when his name was called, walking away, rubbing his arm up and down, pinching his clothes against his skin.

The humans we did find, Vincent took the liberty of either killing in front of us, or ordering that they be kept hostage back at our old base. It depended how old, or young they were.

"Vincent wants you to find Jess," Draven says, walking up to me, out of the blue, whilst on my daily walk this morning.

"Does he now? And are you his messenger?" He rolls his eyes when I look at him and purses his lips into a fine line.

"No. I just heard him telling Achillea and Ambrosia that he's holding a feast for his birthday. He wants everyone to attend, including Jess. And you."

"Of course he does."

"I think he wants you to train him."

"I still think he needs more time."

"How much time are you willing to give him, Jack? Until Vincent snaps and takes it out on both of you?" He stares at me, waiting patiently for a response, but I shake my head. "Are you avoiding the boy? Too many unpleasant memories?"

"I'm just glad Zayne isn't his mentor. That's all."

"He," meaning Vincent, "has a reason to believe the kid won't simply leave. Is he aware of Jess' sister?"

"He won't leave, I know that too. But Vincent shouldn't assume that. There's plenty of dysfunctional families who'd just ditch their siblings at the first chance of safety." He scoffs, looking away from me and at the lake beside us beneath the setting sun.

"I know that all too well." I perk up my brows at him.

"Oh?" It's my turn to question. His scraggly raven hair covers half of his face, but I can still see the way his eyes rise to the sky, then behind, to make sure no one's around.

"Did you have a brother?"

"I have one, yes." *Have.* So he's still alive. "Not who you'd think it is." I suspect it's Vincent. The way he dismisses Draven all the time is unusual even for him. But I've never spoken about it, never having the opportunity to bring it up in conversation.

"Should—" Now, how do I word this correctly? "Should Vincent know better than to assume so too?" He catches my eyes, his bright blues sparking aflame. Hesitation and doubt flashes across his face, before smiling the tiniest bit and nodding.

"Yes, he should." My hunch was right. "Is Jess the older sibling?" I nod. "Are you?"

"Yes."

I chuckle a little, looking away and at the sky.

"Is that funny to you?"

"I thought Vincent was," I admit, and I flash him a smile.

"And why's that?"

"Taller. Bossier. You know, attributes of an older sibling."

"And how would you know what an older sibling acts like?" He crosses his arms over his chest.

"My brother was four years older than me. Always bossing me around, always telling me what to do, even if he never meant to directly. It sort of spilt out, like his 'dad' mode kicked in when parents weren't around. He got better at it eventually. The more he was allowed out, the nicer he was to me, since he was spending more time alone." I shut my mouth, realising I'm oversharing for the first time in months, years maybe. I haven't shared any thoughts of my brother with anyone except Violet. Because she was the only one I trusted with the deepest darkest parts of my mind. But I guess I don't mind sharing with Draven.

I look over at him, and he's smiling.

Then Shane received his driving licence. Then a truck slammed into his car. Then he was put on life support. He was blamed for it all. *Too reckless. Too young. Too carefree.* But I kept fighting for him. They pulled the plug while I was still in the room with him. They all gave up with him pulling through; I never did. His partner by his side, holding his hand. Violet beside me, Mum and Dad at the end of the bed. Sobbing. Everyone sobbing.

A few days later, we were taken, turned into monsters. I was in such a dark place at the time, I assume my friends must have believed I ran off on purpose, or worse.

"I guess I was like that," he says, softly. "I guess before all this, hundreds of years ago, I was too strict on him."

"You sound old," I comment and he starts choking out a laugh, staring at me.

"I am old! Old compared to you, anyway."

"I keep forgetting you're one of the oldest vamps here. Why aren't you a Royal like Achillea and Ambrosia?" He smiles, fondly remembering.

"Because it was their idea in the first place to be here. It wouldn't be right if I had that title along with them." I have no idea what that means but I don't push him on it. We look away, and up to the sky. When I spot a sparkling star, the brightest one peeking through the deep cyan shade, no sun in sight. I think of him. "Don't tell anyone about it. I don't think anyone knows he's my little brother."

"If you start calling him your little brother to me, I'm never gonna get used to it," I mutter, shaking my head and he slows down behind me, cackling out another round of laughter.

"I'll spare you from it then."

It's an odd thing to think out loud, write on paper, or tell someone close. It's an odd thing to consider at all—but for a single moment, goosebumps cross my skin, every single inch of it, and a weight lifts from my chest, breathing in the clear air freely again as I once did years ago. As I stare at this certain star that lights up my eyes, it's truly like I can feel him watching me, and I truly believe he is. I smile to myself, letting the wind blow onto my face, rough and harsh. But I welcome it nevertheless.

I find the house Jess said he would be staying at. I'm only slightly surprised to see the curtains torn from inside of the living room window. I peer in before knocking, finding him lying on the floor, arms stretched out with music blaring from a phone close to his head. He must've been saving the battery. He lifts his hand to itch again. His neck this time. He grits his teeth, suddenly closing his eyes, clenching his hands into fists before returning them to the floor either side of his body. His chest rises and falls in time with the tapping of his fingers on the carpet. He's taking all of this so much harsher than me or Violet did. He has no one. We had each other. *I wish I could help more.*

I step to the door, knock, then open without thinking.

"Whoa! You can't go barging into people's homes uninvited!" I walk into the doorway of the living room and Jess immediately clamps his mouth shut, grimacing at the sight of me. He quickly stands, turning off his music and returns to scraping his nails across his skin, on his arm, more specifically. When he does stop for a millisecond, he twitches, winces in pain, and then reverts back to clawing at it. "Oh, it's *you*. Leave." I drift my eyes around the room, but I don't take a step closer. Family pictures are scattered on the mantelpiece, some have fallen onto the floor, a rush to escape it seems. Or at least they tried to escape. None of those pictures are of Jess though. In fact not one of them has pictures of a teenage boy. All of a happy couple, a baby in their arms. Then a toddler in others, and finally a young kid with dark, black, fuzzy hair. Certainly not Jess.

"Draven told me that Vincent wanted me to find you. I just wanted to know where you were." But I don't want to leave. "I think they want me to start training you." He shifts uncomfortably. "I tried to tell them you need more time." I told Draven, so that's only a half truth. "But I don't think they're very understanding."

"Well." He looks away from me, crossing his arms over his chest. "Thank you for attempting to talk to them." I nod before he goes back to his skin. I think he'd rip it all off if he could. Rashes cover it. He notices me staring, and glares daggers my way.

"What are you looking at?" he demands, but there's hesitation in his voice, dripping off his words. Insecurity. Fear. I'm staring at his skin in all honesty. In this dull lighting, it looks patchy, almost scaly, red, inflamed. He has a skin condition, and with the recent turn of events, the stress hasn't helped at all.

"Do you have any lotion?" His eyes widen.

"Excuse me?"

"Do you have any creams that could help?" He purses his lips together, darting his gaze away, taking a seat on the couch in the middle of the room.

"A few," he reluctantly admits. "This isn't my house. This *was* my friend's. I found a stash of creams in his room. Ones that didn't work very well. He kept them in case of emergencies."

"Why don't you go to your own house to get the lotions that *do* work?" I think I already know the answer, but the way he stares at the floor, emotionless, cements it entirely. The house he previously cried at, was his. And it was in ruins. "If you need me to go in to find anything, then just say the words."

"Since when did you become so understanding?"

"I've been understanding from the beginning. You've just caught me in bad moods and unfortunate circumstances." He smiles slightly, leaning back on the sofa, sighing with his head up to the roof. "I do need to start training you at some point though, Jess." I lean on the doorframe and he opens his eyes to stare at me.

"I know. But not now. Okay?" I purse my lips together. "Please?"

"You need to at least show your face more often then. Lie and say you're on the way to my house if someone questions what you're doing. Vincent hears everything." He nods, folding his arms across himself.

"Alright."

"That way, it doesn't look as bad on both parts—"

"Are you going to leave yet?" He looks up at me through the fringe of his golden hair. "You know where I live now, you've declared what you want with me, and you've figured out my skin problem, what more do you want?"

"I want to make sure you're okay." The words leave my mouth quicker than I register them.

"I don't believe you right now." *Right now.* I echo in my mind. *Right now.* Will he someday? He stands up, crossing his arms over his chest. "Were you hoping I'd be able to train now?"

"No, but it would've been handy." He rolls his eyes, back to his normal ways, the way he was before I became 'understanding'.

"Well, as I said, I'm not ready." He avoids my eyes, his own flicking to the broken frames lain on the floor. He picks one up, then readjusts it on the mantelpiece, pretty and perfect, despite the broken, cracked glass. His gaze lingers on it a moment more, he remembers why he's here, and then glares at me, hands curling into fists. "Leave." I swear, there are tears somewhere in his eyes. He twitches suddenly, giving up, beginning to itch the same spot on his arm until he bleeds, then on his neck, then—

"Jess." I take two steps forward and he takes three back, hitting the mantelpiece with movies and cds on it. They tumble over each other, one falling onto the floor beside Jess' feet.

"Leave me alone!" I purse my lips together, stepping back once again, closing in on the doorway. "Alright? I have it hard enough as it is right now.

I do not want to pick up a weapon for the first time and—"

"I get it, okay?" I mutter, turning my back on him. "I thought perhaps training could provide a distraction—" He begins laughing behind me. *Laughing.*

"A distraction? If anything, it'll remind me of everything I have to bear on my shoulders." I can't do, nor say anything correctly, can I?

He's had near enough three weeks to grieve, and I understand that it takes much, much longer than that to get used to the loss of your friends, but he has a sister to fight for. He should use that for motivation, and get to work as soon as he can. I know I would do that if I could fight for my brother again.

I clench my jaw, rubbing at my chin. His sister's words echo inside my head,

'*"Keep my brother safe, please."*

"I'll try."

"Pinky promise?"

"Pinky promise."

"You need to take care of yourself," I say instead.

"What's that supposed to mean?" he demands.

"It's supposed to mean you have someone to fight for. Therefore, you need to eat enough, drink enough, sleep enough, and work towards breaking her out."

"You're not...?"

"I'm not what?"

"You're not going to stop me? Stop me from getting her out to safety?"

"I told you, I'm not a monster. After all, I'm here against my will too." I turn around and point a finger towards his chest. "She's around seven years old—"

"Six," he corrects in a small voice.

"She's six years old, Jess. I don't want you to live here like I was forced to. I'm not going to stop you, hell, I'll even help you!" His jaw's ajar, expression softening.

"I thought I'd have to work against you."

"I'll help you," I echo Draven's words from when I first came here. He reached out a hand, and I took it. He helped me survive. And stopped me from ending it. "Just...." *Stop being a brat and suck up the orders we tell you to obey, or else we'll both be punished for not doing what we were told to.* "Don't take too long getting ready to train." He begins to hastily clear his cheeks.

"What house can I find you in?"

"I've taken the house on Elvewoods Street, number 8. If I'm not there when you come looking, I'll be out by the lake." His eyes widen once more.

"Why that house?"

"Why do you want to know?"

"Because my friend lived there," he says. "Did you see her?" He takes a step closer, a fire blazing in his eyes. "Did you *take* her?"

"I let them go."

"'Them? You let *them* go?"

"Them. A boy and a girl."

He scratches his head, looking around the room, calculating something in his mind.

"Of course. Luka would have gone to check on her."

"He came in, kicked Zayne down and ran up the stairs to where the girl was hiding—"

"Savannah." He meets my eyes.

"Zayne went to wait by the back gate, letting me take both of them by myself. Instead, I told them to leave through the front door." I pause for a moment, remembering how their eyes widened, a mix of fear and relief in their expressions. The girl—Savannah, appeared hopeful for a split second. The way the boy's hand grasped hers, it was so tight, I thought their veins might burst. "They were terrified. I couldn't—"

"Thank you." I snap back to reality, he's weeping silently to himself. He wipes his eyes, smiling. "You let them go. They could still be alive, thanks to you. You bought them time."

"Don't get your hopes up," I tell him, but his smile never fades.

"Thank you so much." My chest grows heavier instantly.

I already want to give this kid everything I never had when I first became imprisoned within this clan. I want him to be free. So, I spit out, "You're welcome." I turn around to leave, before remembering to remind him, "That offer for your cream is still open."

"I'll let you know if I need it then." I stop before walking out the front door.

"What is it that you have?" I ask, praying I haven't taken a step over the line.

"Eczema," he says in a quiet voice. Stern. But broken. I'm trying to help him gather the pieces back together. Just enough so he can continue soldiering on.

On my way back, voices close by catch my attention—coming from the outskirts of the secondary school building. It's surprisingly close to Jess' new house, actually, and my curiosity gets the better of me when I hear both Achillea and Vincent's voices. So, I edge a little closer, taking a detour to my usual route back.

"It's obvious, isn't it?!" Vincent laughs manically at the top of his voice. "We should burn something down for their attention. Perhaps the one beside us? It's the biggest place by far in this puny town!" What in the world have I walked into— "They're bound to see the smoke, even from so far away. It'll go up in flames, setting the beautiful night sky alight. If the wind is on our side, the smoke will fly towards them! And perhaps I can even consider it my own birthday present from all of you, allowing me to follow my arsonic dreams."

"Calm it! Do we have to do this? It all seems a bit...dramatic. We don't need to scare them."

"Yes, we do," Achillea quips, interrupting Draven. Of course they shut down the only logical speaker there.

"We don't *need* to do anything to them."

"Yes, we do, we need to show them who's truly in power here, or, dear Draven, we risk losing our future!" she yells. "Vincent. Do it. But make sure it doesn't hit any of our clan's houses, or else there'll be consequences. Understand?"

"Of course, ma'am! Wouldn't dream of it."

"And Ambrosia, alert Jade of any such events taking place. Warn her this is all part of the long-run plan. She might think we're turning against her if we don't tell her prior," Achillea orders.

"Sure thing, babes."

"And Draven. Keep a close eye on Jess. Be sure he doesn't take a runner, oh and make sure Jack is training him."

"Yeah, I know, the same orders I've had for the past two weeks." I can practically hear the eye roll.

I haven't stopped walking, I just slowed down to hear their conversation to make sure everyone is safe, but I was too close for some people, evidently. I glance back at an incoming knife thrown beside my head, a Knight guarding approaching me, as the blade lands in the pavement, causing a crack in the path.

"You're not supposed to be eavesdropping, *incruentus*!"

Jack

29th October

The first thing I register isn't sudden darkness, but a jolt of sudden pain in my system. Then a blinding light, shooting through my eyelids.

I squint as I open them, resisting the urge to close them immediately after the light held above my head glares down on me. I'm in a very small room, with four people present, gathered around me. My already stone chest sinks when I see Draven among them, frowning, the furthest from me in the corner. No windows are in this place, it seems to be a basement of sorts with one light shining above us all. Achillea, Ambrosia, and Vincent stand between Draven and I.

I can't help but let my eyes linger on Vincent a moment longer than I should. *Draven's brother.*

I purse my lips together. So, he believes Jess will abandon his sister? Why would he think he'd do that, especially when he came here for her?

He suddenly claps his hands together. "Finally! About time you awoke from your little slumber!" His grin shines brighter than the light above his head. Menacing as always. Draven kindly informs him of how hard I was hit round the back of my head when he continues on about how long I slept. My hand instinctively flies up to meet the back of my head, searching for any sign of blood. Thankfully, I find none. I sit up from the wall, looking up at all four of them, three of which look down on me as if I'm prey. Draven at the back of the pack looks anxiously between Vincent and I.

"You were intruding on our conversation. Why?" Achillea cuts straight to the point. The first to break the silence. So, she's taking the lead on this lecture? Punishment? Whatever it is. After all, she's the founder of it all, she's the leader, she's practically the Queen. The whole idea about her being the Queen of us first came from Ambrosia. She said it half heartedly as a joke, but it caught on. However, Achillea hates being referred to as it, despite her reputation. Granted, Ambrosia has been with her every step of the way, but she doesn't take as much responsibility as Achillea. Ambrosia is more laid back, Achillea is down to business constantly. She's work driven; I admire that about her.

They look incredibly similar too, you'd think they were *sisters* instead of cousins.

Achillea has lighter brown skin, dark black eyes (it's said that they turned black because of all the blood she's drunk that isn't hers). She has long straightened hair with extensions on the ends to reach the base of her spine. On top of her head lies a silver crown with golden leaves laced like branches. It's a beautiful crown, angled to fit perfectly, so she can freely move without worrying it'll fall.

All Royals have crowns to set them apart from the crowd, because they just *need* to be above the rest. It wasn't Achillea's idea originally—it was Ambrosia's. She's the one who made the idea, and put it into effect. She simply wanted the Royals to take pride in their appearance. She's the one who is profoundly more focused on the way she looks and acts than what she does with her time, which is fair, and she's happy doing so. It feeds her confidence. She wants people to not only *know* she's a Royal but to be highly *aware* she's one.

Both Royals in this room are wearing beautiful black dresses. Achillea has a shorter skirt with glittering tights below, with a thin, shimmering material falling to the floor behind, gathered around her skirt, a slit at the front. Sparkles encrust the material, appearing to look like the stars under direct light. Her sleeves are long, skin-tight until it reaches her forearm where it stretches and falls, able to reach her waist. But the most noticeable thing about her whole outfit, are the pearls hanging around her neck, outlined with gold. Knives are attached to the pockets beneath her dress on her thighs. Everyone knows she never leaves home without them.

"Answer me!" Achillea demands one more time, stepping closer, heels clicking against the brick floor.

"I was just passing by. I didn't hear much."

"Much? Then what *did* you hear?" *Shit.* I glance to Ambrosia, and I shoot out,

"Vincent is doing something for his birthday. That's all." I remain poker faced, as she drifts her eyes back to Achillea, crossing her arms over her chest, turning completely away from me.

Unlike her cousin, her hair's in box braids, reaching halfway down her back, a streak of   dark crimson red on one side, falling in front of her shoulder. Her skin is darker than Achillea's, but with brighter and slightly lighter shades of black in her eyes. Her ears are pierced, dangling golden hoops in both of them and then on her right, she has a purple jewelled snake curled at the top of her ear lobe, which she named Delina for some reason. Her crown is a beautiful shade of rose gold, and instead of careful leaves intertwining with the branches, hers are tiny roses with sharp thorns on the stems. Her dress is just as regal. It reaches her feet, a thin glittering material like a veil, it looks like tiny thorned roses to match her crown under the light. The silk over her dress falls to the floor around her, the definition of elegance when she walks.

"Are you sure that's all?" Achillea says, leaning closer.

"Yes," I answer simply. Short and sweet. Exactly what they'll want.

Vincent suddenly rolls his eyes dramatically, looking between the Royals.

"Clearly, he's lying."

"Or perhaps you just think that about everyone—"

"Draven!" Achillea glares back at Draven as a warning, before staring at me again, gaze hard and stern. "You always try to defend him."

"Shouldn't *I* decide what happens to him, since he's in *my* clan?" Vincent exclaims, his dark ginger hair flaming. The terrifying fact about Vincent is that his eyes aren't black like the Royals here. This could indicate he hasn't drunk as much human blood as them, but he looks just as, if not more, horrifying. A deep, dark, blood red spreads around his pupils, alight once again in front of me at the prospect of a fight. He grins, teeth bared, a lighter in his hand as always. "He's mine, afterall, is he not?" He waltzes over, grinning, bending over and grabbing a rough hold of my cheeks, forcing my eyes to meet his. "Look at him! So powerless on the floor!"

"Achillea, maybe we should—" Ambrosia attempts to reason with her on my behalf, but she's shut down almost immediately.

"Leave him be."

"But you know we need numbers now, we can't have him getting hurt and—"

"I said leave him be." I raise my eyes to them in time to see a dangerous spark in Achillea's stare after having raised her voice toward her cousin. Ambrosia spins on her heel and marches out. I look to Draven, waiting for him to chase after her but instead, he stands there, watching me with a dull expression in his eyes.

Vincent pulls me closer to him, so close I can smell the blood tainting his breath. I force myself not to gag, meeting his deathly gaze. "I know you heard more than what you're telling us, Jack darling."

"You're just gonna watch?" Draven mutters to Achillea with a glare, but then Vincent whips his head round to stare at him.

"And what are you gonna do? Stop me? I'd just *love* to see you try, Draven. What I do is out of your control."

My head is still throbbing, so when he looks back at me, that stupid grin on his face, I'd do anything to wipe it off his lips. I spit in his face—an attempt to wiggle free from his grip. In any other circumstance I wouldn't dare, but the way his face lights up at the mere thought of burning down a school with no valid reason is beyond my limits. Dread builds in my stomach as he wipes my blood from his cheek, eyes turning cold and dark, something I only ever witnessed on the day I was transformed.

"You little bitch." He stands up and drags me with him, feet dangling as he holds me above with his abnormal strength, his hand slipping to grasp my neck, fingers digging into my skin. I hold onto his wrists, digging my nails into his clothes, trying to loosen his grip so I can break free, but it does nothing to the monster holding me hostage in mid air.

Then, without warning, he leans down, and sinks his fangs into my skin, closing in on my collarbone. I shriek, feeling his teeth dig deeper into my veins, the pain in the back of my head throbbing more at the sudden sensation of everything being drained from within me. Like he's stealing my life source, taking what he pleases, wants, needs and I can do nothing but squint my eyes close, gritting my teeth, digging harder into his skin.

"Vincent!" Draven yells, sprinting over, grabbing his brother's shoulders to pull him back. So suddenly, he lets me go and I manage to escape out of his grip, dropping to the floor, leaning forward, so I don't hit my head on the stone wall once again. Instead, I carefully lean against it with the world spinning. *I have no control.*

My hands fling to my neck, covering the bleeding gash. I look up, gaze blurry, but I can make out Achillea walking towards me, as Draven shoves Vincent into a wall, shouting at the top of his lungs. Now his Noble title will definitely be taken away. But right now I need to focus on leaving with all my limbs attached.

Achillea leans down, grabbing my face harshly, forcing me to meet her eyes. No way to escape. *No control.*

"You will not tell anyone what you heard, understand?"

"Or what?" I question, shivering. A cruel smile curls around her lips.

"Do you want to find out?" I gulp nervously. I should never have asked. "I'll hurt something you love, should you disobey." I widen my eyes. "*Someone* you love."

"No." I leap forward, shocked at my sudden found energy and adrenaline, the only thing repeating in my mind, *Violet, Violet, Violet.*

"No, you won't. I'll make sure of that." My voice is raw and shrill, as she pushes my back into the wall with such ease. Fear steals my breath away. My hands shake, my heart beats fast, ticking like a time bomb. She can't take her away from me. I only love one person in this world. One flower. One thing my heart belongs to. "Stay away from Violet."

"Or what?" She shoots back at me, her eyes burn a hole into my skull. She pulls out a knife from around her thigh, and with every advance, she closes in on me, until she rests it across my neck. I hold my breath, held up against the wall—my eyes flick between hers, her hair falls in front of and beside her face, nose almost touching mine. "Or what, Jack? Tell me. I'm intrigued."

"Or I'll kill you." But *I'm no killer.*

"Tut, tut...I thought you didn't murder people without good reason? Oh how times change. You've grown Jack. I'd almost be proud if it wasn't for this little predicament we find ourselves in."

"Stay away from her," I repeat.

"And what will you do for us?"

"Anything," I choke on my own words, at my own eagerness to keep her safe.

"Don't tell anyone what you heard today. Not a word about what's happened here." I nod. "And do as we say, without any sort of objections. You will train Jess. Take on more orders, and be our little puppet, do you like the sound of that? We need someone else on the inside, someone to complete our... How would you put it? Dirty work?"

"Anything." Jess better be ready to train tomorrow morning. I'm wasting no time, my dead heart is in my throat and it's a horrible sensation. I want to be rid of it. "I swear it." I give her my word. She grins, taking back the knife, sheathing it below her dress and she stands up.

"Now tell me, is it hard to comply? Was it worth eavesdropping on us?" When I don't respond, she merely scoffs, glancing at a bickering Draven and Vincent, and spits out, "Leave. I have work to do." I stagger to my feet, almost stumbling as I hurry out the door, barely able to catch my breath.

I didn't think I could cry again after they took away my humanity. But once the adrenaline wears off, once I'm out in the open, gazing at my palms shaking, wet and silent tears trickle down my cheeks.

I've lost everyone I have ever held close, I won't lose Violet too. I ball my hands into fists. I'll do whatever it takes. Even if that draws death closer to me. Anything for my flower.

I make it to our house quickly. It's much closer to the lake than I had anticipated. I open up the door, her name escaping my lips instantly, as I lay my eyes on her in the middle of the living room, on the floor, finishing her exercise routine. She looks up, a small smile spreading across her face.

"Jack," she exclaims, and scrambles to her feet. I realise my breath still hasn't returned. I shut the door with an unintentional slam. "Hey." She tilts her head ever so slightly, edging closer to me. "Everything okay?"

I don't answer. I don't have the strength. Because my lungs are begging for more air, my chest is aching for it and my mind needs time to calm the whirlwind. I shake my head, walking to her as fast as I can, wrapping my arms around her body. We fit perfectly together. Like a jigsaw. She quickly returns the gesture, embracing me back as I rest my head on her shoulder, closing my eyes, the last of a few tears escaping, but then complete stillness. She breathes deeply, rubbing circles with her palm on my back and then squeezing me more.

And the worst thing of all, is the knowledge of it, stifled within my thoughts. Because I can't tell anyone what I know, not even my soulmate. I hold on a little tighter, inhaling her hair, an unfamiliar coconut.

"I'm here," she says. And it's the perfect thing she could say at a time like this. "I'm here with you, Jack. What's happened?" I finally open my eyes.

"It's been a long day, my love," I say in a quiet voice. "A long and tiring day. I'm just happy to be with you again." She smiles into my skin, pressing a kiss onto my cheek. She moves some of my hair away from my collar, something catching her eye.

"Oh my god!" she yelps, her fingertips tracing the fang markings on my neck. I turn my head to lock eyes with her, but she's glaring right at me, peering into my soul. I know it's not directly towards me, but there's a rage behind her eyes. Dark and powerful. "Who did it?"

"Is it important?"

"Of course it is," she scoffs, raising her brows when I still don't answer. "Vincent?"

"You already knew."

"He can't keep doing this!" she yells, stepping away from my arms. "I swear to god, Jack, if you don't say anything to him, then I will!" She grabs her bow leaning against the wall, but I quickly grab her wrist, shaking my head more insistently, forcing her eyes to meet mine. "He can't keep hurting you."

"I know."

"That's it? You move on? You just keep *dealing with it*?"

"No, Violet—"

"It's abusive!"

"Zayne's abusive. Vincent's just smart enough to take long enough breaks between bites that it's not concerning enough."

She glares. "We've dealt with both of them long enough! What's next? Draven starts using you and betraying your trust—"

"Hey." I place my hands on either side of her waist, pulling her closer to me. "Remember what we're fighting for here."

"Each other—"

"Yes, but in the long run, love." She rolls her eyes and lowers her gaze. "We're fighting for freedom from him, from the Royals, from them all. We'll run away."

"Why don't we do it now then? We've waited long enough, and I am sick of it all." She looks back up into my eyes, almost pleading. The flame inside extinguishing.

"We can't leave Jess. And not while there's so many people who are locked up because of *them*." I'm hearing myself spit these reasons and I wish I could eradicate them all. Why didn't we go earlier? *It would've been so easier and now we have Jess.*

"It's not our job to pick up after them, and fix their mistakes."

"But do you understand where I'm coming from?" She sighs, resting her arms on my shoulders. "If not us, who will?"

"I suppose you have a point."

I'll hurt someone you love.

"We will though. As soon as Jess is out of the picture and I know Zayne or the Royals won't hurt anyone—"

"Which will never be."

"Which will be sooner rather than later. I swear it."

I lean down and kiss her, our bodies pressing together. She leans into me, one of her hands running over the back of my head as I close my eyes, drinking her all in. Her taste, her coconut scent, the heat on my skin, electric and fizzling. She pushes me and the backs of my legs hit the sofa, but still, she hangs on, another hand sliding down my back through the collar of my uniform.

I hold her, warm and tight as I fall back onto the sofa. One of her palms moves beside my head on the cushions, while the other is softly lain on my chest. She lowers herself down onto my lap, sitting perfectly and comfortably against me. All whilst her kisses become more and more greedy.

I hold her as close to me as I possibly can. Wrapping my arms around her back, resting a hand on her head as she nuzzles my neck, resting her forehead there, trailing kisses all down my skin, my collarbone and then finally my jawbone, until she reaches my lips once again. This time, slow, consuming, and I savour it all.

Let's stay here, where I know you're safe. Where you're here beside me. Where I can keep you with me. And let's never move. Because in this moment we're trapped in, it's all I want, and it's all we'll ever need, my dear flower.

I will protect you no matter what, Violet. Please, don't fret. You have me, always. I love you, more than you could ever know. I love you more than anything else in this cruel world. And I love you. More than words could tell.

Savannah

31st October

I have never felt as powerless as I do now.

Luka was the first person I told about what I heard a week or two ago. I shared the basics—someone told Thena and Selene people were alive in the town, about how someone is helping them with whatever their plan is for this place. Hell, I even told him about my first thoughts linking this mystery person to Jess. I told him everything that was going through my mind, because as soon as I started, I couldn't stop. The weight on my chest lessened. I could finally *breathe* again.

We don't have enough evidence to know whether it's Jess or not. It's a long shot and I know that. But at this point, I'd do anything to make Oskar and Matthew smile again. And I mean *truly* smile. So maybe, I can go back to Hillark to find him. But even the mere thought of it all makes my legs shake under the weight of my own body. I don't think I could do it alone.

Luka's been checking in more recently. When he finds me alone either training with unfamiliar weapons, or in the tent we basically live in, he tries to talk about how I'm feeling. He asks if I want to be alone, if I want company. Whatever I say, he complies with. And I love that about him. Sometimes when he stays, he'll start talking about something completely different, but sometimes, he asks what's bothering me.

Tonight, we're talking for much longer than we should. No filter, no restraints, no boundaries. Just pure chatter. The air around us is colder than usual, so we're wrapped up, side by side, huddled together on my crappy fold up bed, while Zack snoozes on the opposite side of the tent to us. A comfortable silence settles, and I embrace it with open arms, closing my eyes for the moment and inhaling the stifled air. If I focus long enough, I can hear the gentle wind against the fabric above our heads. A second of peace to breathe freely.

Luka slowly rests his head on my shoulder, and my heart skips beats with my cheeks flushing furiously. I don't risk moving an inch. If he does this more often, I'm not sure how my heart can take it.

"Do you miss it?" he asks.

"Miss what?"

"Our home." My chest aches at the mention of something familiar, as he intertwines my hand into his fingers. For a second, I'm on that same damp stone pavement, leaning against the cold brick wall, holding Luka beside me who whispers sweet broken comfort in my ear. We ran away, hiding in alleys, anywhere we called safer. I haven't been apart from him since really.

I look down at him.

"I miss her." He immediately closes his eyes, twitching ever so slightly. A shiver down his spine. "I miss my parents. I miss Jess." It's not the town that's hurt me, it's the memories inside that I'll miss. I'll never go to school again, annoying the worst teachers for fun. I'll never be in my living room again with my family, watching nonsense on TV with the curtains drawn. And I'll never be with Piper again, in our bedrooms, eating junk food and watching shows we've watched millions of times before until we pass out. Tears brim my eyes at the dawning thought.

I've tried so hard to distract myself from thinking too deeply about her. It's been weeks already. I blinked and here I am, beside Luka. And when I *do* allow myself a brief moment of realisation, it's always met with numbness and guilt. I know it's all real, but a part of me *still* wants me to believe it's not, to cling onto the hope that she'll walk into my life again.

Piper Miley. Best friend of seven years. Gone in a blink of an eye. It should have been me, because what did she ever do to deserve what was handed to her?

My mind replays it over and over again, a different twist every time, but when I close my eyes, something is always for certain. She screams for help. But I'm always too slow. Luka drags me away. And instead of being wrapped into his arms, I fall through the pavement. As if he was never there to begin with.

This is the first time I've felt something other than guilt and numbness at the thought of her. Instead, sadness swallows me whole and I have to resist the tears on the verge of escaping onto my cheeks. He says nothing for a moment, and then catches me off guard as he edges closer than I thought was possible, before I would combust entirely. Luka squeezes my hand. Like he never wants to leave. Never wants to let me go. So he doesn't move. And so, *we don't let go.*

"I'm sorry," he murmurs.

"For what?" I ask. He lifts his head up, and meets his gaze with my eyes.

"I'm sorry you saw it." I don't mean for it to shake my world and everything in it, but my eyes widen and my heart stops beating. I part my lips to speak but no words escape my tongue, because what words could possibly fill the void he's created in this tent?

I've never seen him look so upset and guilty.

"Luka," I barely whisper, but that's all I can manage. He frowns, softly, but his gaze remains on me.

"I wish it wasn't her. I really do. If it were any of us, I'd rather it had—"

"Luka, don't say that."

"But you know what I mean?"

"I don't want to think about that!" I exclaim. If it were him instead of her. If Piper were beside me instead of him. If...

He doesn't show any remorse whatsoever for the thoughts he shared, until a few tears roll down my cheeks. His forehead creases at curved brows.

"I'm sorry, but that's just the way I feel. I didn't mean to make you upset. I wish I could've protected her, and you."

"Don't you think I've thought of *that* every day since? *What if it was me instead of her?*" My heart is pounding and my chest is heaving at an alarming rate. My throat's gradually closing up, barely able to speak; barely able to stop more tears from falling, but I manage it somehow.

"Every day?" he mumbles, leaning his head closer to mine.

"That's what I said, right?" I sniff pathetically, rubbing at my nose with my free hand. I finally find the courage to glance his way. And when I meet his broken eyes, I can't bring myself to turn away again. He opens his mouth to say something, but he finds no words to fit the silence, and he clasps his mouth close again.

He lifts a hand to dry my tears, moving slowly, giving me time to push him away. He removes his hand, placing it back onto the blanket we stole, the space between us suffocatingly tight.

"I'm sorry." Of all times to look away, he chooses now? I want him to say something more, but he just stares at his feet.

"It isn't your fault." I choose my words carefully.

"Then why do I feel like it is?"

"Because that's your head feeding you lies." I've said those same words to him so many times, I've lost count. He shifts beside me, getting comfier, head back on my shoulder, and I lean on top of his hair, a moment of silence, embracing the comfort. "It isn't your fault," I repeat. "You couldn't control what happened." It wasn't my fault, I don't think. I just wish it hadn't been her, but myself. He doesn't respond to anything I just said. "Luka?"

"Do you smell that?" He stands, sniffing the air around us. "Or am I officially insane?"

"Smell what...?" I shake my head from side to side until I understand what he's talking about. "Smoke." And where there's smoke, there's fire. *Suffocating fire.*

"Fire," he murmurs, his eyes as wide as mine when he glances at me. And then rushes outside to check the surroundings. I walk over to Zack, battling against my quaking legs.

"Zack!" I exclaim, and start pushing and pulling his shoulder until he begins to stir. "Wake up!" He squints his eyes at me. "We think there's a fire somewhere!" Then he's up too, wide eyed again. He sits up, manages to get onto his feet faster than I did, and he starts talking at me. But I can't hear over Luka's words outside the tent. Talking panickedly about finding the source. Making sure it's not in a tent. Zack holds onto my shoulder briefly, and heads outside. But my legs are weak and numb all at once. I retain my balance with a thumping heart reminding me

I need to move.

Once we're out in the open, Oskar runs too fast, and slams his shoulder into Zack.

"Sorry!" Panic pure in his eyes, glistening and clear. I cover my mouth with the sleeve of my hoodie. It's not *so* strong it's causing my shortness of breath - that's just the anxiety, but stopping the worst of the smell might help me find some solace. "Are you guys alright?" His gaze shoots towards me and Luka as well, taking us all in, looking us from top to bottom.

"We're fine. What about you and Matthew?" Zack questions.

"He's making sure Anna's okay. They're a bit shaken, I think, but he should be out in a sec." Zack walks past Oskar, nodding, a brief hand on his shoulder like he did with me, before beginning to search for Matthew. He glances to our left, looks away, but then does a double take, head turning back slowly in the direction we came from all those weeks ago. Hillark.

His jaw drops and his eyes widen, emotions misting them, before raising a hand to cover his mouth. Matthew emerges from the tent, jogging towards Zack, shaking his shoulder.

"Zack?"

"Look," he whispers. Matthew hesitates before looking towards where Zack's eyes are glued to.

In that direction is *our home.* How didn't I think of it before?

Oskar edges towards them both. Just like Zack, he gawks at the view, the bright orange glow reflected in his eyes. Fire is lighting up our home. Our tiny little town. A building's in flames, igniting the night sky. The smoke is growing closer and closer, before it inevitably engulfs us in its burning beauty.

I march forward. Luka falls in time with me before I can let his hand go. He hangs on tight to hide his trembling. We pass the tents, eyes glued to the horizon, watching it burn from afar, our world illuminated by flames. It emits such a powerful light, it must have been a large building, not *just* a few houses. But what if it spreads? I glance to my right, Zack beside me, Oskar on the other side, then Matthew trailing behind. Zack looks at me and tears immediately spring to my eyes. We stop in a meadow that feels like our own. As if we were always supposed to end up in this spot. Zack's cheeks are similarly drenched with tears.

He lays his hand on my shoulder, glancing at Oskar, who takes deep breath, head tilted higher towards the sky, whilst Matthew's eyes glisten and crease at the edges. He starts sobbing uncontrollably, dabbing at his eyes with his sleeves. Oskar quickly wraps his arm around him, bringing Matthew's head to fall against his shoulder, letting him break into pieces on his clothes. And then I stare at Luka who's silently weeping to himself, and I join him against my will. I bring my gaze back to the fire, and my throat closes up. Zack's hand still lain on my shoulder, and Luka holds my left hand tightly.

As we watch our home, our childhood, our favourite memories crumble, something inside my soul ignites. An aching—a realisation. There's no going back. All this time, I was hoping and praying that I could return home in a few month's time when everything had died down. See for myself what now lurks there.

They've killed my best friend.

They've taken away Jess.

They've stolen my parents.

They've ruined my life. It's time I take it back. Once and for all.

Luka's still holding onto my hand like it's the last chance he'll have. I look down at our feet, having seen enough of what's in front, because I don't know how much longer I can stand this. Luka bumps my shoulder and I look at his eyes—bloodshot and puffy, glued to my own.

"Shall we go back?"

"Yeah." I nod and we turn around, just in time to watch Thena move swiftly behind some tents with two inconspicuous looking figures trailing behind her in black cloaks.

"What the..." Zack notices and stares at us. "Who the heck are they?"

"Survivors?" I suggest helplessly.

He shakes his head. "Why would they be wearing cloaks?"

"I'll go check it out," Luka says, noticing Oskar and Matthew talking softly to each other. "You guys go to one of the tents. I'll find you in a few minutes.."

"Sleep in the same one tonight?" Zack suggests. Not that I think we'll be sleeping much, I nod when I say,

"Sounds good to me." I look at Luka, who lets my hand fall as he walks towards Thena. On impulse, I start to follow, but he turns back and shakes his head.

"No, you go with them."

"I want to help."

"I can sneak around on my own."

"But I don't want you to be on your own." I stop walking completely, but so does he for the moment. "Okay, sorry, that wasn't—" I hold out my hands as if I've attacked him, but instead, he gives me the smallest of his smiles.

"It's okay, I get what you mean." He steps in front of me, briefly brushing some of my hair behind my ears, which catches me off guard, and I blush bright red. "But I'm going alone." He jogs backwards a few paces, and then turns back to see where he's going. "I'll be back soon." He waves his hand back.

"Be safe," I whisper under my breath. Zack steps beside me.

"He'll be okay. Trust me."

In our tent, I sit at the back, leaning against the tent's fabric. Oskar and Matthew sit in front of a fold-up mattress to my left. Zack sits opposite them, pursed lips, softened expression.

"How long will the smell linger?" Oskar says, eyes glued to the ground, unmoving, whilst Zack looks up at him.

"I don't know, a few days? Depends." Oskar presses his lips together, breathing deeply as he leans on the bed.

"What do we do?" I ask out loud, and Zack looks at me.

"What do you mean?"

"What do we do now? Where are we supposed to go? They've taken our town. Do we move to a new one and start again? I know my cousin, Georgia, is in the next town over. We could run to her."

"There's any hope of ever going back. That's for sure," Matthew says in a hushed voice beside Oskar. "We shouldn't bother." *But Jess.*

"Well, I don't want to stay here," Oskar announces, shaking his head.

"We don't have to," Zack insists.

"But where else will we go? And if we can't find Georgia? Knock on random doors until someone takes pity and agrees to take care of us?"

"Maybe there'll be an orphanage there—"

"We're all eighteen in a year and a half. There's no point in that."

"Sorry for bringing it up," I say pathetically, sighing and then yawning in defeat.

"We stay until we're...seventeen then. Then we get a job and find people. Anyone who will help us. Or we stay until one of us turns eighteen," Zack suggests, helplessly. "I'm not sure we have many other options but to stay here for now." I'm sick of this place already.

"Just for now," I echo as the tent's 'door' is drawn back and Luka steps in, zipping it up behind him. Zack sits up and I release the tension in my shoulder. "Are you okay?" I ask first. He nods, planting himself on the floor next to Zack, smiling at me.

"Yeah, yeah I'm fine," he says, staring right at me. "He was there. The guy who saved us, Savannah. A few weeks ago." I don't know what I expected to hear, but it wasn't that.

"What?"

"He didn't look like he wanted to be there." He glances at Zack, then back at me. "And they weren't human, I can guarantee that." I widen my eyes even more, a lump in my throat forming. "They had...really sharp teeth. They were sickly pale and their ears..." He trails off into a murmur.

"So she was telling the truth."

"What's going on? What are you not telling us?" Oskar demands as Luka looks at him.

"We told you someone saved us in Savannah's house, remember? Well, that guy was with Thena just now. And a few days ago, Thena told us that the people who took our town weren't human and... Well, we didn't believe her. And we made that very clear." He looks back at me, and I know he can see the worry in my eyes as he leans closer to me. "We'll be fine," he says, while Oskar exchanges a sceptical look with Zack.

"And if she throws me out?"

"You haven't done anything wrong."

"She doesn't seem like the type to think that way, Luka." I roll my eyes unintentionally.

"Whoa, whoa, whoa, why would she kick you out?" Zack questions. "If she does, we'll go too, of course, but—"

"Agreed," Matthew adds, raising a finger.

"I don't *want* you to follow if she does," I mutter in a small voice, a twinge of guilt in my chest pings.

"Well, tough. We're family," Zack says. When I stare at him, looking so anxious and desperate to hold onto anything we have now, a chill breaks through me. "And we only have each other now. We stick together."

"And if we die when we're out there alone? Either by starving or...or them—"

"Then so be it," Luka exclaims. "If she throws any of us out, we're all going together." He looks at everyone as he says these words, so simple coming from his lips. I don't deserve it.

My lips quiver and tremble.

But I don't want to be alone either, and I've never wanted that.

Maybe if I am forced to leave, *then* I can find Jess. I'd just rather do that on my own now than let them follow. I want them to be safe.

Savannah

1st November

Someone moves on top of my hair, jerking me awake.

I lift my head, wondering what time it is, but they quickly lay their hand on the opposite side of my head, gently pulling me back down to their shoulder. I blink the sleep from my eyes, look over, and catch Zack looking at me. He smiles, and rests his head on mine again. I scan the tent, Oskar and Matthew on the floor in front of us, snoozing and then Luka on the bed that used to be mine. His eyes are open already, just staring at the roof of the tent. The smell of smoke is thick in the air.

I close my eyes again, wanting to slip back into the peace of my sleeping world.

"You alright?" Zack asks.

"Is that a trick question?"

He chuckles softly. "I take it back." Good. I wouldn't know how to answer anyway.

"Anyone know what the time is?" Luka mutters on his bed.

"I lost track of time around a week ago. Or was it two weeks?" Zack remarks.

"Oh ha ha." I open my eyes to watch Luka sit up and stare at Zack. "Seriously though?"

"No clue."

"Does it matter?" I murmur, catching his eyes and my stomach flips inside of itself. "Do we need to know right now?"

"I suppose not." He looks at snoozing Oskar and Matthew, then flops back onto the mattress. "Can we take a sick day?"

"I'm not sure that's how it works around here, Luka," Zack tells him.

"What if I just straight up refuse to move from this bed then?"

"That won't go down well with anyone here and you know it."

"I guess. Stupid thing for me to say."

"It's not a stupid thing. I reckon we're all thinking it," I murmur. I let the silence swallow me, embracing it wholeheartedly. Because I'm not sure when we'll get another blissful moment like this. With all of us in the same place, sort of safe and sound. I don't want it to end, but in order to find answers, we need to move forward.

Unfortunately.

If there's any hope of finding Jess, or Luka's brothers, or any of our parents, we need to get up and face the day with a strong facade. Whether that facade will break as soon as I leave this tent is another matter completely.

Oskar stirs suddenly, knocking his shoulder against Matthew's by accident. Our friend wakes up instantly, hands flying up to his face to protect himself from an invisible danger, squinting his eyes.

"It's only me!" Oskar exclaims, slurring his words together. "Sorry!"

Matthew hesitantly lowers his hands to stare at Oskar, sighing in relief, "Oh."

"Sorry."

"It's okay." Oskar just frowns, looking back at Zack and I. Zack finally sits up, head apart from mine, but I can't bring myself to move. I don't want to. Because my entire body aches. Images of the fire flashes inside my mind and chills spread up my arms whenever I remind myself of the harsh tales of reality.

"I say, we deal with today as it comes, and let's not do anything too drastic," Zack announces. "We don't want to draw attention to ourselves." Oskar stares at him in slight confusion.

"What do you mean? You're making us sound more subtle than what we actually are. And besides, we're not trying to do anything to them anyway, right?"

"We want more information, don't we?" He purses his lips, considering the notion.

"We deserve to know what's happening. That's all, so we kinda have to take matters into our own hands," Luka says from the bed.

"We just need to be careful," Matthew mutters. I lift my head from Zack's shoulder, yawning, and twisting to stretch.

"Very careful," I say. "I don't want Thena to have more of a reason to hate me. "

"True," Luka admits. "But you may have crossed that line already." I look at him, who sits up with a grin. I can't help but smile, blush and look away again.

I spend almost the entire day avoiding everyone except my friends, training on the field. The clouds are grey, either mixed with the ash and smoke from last night, or a storm's coming.

I'm headed back to my tent, when I hear a rustling from close by. My heart skips several beats, eyes darting right to see Thena watching me, with a straight-faced stern expression, head peeking around the corner of a tent.

"Why are you following me?" I exclaim, taking a step back. My hand hovers over the dagger strapped around my waist.

"You're not the only one who can play this game." She smirks, tilting her head downwards.

"What are you on about?" I question.

"You've been following me, haven't you? Don't think I haven't noticed. I'm not as stupid as you think."

"I haven't been following you. I've been catching your conversations, that's all. Even then I get no context and can't understand half the things you're saying," I tell her, which is only sort of true. She merely rolls her eyes at me.

"Like I'm gonna believe that."

"Go away and leave me be. I'm going to bed."

"This early? Having not eaten anything all day long?"

"How would you know that, unless you've been following me all freaking day?" She smirks deviously. "I haven't been hungry."

"Sure, sure, you're gonna need a lot of food tomorrow then."

"Leave me alone!" I shout, stupidly raising my voice at her. *Remember, she has the power to throw you out at any moment,* I tell myself.

She can't keep pushing me around. But I can't risk my friends leaving this place with me, either. I clench my hands into tight fists. "I don't trust you." She edges closer to me. Until I can smell her breath, and I can't quite put my finger on *what* the scent is. She looks down on me, but I don't dare look away, in case she sees some weakness or fear in my expression. "And I'm sick of it."

"Of what?"

"Of the spying. I've caught you taking late night walks, all around camp to clear your head, I've seen you watching us, like you did last night, rushing behind tents, thinking I couldn't catch even a glimpse of you before disappearing." That wasn't me...that was Luka. She saw Luka? "If I catch you one more time, I won't show you mercy." My gaze flits to her teeth, gleaming as she smirks, two tiny fang-like ones attached to the front.

Goosebumps spread up my back. At this moment, I fear that I really was wrong about vampires.

"You'll kill me?" I ask.

"If that's what you really want, of course." She shows off a cruel grin. "But I was talking about sending you back to your precious home town." That wasn't what she was hinting at. "Got it?"

"For the record, I don't trust you, But yes, I get it." I spin around and retreat into the tent and zip it up as fast as I can.

I sigh, chest tight, limbs heavy, turning around hearing Thena's footsteps fade away as I lay eyes on Luka, silently sitting on my bed, gazing up at me. Like he never even moved from this morning. "Do I even need to ask whether you heard all that?" He shakes his head from side to side.

"She won't," he says.

"Won't what?"

"Kill you." The words hit me, like a punch in the gut. Of course he heard that too. "I'll make sure of it." I walk over to the bed beside him, and take a seat. "How could she ever threaten *anyone* like that?"

"It's probably just empty threats." He lifts his head and looks at me.

"I wouldn't put it past her, Savannah," he says, cautiously. "We need to leave this place, we can't afford to wait until we're eighteen."

"We have to!"

"Savannah, she threatened your life!"

"And where do you expect us to go?" I ask softly, staring at him, but he quickly looks away, clenching his jaw.

"Anywhere but here."

"We can't simply leave and hope for a brighter future."

"But that's the only option we have!"

"Or we stay." He closes his eyes, sighing in annoyance.

"But *you're* not safe."

"I don't care." He flashes his eyes back open at me, piercing me.

"I do." The warmth that floods me when those words escape his lips, *overwhelms* me in the sweetest of ways. I edge closer, bumping my thigh with his, resting my head on his shoulder. He relaxes. "What did we do to deserve everything that's happening to us?"

"I don't know," I whisper to him, in the mist of the night, echoing around us. "I don't know."

Savannah ✵

2nd November

My arms are aching, heavy and stiff. My knees are weak, constantly shaking under the weight of my own body. I think it's making me pay for finally crossing the line.

I'm dragging my feet back to the tent under the setting sun. I walk in, surprised at the sight in front of me.

It's Oskar. Lying on the floor, staring up with vacant eyes at the fabric ceiling. He doesn't flinch when I enter and move closer to him. But my heart breaks a little when I see the dark circles under his eyes. He focuses his bloodshot eyes on me and then back above him.

"Sorry," he murmurs. "Matthew and Zack are in the other tent. I needed a minute to myself."

"Don't apologise. I can leave if you want—"

"Nah, you can stay. It *feels* like I've been here for hours, so the others have probably gone. Besides." He fixes his stare on me, a sudden weight planted in my chest. He's been alone, crying in here. He still seems teary. "I'm not doing much." He stretches his arms out, palms facing me. "As you can probably tell."

"I would never have guessed," I say. He gives me a brief and kind smile, crossing his arms over his chest. "Is there anything I can do to help?" I offer, as I step over to his left, and I bend down to sit beside him, unable to hide a groan when I do. I watch his eyes settle on me, like he can read my mind.

"Training too hard?"

"You're avoiding the question."

"But are you?" I look away, lying my head next to him, grimacing as my back hits the ground. "I'll take that as a yes," he says and looks away too.

Just two friends staring into the abyss together.

"Answer my question."

"There's nothing anyone can do, Savannah," he sighs, and I catch him closing his eyes, tilting his head back, taking deep breaths to steady his trembling hands, still holding onto his arms. "I just miss *him*." My heart twinges. "That's all."

"We all do."

"Not like I do though." I inhale sharply, keeping my breath held in my lungs as tears spring to my own eyes. Because it's the harsh truth. The two of them were both too scared to tell each other of their feelings. "It just feels different from when I think about missing anyone else. Like my parents. My cousins. Anyone from school," he continues on, staring at me. "I'm not tryna tell you I miss him more, as if it's a stupid competition. I'm tryna say I miss him in a different way."

"I know." I look at him, at his scraggly hair falling down his face, another tear escaping his eye. "I get it." His expression softens, before glancing away first.

"He was just my home. My favourite person. One of them anyway. I don't know what else I'm meant to think about at the moment."

"What do you mean?"

"I think of him every. Single. Day. I don't *want* to think about the way our world is changing. About the way our town was burned in front of us. About how we don't have many ways to protect each other. I don't want to think about any of that," he goes on. "Jess," He smiles fondly, a spark momentarily burns in his pupils, a memory uncovered, imagining he's in front of him now. Jess' eyes shining right back at him. Maybe he's smiling too, perhaps even laughing. I want to know what memory he's thinking of right now, for him to say, "he was my comfort person, and he got taken from me. From us, sorry."

"Don't apologise." It's the way I keep thinking about Piper. I sometimes forget anyone else lost her, that it wasn't just me.

"We both just found each other in the middle of this whole build-up of stress. Like in the middle of family issues, in the middle of school shit, in the centre of it all we just found each other, and now—" He hiccups, crying a river, his lips quivering, teeth chattering, eyes squinting. He moves his left arm to be beside him, his right flinging to his eyes, trying to wipe the emotions clean off his face. "He felt like my home through all of it, all those years, he was just always there. And-and now, because he's not in our lives anymore, it's like a part of my life has been ripped from inside of me. The moment I stepped into his house, I could sense it immediately." He lifts his right hand up, stretching his fingers out, trying to grasp something that's always out of reach. "The sense of 'I'm never feeling this way again, am I?'"

He completely loses himself, letting his hand fall from the sky, closing his eyes and letting his soul pour out onto his cheeks. "I miss him, damnit." I find his hand and I hold onto his pinky, hooking his with my own. He lets out a short, sudden exhale.

"And there's no bullshit lie anyone could tell me to make it all feel better than it is," he cries, and stares at me. I see a side of him I never thought I'd witness. Broken. Shattered. Unsure. All I want to do is wrap my arms around him, but right now, all he just needs is someone beside him. "There's nothing anyone can do, because he's already gone. There's no going back to save him, no searching one last time. The chance of *him* is over."

"Oskar," I murmur, wishing nothing more than to take his pain and add it to my own.

"I think I loved him," he whispers, smiling through his tears. "And I never told him. I was too late," he sniffs, taking his hand back from mine and rubs his eyes with them. "I was too slow. I was never ready."

"I'm so sorry, Oskar."

"It's not your fault, Savannah," he says and looks at me again. "So don't say you're sorry. None of us could have done anything. We all got there as fast as we could, and—"

"Even if we did, it wouldn't have guaranteed his safety," I mutter, voice breaking. He holds my whole hand again, tightly. Like an empty promise.

"It wasn't your fault. It wasn't anyone's with what happened to *her*, or *him*." *Piper* or *Jess*. I nod, but a part of me doesn't believe it. He looks back at the tent fabric above us. I do too, the silence enveloping us into its warm embrace.

"Why don't they just kiss already?" Piper whispers into my ear, before trailing off into a series of giggles, watching Oskar fumble over his words. Jess stands a few feet in front of him, arms crossed over his chest, tapping his feet on the ground with an amused smirk dancing across his lips. "The tension—"

"Shut up." I slap Piper's arm, trying to remain straight faced, ignoring that grin splitting her face.

"Did I prove you wrong, Oskar?" Jess chuckles.

"No! 'Course not! You just have me, erm, stunned. I don't know what to say now." Jess simply nods along, smiling at Oskar.

"Sure, sure. You really don't like it when you're wrong."

"No, it's not that—" He shuts his mouth when Jess steps in front of him, pushing up on his tiptoes to get closer to his face.

"Then just admit it. I won't tell anyone else you thought gullible meant something completely different." It's not what the word was, it was the context he put it in with a sentence. He thought it meant it was able to crumble. *"What's so*

hard about that?" He moves back to his original distance from a bright red Oskar.

"This is hilarious, we should get some popcorn."

"Shush, I'm watching too," I tell Piper, elbowing her side.

"Jess."

"Oskar," he purses his lips together.

"I did not know what it meant." Jess' jaw drops dramatically. "What I meant was—"

"We know what you meant—OW!" Piper pinches my cheek making me clamp my mouth shut before saying anything more.

"Not helping," she remarks. Oskar clenches his jaw and Jess starts laughing, covering his mouth and bending over his stomach. A laugh straight from his core. Wait 'til Matthew hears about this. Oskar turns to look at him and he blushes an even more furious colour with wider eyes.

"It's okay." Jess waves his hands across him. "Oh, god, you're funny, Oskar."

"I was tryna sound smart." To impress Jess, I assume. He's so head over heels for him after all.

"Sure, sure."

Piper rolls her eyes onto me and I shake my head at her. She smirks and I return it. I don't know if they know we know. But it's so painfully obvious they're madly in love with each other.

"I forgive you, Oskar." I watch them stare at each other for an agonisingly slow moment. Before Oskar finally smiles back at him, shaking his head in disbelief.

"I should know better to say words I'm unsure of in front of an English student."

"Perhaps."

"Look at the way they stare at each other," Piper whispers under her breath. We gaze at them, and they both stare at us immediately, catching our eyes glued to them. Piper immediately looks back at me, brows flinged up, muttering into my ear, "I think they caught us staring."

"No shit, Sherlock." She starts laughing.

Her melody fills the air around us, invading our lungs with her warmth flooding through.

I miss everything.

But I'll go on for them.

And I'll live for her.

"I've been looking everywhere for you!" Matthew bursts into the tent. We jolt up, both flinching.

"And *you* almost just gave us a heart attack," Oskar mutters breathlessly, pressing a palm to his heart, collapsing onto the floor again.

"Have you been in here the entire time?"

"Yeah, why?" I question.

"I thought you had disappeared. It's Selene. She said to prepare for an incoming attack. She seemed eerily calm telling people about it, and I'm not even sure I was meant to hear or—"

"Matthew." Oskar stands up, stepping closer to him while I breathe it all in.

"An attack?" I ask.

"Calm down, okay?" Oskar insists.

"People are coming to fight us tomorrow night and I-I don't know enough self defence to protect myself, or you, or—"

"We'll stick together and protect each other, Matthew, alright?" He tilts his head when he closer inspects Oskar's appearance.

"Have you been crying?"

"Yeah," he admits. "So?" Matthew wraps his arms around Oskar, leaping around his neck.

"Are you okay?"

"I'm fine." He smiles, grasping his shoulders. "We're all gonna be fine."

"Why was she overly calm about it though?" I think to myself outloud. "Unless she has something to do with it."

"Why would she want a fight to break out here?" Matthew asks as he steps away from Oskar, staring at me with desperation in his eyes.

"I don't know." Something doesn't add up.

"Doesn't Thena want you out too?" Oskar questions, pointing at me. My mind flashes back to her death threat last night. *How Luka heard.* "I wouldn't put it past either of them to initiate something like this."

"We don't have proof though, so we can't say anything." I sigh and flop back onto the ground. "It's one thing after another, huh? Can't get enough of it." I'm struggling with the bow at the moment anyway, and the knives I'll never get used to. *I'm failing.* I press my palms to my eyes.

"Savannah, you alright?" Oskar's words cut right through me. I drop my hands, staring up at the empty fabric above—feeling everything all at one, yet nothing at all. Then he sits down beside my head and his hand reaches my shoulder, and then his touch freezes the skin beneath my clothes.

Am I alright? Does it matter? I need to focus on more important things. Oskar squeezes my shoulder and tightens his grip.

"Savannah?" he asks.

"Hmm?" I hum, forcing myself to look at him on the ground with me. Is he feeling the same as me right now? Like the world is caving in? Like it's crumbling to our feet and there's nothing we can do about it? *I know he is. It's just so easy to forget others feel like you too.*

Oskar gives me a small smile, that modest smile that made Jess feel safe and happy in his time of need. My eyes are burning as I close them, listening to Oskar and Matthew's soft and murmuring voices.

"I've been meaning to ask for a while now," Matthew starts. "Are you guys sleeping well? I mean, I know Zack sleeps like a log, but that's Zack. I don't know about you two. We haven't really spoken about it."

"I'm not sleeping well, no. But I never do," I reply.

"It depends on the night," Oskar admits.

Matthew pauses, debating all the words inside his head, battling with his mind. I glance up at his emerald eyes, that look dull and almost lifeless.

"Are there any specific reasons?" Oskar prompts before me.

"Nightmares." About Fire? Flames? *Death?*

"About?" I ask.

"Turning into a vampire. At least, I think that's what it is. I mean I get fangs like Thena's. When she told us it was vampires, it just stuck with me." His voice trembles with a mix of fear and hesitation. "I always end up dying, but I can never remember how."

"That's rough." Matthew nods to the floor. *Thena got into his head and caused him nightmares of becoming a monster.*

"I'm so sorry, Matthew," I say. "I don't like her. She's been spying on me. I think since the fire, maybe even before then."

"Spying on you? Why you?" Oskar asks, as if I have an answer. I simply shrug my shoulders.

"She thinks I've been watching her, therefore, she returns the favour." I roll my eyes. "She's hiding something."

Matthew quickly shrugs off any more questions of his dreams, so we don't press him any longer. And soon enough, it's time to try and get some sleep. Zack comes searching for me and Luka comes into the tent, talks briefly, before lying on his bed, back facing us, eyes closed, but he's not asleep and I know he's not. He's struggling like me. Like Oskar. Like Matthew. Like Zack. We're not alone in that way at least.

I can't sleep for hours, until I eventually pass out due to exhaustion.

Jack

2nd November

I hate it here, and so does everyone else. The mood is glum and miserable when I walk in the midst of town, decorations for a perfect feast hung up. Draven's beside Ambrosia, watching from a distance.

"Happy birthday," I say and stand on the other side of him, trying my best to ignore the burning stare from his best friend.

"Oh, thank you. You're the second person to have said that to me today," he tells me. He points at Ambrosia. "She was the first." To my complete surprise, she smiles and waves at me. She doesn't seem so terrifying under this light.

"At least someone else remembered," she says. If these two really were from down in some lost city, then how do they know what their birthdays are in this timescale? Or was it really that easy to remember? *Did they choose a day?*

"Indeed." He crosses his arms over his chest, watching Vincent ordering his pawns around like there'll be none tomorrow.

"I'm surprised not even *he* has said it to you, Draven," Ambrosia says, nodding towards Vincent, his younger brother—which still baffles me.

"You're lucky he," Draven nods towards me, "knows about it." He shoots her a stare.

"Oh, I assumed. You seem close." She shrugs her shoulders, leaning forward to look at me. "It's weird, isn't it?" I nod.

"You better not be agreeing because she's a Royal," he exclaims, for once a dangerous sparks in his eye.

"What gave you that impression?" I smirk.

"Oh." He rolls his eyes. "I don't know, the minor inconvenience that took place the other day?"

"I hated everything about that." Ambrosia's sudden distaste for her own cousin shocks me to my core. She's usually the one to run to her side, should she be in any form of trouble. The fact that she's against the things she said, says a lot, in my mind. "I don't think Achillea nor Vincent were thinking straight."

"It's too late to change that now," Draven tells her, and I look to Vincent. He stands on a garden bench, overlooking everyone. He catches my eye and waves with a lighter in his hand, a creased grin across his face. He drops the flame, a small fire breaking out in a few strands of grass, so he jumps down, putting it out before stepping away from the tiny pile of ash and smoke.

"I wish they would just listen to us," Ambrosia remarks. "Seems I barely have anything to my Royal name. Like it truly is worthless." It is. Hierarchy is something the highest people made out of thin air, like Achillea and Ambrosia did. They just take charge of things. Other than that, they have no more right to ask requests from people than I do, or Violet, or Jess. And it's depressing to think that without the hierarchy, everything would fall apart. Riots would break out. Without these two cousins as Queens of us vampires, they'd be war, they'd be hell.

"Oh, boo-hoo," Draven scoffs, but a slight smile tugs at the ends of his lips. "You're a Royal, Ambrosia. You deserved it then, and you deserve it now. Nothing has changed." They stare at each other and Ambrosia pushes into his shoulder, a little too harshly. He bashes into me and I have to steady both of us to regain our balance.

"Shut up." But she wears a gleaming grin. "Thanks." I know they've been friends for a couple centuries, but I never admired the depth of their friendship before now. They share everything and anything with each other.

Ambrosia says goodbye to both me and Draven, waving to catch up with a couple of guards walking around, and a random thought strikes me. Have they ever dated?

"What's going through that head of yours?" Draven asks, not bothering to look at me, crossing his arms over his chest.

"Admiring whatever you have with Ambrosia, that's all."

"Why did you word it like that?" He smirks.

"Because I don't know what's going on behind closed doors."

"Are you implying we have a *'thing'* going on between us? That we're an *'item'* like you and Violet are?" I shrug my shoulders.

"I don't know. It was just a thought." He glances at me, then at anyone who's close by. As a pair walk past, he turns his body to face me, leaning on the wall behind us.

"We don't have anything going on and never have. Never will."

"Ah." I nod, fearing I've hit dangerous territory with him.

"Because I'm aroace." I stare at him. Oh. That explains it then. I wonder how many people know. "You're not the only one to have asked me before. She's had flings though. Mostly with girls, but some guys too. She's a casual dater, not a settling down and sticking with one person type like you or Violet." I smile at the mention of her.

"I understand now." He grins back at me, glancing at Vincent.

"I'm pretty open with it."

"Does he know?"

"I think so. I don't see how he could've glanced past it. For a while he actually had a two year long relationship and for him, that's huge." I know how huge it is, my jaw drops to show it.

"Vincent? Committing to something like that?"

"They were really sweet as well. We were good friends, but I think they were part of another clan that's not so close by. Long distance was part of the final few months, but he couldn't keep it up. I remember, because he was...literally heartbroken from it. He wouldn't admit it though. That was when he went on his worst rampage ever." He glues his eyes onto me. "He went off on his own for a little while. A week later, you and Violet showed up at our door." My eyes widen, taking a breath.

"That's why?"

"He didn't *understand* what he was feeling at the time. Remember, he's a vampire. He doesn't deal with emotions very well, let alone such strong ones. He was confused." He exhales sharply through his nose. "All I wanted to do was to help him, but he isolated himself. No one could approach him except the Royals, since, y'know, higher importance or whatever. It was terrible." The twinge in my chest settles down.

"God. Vincent being in a two year relationship then cutting ties because of separate lives. Didn't see that coming."

"They were kind to him. The opposites of each other really. They mellowed him out, I think. I know he misses them."

"Isn't there still a chance for them?"

"I guess. The chances are slim, but if we get into contact with their clan specifically, then, maybe. Definitely maybe."

"Wow, Vincent was in love."

"Vincent was in love." I can hardly believe he was ever capable of it. "It was sweet while it lasted." He gives me a glum smile, leaning off from the wall, arms over his chest, still crossed. "But yes, Ambrosia and I have never done anything like that, because I'm not into that." Oh yes, that was the conversation starter that led to Vincent's 'history'. "Anyway, does Jess know about the feast for later on?"

"I don't think so." He stares at me, and I roll my eyes, already knowing what he's about to ask. "I should go find him, I guess." He nods.

"Yes, you should."

"Well," I dig my hands into my pockets, walking backwards. "I'll see you around."

"See you later."

I knock on Jess' door. Then again. And again.

But no one responds. So, I let myself in, uninvited. First, I peer into the open living room, but no one's there. No light, no nothing. I head upstairs, a sign on the first door I lay eyes on reads, 'Oskar' in messy handwriting scrawled across it. Just a simple name. But a name Jess basically screamed the first day we came to this town.

So this is his house. I probably should have assumed.

I walk into the bedroom to find Jess lying on the carpet, headphones on, nodding along to the music. He flinches when he hears movement in the room that isn't his own, sitting up immediately. His chest heaves, pressing a hand against it, collapsing onto the floor once again, out of breath. A little on edge it seems.

"*Please,* knock in the future. You scared me."

"You wouldn't have heard it over your music. I can hear it from here." He rolls his eyes and takes the headphones off, sitting back up to give me his full attention.

Another love. The song plays. *All my tears have been used up.*

His eyes glance to the cream pot beside him, before looking back at me.

"Why are you here? Should I pop out the wine?"

"Oh, ha ha. I don't like wine anyway."

"You don't?"

"I'm more of a whiskey fan."

"Of course you are." He cracks the first real smile I've seen from him. Brief, but it's enough to know he's still there, not completely numb just yet.

"What's that supposed to mean?"

"Nothing."

"Anyway—"

"Yes, anyway." I take a breath, and choose my words carefully, because I know he's going to hate this.

"There's a feast tonight," I say. "And everyone is meant to be there." He grimaces, scrunching his nose up.

139

"Everyone?"

"Everyone."

"I heard someone mention. I thought they were joking about it to be honest." I purse my lips together and shake my head. "I won't eat anything."

"As long as you're eating in your own time, I don't have a problem with that." I shrug my shoulders, and he nods hesitantly. Soon enough, he won't need it anyway. I glance around at the long but narrow bedroom. A plain grey bed made to Jess' left, a desk to his right with textbooks, a laptop, and a phone. Above the bed has pictures scattered all over the wall, most of them with Jess, all of them including a boy with black fluffy hair, a gummy grin on his lips. Then the biggest one, which includes Jess, I'm assuming Oskar, a blondie, another black-haired guy with thinner hair, and the kids I saved.

What were the odds that all these kids were entwined with each other?

I tear my eyes away from the pictures of everyone so happy together, simply existing and smiling, and I notice the stash of creams on top of the bookshelf behind the opened door. Oskar must've brought them.

"Is that all?" Jess snaps me out of my trance. I stare right back at him.

"When will you be ready to train?"

"Soon," he replies, putting his headphones on. "I swear it." My job here is done, so I take my leave, shutting the door behind me to let him listen to his music in peace.

The long awaited feast is soon. So Violet and I make our way towards the small meadow Vincent has set it up in. Sunset dawns on us, and Jess is already hovering at the entrance, waiting despite everyone walking past him to find seats. I step beside him, with Violet's hand safely in mine. People are already discussing what their plans are for after the feast. Already discussing what food will be there, *who* will be there. An archway presents in front of us, but none of us move.

"Draven seems to have saved seats for us," Jess tells me.

"What makes you think it was him?" I roll my eyes onto the table in question, with Vincent at the head of it, Draven sits with Ambrosia and Achillea seated close by. He looks at me, shaking his head briefly. I squeeze Violet's hand, taking in a stifled and tainted breath. I look at her.

Knowing Draven will protect her just as I would, I say, "You can sit next to Draven, I can sit on the other side of you, and then Jess." I glance at him and he nods, slight confusion conflicting his expression for a split second before swallowing down whatever question he was about to ask.

An overwhelming, sudden smell floods my system. I repulse, covering my nose with my free hand. Jess is the one to gag, covering his mouth and then looking to where the smell comes from. The smell of rotten flesh and dried blood.

"Ugh, that's disgusting." Violet shakes her head, and faces me, her hand attached to her face as well.

"It smells like a body," I mutter and when I look at Jess, he's wide eyed and literal tears are leaking from his eyes. He doesn't seem to be doing anything else. No breathing, no blinking, not even twitching. I follow his gaze, and I have to deny the impulse to look away.

There's a head in front of Vincent, on a plate, and he seems to have lifted a lid from it, sniffing in the stench, smiling to himself. It's the head of a human's shocked face, jaw ajar and hanging off its skull, the skin pale and lifeless, eyes faded and iris colourless. Someone with short brown hair—a pixie cut with lumps fallen out and now on the table. Whose skin has had the life sucked out of it. Her eyes still open.

Paralysed. Dead. Soulless.

"Excuse me." Jess turns around, finally taking a breath and he walks away. Not too far, he knows he still has to attend whether he likes it or not, instead he walks down a darkened alleyway.

"A friend?"

"Perhaps," I echo and look at Violet, holding both of her hands. "Are you okay?" She nods, hesitates, then shrugs her shoulders,

"It's Vincent. Are we surprised anymore?"

"No, but it doesn't mean things like this should still be happening."

"Again, it's Vincent. He doesn't change overnight." But, god, how I wish he would sometimes. "Hey." She knocks our joined hands against my chest. "It's gonna start soon, go talk to him." The thought of leaving her side sends shivers down my spine. I glance at Draven, who's watching the entire thing. Then at Vincent who's busy with something else, then to Achillea who's talking to Ambrosia. They're all busy, and Draven would help her if anything goes south. I meet her eyes again, forcing a nod.

"Wait for me."

"Of course." I lift one of her hands to my lips and I kiss her knuckles.

"I mean it. Don't go without me, I won't be long, darling." And before I can wait for a response, I let her soft hands go, and turn to find Jess.

I turn a corner, and Jess is on the floor, hugging his knees to his chest, eyes tightly shut. I feel a twinge of sympathy for him when staring at the broken mess, crying through staggered breaths. He's been through a hell of a lot, and all of that I know he doesn't deserve. Neither him nor his friends. But I mustn't be helping either. So instead of telling him to get up, shrug it off and deal with it, I edge closer and silently, until I'm in front of him.

I kneel down.

"Jess—"

"I'll be fine in a minute, just- just go to Violet or something." He props his elbow on his knee and rubs his eyes with one of his palms, tears streaming down his cheeks.

"Who was it?" I ask softly. He opens his eyes, leaning his head back, rolling the name over his tongue a few times before saying it outloud.

"Her name was Piper Miley. Savannah's best friend." His voice trembles with every word. "She was a dear friend of mine." The gaze in his eyes is all too familiar. The way he talks, the way his eyes dull down with every breath, before turning suddenly stern, glaring at me. "Was it you? Did you know they killed people my age? Why didn't they kill me?" He shoots these useless questions at me in a frenzy. Eager to receive any answers to cancel out the thoughts in his mind.

"Jess, I had no part in this, and I thought you would assume that to begin with."

"But how can I take your word for it?" I sit down, cross legged, sighing.

"I didn't kill Piper, I let Luka and Savannah go, and I've never met Oskar. Or your other friends. I would never kill anyone, because I made a pact with Violet, swearing we'd never become monsters - that we would never take someone's future from them." I wait for him to belittle me, but when nothing comes, I continue. "The exception was if one of us was in immediate danger, we wouldn't hesitate to protect each other. Or ourselves. So unless you or your friends threaten mine or Violet's lives, you're safe. Besides, you have a sister to save. I'm not gonna take that away from you." He widens his eyes, then wipes his cheeks, sniffing once again and I notice the way his hands shake with every inch, the way his lips quiver, fight or flight set in.

"I miss her, but you've seen her, right? She's okay?"

"She's okay," I nod and it gives him enough strength to at least breathe deeply again.

"I miss my friends." *I do too.*

"They could still be alive, Jess. You've got a reason to keep fighting. Don't give that up so easily." He looks down at his knees, pursing his lips together. "I'll give you a moment alone, but *please* don't be long." He nods, watching me stand and leave the alleyway. I don't dare glance back at the mess he is right now. I want to help him. I wish I knew how. I can't even help myself.

"Is he okay?" Violet asks, as soon as she sees me.

"He just needs a moment more. That head," I say in a low voice, nodding towards Vincent, still standing over it, laughing merrily. "Is one of his friends. So you can imagine what he's feeling right now." She frowns, looking back at the Noble.

"I hate him," she grunts behind gritted teeth.

"We all do, flower." *Well, not everyone. There's Draven, and then that mystery partner he had years ago in a separate clan.*

During the entire feast, Jess doesn't touch any of the food lying on the table, not even the bread and butter, or the pasta, and I'm not surprised. If I were him, my appetite would have disappeared completely. And I fear it has, Violet is the only reason I actually remember to eat instead of constantly making sure no one even *looks* at her. Not out of obsession, but out of protection. I feel like I can't even turn my back on anyone, but I need to remind myself she can protect herself. She's stronger than me after all.

"Thank you, thank you all!" Vincent begins to make his grand speech around an hour in, sitting at a table surrounded by people I despise. I catch Violet rolling her eyes before staring right back at him. "Thank you for attending my little birthday feast, and I know, it's a few days late, but! Better late than never!" Jess' eyes are on Piper's head. Still on the plate in front of Vincent. I tense, clenching my trousers in my hands out of anxiety. He hasn't touched it, so what's going to happen next? "I have an announcement, my friends! There's a camp within the meadow, neighbouring our home." Violet glances at me with warning eyes, flashing with flames, or is it fear? "They have a stash of humans there!" *Savannah.* I never told Jess I saw her a couple days ago, when I got ordered to go there with Ambrosia as her guard. To meet whoever we were trying to intimidate with that fire. To be civil. Neither of them ever mentioned an attack. A planned attack. I never told Jess in fear he would have made a break for it. But if he gets told to attack with us, then he'll see for himself. Savannah and Luka.

Oskar?

"We need more blood supply, so I say, and order." He holds up a knife for everyone to see, glinting in the lamps that surround us, tilting it down towards his prey. "For us to take them out tomorrow night!" He breaks into a manic laugh, his fangs shining even from this far away whilst a few people begin cheering, while others start clapping and more start murmuring."For more human blood!"

He slams the knife into Piper's head, cutting through way too easily, and Jess flinches, turning away, biting back a gag.

"Is there anywhere and anyone he won't attack?" Violet questions beside me.

"I think we both know the answer to that," I mutter.

"Now, since the camp is only a puny one, we'll only need a few Knights. I have a list!" He starts calling out a few names before the inevitable, "Jack." But I'm not expecting Violet's name to follow quickly after. In total, there's only six people going. Admittedly, it is a small camp, but these are all carefully picked skilled fighters—I'm the weakest among them.

Thankfully, Jess' name is not called out. "We will move out at sundown tomorrow!"

Jack

Familiarity.

It's a lovely, but addicting feeling. I gaze around at my surroundings once more. A field unfolds around me, the one I spent time laughing in—the one just behind my house when I was growing up.

I've had this dream before. Fear clogs my throat up immediately.

Shane.

He's nearby. I pinch my skin, which never usually works, but I try anyway. Then I search for the highest building, but none look particularly high, none I can jump from for me to just. Wake. Up.

Dread freezes my veins, echoing in my ear when I feel the vibrations in the ground of someone's footsteps behind me, closing in on me. I choke on unspoken words, walking forward.

Then I'm running.

I'm sprinting through familiar street corners, shops, roads, houses, everything. I'm seeing it all except humans. But the person behind me is still following, and no matter how many twists and turns I take in this town, they only gain on me, huffing and sighing in annoyance. But it's only a matter of time before they catch me, before I see him, before—

"Come on, Jack! I thought you knew how much I DIDN'T like running! Slow down and let me talk to you!" I grit my teeth, grimacing so hard I slow down, but that was a mistake. He grabs my wrist, and then my shoulder.

I yelp, squinting my eyes shut as they turn me around, but I refuse to see him in the flesh again. Unscathed, safe and not unconscious in a hospital bed. How long has it been since I saw him in a dream—two, maybe three years? And yet it still shakes me to the core, still makes my heart rattle in my chest as if encaged behind iron bars, especially when he begins talking again.

"Jack, why won't you look at me? Have I done something wrong?" His voice drops, and I don't want him to believe I've pissed him off. I bite my lip and shake my head. "Then what is it?"

There's no point running. There's no use denying that he'll always be a part of who I am. He will always be there in the back of my mind, one of the reasons why I'm fighting for life.

But it hurts seeing him in dreams. I want him to stay in the past. Where he will forever remain in my mind.

I open my eyes with a stifled breath, staring at his brown leather shoes first, then his flared black jeans, his favourite pair with a tear in one side. Then his baggy grey top, hanging over his gold embedded belt, then his broad shoulders, his arm still outstretched towards me. His hands are still holding my wrist, refusing to let me escape, burning my skin.

And then I spot the chain. The one I gave him for his 18th birthday, hanging loosely around his neck, and I feel a shock of tears behind my eyes.

He meets my gaze.

And smiles his normal gummy smile. Before he was battered, broken, and bruised.

"That wasn't so hard, was it?" The exact same shade of blue as mine stares back at me. His deepened dimples are showing, and I spot the moles in front of his ears, above his eyebrows and below his chin. I haven't seen this face in years. As a monster, I'm only able to dream once every two years or so. Most vampire's can't, almost all the vampires turned humans can't either, even Violet can't. Something in the brain that lets some humans visualise turns off when the new blood is injected into our system. Something screams 'this isn't right' and then shuts down completely, which is why it's so dangerous to turn someone into a monster. Any vital organs can react like that too. So when Vincent was turning Jess, he was bordering on killing him. A thin line between immortality and death. "Jack."

"Shane." It's been a while since I've said his name. It's scary how easily it rolls off my tongue.

"What's wrong?"

Then it overwhelms me, that he's here in front of me. I could talk and talk and talk and no one would ever know, because this isn't real. He's dead, and yet he feels so real to me everyday of my pathetic life. Like he never left me at all.

"What's actually going right?"

"You're still being edgy then."

"Still?"

"I figured, since you're older now, you'd have outgrown that," he smirks, and finally lets my arm go. "That's all. Nothing negative, I promise." He holds his palms up, as if to say 'I'm innocent'. But he was always *innocent. "Anyone would've thought I was stalking you or something."*

"There's no one here TO think that, Shane."

"Anyway, I thought we were gonna go to the lake today, the meadow or even the park. It's an 'us' kinda day, right?" I shake my head, hardly believing a

word of this. "No? Oh, is it Vi?" *His nickname for her.* "Are you hanging out with her? She can always join us!" *Maybe on another day, I'd play along. But right now, I don't have the energy to pretend.*

"No, there are other reasons."

"Other reasons that are more important than your own big brother? I'm honestly surprised and offended. Just slightly though." *He shows just how offended with his thumb and finger, the gap practically closed, and he laughs a little.*

"I don't think you understand."

"Please, enlighten me, brother dearest." *I grit my teeth together once again, staring into his dark pupils, trying not to let any sort of tears escape.*

"Do you really want to know why? Or are you asking to be nice?"

"Would I lie to you?"

"You're dead," *I spit. His eyes widen, and it makes it a whole lot worse when I know this is my mind, my own head playing stupid tricks on me. Why would I ever have to tell him he died because a truck slammed into his car when he was nineteen? Why am I telling him, I'm the only one who fought for his life support never to be pulled? Even if it was a minor chance of him surviving, everyone turned their backs and said with solemn expressions, 'We understand, doctor, just do it,' when they could have let him hang on a little longer.*

I believed he would make it, and maybe he would still be alive if they had just never touched the plug. I could've fought harder. I could've–

"Jack." *He steps forward, and wraps his warm and protective arms around me.* "You're crying." *A tingling settles on my cheeks where damp tears are falling down my skin. I wasn't sure I could cry after being turned. It was like they turned off my feelings. But I'm standing here now, in my dream, with my brother's arms around me–*

I choke back a set of words, hiccuping helplessly in my brother's arms.

In my brother's arms.

"Who hurt you?" *he whispers quietly in my ear.*

"Everyone." *I give up, sobbing onto his shoulder, gripping his clothes tightly in my hands, letting it come in waves.* "They didn't let me save you, and I watched them hold your hand as you died. Mum and Dad sobbed, nothing like I had ever seen before. And I see Vincent completely rejecting his big brother and I–" *Shane holds me up as I grow limp, my own words failing me.* "How can he be so heartless? I don't get it." *My cries turn into anger, clenching his clothes in my palms as tight as I can make them.* "How can he just...forget? I'd do anything to have you back–"

"Jack."

"Because how can someone who's dead be one of the most important people to me?" I yell, not at him, not at Vincent, not at those damned doctors, but at the universe. I squint to see a crack in a house, then a window shatters. A scream's heard from afar, and the world seems to be spinning, so I cling on tighter. "Sorry, that came out of nowhere."

"Jack." He steps away, hands slipping to my arms, staring into my eyes with a softened and broken expression. "You really need to learn to let your emotions out rather than letting them build up and then explode like this."

"It's not like it's in real life, is it?" I wipe my eyes and he merely tilts his head.

"Is it not?" He begins to slip from my grip, beginning to fade away into nothing, his smile see-through.

"Don't go. Don't you do this to me." I shake my head, holding on tighter. "I want to talk some more, I don't want this to be over so soon, and I'm sorry I ran, but—" The wind sweeps him backwards, but I go with him. "Say something!" I shake the almost lifeless ghost in front of me. He smiles.

He smiles. And shakes his head.

As if I'm too late.

As if our time is up.

As if I have to wake up again.

"I don't want to go!" I scream, leaping forward to wrap my arms around his neck, but no one is there to catch me when I fall into the meadow.

Jack

3rd November

Violet and I sleep late into the morning, and I bask in the warmth of her arms, like no harm can be done to either of us.

However, the tranquillity is ruined when we flinch at the front door opening and then slamming. I lean forward, covering Violet on instinct with my body, as they stomp up the stairs, heavy footsteps.

"Who—"

"Ssh." I lean over the bed and grab my sword whilst she reaches for her dagger, both blades pointing at the door, waiting for whoever's turning the knob from the other side

My shoulders hunch back, and I find Violet's hand, gripping it tightly. No knock.

The door opens.

It swings wide to reveal—

Jess.

"Goddamn it, Jess," Violet exclaims, dropping the dagger onto the floor and then leaning her head on my back. "You gave us a heart attack."

"Knock in future." I roll my eyes, lowering my weapon.

"Sorry, I figured you'd already be up," he says with a slight smirk on his lips. "You're going to that camp tonight, right?"

"What of it?"

"If you see any of these people," he leans forward and drops a picture onto the duvet. One of him, Luka and Savannah, two black-haired boys and a blonde. All smiling at the camera. I pick it up, seeing the wrinkles around all their eyes, Savannah seemingly on Luka's back, both of them mid laugh at the top. Jess on the blonde's back beside them, with the longer black haired guy in the middle with the other in the bottom left corner, taking the picture itself. The middle guy seems to be looking at Jess. Oskar? "Tell me." Jess seems happy in the picture, frozen in time.

"And you'll leave for them?"

"No, I just want to know they're okay." I nod but make no promise. "Try to keep them alive. I know you wont kill them, but...others might."

"Who's who?" He points at the blond kid first.

"Matthew." His finger traces around the middle guy's gummy expression, the one with the longer, fluffier, darker shade of black hair. "Oskar." He then taps the final guy's nose, the one taking the picture. "Zack. And you've met Luka and Savannah."

"Jack, don't make any empty promises," Violet warns me from behind.

"What does she mean?" Jess stares at her, a hardened expression in his eyes.

"She means I shouldn't make any promises I can't keep." He looks back down at me with uncertainty. "I can't promise they're there, and I can't promise I can keep them safe. But I *can* swear that if I see them, I won't kill them." I will not, however, promise to tell him if I find them because if I do tell him, there's no guarantee he won't just leave to go after them.

And then it would be my fault. Then they'd take Violet away from me.

"Is that all you came for?" I ask.

"No, I came to visit Savannah's room."

"Any reason?" I yawn, as he snatches back the picture from my grip and scowls.

"Because I miss her." He turns around and leaves, slamming the door after him.

I fall back onto my bed, head hitting the pillow whilst Violet swings her legs off to change and prepare.

"You gonna move or what?" she asks.

"I was thinking of just staying here to piss Vincent off actually." She rolls her eyes with a smile.

"Excellent. I'll make sure he throws a proper funeral for you then."

"Thank you, love."

When I'm in the living room minding my own business, the front door bursts open and this time, Vincent walks in, arms wide, grinning widely. It's 12pm. And somehow it is still too early to deal with him. *If we didn't have Jess to deal with, we would've left by now. We would've told Draven already, he seems okay for now, and we would be in the wilderness somewhere.*

Away from this lunatic.

"Good afternoon everyone! Such a wonderful day!" Vincent snaps his head down to look at me. "Don't you think?"

"Yes, just lovely." I force the fakest smile I can manage at him before looking back at Violet where I roll my eyes.

"Violet, darling." My eyes flick up, turning my head to glare at him. "Would you mind—"

"What do you want?" I say.

"I need to talk to *you*." His eyes stare into the back of my skull. "So I may need her to leave the room, that's all." I clench my fists.

"Why?" Violet demands before I can.

"Now, now." He glares at her. "If I told you, it wouldn't be a secret. And aren't secrets fun to keep from one another?" Anxiety twists in my stomach. I glance at Violet and she scowls before walking past us and up the stairs, and with one more glance at me, she disappears into Savannah's room to join Jess. "Thank God she went without a fuss, huh?"

"What do you want, Vincent?" I say, slow and careful as I draw my eyes back to his flames.

"I need you to check out a location for us." Us? "It's by the side of the mountain. Check if there's a dent in the rock side, and see if there's an outline in the grass, if you would be so kind."

"The mountain is miles away, I might not make it back in time for the camp thing today." A smile curls at the sides of his lips and a dark shiver of fear runs through my veins. Violet. He wants me away, so he can get to Violet.

"Oh, pity." He turns his back on me and heads back towards the door.

"Do you not want me to join?" He looks over his shoulder at me.

"I never said that now, did I?"

"That's the impression I'm getting," I say. "Why can't you go? Or Achillea, Ambrosia, maybe even Draven?" He stops at the mention of his brother's name. He turns around, staring down at me through his nose, eyes stern and rage burns in them, intertwining with the blood of his irises.

"Because we are *all* busy. Jack, I suggest you go now if you want to be at your precious *darling's* side tonight." And with those parting words, he leaves, slamming the door behind him as Violet opens up the door upstairs and races down the stairs.

I grind my teeth together as she appears in front of me, concern in her brows, a softness in her eyes. Her hand rises to my collar and checks to see if another mark was made. After finding none, she simply rests her hand on the back of my nape.

"What was that all about? You okay?" I raise my palm to hers and I hold it tight, leaning into her touch, and I nod, closing my eyes.

"Tired."

"Of him?"

"Of everything."

"Who hurt you?" he whispers quietly in my ear.

"Everyone."

"What has he done now?"

"Just some pointless orders."

"Why did he need me out of the room?"

Because he wants me to fear what he'd do to you if I go against these orders. There's a possibility he's just messing with me. But that's not a risk I'm willing to take.

"I don't know," I lie. And I can feel my chest growing heavier. She frowns and leans in to kiss me. "Violet," I break away. "Don't leave without me."

"What? For the camp?" I nod. "Sure, how long will you be?" I grip both of her hands tightly.

"I'll be back before you go." She nods.

"Okay." She smiles.

"Okay." I kiss her, longingly and deeply. I don't want to ever let her go. But I need to leave now if I have a chance of coming back in time. My weird *Alatus'* ability may not hold up for as long as this journey will last, so I leave her standing in the middle of the living room with a final kiss bestowed on her lips, as softly as a flower kisses the breeze. I bid my farewell and walk out the house. Everything is tearing us apart. Be it Vincent, or the world itself as it crumbles under our feet. I'm sick of it.

I swear, if Violet and I weren't set on leaving sooner rather than later, I'd stay just to make Vincent, at least, *feel* threatened. Maybe grow powerful enough to fight him and Zayne and Achillea. I'd show them the kind of torture they put us through, and let them taste it.

At least Zayne has backed off since moving here. I've seen him less and less because of my involvement with Vincent. Maybe he wasn't Vincent's favourite person after all.

I turn my head to see Jess outside as well, watching my every move.

"May I ask?"

"No, no you may not." I stop, facing him. "But please." Am I really trusting him with this? "Keep Vincent away from Violet best you can."

"Is there something more I should know?"

"No. I just don't trust him." Jess is safer than both Violet and I in this situation, so can I really drag him into this any further? After all he's been

through and dealing with - both his skin and his transition. *Is that right?*
"Actually, nevermind." I turn back around and start walking off, when he
calls my name. I fling my head back over my shoulder to see him slightly
smiling at me.

"I'll keep her safe." He may be younger than us, but he has spirit, I'll
give him that. There's not much he can do in order to protect her, but I
know he'll keep an eye out, at the very least.

"You have my thanks." He nods, and jogs off back the way he came
from.

"It's the least I could do for all that you've done for me," he shouts back.
I thought he wouldn't think much of it.

I spread my deathly black wings with a dark glow. Times like these, I'm
thankful I'm an *'Alatus'* vampire. I inherited it from Vincent since he's the
reason I am the way I am. His other ability is *'Sanguis Potentia'* which means
he needs blood to survive. I fear Jess has inherited from him.

Of course, there are two other types, *'Sol Sensitivo'* where you're
sensitive to the sun, and finally, *'Intelligente'* which means you're basically
smarter than the rest. They can hold more information than others, are
more observant and some other stuff I can't quite remember. There were
other types, apparently, before Achillea. However, only four remain now,
because those four were all a part of her original group who came to the
surface hundreds of years ago – if that even happened.

Achillea is all four of them, which I hear is rare, Ambrosia is an *'Alatus'*
vampire. Vincent is a *'Sanguis Potentia'* and an *'Alatus'*. And Draven is an
'Intelligente' vampire and *'Alatus'*.

It takes an hour to the mountain side. I land unsteadily, leaning my
back onto the rocks, panting until I catch my breath. It's gonna be a pain to
fly back, *and* make it back in time for them to leave the camp.

I shake my head free from those thoughts. My back is already aching.
One thing at a time.

First, find an indent in a mountain side.

I keep to the side of the mountain, hand on the rocks. I pick up the
pace, jogging until eventually, I think I find what I'm looking for. Quite
literally, a circular indent is part of the mountain. On top of that, it doesn't
look natural. I look up, stepping closer to it, laying a hand on the cracked
mountain.

A *crack* that spreads up and onto the curve of the highest peak. Why do
they want me to check this location?

I step closer and I feel the earth shift beneath my feet. I hold my breath, looking down at where the grass meets a burnt stone outline beside this indent. The stone falls deeper into the mud itself, hiding a platform. I quickly stagger backwards as the ground shakes, and the crack in the mountain spreads deeper and deeper. And then passes onto the platform. Before suddenly stopping.

Just before it reaches my feet.

Was that an earthquake? Or was this a trap? A diversion?

A diversion.

I turn around, leaping up into the air, summoning my wings.

I spot the small group departing town from afar. It's taken longer than I had anticipated on the way back, since my wings are giving out, burning with aches.

Violet's at the back of the pack, looking around nervously, before narrowing her gaze on Vincent at the front of the pack. Leading.

"Violet." I lose the grasp I had on this force I use to keep my wings raised. I glance back, as they disappear into thin air and I fall, tumbling onto the grass in a heap, a big enough leap to make me roll onto my front, yelling, and making my knees buckle.

"Jack?" I lift my head up. She's sprinting towards me. "Jack!"

"Violet," I murmur, pressing my palms to the ground, lifting myself up, spitting grass out from my mouth. She leans down, grabbing one of my shoulders and one of my arms, pulling me up to be sitting right again. She looks back at Vincent just watching, with a plain expression. No anger visible. No remorse evident.

"We'll catch up!" She turns back to me, softening her gaze with a small smile, shaking her head side to side. "You pushed yourself too far, didn't you?"

"What makes you think that?" I smirk and she lets out a laugh.

"I would be fine on my own, love. Go back and relax—"

"No." I clasp her hand, as she helps me up to my feet. "I'm coming too. Jess would kill me if I stayed back whilst his friends could be in this camp he's fixated on." She merely purses her lips into a thin line.

"Just take it easy, okay?"

"Of course." I lean down and kiss her, squeezing her hand tightly, with her arm knocking into my own.

Familiarity. Such a lovely feeling.

Violet and I don't let go of each other's hands, not even to ready our weapons as we draw closer to the camp. We flinch at the sudden shriek of what sounds like a young kid screaming. We shouldn't be here. This isn't ours to take and yet here we are. Vincent spins around to face us, shouting over the chaos.

"'Take what you need, and take what you want! The only rule is to leave survivors!" What? That's out of character even for him. He winks before turning back around. "We need someone to keep our legacy close, and to scare their children at night for halloween time." To pass on the message? He drops his cape onto the ground, as if it never mattered anyway, to let his dark ginger hair glow vibrantly in the dimming sun, his eyes as piercing and as crimson as ever. He sprints forward, sword behind him, laughing as he slices a strip down a tent in his wake.

Meanwhile, Zayne turns to me with warning eyes.

"Don't fuck up again, Jack. If I find out those kids are still alive, I'll make it my own job to plot their demise, and your heroic actions would have been meaningless." He runs off with the rest of the group as Violet shakes her head, leaning onto my shoulder.

"We could turn back now, no one would ever notice."

"Jess would." Therefore, I march on, with her in my grip around my arm. I draw my sword, not that I have any intention of using it, and we squeeze through a gap of two tents.

The first scene I set my eyes on, is Zayne gripping a human's neck, lifting them up from the ground to leave their feet dangling helplessly below. He licks his lips when the human trembles in fear, wide-eyed, staring into an abyss. They don't even scream. Or cry for help. Or yell and sob. They let him grin, they let him lean down, biting into their neck, pulling a chunk of their flesh out. I grimace, looking away, hearing him drop the human to the ground, his sword digging into their body.

But as I turn my head away, I catch a glimpse of someone's head looking round the corner of a tent, with wide, bulging eyes, clenching daggers in her fists, clearly unfamiliar with their weight, with a bow strapped to her back. She's watching Zayne. Intensely.

And I know who she is. I could never forget the fear in those eyes. The girl named Savannah. I turn to Violet as she looks at me.

"Be safe, I need to talk to her for Jess' sake."

"He spoke to me about his friends, whilst you were talking to Vincent," she pauses, biting her lower lip, glancing at the girl behind me. "He needs them alive, Jack." She looks back at me with stern eyes. "Go, I'll distract anyone coming close."

I let her go and sheathe my sword, approaching the girl, glancing at Zayne to make sure he's got other things on his mind. When my eyes are back on Savannah, she's backing away and out of the tent gap, holding her breath, staring at me. I lift my hands up in a '*I come in peace*' way, as I grab the wrist she's holding her weapon in. I say nothing but try not to glare, and I drag her back into the tent's 'alleyway'. She begins breathing in and out, shallow in panic, tilting her hand ever so slightly to scrape the end of the blade on the inner side of my elbow. She slices down, so suddenly, I don't have time to react or even defend myself. I fling her off me, and she stumbles back, hissing out an abrupt gust of air.

Blood seeps down my uniform, a gap in it's fabric, quickly growing damp. I whip my clothes up and over the cut, seeing the dark liquid fall from my skin and onto the ground. I glare at her, the pain stinging, spreading through my veins in a rush of adrenaline.

"I wasn't going to hurt you," I spit out.

"What else was I supposed to do?" she questions, and I roll my eyes. "It's just self-defence."

"For one thing, I wasn't holding a weapon! I showed you my hands and I was leading you somewhere, out of sight of that *monster* out there." I fling my unscathed arm towards the direction Zayne was in. She clamps her mouth shut, still not grabbing her main weapon. "And you clearly don't want to do anything to me, since you're not advancing."

"What do you want?"

"You need to hide. The guy just round the corner - he was the other one in your house *that* day. Zayne." She purses her lips together.

"Oh."

"I'm surprised you even survived." Jess will be pleased – at least, if he finds out. I open my mouth again but it's cut short, because a blood curdling scream erupts from close by. Savannah's out in a flash, running away from me and out of the tent to their aid. At least I don't have to lie to Jess if I do decide to let him know Savannah's safe. But that scream – please don't be Oskar, please don't be Matthew, or Zack or anyone.

Please don't be Oskar.

I march out from my hiding spot. Where Violet once was leaves no trace of where she is now. Quick and sneaky. Just the way she's always been.

"Oskar?" I whisper into the air, walking beside tents, because if he's hiding anywhere, it'll be in a tent. And if he's anywhere outside, then I'll be able to recognise him thanks to Jess' pictures. I look around, on the verge of giving up when I hear Vincent's voice from close by. I panic, fight, flight or freeze kicking in.

I flee into the closest tent, so rushed, my brain can't grasp why I'm running, except for the only rational reason, *I don't want another meaningless order that separates me from Violet for any longer.* I zip the tent up, sighing in relief until a voice behind me calls,

"What the hell are you doing?" I turn around, trying not to show my disbelief so plainly on my face when the exact same face from Jess' picture appears before my eyes.

Oskar.

"Apologies, I don't particularly like my clan leader. I'm hiding from him." He looks hesitantly between me and his sword lying on a fold up bed. "I'm not gonna hurt you."

"And I'm supposed to believe that?" he scoffs, and rolls his eyes. I begin to speak again, but he raises his hand to stop me. "Don't worry, I don't have the energy to fight back so if you wanna cut my head clean off, do it quickly." The fact he's so willing to just die like that – embracing it with open arms – alarms me on several different levels.

First, Jess is fighting hard to see this person again another day. Secondly, I've been there, done that. Despair and helplessness is an awful feeling. Thirdly, does he not want to fight for Jess too? Or any of his friends?

"I said I'm not here to fight, and I stand by that."

"Oooh, noble, I see," he says, "Well, stay for as long as you want." He opens up his arms, a blank expression in his eyes, completely vacant and glazed over. Hopeless. "Why are your people—"

"They're not my people," I snap. He holds up both of his hands this time, taking a step back with raised eyebrows.

"Okay then, why are your other *guys* here?"

"Because my clan leader gets bored from time to time," I reply and he snorts.

"Oh, poor him. So he drags everyone else down with him?"

"Pretty much."

"Jeez." He glances up and down at me. "You seem pretty chill as well, for someone who's meant to be attacking me right now." He notices the patch of dried blood on my arm. His eyes linger. "And it seems someone thought you were an enemy."

"It was more self-defence," I echo her exact words and he smirks. "I had to warn them about something. Didn't take too lightly to it."

"Damn." He visibly hesitates once again, but ends up diving under the bed, pulling out a first aid kit. He takes out some wipes and bandages, standing back up, looking at me, holding them out.

"No, you as a camp will need them more than I do."

"What's that supposed to mean? I'm tryna do a good thing here, man," he smiles again. Nowhere near as close to the one I saw in that picture though.

"Well, if Vincent has his way, he won't just stop with a random short attack like this."

"So, I might be seeing more of you?"

I chuckle. "Maybe, but not for the reason you think right now." He pulls back the first aid stuff and chucks it on the bed, tilting his head.

"I feel like I've said this quite a lot, but what do you mean?"

"I mean," I take a breath, watching him just wait patiently for an answer while I decide how to word it. *Jess is alive? Jess is my 'student'? He's one of them now but he still thinks of you?* How will he react? Will he press for answers? Will he rejoice in happiness?

This is the person Jess has spent weeks *grieving* over, because he was unable to see him, unable to know if he was dead or alive. I can practically hear his voice at home, begging for them to be alive, crying to himself. The uncertainty of the unknown *tortured* him.

When I look back at Oskar, I see the boy Jess fell in love with. With soft brown eyes, his head tilted in curiosity, seeming so casual to even talk to strangers, and I notice the way even his hair doesn't seem to need any sort of maintenance at all.

This is the boy Jess misses ever so dearly.

"Jess speaks of you often."

The definition of the word 'broken' means: when something falls, hits a surface, or is pulled apart, it shatters. Sometimes, it can't be fixed, and sometimes it can be mended with some simple tape or some glue. But there's another, more commonly used definition to it.

It can mean to have lost all hope. And to give up. And if I could watch someone break so simply before my eyes, this is what it would look like.

Oskar *breaks* in front of me. His lips ajar, chest frozen, shoulders falling and his eyes – his vulnerable and beautiful eyes fill with tears. He quickly looks away, clenching his fists in complete anger.

"And how in the world would you know that? Actually, no, how would you know who I am before I tell you?"

"He showed me pictures of you. When he heard I was coming here, he told me to make sure you're alive. Safe and breathing." He bares his teeth, and quick as a flash, he's light on his feet to grab his long sword, and then points it at me with two hands gripping it tightly, until his knuckles are a paper white, shaking furiously.

"He's dead."

"And if he were, how would I know who you are?" He shakes his head, and advances so I unsheathe my own sword, pointing it right back at him, the blade lain between his eyes.

"Then you have no right to speak his name." He shakes with fury or is it fear? Either way, his words escape twisted and cracked. His lips tremble and he steps even closer towards my weapon. "It's a real sick joke to play on a guy. And what? I assume you killed him after he told you who I was? Who any of his friends were?" He raises his voice at me in a frantic frenzy, but I see the boy behind the broken expression, begging for questions, begging for any sort of hope to hang on to. Anything to fight for.

"I didn't kill him, and he's alive and well. He wants to see you, and he misses you—"

"Shut up, shut up, shut up, shut up!" he screams, shaking his head from side to side, as if it'd cancel out the noise, but I drone on, having not finished my lines,

"But Vincent is too tight on his instructions to have allowed him to come here with me."

"Bullshit."

"Believe what you want to believe! I'm only doing him a favour." I drop my weapon to my side, but he refuses to, his grasp frozen in time with his breaths.

"Oh, ha ha ha," he forces out, tears now falling rapidly down his slicken cheeks. "Get out." I chew on my inner lip, stepping forward to rest his blade on my neck. "What are you—"

"Do you really want to hurt me? Or are you bluffing? I'm curious." He glares daggers at me.

"I have no more words for you."

"No questions about your friend?" His brows fling up. "I'm not lying." I use my fingers to push the sword away from me, and he drops it to the floor with a crash. "Why would I?"

"Because you're on *their* side."

"And you think it's by choice?" I say. "I will say this though, you can't rescue him." His jaw drops open in dismay, brows curving under the weight of my words crashing down on him. "Yet."

"Yet?"

"It's too hectic right now. His sister's trapped and he's working to get her out. If you come now, it'd complicated everything for both you and him. It could get us all killed, understand?"

"Tell me something about him. That a picture can't tell, or that his sister can't prove." I rummage through my brain for anything, because in fact, I don't know him well. But I do know one thing for sure.

"He has eczema." His eyes widen, taking a step back, even more tears flowing onto his cheeks, as he grips onto his hair, as if ready to pull it out by the roots.

"So he really is...with you? Is he one of you? As in a- a-"

"Monster?" He doesn't say anything, but I nod for him instead. "He's not a monster. He's a vampire. And it wasn't with his consent. He hates himself for it. He hasn't said out loud but..." It's in the way he treats himself. "I know he does." He grimaces, and creases his eyebrows together, sniffing and wiping his nose on the back of his sleeve.

"Jess," he weeps silently.

"Anymore questions before I leave?"

"Is he well?"

"Are you?" He purses his lips together into a fine line. "I don't think anyone is in this world, Oskar. And this goes the same for him, as I assume it is for you."

"He's alive, he's really alive." He looks up from the ground, as I turn to make my leave. "Wait, wait, tell him I promise to make it to him one day. Please?" I nod ever so slightly. "Take care of him," he says before *breaking* down once again. I look over my shoulder reluctantly to watch.

He weeps to me, and then he cries, and then he sobs to me, as he holds his hands close to his head, looking down at them, at the tears falling uncontrollably, before staring up at me with glossy, misty, and helpless eyes.

"Please, don't let him die."

Savannah

3rd November

Roots wrap around my feet.

We're watching a group march towards us from the distance. Luka, Oskar, Matthew, and Zack are beside me, spotting a winged creature land close by and a silhouette of a person rushing towards them. *Wings. Actual wings.*

"This is bullshit." Oskar rolls his eyes, turning back, starting to walk off. "We shouldn't be the ones to fight *their* fight in whatever mess they've created for themselves."

"They saved us, shouldn't we save them?" Zack questions.

"It's not just Thena and Selene in this camp. There's innocent people, like Annabeth. They've done nothing wrong. Just like us," Matthew pipes up, glancing back at him with furrowed brows. "I'm not fighting for Thena."

"I want to protect as many people as I can," Zack mutters.

"None of us are prepared! Am I the only one who sees this?" Oskar yells. And just like that, he leaves to go back to his tent to hide in his own self pity. Matthew glances at us, a moment of silence in understanding, and then swiftly follows, whilst Zack finally lifts his gaze to the group nearing us.

"I'll go let them all know," he says glumly, and turns away.

As the attackers approach, Luka and I glue our sight onto them. I grit my teeth together, taking a silent breath, over and over again, until I'm steady again. I'll be able to fight this time. I hope I don't freeze up.

Luka glances at me, and then away as quickly as a sudden gust of wind. He hooks his pinky with mine – as if too scared to go the full way. I relax my limbs, spreading my palm over his, intertwining our fingers, grasping tightly. I'll never let go. The bitter breeze quickens, and I shiver under the chill, but when I look at Luka already staring at me.

"We'll be fine," he says gently in a hushed voice, fading into the wind. "We'll be fine," he repeats and circles his thumb around my skin.

"Hopefully," I remark. He gives me a strong, deceiving smile.

"I promise." Despite it being nothing but an empty promise, a part of me wants to believe his words wholeheartedly.

And then I smile at him. And he smiles back. A moment shared between two lost souls. And then he's leaning closer to me, his gaze flicking between my forest eyes, calculating his next move. And then I'm holding my breath, because I forget where I am, what I need to prepare for, and who surrounds us.

My skin is alight.

And then I lean towards him. Adrenaline fills my veins.

His breath brushes over my skin, his eyelids flutter close, all for a split, ecstatic moment. And then—

"We need them to continue their legacy!"

The voices are too loud. We snap our heads to our left, finding them closer than expected. *How did we lose track of time so simply?*

"Shit— Sorry—" Luka tugs me behind, fleeing deeper into the camp on heavy feet.

But people are rushing around, retrieving as much food as possible into bags and hiding it in tents. They're shrieking, they're crying. They're terrified.

"Hey—" Luka lets go of me, drawing his sword, sprinting forward at someone being cornered from an attacker in a cloak. *They're already in the camp? Did they go around the side? Why did no one warn us?* Luka hesitates, stumbling in his step, as the girl shouts for help. He grabs the enemy's shoulders, pulls her around, ducks a dagger swiping at his head and digs his sword into the woman's legs. Enough to shock her, enough time for the innocent to run, enough for Luka to push the attacker into the tent's fabric.

He glances at me.

"Stay safe."

"Luka!" I lunge forward as he grabs her collar, and she grumbles in response.

"You're gonna pay for this—"

"Come get me then!" Luka leaps away, and starts walking backwards, away from me. The woman's attention is all on him. He grips his sword, and glares at her. She takes the bait, chasing after him, even throwing an axe at his head. It narrowly misses his head as they turn a corner, out of my sight.

Voices float behind me. I flinch, sprinting to a tent. I peer out to watch as a guy that looks too familiar rush forward, trapping a younger boy's neck in his grip, slamming into a wooden stall. He raises the boy into the air, feet dangling helplessly, struggling to breathe through a closed throat. I widen my eyes, as the predator *laughs* and bites down on the boy's neck. *And I almost recognise it.* I watch when he gives up, growing still, holding in his breath when he should desperately be trying to find it again. I swallow a lump in my mouth, gripping a dagger in my left hand, the dagger I forgot I unsheathed. The one I forgot I drew when I saw Luka in danger.

I look away when the attacker pulls out a chunk of flesh sitting in his mouth to have my eyes land on – the man who saved us on the 8th of October.

And he's approaching me.

I back up, his hands outstretched and empty, like he's ready to hold me hostage. I bite down on my lip, continuing to walk away, unsure of what to do, bending my legs, light on my feet, twisting my dagger so the blade is pointing at him. He looms closer and quickly grabs my wrist, dragging me into a gap between two tents, a place where no one could see me die in the darkness. So, without thinking too much, I twist the dagger, slicing down his arm in a hurry so I can be freed. So I can run.

Wasn't I meant to be brave today? But when I'm face to face with someone who might hurt me, all my nerves are on high alert, my mind racing, immediately thinking of the quickest escape route.

He shrieks, bouncing back, holding onto his arm, glaring at me. But I don't care. I'm free again.

"I wasn't going to hurt you!" he exclaims.

"What else was I supposed to do?" He merely rolls his eyes at me, and I can hardly believe I am *talking* to a stranger who I just made bleed. "It's just self-defence."

"For one thing, I wasn't holding a weapon! I showed you my hands and I was leading you somewhere, out of sight of that *monster* out there," he says, as if it was obvious all along. He points in the direction I witnessed that attacker killing an innocent teenage boy. "And you clearly don't want to do anything to me, since you're not advancing."

"What do you want?"

"You need to hide. The guy just round the corner - he was the other one in your house that day. Zayne." I purse my lips in an attempt to hide my shock at the thought of someone who's meant to be a 'bad' guy trying to look out for me – a tightness forms in my chest. *I've got to warn Luka.*

"Oh."

"I'm surprised you even survived." I can't tell if he's impressed or disappointed. But I can't ask anymore questions, because his next words are cut off by a blood curdling scream.

My heart stops beating, now just a lump in my chest weighing me down. *Zack.*

I turn back and sprint towards the sound without another moment of hesitation. I take a left. Watching humans dodge swords and daggers whilst the vampires avoid bullets and arrows. But neither looks like they're winning. Many vampires wound us just to try our blood, and then they're speeding to the next victim, stronger with an even more bloodthirsty glint in their eyes. A human falls to my feet at one point, with blood covering their hands, cheeks, and a gaping hole in their chest. Their lifeless eyes stare up at me, *until nothing.* I screech, leaping over them, and after that I try my best to ignore anyone else who might be watching the lunatic scramble towards danger, panting heavily, but no air held in her lungs.

The world is in slow-motion, finding Zack on the floor, blood staining his hands and a gun beside him. I widen my eyes at the look on his face.

He's breathing heavily, chest heaving, hands shaking. Looking down at the mess, crimson red on the floor in front, tears streaming down his cheeks.

How did he get so much blood on his hands? And then I notice the body beside him. A gaping hole in their back, blood pouring out, trailing all the way back to Zack.

Luka drops in front of his best friend, but I don't remember him being close by. I see his lips moving, but no words escape his mouth. Zack looks up through all of his emotions at the simple words Luka speaks that I catch.

"You saved my life."

My gut drops ten more feet. I step closer to them, with numb and unsteady legs, and I turn my own back to them, looking out for anyone who might interrupt their moment of broken comfort. I glance back to see Matthew doing the exact same to me on the other side, protecting from both ends, but he looks just as shaken up as Zack, wide-eyed, quaking legs, as if he could topple at any moment. I look up at the cyan sky bleeding into midnight, before dropping my gaze back to the corner where danger could spring from.

"Zack, look at me—" Luka exclaims.

"I *killed* someone! Their blood is on my hands!"

"Then let's get you cleaned up. She was going to kill me. You made your choice to protect me, so Zack. I- I owe you." He doesn't reply. "Let's go somewhere safer, okay?" I glance back at the same time as Matthew, watching Luka help Zack to his feet, leading him away in a hurry, not bothering to pick up the murder weapon. Matthew looks up to me first before edging closer to it, kneeling down beside the body and taking the gun, eyes lingering on the corpse.

"I could see if they really are vampires, Savannah." He looks at me with curiosity and fear in his eyes. "It's the safest way. They're not getting up any time soon." I bite my lip.

"They *are* vampires.."

He looks up at me again. "Did you confront one?"

"Have you been ignoring Thena's teeth?"

"She could just be filing them down or something weird."

"I spoke to one. You know the one who let me and Luka go?" He nods. "He told me to stay away from one guy in particular."

"Them?" He points at the corpse. I shake my head.

"No, someone over there." I point in the vague area, gripping my dagger tight. "I can't say I was looking at his teeth when we spoke though."

"Then let's..." he motions towards the body and I sigh heavily, looking back and then at the body.

"Quick." He holds onto their shoulder, and I hold onto their knees, and I cannot begin to tell how wrong this feels on so many levels. Be it my light-headedness, or the anxiety in my stomach. *Did they deserve this?* I suppose if they were going to kill Luka, then it was either them or him. And I'm glad it was them in that sense.

"Three. Two. One!" Matthew counts, and we flip them over, more blood oozing from the hole in their chest, eyes still open but glazed over and her skin colourless, hair already falling out in clumps. How is she deteriorating so fast? "Right," Matthew grimaces and bends closer, whilst I check our backs again. "Here goes nothing." I force myself to watch as he grabs a nearby stick and lifts the corpse's lips up, to reveal sharp fangs embedded in her gums. He lets out a stifled breath, dropping the stick and staggering back in a panic. "Shit, so Thena was right!"

"Thena was right," I echo, and I look at him, wide eyed and lips ajar, dropping the gun on the floor again.

"She wasn't bluffing," he says breathlessly. "She wasn't bluffing! How the hell—" I frown, glancing down at the body, pursing my lips together. I had expected as much, so it doesn't surprise me half as much as it should, but Matthew – he's been begging for them to remain fictional. "How?" I look back at him, his eyes searching mine for an answer when his voice breaks, "How long have they been real?"

"I don't know," I tell him, sheathing my dagger. "Matthew." He clasps one of his hands to his hair, fidgeting on the spot. "Hey." It's catching up to him. Everything happening to us has hit us all full speed ahead at some point, and it's happening to Matthew now. I step in front of him. He smiles sadly and I throw my arms around his neck, his head falling to my shoulder as he hugs me back, as tightly as he can, squeezing my clothes.

And Matthew is no hugger. But everyone needs a hug sometimes.

"We have each other. And for that reason, it's gonna be fine. Vampire or no vampire. It's just another...species."

"The ones they tell horror stories about."

"I *know* some are different from that. Remember? One of them saved me and Luka, and another brought us to this camp."

"Can we count Thena as a good person though, Savannah? I'm not saying all of them are bad, it's just—"

"What?"

"Nightmares." My eyes fling open again.

"Dreams are just dreams. A twisted distorted reality our brain conjures up at night. We'll protect you." I lean back, remaining my hands on his shoulders, maintaining his full attention. "I promise." He takes a deep breath, reluctantly nodding.

"I guess," he barely whispers above background noises. "I don't want to fight anyone."

"Then you don't have to, I'm here in case I can save someone else's life."

"I'm *meant* to be strong though."

"Are you hearing yourself?" I smirk.

"Shut up, I *want* to be strong!" He opens up his eyes, sad and exhausted. "But I'm scared."

"That's okay, go find—" His eyebrows rise abruptly, a thought clashing in his mind, a question upon his lips. "What?"

"Did they kill *Piper*?"

My heart aches, as I slam my mouth shut, my entire chest suddenly squeezing tight.

"Do you think that's who killed *him* too?" Jess.

"I don't know," I say, instead of feeding him the hope I secretly stash away. Someone told people we were in that town. Alive. Was it him?

I shake my head, free from the dawning thoughts and the heavy burning loss of them. And somehow, it's not getting better. Because instead of feeling it all wholeheartedly, I feel as though I'm getting used to it in a horrible way.

"I'll go find Zack and Luka, do you want to join?" I shake my head. "Thanks, Savannah." He walks past me.

Numbness is a horrible feeling.

I turn around, nerves freezing my system to see a woman standing close by, who appears to just be staring at me. She has a bow and arrow in her hands, so I reach for my dagger.

"No, no, no, no, no!" She shakes her head, clashing with her long raven hair, moving alongside her bow, before returning it to her back. "I'm not gonna hurt you!"

"For something that's meant to be an attack, you guys seem awfully nice," I murmur. She cocks her head to one side before widening her eyes in realisation.

"What? Oh, you must've met my boyfriend, Jack."

"I think so." How are all these people linked together? "He found me," I tell her. "Who are you and why aren't you attacking me?"

"I'm Violet," she says, her bright green eyes piercing through my skull, her smile meeting the wrinkles on either side of those eyes. "I come in peace." I smirk a little. "So you're Savannah?" I raise my eyebrows in surprise. "Oh, I know you through Jack. And—"

"I never told him my name."

"You didn't?"

"No." She looks hesitant.

"Then I'm not sure how he got your name." She takes a small moment of realisation, pausing her train of thoughts, then she nods, and makes an 'oooh,' sound.

"What?" I press her.

"I think I know how he got your name." My heart skips a beat, goosebumps appearing on my arms and down my legs. *No way.*

"Jess?" His name escapes my mouth before I can think it through. She nods slowly and I release mist into the air, eyes drifting away from her, brimming with hope in the shape of tears. "He's alive?" I exclaim.

"Funny, he would say that if we told him you're here." She gives me a sweet smile. "He misses you."

"Jess is alive?"

"Look." She holds up her hands. "Hate to break it to you, but I'm not sure I was even meant to tell you, kinda spilled out, that part about your name, but I'm sure you have many questions. However, I'll be real with you. I'm tryna find *the* boyfriend."

"*The* boyfriend?"

"*The* boyfriend." She nods. I find myself blushing, thinking of Luka.

"You say that was who warned me?"

"Jack? Yes. He said he saved you and another kid at the beginning of the month." I nod. "Ah, okay." She marches closer to me. And it takes everything in me not to back away from her on instinct. But then her lips burst into a grin, showing off her gleaming fangs. "Farewell for now, and listen, dont tell anyone about the Jess thing – unless they already know 'cause of Jack." She winks and walks away, waving behind her. "Good luck and stay safe."

My mind is reeling, the world is spinning. Overwhelmed. Too much happening. Cries echo all around me.

Zack killed someone for one thing out of self defence. And then strangers are hoping I stay safe – and Jess.

Jess was the one who told them. Surely! Jess is alive. He's alive. Can I even tell Oskar? What about Matthew? Would he know? *Would they believe me?*

I look down at the dagger in my hands, gripping it tight.

Never thought I'd see the day where I'm the one holding the weapon.

My eyes burn as a wave of headrush overcomes me beside a tent I'm walking by. I almost fall into it, carefully steadying myself, realising the pain in my head for the first time. My entire body's aching, limbs heavy so I sheathe my knife.

I glance up as a human leaps to Zayne, but he simply slices his sword across her stomach. She doubles over in pain and shrieks to the sky. She crumbles to her knees, her weapon lying beside her as Zayne swiftly lifts his sword above her hair. She bows her head.

He grins.

And—

I turn away as quickly as I can. Different way. Different tents. Different people. But the cries remain the same. I cover my ears. *I can't drown anything out.*

Suddenly, the man who stopped me earlier walks out of the tent in front of me. He stops, glancing at me and then at the tent.

"You're Oskar's friend, right?" I widen my eyes, my breath clogging my throat. "He might need someone right now." Without waiting for something more, I hurry into the tent, pulling back the fabric, letting it fall behind me.

Times like this, I wish there was a way I could transfer someone's pain onto me. Let me absorb it. Let me take it from them. Because Oskar is in tears, hands in his hair, eyes closed tightly in the middle of the tent. My heart sinks six feet below, lips breaking into a frown.

"Oskar," I say softly. He slides his hands to be over his eyes and cheeks, sobbing into them, greasy hair brushing over his skin.

"I should be happy, right?" he barely whispers.

"About what?" I edge closer, as he drops his hands, finally staring at me with swollen and bloodshot eyes. He whips his hair out of his face, raised eyebrows, and he heaves heavy breaths.

"This guy came in, and he told me that Jess is *alive*," he cries. "Jess. He said and I quote, 'Jess speaks of you often'. What kind of thing to say is that?" he exclaims, flapping his arms around, gesturing furiously. "And he could prove it, Savannah." He walks closer to me, hands out in front of him. "He said he had eczema. He said he had a sister. He knew my name and he knew what I looked like. He said he- that he-"

"Hey, hey, deep breaths, Oskar."

"He said he hates himself for being turned into one of them," he breaks down into a series of tears. Shaking his hands, uncontrollably. "But he's doing it all for his sister. He never abandoned us, and- and we can't go to him or else he could die."

"It's not impossible."

"It feels like it is!" He sinks to his knees, and sits back down, unable to stop the flow of tears down his cheeks. "It always feels like it is. With anything to do with him. But I suddenly saw that it wasn't the day *we were attacked*." I kneel down in front of him with my hands on my lap, watching him give up. It's heart wrenching. "Suddenly, I thought I could try, and the impossible didn't feel as far away as it does now."

"Oskar, I swear, we can see him again."

"And if he doesn't want that?"

"This is Jess we're talking about." He looks up at me with a literal broken expression in his eyes. Worry wrinkles spread over his skin, tears separating his cheeks, brows curved in a way to match his lips.

"I really miss him. And I hope he misses me too," Oskar whispers. I smile ever so slightly, resting my hand on his shoulder.

"I can assure you, he does." His lips tremble when he tries his best to mirror my smile. "Hug?" I ask. He chuckles a little breathlessly, before nodding, sobbing some more, leaning forward to rest his head on my chest whilst I wrap my arms around him, hovering my head beside his. His tears dampen my shirt as I rock us from side to side, whispering,   "It's okay, you're gonna be okay," every now and then to help calm him down.

He mumbles a few times, and only once do I catch his words in thin air, "Why can't I be at his side when he might need me the most?"

I rub circles on his shoulders and back until he grows still, and I hear very light snores escape his mouth, reassuring me that he's asleep in my arms.

Then the tent fabrics pulled back and someone steps in from behind me. I quickly wipe whatever tears were in my eyes away when a voice calls out to me,

"Savannah? Oskar?"

"Luka?"

"What..." he trails off, walking past to look down at a sleeping Oskar in my arms. "What happened? Is he okay?"

"Jack," I say as he sits down in front of me, laying a hand on Oskar. "He came here to tell Oskar that Jess is alive. And he just lost it completely, broke down and here we are."

"Poor thing." His eyes flick up to mine and a sense of relief washes over me. "Jess is alive?" I nod. "I wasn't expecting it, that's for sure. I'm glad he's okay physically at least."

"He must've told someone we were in there still when Thena came to find us."

"Since when would he have gotten a chance to come here then go with the other guys?" I shrug my shoulders, tightening my grip on Oskar. He looks between my eyes, sighing. "You look exhausted." I give him a weak smile, tilting my head at him.

"What gave you that idea?" he shakes his head low. "I am incredibly tired, are you?"

"Yeah, I am."

"How's Zack?"

"Zack is..." He heaves his shoulders up and down, glancing around the room. "Managing. Matthew's with him in the tent beside us. He's-" He shakes his head again, looking down, itching the back of his head. "It's something else, you know?" He saved your life. It's the only thing he could've done. Surely he would've felt worse letting Luka die.

Luka dying is something the world would have to pay for.

"Shall I help you get Oskar to bed?"

"If you could? My muscles are on fire." He nods, stands, and starts to lift Oskar up under his armpits. I help, standing up and I pick him up by his legs. He's surprisingly heavy, as we lower him onto a bed, pulling a blanket over him, and I don't have time to think afterwards, because Luka just engulfs me into a tight embrace immediately, flooded with the warmth and protection of his body around mine.

"Are you okay?" *No. Help me.* "You hugged everyone else tonight, Matthew and Oskar." He saw Matthew? "And no one offered *you* a hug." Tears swell up into my eyes, widening them as I fling my arms around him, melting into his touch, completely and comfortably.

"Back at you," I whisper. So we stand here for a few more minutes, hearing the wind blow against the tent, the clambering outside fade away, footsteps retreat whilst Oskar is beside us, snoring ever so gently.

It doesn't feel like the cries ever stop. But suddenly, I'm in between Zack and Matthew whilst Luka snoozes beside Oskar. It doesn't feel like this needless attack ever ends. But I know it does, and I know it's been quiet for a few hours because no one peeks inside the tent to find us. To spill blood.

But in my mind, and in my ears, *the cries ring out forever more.*

I know my next step. Jess is alive. And I need him to know we are too.

Savannah ✵

10th November

I've rested. I've had a proper night's sleep. I've even eaten enough.

Now it's time to find Jess in our lost Hillark.

It's all I've been able to think about for the past few days. It's been around a week since that attack. And I've tried not to think about the almost-kiss with Luka. I'm sheathing my knives, strapping my bow to my back, and eating and drinking as much as I can before departure.

"Savannah, listen to me," Oskar says outside, holding onto my shoulders, and looking into my very soul with an intensity that burns. "If you are not back within the next three hours, I'm telling everyone about this and we're coming to get you, got it?" I nod. No one else knows about me escaping in the middle of the night to go back. Oskar and I decided that if we told Luka, Zack or Matthew, they'd either beg for them to go with me, or they'd make sure I stayed in the camp with them.

I don't think that's the right word. Not after meeting Violet and running into Jack again. They're not all against us, so calling them our 'enemies' is wrong on so many levels.

"Got it?" he repeats.

"Yes, understood." Part of the reason Oskar isn't going instead of me, is because it was my idea to begin with, and I know he isn't ready to see Jess just yet, in a weird bizarre way. After a month of believing he was dead, and then all of a sudden he's alive – it's a shock to the system. A sense of false hope would blind him. When I said I'll go and it's best to be alone, he didn't speak against it. If Jess is there, it gives Oskar time to prepare on how to approach him when he does see him again. And I think that goes both ways as well. Reuniting like this would mean the world to them.

I know it would mean the world to me if it were Piper.

So with that aching thought, I nod once again, wave to him, and walk off into the long grass meadow.

"Please be safe," he calls after me.

The walk back to our old home town seems much shorter than what it was when we first arrived at this camp. I blame the anxiety in my stomach, but surely it shouldn't feel *this* short?

As long as I avoid my street, I should be fine. I should be able to keep this nausea at bay. I take a deep breath, settling my chest with my hand on my knife, as I close in on the road surrounding Hillark.

Before crossing, I look back at the camp in the distance, barely able to make it out through the thick darkness. I wonder if Oskar is asleep or not. I wonder if Luka's awake. I wonder if Zack is snoring. I wonder if Matthew's able to calm his mind.

I purse my lips together. I have to hurry. I cross the road.

In the dead of night, I expected more vampires to be outside, wandering the streets, patrolling maybe. Surprisingly, there aren't many defences to keep outsiders out. So, I hop over a small wooden fence, and I pass through familiar streets. The street lamps are on, or at least some of them, and lights inside the houses are dull, those which are on at all that is. If I'm quick about this, I can get to Jess' house without having to pass by mine or Piper's. But maybe Jess isn't in his old house.

I don't make it very far before fear tries to freeze my limbs up entirely. I hear voices from everywhere suddenly. Maybe I should've disguised myself as one of them instead of entering with knives in my hands. I swallow tightly, trying to steady my shaking hands, but when nothing seems to help the shallowness in my chest behind the bushes, I turn back, ready to call it quits for being too dangerous, but someone is walking towards me, mindlessly as if they haven't realised *I* am a stranger. Why are they in the shadows as well as me? Do they not like the lights casting down on them?

Before I'm able to turn back around, they look up from the ground and stop in their tracks, drawing their bow almost immediately. I widen my eyes as they advance on me, cocking their heads to one side, eyeing me up.

"Who are you, and what are you doing in Ash's area?" they demand. Ash? Are there tribes? I puff my chest out, staring into his crimson red eyes.

"I-" Don't stutter, don't show weakness. Can't show fear, can't show my breathing patterns, *can't show my teeth.*

"Come on! Straight answer, girl!" I tighten my grip on my knives.

"I'm a part of a nearby clan. I was looking for someone that's none of your business. However, I don't really care for names, so I can't remember what clan that is exactly." Did that even make any sense? I straighten my back, trying to show authority, ignoring the rate of my heart's ticking time bomb. "So, I cannot give you one." They glare at me.

"Sure, sure." He leans his head down, glancing at my mouth, looking for my teeth. "Everyone knows whose clan they're a part of." *I'm on my own.* "Are you questioning me?" I force out.

"They're a part of my clan. Cinus. No reason to be so hostile," a voice speaks from behind me and my mask drops instantly. *He's alive.*

I turn back to a neutral expression, as the stranger looks down at me, stepping back, brows arched and knitting into each other.

"And I can believe you?" the enemy demands.

"You're part of... Ash's clan, correct?"

"What's it to you?" I glance to my left, to Jess. A little taller than before, or maybe it's his better posture beside me. His golden brown hair a mess, his eyes a normal bright, shimmering brown, but his facial expressions harsh and sharpened.

"I have a dear friend who is rather close to Noble Draven, and he allowed me to take this one." He doesn't hesitate to loop his arm through mine, closing me to him. "I wasn't meant to tell anyone to begin with. They might get jealous, so if you would be a good...little thing and don't tell anyone?"

"And who is this friend close to him? I've never seen *her* around here before." He tosses his wrist away from me.

"Jack. Go ask Noble Draven that Jack got her for me, and he'll be sure to confirm. Or do you think you can question a Noble's choices?" Jess shakes his head at the stranger while the guy's jaw drops open a little bit. "Now if you'll excuse me, I have work to do." Jess turns around and drags me with him, holding me close, but this time, he's softer, he's trembling. I can feel it, so I lay my hand on his arm as he leads me away and down the streets I once called home. "Why are you here? It's not safe," he whispers under his breath.

"I'll explain everything when we're inside." He looks at me for the first time. And I look right back at him. He can't help but smile the tiniest bit, before shaking his head again, inhaling heavily, and continuing his way down the streets.

Jess welcomes me into Oskar's home.

I'm desperate to see what's changed, but as I step into the living room, it dawns on me that *nothing* has. All the photos are still hung up, the sofa's still where it was years ago, and the rug's still in the middle of the room. I step in, looking up at the simple light, as he closes the front door. I turn back around, holding my breath when he stands in the doorway of the living room, a solemn, saddened expression slipping onto his face, as he crosses his arms over his chest. The little things about him, though, *have* changed. His jaw is clenched, making his facial features appear sharper than before, his eyes a broken mirror, shattered pieces brimming in them.

We're such different...people, and yet all the same.

I split my face into a smile, letting out a stifled breath. I rush towards him. Because he's proof hope is not so lost. He watches with a gobsmacked expression, brows rising with lips parted, as I throw my arms around my smaller friend.

He's alive, I think to myself as he holds me back, grinning into my clothes, feeling the patch dampen.

He made it.

A sting in my chest becomes apparent all in a moment. Jess is here, right now, with me, and for that reason alone, any hardship I've gone through in that camp was worth it. The attack last week, dealing with Thena, facing my fears. Holding a knife for the first time. *Jess is okay.* I squeeze him tighter, closing my eyes, holding back pathetic shivers and sniffles.

"You're alive," he says when he moves back for a moment to breathe, and then he lays his cheek on my shoulder.

"You're alive," I repeat. He chuckles softly, grabbing my clothes in handfuls.

"Hey, I said it first. No copying."

"I can't believe it."

"Did Jack tell you?" he asks.

"Kinda. Violet told me, Jack told Oskar." His breathing stops completely, leaning away from me, looking up into my eyes and letting go.

"Oskar – he knows?"

"You don't want him to?"

"I don't know. I didn't think Jack would *tell* you all I was here. I wasn't even certain you all were alive either!" His brows suddenly shoot up and even more tears fall down his cheeks. "Does he hate me?"

"Hate you?" I exclaim. "Why would he ever hate you?" His eyes turn sharp and stern.

"I thought Jack told him that I'm- I'm-" he grimaces.

"We don't care, Jess." The words escape my lips before he can even finish his sentence, and he takes a step back, balling his fists up, scrunching his nose, and looking away from me. "I promise." He purses his lips together, watching the ceiling. "Are you okay?" His shoulders rise and then fall, as his bottom lip trembles and then looks back at me, tilting his head to the side.

"I thought you'd hate me. I thought this would change everything. I'm here for Sierra, that's all. I swear!" He chokes on his words, stepping closer. "I never wanted to leave you or Matthew or Zack, Luka, Oskar. God, Oskar." He digs his fingers into his hair, squinting his eyes close. "Oskar," he barely whispers. "I miss him. I miss you all." He drops his head down, and I quickly lay my hands on his shoulders.

"Oskar's okay." His head flings back up with wide eyes burning into my skull. "We all are, and we'd never hate you over something like this. You're still Jess, right?"

"Right," he whispers. "Just you know," he gives me a forced smirk, "with spice." I chuckle lightly.

"That's one way of putting it," I smile right back at him. And yet tears still fall down his cheeks. "Oskar's missed you a heck of a lot."

"Well, I've missed him a heck of a lot too, be sure to let him know. I'm bummed I have to wait longer to see him. And Matthew, gosh, how is he?"

"He's managing."

"Managing?"

"Managing," I echo. "I think we all are."

"I wish I could be there."

"You have to do this though. If anything, we should be here with you."

"That's not safe." He leaps down my throat. "Too risky."

"We know, and it's hard knowing you have to do this, for the most part, alone. But we'll come back to help you, when all of this has died down, okay?" He hesitates, but ends up nodding anyway, a glazed expression in his eyes when he faces me again. "What? What is it?"

"Piper." I soften my expression, chest getting heavier. "You already knew?"

"Jess, I watched her die," I say simply, in defeat. "So yeah." His eyes widen again. "I knew."

"Who?" he suddenly spits out. "Who?"

"I didn't exactly catch his name!"

"Looks?"

"Why?" He simply shrugs his shoulders. "Basic black hair and red eyes. His voice sounds like fingernails on a chalkboard," I shudder. "But it's a blur." He looks out the window, clenching his jaw.

"There's so many people here like that." He shoots his gaze back to mine. "If I do find out, I swear I'd—"

"Yeah. I know," I say softly and he drops his fists. The thought of my best friend preys on my mind along with the fact I have to get out of Hillark now. Unscathed, Avoiding Nobles. Avoiding everyone. "I guess I should get going then." I don't want to leave him but they're going to freak out soon. "I'll let Oskar know you're here," I tell him. He nods, taking a step away from me, digging his hands into his trousers.

"I suppose so." I purse my lips together, glancing around at the house once again. "Tell him I love him," he whispers in the quietest voice known to man. I flash my eyes back to his, but his are glued to the floor.

"Why don't you tell him yourself?"

"Because it's now or never? Anything could happen, Savannah." He looks back up to me, and sighs. "There's no guarantee for tomorrow."

"You'll have to make it work, book out a slot in your busy schedule in about a month's time, because you're going to be the one to tell him." I step in front of him, embracing him one more time, as close as I can. "There's no way Oskar would believe me anyway."

"But—"

"I refuse."

"You're a lovely friend, aren't you?"

"And so are you. I hope you weren't being sarcastic." I play a grin on my lips to hide the sourness on my tongue.

"I love you."

"You're one step closer, now imagine I'm Oskar."

"Oh, shut up."

"I love you too." After a short while, I finally let him go, giving him my strongest smile, as I walk past.

"Savannah," I look over my shoulder at Jess peering at me. "You truly don't care about me being one of them? A monster?"

"You're not a monster, Jess," I say simply.

"Tell them I miss them."

"Of course. We miss you too. But we'll figure out a way to be together again, I swear." He nods and gives me a small and weak smile, taking a deep breath.

"Please be safe." Aren't I always? I leave his house, and that was the last vivid memory I have before everything else becomes frenzy and frantic. Blurry and blind.

I make it to the edge of the town, by the meadow. But a voice calls out from behind me and I stumble over the wooden fence.

I peer back, to see a ginger-haired vampire, cocking his head to one side, staring down at me with a man behind him, holding onto his arm, trying to pull him back.

Panic surges through my veins, sprinting through the meadow, a laugh erupting from the man as I make an escape. When I look back again, Jess is there, pulling him with the other man in black. He pulls out a knife and leaps at the ginger, screaming something inaudible but he slaps and pushes Jess away. Jess swipes his dagger across his cheek. He backs away while ginger steals the other man's bow and arrow, mutters something and starts shooting at me.

I yelp, sprinting through the long grass, hoping it'll help my escape and lessen his visibility on me. I run and run and run, realising Jess could have ruined everything for himself in order for me to be able to get away.

He brought time for me. He saved me. He's no monster, he's my friend, my family. And I swear this isn't the last time I see him.

I run until I fall.

I run until I can't breathe.

I run until I feel something sudden and sharp dig into the bottom of my ankle.

I cry out, tears rushing to my eyes, looking back, squinting through the grass at the monster merely laughing as the other man in black pulls him back.

Ginger disappears. I don't know where to, but I flip onto my back, hissing out in pain, at something digging into me, blood oozing down my skin and dampening my clothes.

I see stars overhead.

Black splotches cloud my vision. The world spins around me.

But the stars. They were ever so bright above my head.

I blink, eyes fluttering close. I must've had them closed for longer than I had thought because when I open them again, the man's head, the one with long black hair and bright blue eyes appear above my vision.

"Stay awake," he says. "This is gonna hurt," he tells me. He pulls an arrow out from just above my ankle and even more blood pours down my skin and onto the grass surrounding it. I howl out in pain, clenching the mud and grass in my hands, spreading under my nails. Pain surges through my veins, overtaking my system, the only thing I focus on as tears roll down my cheeks. "Where are you from?"

"The camp," I grunt out in a small voice. He looks up at it. "Who are you..." I manage to bite out, before my muscles go limp and the weight of the world crashes down on me.

Suddenly, the stars are falling.

"Draven," are the last words I hear from the stranger, before I black out completely.

Savannah

11th November

Someone named Draven saved me.

I gasp for air, sudden pain stabbing me at the back of my ankle.

"Savannah?" Luka?

"Thank God!" Oskar's here too, of course he would be. I turn my head, flinching at the light, Luka's head beside mine, one of his hands on my lower arm and the other on my shoulder, creeping up to cradle my neck, breathing fast and shallow.

"Hey, are you okay? How are you feeling?"

"I'm fine?" I'm not sure. "What happened?"

"Someone called Draven carried you over here. He found Luka who was looking for you anyway and he panicked an—"

"I think she gets the idea."

"Draven." I lay my head back, staring back at the tent, trying to rewind my mind a couple hours. Draven came to my rescue when someone shot me with an arrow. Draven had black hair that hung over his eyes and he remained calm the entire time, asked me where I was from, never why I was there.

"Savannah." Oskar leans over with a saddened expression, "Draven said it was someone called Vincent who hurt you. But did Jess help?" I widen my eyes, shaking my head, clenching my hands into fists as Luka backs his hand away from my face.

"Of course not! He misses all of us. You have no idea what he's doing just for his sister," I tell him and his eyes soften, taking a step back in surprise. "He," *loves you*, "misses you so much. Jack was telling the truth." He purses his lips together, tears brimming his eyes, before splitting his face with a grin so wide it's like Jess was in the room with us.

"Oh. My. God," he says, beaming.

"That's amazing," Luka adds, flicking his gaze onto a happy, bouncing Oskar.

"He saved me." I sit up.

"Draven mentioned that," Oskar tells me, breathless whilst Luka's jaw tenses. I find his hand and I grip it, bringing him back to his senses. He looks back at me, no longer glazed over in a hazy expression. "He's alive," Oskar mutters, practically jumping on the spot. "We can see him again! We could run away together and—" He suddenly grabs his bearings looking down at my ankle and then at me. "Are you okay? Vincent's gonna have it if I ever meet him."

"I'm okay," I chuckle, but Luka remains silent beside me.

"Right." He nods repeatedly, back to smiling again. "Right."

"Oskar, go get some sleep."

"You sure you don't want me to stay with you? I can help with bandages and stuff."

"I'll be okay, don't worry." I give him a mirroring smile. He nods again, head in cloud nine as he leaves, bidding his goodnight and farewell. "I'm glad he's happy." I let my head fall back onto the pillow positioned beneath me, taking a breath. "How bad is it?"

"The wound?"

"Yeah."

"Not that bad, so don't worry about it, Sav."

Sav?

I twitch, shifting uncomfortably under the weight of a single word he speaks. Sav. The name only Piper ever called me. My heart aches at the recognition. "You okay?"

"Haven't heard that name in a while."

"Oh," he mutters. "If you don't want me to call you that, then just say." I peek at him.

"I don't know, I can't think straight," I say. His eyes saddens and he slowly nods for me. "What's wrong?" I ask, sitting up again, still hanging onto his hand with my left. He looks away at everything but me and my damned eyes. "Luka?"

"Why didn't you tell me about going?" he says in a small voice. "You didn't trust me."

"I knew you'd worry and I knew I needed to go alone because the fewer numbers, the easier it would be to get around—"

"I worry about you anyway, Savannah." He leans back, yet still hangs onto my fingers. "A lot more than you think. Nothing would change that."

"You don't have to." *Hypocrite.* He's always in the back of my mind. He's never left it, ever since this whole thing began.

"Force of habit."

"Is there something else?" I press. He lifts his shoulders up to his ears. "I don't like seeing you hurt, that's all." I clamp my mouth shut, as he flashes his mesmerising blue eyes at me again. I frown, a drop in my stomach when I realise his grip is loosening around my hand. *Don't let go.* "I want you to talk to me more. I want you to be able to trust me with these kinds of things."

"I felt like if I *did* tell you, you would insist you came with me when it would be more practical for just me to go alone," I exclaim, shrugging my shoulders, staring right back at him. "That's all, it's not about anything else."

"Okay."

"Why?" I pause. "What do you think the reason is?" He pulls back, recoils his head, and inhales deeply again.

"Nothing."

"You're not telling me something," I point out, edging closer.

"Honestly, I think I was just paranoid." He grips on tighter too.

"Do you not want to talk about it?" I know he does. The way he hesitates over everything he says. The way he's choosing his words so carefully, that his gaze drops away from me every time he opens his mouth.

"I just worried you were getting sick of me." My chest grows a little heavier. The last time he said something like this to me was a couple months ago when he was going through a depressive episode. He said I was one of the only people who he directly told about it. Me and Zack. "I guess that's it."

He's so quiet today. I should have realised it sooner, but instead, I was too busy thinking about tonight. About finding Jess. About keeping a secret. "I know, I know." He forces a weak smile, as if that's the best he can do and he goes to shuffle away from me. "Stupid of me," he chuckles nervously. "Sorry," he murmurs. He flicks his head up to stare at me. "But that's what I was thinking."

"Luka," I say, "I think you're one of the very few people in the world I would never get sick of." His eyebrows fling up and his cheeks blush bright red. He shakes his head, then laughs a little more, right from his chest. "I promise!"

"I was going to say you don't need to lie, but you seem genuine," he chokes out, smiling more than before. "You've changed a lot."

"I guess. I want to be stronger."

"I've seen you training. You certainly are stronger, but you've been pushing yourself over the limits too." He pushes forward onto his knees, getting even closer to me with his beautiful ocean eyes. "Just be careful. I can help with anything if you need it. Just ask. I'll be there."

I blush a soft pink against my cheeks, spreading to my ears, nodding and smiling. My heart begins to pound as I glance down, searching for his hands. I lean down and hold both of them with mine, lifting them onto the mattress, against my hips before lifting my eyes to his again.

"Thank you, but, Luka?"

"Yes?" he says, almost cheerfully. He's so good at masking his emotions, he forgets who he can be real with.

"Are you alright?" I tilt my head to one side, looking between the Pacific and the Atlantic. I see my whole world in them. "And be honest."

"Damnit, I was hoping you wouldn't say that," he smirks, playfully. But I wait patiently in this excruciating and suffocating silence. I watch his eyes glance down at my lips, and my heart skips a beat, goosebumps appear everywhere on my skin, adrenaline in my veins pumping all around my body. *My lips. His lips.* "Right now, I'm fine. But in general? Could be better."

"Am I able to help?"

"I don't think so."

"You'd tell me if I could?"

"Well, for one thing, let me know when you're gonna do great and dangerous deeds like that."

"Noted."

"Thank you, and I'll do the same with you." He moves even closer to me, so close I can feel his breath on my skin, everything on fire, everything in my body is begging for more. *Now, now, now.* "Savannah," he whispers, gulping nervously, eyes flicking over every feature on my face, anxiety pooling in the bottom of my stomach. It drops ten feet below.

"I'm sorry I kept it from you," I mutter. "I..." *love you?*

"It's okay." *What if I closed the gap? What if I said I had enough of dreaming? Of hoping?* "Savannah." *What if I leapt for it?*

I drink him in. The five freckles across the bridge of his nose, his dilated pupils as he grows forever closer, his soft perfect lips, his button nose, strands of brunette hair falling down his forehead.

What if I don't want to wait anymore?

"Yes?"

"Is this," his voice drops lower, one of his hands spreading up my right arm against my bare skin. "Okay?" I nod, slowly and gently, as if I'd scare him away if I said something more. "May I?" I smile as a response, anticipating his next move.

His hand catches the back of my nape. He glances back down to my lips, and I catch sight of his, before he's pressing his own into mine. Anticipation blends into safety and warmth in a matter of seconds. As he leans in to me, he holds me even tighter, and then pulls me to his body, clasping us together. I lay one of my hands on his chest, and I kiss him again and again and again. Never having enough, never being satisfied, always left yearning each time we break apart to breathe.

I melt into him, his touch, his taste. His familiarity relaxes my muscles all together, forgetting about everything around us. Just for this precious moment of bliss and privacy.

I smile brightly when he tangles his fingers in my hair. I chuckle when he pushes into me again, knocking me back. I breathe when I get a chance. And I drink him all in, all over again.

He slowly leans back, fluttering his eyes open to look at me, hand slipping to my thigh, the one which held my hair intertwined with his fingertips.

"We should probably sleep, get some rest," he laughs softly, panting ever so slightly like me, eyes flicking between both of mine.

"I guess," I reply, wondering what happens next.

Another kiss. But this time, soft, slow and distant. Like a goodnight kiss, but I know it's not when he holds onto my hands tighter, as if he never intends to leave.

"I'm sorry about snapping. About Sav. I- erm," I murmur. His face grows solemn. I hold my breath as he wraps one of his hands around my head, pulling me to his shoulder, pressing his lips to my hair.

"I'm sorry. About her." *I know. And you shouldn't be.* But saying that wouldn't help. So I hang onto his arm, closing my eyes, leaning into his touch, an awful amount of relief overcoming my system.

"I miss her."

"I miss her too," he says.

"I'm sorry I've been preoccupied recently. And I'll tell you in future, I just wanted to go alone to Hillark. Only Oskar knew. No one else."

"It's okay! I said it was okay like ten times already!" He kneels back down on the floor beside me and this trashy fold-up bed. "Maybe I was overreacting," he smiles sadly.

"I don't think you are. I haven't been the greatest person recently."

"You're taking care of yourself now, and it can be hard. But you're better than before, and, Savannah." He takes a breath, steadying his hands, wrinkles creasing his eyes. "I want to help with that too." I widen my eyes ever so slightly, I hope he didn't notice. But it's Luka. He notices everything. "I want to help you train, help you sleep, help you when you're stressed or scared, and I have for quite some time now. But I never knew how to put it into words until now." My cheeks are on fire, and my heart is beating so fast I can hear it. "I know that," he gulps and swallows something down, "I'm not the greatest person either." He looks down again, avoiding me. "And I know I have a lot to work on, but I want to work on it with you." He starts to shake his head, and now I'm able to feel his hands shaking in my grip. "And I want to be better for you."

"Oh, Luka." I lean down, cupping one of his cheeks, stroking my thumb under his widened beautiful eyes. I lift his face up, his gaze meeting mine once again. I smile. "You're perfect, and you always have been." I lean down, pressing my lips to his, meeting as one.

Feeling nothing but safe and warm, even in the freezing late autumn night.

Jack

12th November

Jess knocks on our bedroom door this morning instead of just barging in like he usually does. At least he's learnt from his mistakes, but I'm not amused when I find it's 6:00am.

"Don't come in—" But as soon as I start mumbling, he begins to open the door to storm in, so I quickly pull the duvet over Violet and I to our necks before he sees anything. One of my arms drap over her when she begins to stir lightly. "I said don't—"

"You told them? You told Savannah?"

"I never told Savannah anything."

"But you *spoke* to *him*? You told him I was here, alive and— and—" His voice cracks under the pressure of his own words, before he takes a breath and relaxes his shoulders, shaking them briefly to de-tense himself.

"Jess, what's happened to get you so riled up? I assure you, you're overreacting."

"Overreacting?" he mutters breathlessly. "Overreacting?!" He raises his voice at me and I roll my eyes at his dramatic gestures.

"Violet is trying to sleep," I tell him through a clenched jaw.

"Savannah came to me in the middle of the night, Jack, because she knew!" What?! "She came for Oskar because he was struggling with the knowledge of me being trapped here!" I sit up with wide eyes, duvet falling from my shoulders to cover Violet more.

"Boys, boys!" Violet mumbles, raising her hand up to answer. "Firstly, it was I who told Savannah. And secondly, get out if you're gonna argue."

"I'd quite like to go back to sleep," I mutter.

"Why did you talk to Oskar about me? I told you to see if he was alive, that's all! And now he—"

"Shut up, will you? It's too early to be discussing this."

"It's your fault if he comes," he says, seemingly meant to be more threatening than what it really was. "God, why don't you just listen to me?"

"Get out." He slams the door, banging across the landing. I lay my hand on my forehead, gazing down at the bed. *It's too early for this.* Violet shifts beside me, twisting onto her back, laying one of her silk smooth palms on the back of my shoulder blade.

"Hey," she says softly. "Talk to me." A lump forms in my throat, weight pushing me down, stifling all the unsaid words in my chest. I can't tell her about the trip to the mountain. About the fear Vincent inflicted. How it feels to be the only sane ones in this world. *We should've left when we had the opportunity. Before all this. And now Jess is here, and Sierra, and we can't leave them alone.* **We just can't.** "Jack?" she repeats.

"I'm tired." I lift my head up from my hand, now resting beneath my chin, eyelids extremely heavy.

"In what way?"

"All of the above." I look back at her saddened expression.

"Can I help?" I smile a little, falling back, flipping onto my side to gaze into her bright emerald eyes.

"I just need more sleep." Despite not *actually* needing it as a vampire. It's more of a privilege. I'd sleep forever if I could.

"What about Jess?"

"What about him?"

"He went into Savannah's room, didn't he?" I shrug my shoulders, shutting my eyes as she finds my hand to hold close.

"Should I have spoken to Oskar?"

"Should I have spoken to Savannah?" She pauses for a moment, letting our words float in the air. "It's the same thing, and I don't regret it. Neither should you. We were just talking to some humans who are friends with Jess."

"I can't believe Savannah came here. What if she was caught?"

"Jack, all she did was sneak in and out to be sure Jess was okay. It's understandable. Wouldn't you do the same if it were me or...?" *Shane.*

"I guess," I mutter, her arm slowly wrap around me, letting go of my hands to pull me closer to her body's warmth.

"If he leaves, it's up to him. And if they come to save him, then he'll be the one to hide them. Not everything is down to you to sort out." She presses her collarbone to my forehead. "You're doing a pretty good job doing everything yourself, and I'm proud." I smile again, holding her back, cheeks flushing. "But you don't need to do everything on your own. You don't need to take all the fault onto your shoulders, my love."

I can't help but feel as if I need to be doing more, though. Constantly.

"I guess."

"Just remember." She tilts my head up and I open my eyes to gaze into hers. She smiles immediately, glancing down at my lips for a moment. "One day, we'll get out. And that day is getting closer and closer." She edges down. "Keep that in mind." She kisses me, quick and soft, but I deepen it, pushing upwards more. She giggles, grabbing the back of my nape, I spread my hands onto her bare back.

"Tomorrow's another day."

"Tomorrow's another day," I echo back to her. Silence quickly follows, and I drift in and out of consciousness in her arms.

On a walk to clear my mind, it's suspiciously empty everywhere I see. I hover my hands over my weapons strapped to my belt, scanning my surroundings in more detail. Something's not right.

Then I spot Vincent, furiously talking to a stranger in the town square he held the feast all those nights ago. The stranger in question has long, wavy, white hair, and I'm more starstruck at the fact that it looks all natural. Her dress is a dark, sparkling green, which reaches all the way to her ankles, it's amazing she can walk without tripping. She's around 6'2, I'd guess, judging on the height difference between her and Vincent who's 6'3. The pair are death glaring each other, her head held higher, chin sticking out whilst Vincent's is dug in, looking up at her through his eyebrows. I edge closer, regretting it immediately when both of them turn to stare at me. Her stone-cold glare bores into my skull with piercing and dazzling jade eyes.

A golden and beautiful begonia is perched above her ear, placed perfectly in her hair.

"Ah, pet. You've arrived just in time," he says. But I'm focused on this mystery woman.

I recognise her, but my mind's hazy.

Vincent rolls his eyes, "Don't just stand there gawking!" He lifts his hand up and his cape flows in the wind. But then possibly one of the strangest sensations happens when I find him, *pulling* me closer to him, staying where he is, merely pointing his index finger at me, and making a motion to edge closer to him.

But I feel it. An aura. An invisible rope tied around me, something *dragging* my waist closer to him. Tight against my skin, burning into my flesh. It's like I can't *control* myself. And it's all Vincent. But I was told we didn't have *that* kind of abnormal ability.

The smirk on his lips never lies.

I tense the closer I get. I should never have left my bed. I should've stayed with Violet, beneath the covers, hiding from all this mess. It would have been much easier that way.

"I have a task for you, my pet."

"Do not call me your pet," I spit out when I'm face to face, centimetres away from him.

"Sure thing, sweetheart." I roll my eyes, back onto the stranger, watching us closely with an emotionless expression that's impossible to read. "I'm not sure if you heard, but an intruder managed to enter and escape our perimeter last night, unscathed," I shoot my eyes back to Vincent, his sour face looking right back at me. "And our Jade here," *Jade?* "Is unimpressed, to say the least."

"What do you want, Vincent?" I bite out.

"Assign new Knights to be on patrol all hours of the night. Sort a schedule. And do not let this happen again."

"Isn't that a Noble's job?" His cold stare hardens.

"Well, *maybe* you're easier to talk to than the Nobles who are close by!" he exclaims before looking back at Jade, taking a breath and forcing his smile to creep back onto his face.

What on earth happened for him to hate his own brother this much?

"Anyway," he starts readjusting his coat, and pulling a lighter back out of his pocket to fiddle with it. "You'll do that."

"Do we have enough people for night time patrols though?" I press.

"Then *you* do night patrols." My stomach drops as he turns his gaze back onto mine. "Sort something out, Jack, or you know what'll happen." I clench my hands into fists, about to turn away, but he quickly grabs my shoulder, pulling me back. "Uh, there's another job for you, this one may take longer." He nods to Jade who locks her eyes onto mine. But Vincent said 'uh'. He never stutters. He's never uncertain.

"We need a sacrifice," she says.

"A sacrifice?"

"In order to enter the sealed city." She's soft-spoken, even when talking about death. This gets all the hairs on my arms and neck to stand up, all at once, alerting my nerves to be on edge. "Preferably a vampire sacrifice. But any will do really."

"And *I'm* in charge of killing them? Sentencing them to their death?" I raise my voice, pulling my shoulder free from Vincent, shooting daggers at him with my eyes, if only that were actually possible. "I'm not a killer!"

"You won't be killing them personally, all you need to do is find one that's willing! For the good of us all. All by the...let's say 22nd of November?" He smirks. "It's about time you help with spilling blood in whatever way I ask." His eyebrows rise, before cackling out in delirious humour, "Or else it'll be your *darling* by default." My blood boils beneath my skin.

"I have someone I'm looking into. We just need a backup in case," Jade says naturally, unaffected by his outburst of laughter and my complete silence.

"And that's your job." Vincent points his index finger, digging it into my chest, but my glare does not falter.

And my mind is not thinking anything else, when I spit out in a low and threatening tone, "If you ever do anything to harm her, you will not live to see tomorrow. Is that the sort of blood you want me to spill?" I slap his wrist away from me, and I'm half amazed he's letting me walk away without a fatal injury and with all limbs attached.

With my mind racing, I don't make it very far before Achillea practically cuts in front of me, grabbing my wrist, dragging me into a darkened alleyway out of plain sight. For a moment, I think she's gonna kill me as she looks back, slams me into the wall, and watches my expression blend from shock to puzzlement.

"Has Vincent spoken to you?" She crosses her arms over her chest, taking a step back and tilting her head up, chin sticking out like Jade, and yet her chest is heaving, as if she's been running errands all day, and it's only 11:30.

"Yes. Why?"

"About?" I try to refrain an eye roll.

"Sacrifice and patrols."

"Okay, he told you we had a break-in last night?" Why is she rushing through her words and why on earth is she treating it as if someone stole something dear to us?

"Yeah, what of it?" I shrug my shoulders and she shakes her head from side to side.

"Nothing, but we're so close to going home, I don't want any complications. I was just making sure he spoke to you." She drops her hands and her cape flows in slow motion behind her, nodding at me. "Better get onto it."

"What's going on? Why are you rushing everywhere for such mundane things?" She looks back before she leaves the darkness, and she smiles for the first time I've ever seen.

"It's almost time to take back what's ours, of course."

"And what's that?"

"Our lost city, our kingdom, our home." And then she disappears.

She's really full of this city crap, isn't she? Sometimes I wish I were still mortal just so I could simply die and get it over with, naturally. I wouldn't be in this mess, and have no obligations to stay. Let my time come instead of being killed one day.

But then the thought of living another century with Violet is comforting. We could go when we're both ready instead of suddenly. One day we'll leave and we'll never have to see another one of these monsters. It'll be just the two of us. No one else. No Vincent. No Achillea. Just us.

Now Jess is the one who's following. He calls my name repeatedly from behind and I shrug it off. After his outburst this morning, I don't feel like talking to him. I might say something I'll regret.

"Jack," he presses. "Jack! Stop for just one moment, please!"

"What is it now?" I grumble, but I don't bother slowing down. He stops walking entirely to say one single word,

"Sacrifice?" I stop.

"Sacrifice?" I echo, looking back and over my shoulder at him. "You heard?"

"I *over*heard." I turn away, thinking things through.

"You better have been."

"You're going to find someone to kill?"

"As a backup, yes, and at this rate, I'll volunteer myself."

"No, you won't. You have Violet," he tells me. But at this pace, she'll be the sacrifice too.

"Don't tell anyone." I begin to walk forward but he catches up, and runs in front of me, both arms outstretched either side to stop me from passing. I roll my eyes, digging my hands into my trouser pockets. "What now?"

"I came to ask you something."

"No promises."

"On what?"

"Whatever you wanna ask I can do." He purses his lips together.

"I want to see my sister."

"That's not a question." My chest burns, because I'm familiar with the yearning to see your sibling again.

"Please," he huffs, finding the words seemingly difficult. "Can you let me see her?"

"Jess—"

"I know, I know, I know, it can get you into trouble and whatever, but it'll be quick and painless." He shakes his head, and when his eyes blink a second time, tears spring to them, "I've thought of her everyday since she was taken from me. Please, Jack!" I slam my mouth shut, considering the risk. If anyone catches us, they'll hurt Violet. That is, if anyone knows about the threat, find us. Apart from Draven. I could get him to keep an eye on them whilst we found her.

If Vincent catches us, it'll be our necks. We'll be the sacrifices and he'll kill Jess out of cold blood. Possibly right in front of our eyes. Or he'll force me to be at the handle of that blade.

But I'd also do anything to see my brother again, alive and breathing. Not strapped down to a hospital bed, millions of injections, wires and IV's surrounding him.

"I miss her," he begs so much he might as well be pleading on his knees.

"I'll see what I can do."

Jack

14th November

I'm drowning.

I'm not and I know I'm not. But it feels like it. And it's something I'm not able to escape so easily – like it was once upon a time. It's always something after another thing, and all I want is to hold my favourite person in my arms while we do whatever she wants to do. Stargaze. Listen to music. Or perhaps just sleep. That seems much better than dealing with whatever the rest of this day holds for me.

I know where the hostages are. And I've always known. But in order to be as safe and as careful as possible, I leave Jess at my house and I go on a hunt for Draven around town. I need him to keep an eye on the Royals and Nobles to make sure no one follows us. Besides, I'd like to make sure he's okay.

I find him sulking between two houses. I call his name and he turns back, arms crossed over his chest, wearing his longer blazer jacket, his hair slicked back over his head as always.

"Jack. I'm glad to see you well."

"I was going to say the same to you." I give him a smirk, but he shrugs it off instantly. "Everything alright?"

"Just dealing with some personal matters. Worried about something not in my complete control," he says, dismissing it as he holds his head high. "What do you need?"

"A favour."

"Ah, I knew this day was coming." I give him a sceptical look, asking more with a glance of my eyes than words, and he merely looks away at anyone passing by, mentioning under his breath, "You're leaving with Violet and perhaps even Jess. I knew this would come, sooner than I had thought—"

"I'm not leaving." He shoots his eyes back to mine. "Yet."

"There it is."

"When that day arrives, you'll be the first to know."

"Oh, I'm ever so thankful." He presses a palm to his chest, acting dramatic with an open mouth. "That you would let me know when you decide to ditch me to deal with obnoxious Nobles and Royals."

"They'd be thrilled to know you refer to them as such. And you're welcome to join us." He chuckles grimly, nodding in agreement. "Anyway, I need you to keep an eye on Vincent, Achillea and Ambrosia."

"Oh? Are you committing a scandal?"

"And what scandal would that be?" He merely shrugs his shoulders. "Use your imagination."

"I'm taking Jess to see his sister." His eyebrows shoot up, wrinkling his pale forehead, almost covering both of his eyes entirely with his fringe.

"Oh, that seems far more...ambitious than escaping with your beloved."

"Somehow, I agree."

"Right, so you want me to make sure they don't follow you, or..." He holds his limp hand out, motioning for me to continue with the roll of his wrist.

"Yeah, exactly that. Make sure they don't head towards the mansion."

"I could be wrong, but there might be another clan situating there instead of us, for now."

"Why don't they come here then?"

"Why are you looking to me for all the answers to your impossible questions?" He smirks playfully. "I'll do my best to keep them occupied." I return his smile.

"Thank you." I can always rely on Draven.

"If anyone understands how much a sibling can mean to someone, it will most likely be us," he comments. Too right it would.

"I hope she's still there." He nods and begins to walk past me and I join him.

"She should be. I can't see why not."

"People will be feeding them, right?"

"Of course, new people means new rules." He looks at me. "I don't think Vincent's gone back there since the new people arrived." I look back at him.

"Oh?" He purses his lips together, glancing away.

"Yeah, suspicious, isn't it?"

"Didn't you say his lover was in a different clan?" He smiles ever so slightly, tugging at the ends of his lips.

"Exactly."

"Surely not- What are the odds—"

"Slim. That's what they are. But anything's possible. I could ask you the odds of a vampire coming into your home village to attack, and you'd say it's impossible." He looks back at me. "Yet here you are." He glances his eyes over my appearance. "Looking a little worse for wear."

"I suppose."

"Be careful," he insists.

"Yes, *Dad*." I smile and he rolls his eyes.

"I could be old enough to be your great-great-great-great-great-great-granddad or some shit."

"Okay, *Dad.*"

"Shut the fuck up." He walks away from me with a laugh, heading towards the town square like I did this morning. I can't help but wonder if Jade is still there. I wonder if I should have told him to be careful too.

Jess and I sprint towards the mansion, praying that if anyone's living there now, hopefully they've gone out on a commission by a Royal or something. *Anything's possible.*

Jess keeps glancing back nervously, then at his feet, and then at the mansion in front of us. Our destination. I keep my eyes forward, taking a deep breath, standing in front of the grand double doors.

I was standing like this around twelve years ago in this exact position with Violet beside me. I was looking at it, only much smaller, and much more gullible. I had no idea what was held behind these doors. We came after realising Vincent had ruined our lives a few days prior. He gave us the address. And we realised we couldn't see our friends again. Not in the state he created. We were sick of watching them run from house to house, asking for us, which was the most painful experience I've ever endured.

"What are we waiting for?" Jess asks, softly. Calm and patient. I look at him again, catching him staring at me. *We've got all day, take your time,* his eyes read. So I quickly look back to the door. I'm taller than I was twelve years ago, but I still feel as tiny as I did that day.

"Sorry. Unpleasant memories." I knock on the door, half expecting two Royals to answer like last time, but instead, no one responds. Did we get lucky?

"Maybe Draven was wrong," Jess suggests helplessly.

"Or maybe no one's here because they're out on an errand." I glance at him before opening the doors, peering into the darkness. The hall is completely empty. No lights, no guards. Nothing. Maybe the prisoners aren't here after all. I look at Jess.

"Don't get your hopes up, Jess."

"What do you mean? You said she'd be here!"

"Not even guards are here!" Or maybe the prisoners aren't as important as Vincent made them out to be. Does this mean no one's been feeding them if she *is* here? I swing the doors wide, stepping into the cold and damp air, slamming them behind me as Jess lunges to my side. "Straight ahead, go into that office and wait for me. Don't make a sound and keep your guard up."

"Understood." He rushes off whilst I run right and into the hallway, finding the kitchen at the very end of a familiar hallway. I rummage through cupboards to grab bread, bottles of water...crisps, cold beans, anything that they have excess in.

I run back, conscious of time working against me, heavy footsteps in an echoing hallway with light streaming through the windows to give the place an ominous glow. Through the magnificent hall I once admired and stood in awe under, the one with the curved stairs either side of an office way with the golden, old chandelier above our heads. Jess keeps the door open for me as I rush in. He helps by taking some bottles from me.

"Why didn't you get a bag?"

"You think I had time to get a bag?"

"Fair enough." I move the desk out the way, opening the trap door, the stone pathway lit up beneath us by torches below, hung on the walls. I stick my head under, checking for guards but no one's there, so I count ourselves lucky, think nothing else into it, and rush down with the food in my arms and several pockets.

"She should be down here," I say as Jess follows.

"You really think they wouldn't have any food?"

"I don't know, but it's better to have more than enough. We need to be quick. If they still had food up there, people would be living here." I shoot him a glance, watching him walk past empty cells, counting each one, mouthing the numbers, but no need for that. Because I hear her voice before I see her.

"You came back, mister!" the little girl's voice calls. I land my eyes onto the kid with light brown tanned skin, bright sparkling eyes and frizzy hair. She holds onto the bars until her knuckles are white and her elbows poke out, smiling widely, with dirt covering her from head to toe in patches.

"Sierra?" Her thick brows fling up, eyes widening, as she twists her head to look behind me. I glance back, catching Jess drop the bottles through shaking, trembling hands with the exact same expression plastered on his face.

"Jess!" she cries. He runs forward, dropping to his knees in front of the bars, fumbling his hands through them, crying out her name repeatedly until he needs to breathe. Tears dampen his cheeks, holding onto her hands as tightly and as close to him as he possibly can without hurting either of them. Then he lays one of his palms on her cheek, clearing the tears she weeps despite the both of them smiling at the sight of each other. I should look away, this feels too private for my own eyes to witness, but I can't.

It's a long awaited reunion.

"Sierra," he whispers breathlessly, and she simply nods over and over again, bouncing out of her own skin.

"You're alive!" She looks at me. "You kept your promise!"

"He did most of the work," I say with a smirk, before she stares back at Jess with eyes full of love, adoration and admiration for her protective big brother.

"Are you okay?" Jess asks, barely able to choke out enough words for the question itself.

"I miss Mum and Dad." He breaks into another round of sobs, wrapping one of his arms around her through the bars to stroke her poofed up hair.

"I know." He rests his head on the bars separating them from a hug. "I know. I do too."

"I missed you."

"I missed you more." A sudden pain in my heart forces me to realise I'm holding arms full of food. Too meaningful to watch any longer, I walk past Jess to inspect the other prisoners. One to each cell, and I wonder how any of them are surviving the claustrophobia of it all. I sure as hell couldn't.

"Are you here to finish us off then?" the girl in the next cell spits out. I look at her, cutting through the darkness, then down at the food in my arms. She's a human. And already assuming I'm here to kill her before I can help her.

"Do you want food and water or not? I was thinking about sharing," I remark and she widens her eyes, edging out of the corner and towards the bars. She grips onto them hesitantly, tilting her head at me.

"You aren't really here to give us that. It's some sick joke." She rolls her eyes and I bite back a snide reply.

"No, I wasn't. But times change. Do you want something?" She looks at the food and then at me.

"Is it poisoned?"

"It's all in packets."

"Then yes." I hand her a bit of all before retrieving the bottles of water and passing her one. I watch her chug half the bottle in one swell gulp, before ripping out a chunk of bread, as if she's been starved for months on end. I wonder how long it really has been since she last ate.

I make my way further down, feeding around eight prisoners in total, food left for only Sierra now. I lean on the wall after passing Jess the remainder of the food and the bottle. He looks up at me, smiles briefly before opening the tin of beans and passing them to Sierra. She laughs when she spills some down her shirt, and Jess does too, a true heartful laugh, one I haven't heard him sing before. He talks to fill the silence, to stop the inevitable 'goodbye for now' conversation. Then Sierra turns to me.

"Thank you, mister. Thank you very much." She gulps down some more water.

"Yeah." I look down at Jess who's staring at the ground, his eyes meeting no one's when he continues, "Thank you." He grips onto the bars tighter. "Truly. Thank you for all you've done for me, and I know it must be difficult, but I appreciate it."

"Don't mention it," I brush it off in a smaller voice than usual, glancing back at the trap door exit and then at him again. "Jess—"

"I know," he mumbles quietly, gulping nervously, staring back at Sierra with a forced, but hopeful smile on his lips. "Listen."

"Do you have to?"

"Yes, I need—"

"Will you promise to come back?"

"You don't trust me to return?"

"I'm scared when I'm alone."

"I'm scared too, Sierra. I'm terrified." He holds her hands tightly, trying not to lose it completely again. Refusing to break into millions of shattered pieces, piled in front of his little sister he needs to protect. "But I pinky promise," he hooks his pinky around hers and her smile brightens instantly, a little more strength filling her veins, filled by her brother in front of her gaze, "that I will come back, and next time, I'll be ready to escape. We'll run away together."

"Really?"

"With Oskar." Her face lights up again, jumping a few times, giggling out of pure giddy excitement again.

"With Oskar?"

"And Luka, and Savannah. Zack and Matthew too. Everyone, we'll all go someplace else. And we'll be okay." But it'll never be that simple. He's a vampire. When will he accept this? Unless he never plans to make it out.

"Pinky promise!" He nods, but holds onto her trembling hands for longer than he should. His smile fades, taking a deep breath in, and a deep breath out.

Seeing his sister will give him hope. It'll bring him some sort of closure. His anxious mind replaced for a moment, as he sits with his family in front of him, staring right back at him.

Sierra sobs a little more, everything sinking in around her that she's going to have to say goodbye to him again, even if it is just for a short while. Or maybe she's crying more at the fact that he's alive. Happy tears, instead of sadness.

I wonder if Shane would cry at the sight of me. Or maybe he'd laugh, trap me in a headlock and hug me until I couldn't breathe. I wonder if I'd cry. What would we say? I wonder what we would do, what I'd tell him.

"I love you." Jess takes a deep breath, one that shakes his entire world, giving her a reassuring smile, the one that's hiding a broken boy. "I love you more than words could ever tell. And I'll save you, and I'll get us out of here." He strokes her messy brown hair ever so gently, his hand slides down to her cheeks, clearing her tears until she smiles, nods confidently and stops crying entirely. "I *pinky* promise. Then maybe me and you can get ice-cream and go to the park and do whatever you want, okay?"

"I love you to the moon and back, Jess. I'll miss you. But bring Oskar next time!"

"I'll see what I can do," Jess' voice breaks again. He presses a kiss on her hand. "I'll see you soon, Sierra."

Jack

18th November

Achillea has not stopped rushing around, circling town, panicking. Some days, it's like we're moving backwards. And then sometimes, it's like we're 'ready' to go find this lost city. Achillea and Ambrosia are ecstatic. Ambrosia hasn't been caught with a frown; Draven looks as exhausted as ever.

Then there's Vincent. Who seems to be trying to win the good side of this 'Jade' person. She's been here more often than not and it's setting everyone on edge.

It hasn't stopped the random burning of small parks though. I don't think there's a single one left in the east side. But since the parks are relatively harmless, and there's no children here, it was the only thing the Royals would let him take his anger out on. The more stressed he gets, the bigger the fire is, and the more frequent his arsonist duties. A coping mechanism if you like. He hasn't been seen without his lighter alight, dancing between his fingertips.

I don't mean *poor* Vincent. And I certainly don't mean let's *pity* him.

I figured out the midnight rotation. And unfortunately tonight, it's me. Thankfully Jess has volunteered to help out too, so I'm not completely alone and I've got someone to talk to at least.

In the darkness of the early night, Jess and I wander the streets alone, as if we're the only ones awake from miles around. And I'd like to keep it that way.

I miss Violet though. All this time doing *their* errands is less time with her.

Holding her, kissing her, sleeping beside her.

I want to spend an eternity with her before doing any of this. But I have to in order to keep her safe and protected. I'm doing this for her, and I remind myself of this everyday. When I wake up, when I see Vincent, when I go to bed.

All for her, Jack. All for the sake of the future - the one without Nobles, Royals and these vampires surrounding us. Once Jess and Sierra are free, that will be our sign.

I haven't found a sacrifice though. I didn't try to. Achillea didn't seem as disappointed as I expected when I told her. She merely shrugged it off, saying it's fine. She says Jade has someone. I don't question it. With everyone so focused on finding their fictional city, I don't dare step out of line with anyone.

It seems everyone has a 'job' in this city hunt. Gathering food, preparing weapons and armour (not that we need it), or whether that job includes planning to take out a couple of close by camps. When we go to the city, they're moving the prisoners down there with us, so they can keep them close and have more for blood supply for when they're desperate. Which explains the food aspect of gathering. And on top of that, a new clan *has* in fact moved into the mansion. And funnily enough, Vincent stiffens up whenever anyone mentions it. It touches a soft spot, and he walks away without saying a word.

So it's practically confirmed his once lover is part of this clan. Being so close, you'd think he'd go over there and make himself known, but no. He stays far, far away.

Draven claims his partner is now a Noble themselves, but he couldn't be sure, and he's with the whole fate crap. That if it's meant to be, it's meant to be and they'll end up together if they should.

I think he should just go and find them. Find the fucking courage and just go for it.

Violet's leading a small section too. She still has no idea about the threat hanging over our heads. Every now and then, when I lie in the dark with her head on my chest, temptation claws up my spine and I want nothing more than to let it off my chest. Telling her everything I know. Nothing I heard is huge and life altering. Just them being judgy towards Jess and I. And yet Vincent still threatens to hurt my flower if I step out of line. That's what bites my tongue, holding me against spilling it all.

Pathetic, I know. But when your only family's life is on the line, no risks can be made. It's just not worth it.

"It just seems too difficult, Ambrosia." I steer Jess away from the sound, relaxing knowing it's only Draven's voice, but nonetheless, it sounds like a private conversation. "I saw you, Jack. I'm not blind just yet." I roll my eyes, stepping out from the corner, watching Ambrosia and Draven approach us.

"You can start by telling them."

"Again, why does it seem so hard? And why does it matter?"

"You're the one who said you wished more people knew."

"I guess." He crosses his arms over his chest. "Still. It's difficult. Why?"

"Because you don't know how they'll react," she replies simply, tilting her head up for her crown to glitter beneath the moon and the stars. "No pressure."

"I was just saying." He takes a breath. And then another, then looks for Ambrosia with almost panicked eyes as Jess and I walk closer to them. She shakes her head, then looks at us in shock.

"It's a tiny thing that doesn't affect people and they're scared you won't... I don't even know." She looks almost disgusted. "Accept you? It's literally just Jack," she points at me. "And just Jess." *They?*

"Accept?" I ask. "Do you use other pronouns now?"

"He *and* they," Draven says and his cheeks flush a furious red, scrunching his nose up.

"That's all?" Jess asks. "It seemed more threatening than that."

"I know, right?" Ambrosia's jaw drops, eyes wide in amusement before chuckling to herself, slapping a hand onto Draven's shoulder. "As I said, it's only Jack and Jess, they're all good with it, babes. You overthink such basic stuff."

"I'm gonna have to agree with Ambrosia here," I join, staring at Draven, pondering how long he's thought like this. "Do you even know me?" He rolls his eyes.

"Don't throw that accusation. I was just nervous, and Ambrosia's the only one who knows and—"

"Stop rambling," Ambrosia puts a stop to him, and then she smiles, grinning from ear to ear as her teeth shine. "The important thing is, you did it."

"Because they caught you out."

"Do you always bicker like this?" Jess mutters, shaking his head and I smirk slightly. Fitting in, I see, with the group of outcasts we are, standing outside in the cold, in the middle of the night, laughing and bickering over something so small.

"All the time," Ambrosia smiles fondly at Draven, and he returns the gesture, meeting her eyes again.

"Well, Jack, that is what I wanted to say." They look at me. "I don't *need* to tell anyone else."

"Oh?" I press.

"You and Ambrosia are the only ones I talk to." He glances at Jess. "I guess you're in on it too now."

"Hey," Jess holds his hands up, smiling. "I accept, you're valid, you're you. Anyone who disagrees can suck it." Draven chuckles at that response.

"Fair enough." They grin and look back at Ambrosia, and subtly shakes their head as she just smirks knowingly at them. "Don't gloat."

"I'm not, I'm simply smiling."

"Same thing, in your case." She rolls her eyes, nods at us as they pass us, continuing their argument into the night, whilst Jess and I stare at each other.

"I hate that people don't know if it's safe or not to come out," he mentions glumly.

"It's a sad world."

We find Vincent on the outskirts of town, close to the house Violet and I stay at.

And against better judgement, we both make our way over, curious as to what he's staring at and why he's out so late. For once, he's not fiddling with his lighter, because no, his gaze seems much too focused on something for his hands to be preoccupied with that right now. I squint, eyes adjusting to the landscape behind the low wooden fence of this small field.

A small group of humans are headed straight for us.

I widen my eyes, raising my brows. I shoot them straight to Jess who's as starstruck as me. Why them? Why are they back?

"Matthew, Oskar—" Jess speaks breathlessly and quietly beside me. And before Vincent, he sprints over the wooden fence.

"Jess!" I call after him.

But Vincent is quicker.

Vincent is faster.

Vincent is smarter.

And his psychotic laugh erupts into the night.

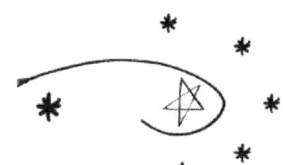

~Amissa Civiate~

Savannah ✦

18th November

"So, we're leaving this shit hole then?" Thena's voice floats by the tent we're huddled in. Luka's beside me, his shoulder against mine. Zack leaning on the fold up bed in front of Luka, Oskar and Matthew opposite Zack.

"Our work here is done, so why would we stay longer than we need?" Selene responds.

"It's about damn time! Feels like we've been here for a decade already!"

"Why am I tagging along though? Won't Matthew and Oskar get suspicious of us suddenly disappearing?" Annabeth?

"I'm sure they'll barely notice you're gone." Oskar's jaw drops open and Matthew shakes his head from side to side.

"Oh, really?"

"Does it matter, Beth?" Thena grumbles. "Suck it up. We'll be back before you know it."

"Okay...?" Beth mutters under their breath, sceptical of the entire thing, I would be too if I were in their shoes.

"It's better *not* to ask questions," Selene speaks over Thena's delusional laughter.

"Can you at least tell me where we're going?"

"Hillark." I widen my eyes even more. *Jess.*

"Oh." Their feet falter, conversations becoming silent, and only when I'm sure they're gone do I open my mouth to say,

"What about Jess?"

"What about him?" Zack asks.

"What if something happens to him while they're around? Do you really trust them to go to Hillark without sparking some sort of fight?"

"And if they're going for someone else?" Oskar murmurs. "We know he's alive, but that's all we know. We can't make accusations and assumptions about whether they're gonna hurt him or not."

"And there's nothing we can do either way as well," Matthew says.

"Well." Oskar tilts his head backwards. "That's debatable."

"What do you mean?" Zack questions, leaning forward.

"We could just go into Hillark, hide out in a house. Savannah got in and out, didn't she?" I drop my head, pursing my lips together, eyes glued to the ground. Ah, that was an enlightening turn of conversation. Zack and Matthew were certainly displeased when I told them the story of my limp these past few days, almost a week. Matthew smothered me in questions of comfort, and if I needed help and then Zack went on a rant about how we should tell each other these things rather than going behind each other's backs about it. "We can do the same."

"Right, let's think about this logically." Zack slaps his hands down on his knees. "What reasons do we have to believe they'd hurt him?"

"Didn't Savannah catch them talking about someone new to their ranks who could be trouble weeks ago?" Luka finally speaks up beside me.

"And what makes us think that was about Jess?"

"There's not a newbie in their ranks apart from him. Jack would have said something," I agree.

"Okay." Zack closes his eyes, biting on his lower lip, momentarily before looking at Matthew and Oskar. "What else?"

"They're dangerous," Matthew says simply, shrugging his shoulders. "And we can't trust them. They seem to have some sort of communication with them."

"Look, the point is, we don't have concrete evidence that they're going to hurt Jess," Oskar sighs heavily. "But." He purses his lips together, glancing between all of us as Luka slips his hand into mine. I tense before relaxing and melting into his grip. "I mean, look at us. What are we waiting for? If we don't leave this place now, when will we? If they're going, it'll turn into chaos and you guys know it. This is perfect!" Hope glitters in his eyes for a millisecond. "Perhaps this is the excuse we needed in order to leave and find Jess."

"It would be nice to see him again," Matthew comments, sitting up. "It's not been the same without him."

"Are we really going?" Zack questions.

"I say we go," Oskar states. As he said, if not now, then when? We're never going to be ready, so why *should* we wait?

I rest my head on Luka's shoulder, closing my eyes and he rests his on mine.

"You okay?" he says low enough to not be noticed by the others loud conversations.

"Tired, you?"

"Also tired." He pauses for a moment. "Do you want to go back?"

"Where else are we going to go?"

"I don't know." I don't know either. And maybe I don't want to know. For now anyway. Maybe I just want to watch it play out, instead of being a part of it all.

So, we wait. We endure the final day. We take our weapons, and we take early naps. Or they do. I lie awake for hours until Oskar comes into the tent, telling us it's late and we should move. Matthew wakes Zack, giving me a sceptical look, and then a small smile. Hope in his eyes. Hope in everyone's eyes.

They all gather outside, talking in low voices, grabbing their supplies from other tents which leaves me and Luka alone for a moment more.

He steps close to me, and holds onto my hands.

"Stay close," he says. I look into his ocean eyes, blushing bright red. "Yeah?"

"Of course." He gives me a small smile, leaning forward, placing one of his smooth hands on my cheek, before kissing my lips, softly, gently and slowly. "Are you scared?"

"A little." He nods. "But I'm sure everyone is." *I'm sure everyone is.* "Right?"

"I suppose." He glances between my eyes, kissing me again and then he heads out of the tent, but I hold on tighter to him, following close behind. I don't plan on leaving his side any time soon.

We step outside, interrupting their conversation as all heads turn to us. Only Zack glances down at our conjoined hands, smirks at Luka and chuckles to himself, nodding along.

"Anyway," he says. "Do we have a plan?"

"Should we just sneak in and out to get Jess?" Luka suggests.

"No," Oskar announces. "Jess is there for Sierra. If we go, we stay."

"Leave no one behind," I mutter and he nods at me, glancing between all of us in a circle, a dim light close by, the only thing illuminating our faces.

I admire them. Like brothers, they always have been. After all that's happened, they're still standing beside me. They still care enough to stay.

"I thought that was self-explanatory," Zack smirks, throwing an arm around me and Matthew, bringing us onto his shoulder, holding tight. I giggle and Matthew drags Oskar with him as an impulse.

And we're all smiling.

"Right, are we all ready then?" Matthew asks as I tug Luka closer, and Zack lays the end of his hand on his shoulder.

"As ready as we'll ever be," Luka comments, squeezing my palm.

"Let's go see Jess," Oskar smirks.

To Jess.

Matthew slows down beside me whilst Luka jogs ahead to speak to Zack. I look at him, reading the nerves on his face, the fear and anxiety drenching him. Or is that the rain itself?

"Matthew, you okay?" I ask. He looks at me, smiling small and nodding briefly.

"I'm kinda worried actually."

"Understandable." His eyes drift around everywhere all of a sudden, everywhere except what's lain ahead of us.

"I'm worried he'll be a different person completely."

"Remember. This is Jess, after all. He's doing it all for his sister, so how much could he have changed?"

"You have a point." He purses his lips.

"Matthew." I lay one of my hands on his shoulders, making him glue his eyes back onto mine. Beautiful emerald shade, so mesmerising. "He misses you a heck of a lot. He's okay, and so will we be."

"We're seeing Jess again," he echoes. His smile only grows, spreading across his cheeks, revealing his one and singular dimple on his left cheek. "We're seeing Jess again!" I chuckle a little as he starts shaking a little out of excitement, his eyes wide and thin brows shot up his forehead. "I'm looking forward to it."

"So am I." He flips his head up to the sky and I loosen my grip on him, sliding my hand down to his arm. I watch as splashes of rain hit his skin, he flinches and twitches, relishing in the touch completely.

"I do love the rain."

A tiny wooden fence comes into view, closing in on our home town. The place we once called safe. It seems like so long ago, like *this* is the beginning of a new era completely. We're such different people, under such different circumstances.

We spot three people watching us from afar on a small hill.

One sprints out of the perimeter, over the fence and towards us.

The other screams.

Oskar glances back, draws his long sword with panic written in his eyes. When he faces back to the stranger, who's laughing out loud, he's stern, sharp and furious. Zack looks down at his weapon, sitting in a hold around his waist but decides against drawing it, whilst Matthew pulls out his sword too, walking around everyone with trembling legs to be beside Oskar.

Another, smaller guy, sprints towards us but the one who bears red flaming hair, and an unforgettable and deadly smile is closest.

"We need to move–" I start.

"Not without Jess." Oskar instead steps forward, readying for a fight, tensing his arms, and pointing the blade at Vincent himself. "I leave either with him, or in death."

"We should run towards the town then! We don't need to run away from Jess directly!" Zack begins, but I'm pretty sure Jess is the one running behind Vincent, whilst Jack is staring helplessly from afar. We all have our battles to fight and this is ours. I ready my bow, resting an arrow, preparing for the worst.

"You guys run that way! Oskar and I will take him then." Matthew glances back and his eyes meet mine immediately, an unfamiliar mist clouding his eyes. No shine in sight. No hope sparks. No comfort to offer. "Now! No time to argue!"

"Don't think you can get away from me little ones!" Vincent's voice carries into the air. Luka grabs my hand, and stares at me. Then he grabs Zack's.

"Come on!"

And we start running. And I don't think we'll ever stop.

I hide away my arrows, freeing my hands to run beside the two boys, letting them lead. I glance back once in time to hear a shriek from Jess, swiftly followed by a struggled cry from Oskar, holding his claymor against Vincent's sword, pushing him away. Matthew steps forward to slice his side. Missing, he ducks from the villains weapon as Jess reaches them, sliding in front of our friends, arguing back at Vincent.

I look forward, Luka jumping over the fence whilst Zack climbs over it. I swing my legs, stepping in between them, watching from afar, powerless as to what we can do to help. I hear rustling, Zack draws his gun finally in trembling hands. I glance at him, and he glances between us and Luka.

"In case of emergencies I suppose."

"You don't have to do anything," Luka objects. He pulls out his own sword. "I can protect us."

I show him the bow, now back in my hands. "I'm a good shot," I say. He reluctantly puts his weapon away.

We all turn to watch Vincent slicing his sword down on Jess. I choke on air, but relief washes over me in an instance when Jess recovers and doesn't double over in complete pain. Vincent shoves him behind, grinning the entire time.

He pushes Oskar away. Blade against blade.

He turns to face Matthew.

"I think I'll choose you."

"No!" Jack screams, finally running across from his hiding place. "Jess, he's gonna—"

Vincent grabs Matthew's neck. Lifts him up, with his feet dangling, and his weapon dropping to the grass. His head flings back in a cry for help, holding onto Vincent's hands.

And Vincent begins *to transform him.*

"Matthew!" Zack immediately leaps over the fence, stumbling and dropping to the floor. He staggers to his feet, sprinting closer and I follow. Luka does too, breath caught in our throats.

"Vincent!" Jess shrieks, lifting himself to his feet, and grabbing Vincent's shoulders, pulling him back, rolling him onto the ground. He drops Matthew, who covers his mouth, turning over, spitting out blood, with wide and bulging eyes. His hand on his chest. No air fills his lungs.

"Matthew, are you alright?!" Luka yells, whilst Jack makes it over in time to grab Vincent's neck, and smashes his head against the floor. Leaving him there, he plunges the back of a sword handle onto him, knocking him unconscious. He looks up to Jess who's nearing Matthew, slowly and carefully.

"What's going on..." Oskar stutters, still on the ground. We slow down, metres away from everyone, as Jack begins to drag Vincent away, who's muttering something about how he was never going to kill him.

"I know his name," he says. *"I wouldn't."* Jack's taking him back towards the town, briefly nodding to me, looking sorrowful and solemn. What happened?

We look back to Matthew. He's shaking his head over and over again, and in his panic, he finds his sword, holding it close to him, coughing and spluttering. He's not holding it close to protect himself.

Not anymore.

"Matthew," Jess starts. Trying to remain calm, despite his voice shaking with fear. "Look at me." Matthew looks up from the ground, tears streaming down his cheeks, shaking his head over and over again still. "You're here. You're all here. I'm so grateful, thank you." Matthew stands up, wobbling, wiping blood-caked lips.

"I can't— I can't—" speak. He can't even speak. "What did he do?"

"I'm so sorry."

"Do I want to know?" He sobs, arms dangling beside him, limp. His lips tremble, nose crinkled, and forehead wrinkled. Dimples hidden. Hair damp and wet, stuck to his sticky face.

"No," Jess whispers. "But Matthew—" He breaks down, and lifts his sword.

Pointing it at his chest.

"I don't want to become what I fear," he sobs, shaken by fear.

"Matthew!" Jess shrieks, lunging forward.

"I love you all."

"Matthew! No!" Oskar yells, reaching his hand out.

"More than words could ever tell." He pushes the blade through his chest.

My hands fling to my mouth. Zack sprints past a paralysed Jess, and catches Matthew in his arms, falling forward, slowly bringing him down to the ground, as carefully as he can with a hand on his head, pulling out the sword which went directly through. The end, bloodied with his insides.

"Matthew, no, no, no, why did you do that, why did you do that? We were so close, Matthew, I—" Zack mutters more to himself, holding Matthew's fading body on himself, lowering onto the floor, cradling him as close to his chest as he can. "Fight, Matthew, fight, for- for anything."

Tears gush down everyone's cheeks. I just stand and watch because I can't move. I see Zack cuddling a dying, a *dying Matthew in his arms,* swaying back and forth with the wind.

"Matthew, no." He shakes his shoulders, squeezing, closing his eyes tightly, trying to mend a broken Matthew back into his original self. "Why is it always the good guys?" he rasps, proceeding to rest his head on Matthew's head, as he releases his final breath into the night air. Without a fight. *He spent his last breath giving up.* He'd rather have died than become something he feared to be.

I break into my hands. Luka embraces his arms around me, pulling me onto his body, head resting on his chest, as I close my eyes.

"He killed *my* Matthew," Jess whispers through stricken tears. "He's going to pay for this!" he screams, hearing his footsteps fade away. Then he's sprinting. Then crying, then barely breathing.

Luka rests one of his hands on my hair, making its way down to my shoulder. And I look up at him, bloodshot eyes staring right back at me. I turn my head to see Oskar nearing Zack, laying a hand on his shoulder, kneeling down beside him, looking down at Matthew in his arms.

I take Luka's hand and I lead us towards them, in complete silence. I sit down in front of Zack, trying to avoid my eyes from leading down to Matthew's pale, and colourless, already faded corpse, pointed straight at the sky.

Rain hits his cheek. Harsh and bitter.

I fall into another round of tears. I wrap my arms around Zack's neck from in front, Luka kneels beside me, hand on my back, another hand on Zack. The four of us huddled, in the middle of the night, in the freezing cold and pouring rain, holding the body of our best friend.

Our family.

And our brother.

Savannah ✫

18th November

"You should leave before anything else happens," Jack says. I look up to see him standing in the pouring rain, watching everything. "I—" he hesitates and swallows a lump in his throat. "I'll make sure he's buried."

"We came for Jess," Oskar says, standing. "We intend to stay for him too."

"Bad idea—"

"I don't care." He shoots back, glaring at Jack, hand on Zack's shoulder. "We'll support him, we'll hide for him, and we'll be here for him. That's what we came for, and that's what we'll stay for." Jack walks closer to us, but I don't bother drawing my knife, and neither does Oskar. If he was going to hurt us, then he'd have done so already.

"Fine." He stares directly at me. "Your house – the one I first met you in." I nod. "I'm staying there with Violet, I've not moved anything, nor touched your room. You are welcome to stay and take your house back." My eyes widen. Back to my house without my parents waiting in the living room for me? A hand rests on my back, Luka stepping beside me. I take a deep breath, finally nodding, glancing at Zack who's still clinging onto Matthew for dear life. I tear my eyes away, tucking my hands around me and under my arms. I shiver when Jack edges closer, so close he's behind Zack, kneeling down, and laying a steady hand on his shoulder. "I'll take care of him." Zack purses his lips together, holding back a sob. "I promise."

"Okay," he replies in a small voice, loosening his grip on the corpse. With trembling fingertips, he closes Matthew's eyelids. I sigh shakily, looking away again, shuffling as the rain picks up above us, slamming onto our heads. Luka rubs my arm, warming me up in silence, but I shiver anyway.

"Head over now. Stay in the shadows. If you see a Noble with black hair over his eyes, he's friendly. If he's with a woman," Jack heaves the body into his arms, standing up straight whilst Oskar helps Zack to his feet, "she's probably friendly too."

"Probably?" Luka asks, letting go of me. Jack glances at him, nods, and begins walking away, with our best friend dangling helplessly in his arms.

"So," Oskar starts, "we're going to Savannah's house?"

"Apparently," I respond. He nods, and as before, he takes the lead, walking with Zack under one of his arms. Luka holds onto my hand, raindrops sliding between our fingertips, squelching forward in the mud.

In an unbearable silence.

I step over the fence, tears mixing with the rain, keeping to the shadows like Jack had suggested and towards my house. Last time I was here, I had a thrill of adrenaline from sneaking around. Now, I'm exhausted and terrified of what'll happen if we're caught. We turn a corner, my house in sight, and I have to slow to catch my breath whilst Zack and Oskar rush off. I flinch, leaping out of my skin when voices are heard behind me. I watch Zack and Oskar make it into the house, but Luka suddenly drags me into an alleyway, as the door shuts quietly from afar. The voices grow louder.

"*Apparently* we need to check this area around the fence because someone's close by the perimeter, babes, that's why we're here," a woman speaks to a stranger.

"Do you think they're people from the camp?" A male voice grows louder. A familiar one at that. I begin to shake violently, in twitches. Luka pulls me closer to him, making me look up. He presses a finger to his lips.

"Probably. Who else has Vincent pissed off?" she questions.

"It's okay," Luka whispers in my ear. "It's gonna be just fine." I shake my head over and over and over again, fear freezing my muscles. No Jess to save us. No Jack to steer anyone away from. We only have ourselves. And that's not enough. I take a deep breath, the voices completely silent, and yet they're closer than ever. I can hear their footsteps. Before abruptly stopping.

Right outside the alleyway.

The light is blocked, two shadows cast beside our feet.

Only means of escape, gone.

"Oh, hello there." Tears glide down my cheeks, gritting my teeth together, as Luka looks first. "And who might you be?" The woman is so soft spoken, I almost mistake it for kindness.

"Please don't hurt us," Luka begs.

"Who says I'm going to hurt you?" I glance over Luka's shoulder at the man with black hair and a fringe covering one of his eyes. Is he the man Jack was talking about? Who won't hurt us? He looks at the woman and says in an even softer and calmer voice,

"Ambrosia." A pretty name for a pretty face.

"I wasn't going to, and I mean it, Draven, have *some* faith in me."
Draven?

"Draven?" I ask.

"Draven!" Luka realises, and finds my hand, and then my arm, tugging at my clothes. "You're the one who saved her!" Draven flicks his eyes back onto him, slight confusion clouding his gaze before he stares at me. His eyes widen.

"Oh."

"You saved her?" Ambrosia asks, flinging her arms up at him. "What the hell?"

"It's a long story and it involves Vincent." He brushes it off just as easily as it had entered this whole conversation. Draven steps closer towards us and I step beside Luka. I blink and Draven's in front of me.

And then I'm admiring why Jack trusts him. He must be the Noble he was talking about.

"Are you okay?" he asks.

"Such a broad question," I reply lightly, shaking my head. "Next?" His expression drops and softens, glancing at Luka.

"What are you doing here?" He pauses and purses his lips together. "Or rather, who are you here for? Jess again?"

"You knew?"

"I saw him watching as you left that night whilst I watched Vincent. He stopped him. Whilst I found you," he answers.

"What in the world happened?" Ambrosia exclaims from behind.

"I'll explain later," Draven tells her.

"Yes, we're here for Jess," Luka says and steps beside me. "But something happened. I think he went to find...Vincent?" He looks at me. "Right?" I nod.

"I think so."

"Oh god." Ambrosia shakes her head low. "That's gonna end well. I'll go find them, shall I?" She looks at Draven who merely nods and glances her way. She looks at us, bows, grinning. "Your secret is safely kept with me. I won't tell a soul you're here, just don't get into any trouble." She lifts her head, winks and runs away, "Vincent! Jess! Don't do anything stupid!" Draven chuckles to himself.

"That's Ambrosia for you, always picking up after other people's messes."

"Are you going to let us go?" Luka advances. I tug him back, he looks at me.

"Words of advice," he crosses his arms over his chest. "Be careful. If there's a possibility you might be caught by Vincent, or Achillea, someone who looks like Ambrosia but with straight hair and darker skin, don't do it. It's not worth it." Draven glances between us. "I'm not like Vincent, I'll give you that," he grimaces, flicking his hair back with a toss of his head. "So what exactly happened in order for Jess to go after Vincent?" I swallow hard with a heavy heart. He crosses his arms over his chest, waiting patiently.

"He hurt someone he loves," Luka says under his breath. "It's irreversible." Draven's expression reads shock, shifting to surprise and then anger.

"That little bitch. He needs to learn when to stop," he spits, and Luka squeezes my hand tightly against him. "Sorry for the questions, just understand you're safe with at least me and Ambrosia. But that doesn't mean you can become reckless." He points at us, waves briefly and simply walks away.

I release a breath, looking at Luka, resting my head on his shoulder. Anxiety melts into my veins.

"You okay?"

"Yeah," I murmur under my breath. "What about—" *You?*

"Come on. Zack and Oskar might be worried." He didn't even let me finish.

We run to my old house, begrudgingly, because I can't stand the sight of it. It brings back too many unpleasant memories – ones I'd much rather never look back on. We stumble through the front door where Zack and Oskar are waiting for us, looking uncertain and fearful between each other. Zack immediately rushes into Luka, arms around him, shutting the door behind us with a slam of his foot.

"What the hell, man?" His voice cracks. "What happened?"

"Why did you take so long?" I want a hug from *my* best friend.

Luka and Zack are holding each other ever so tightly, an emptiness sweeps over my soul. As I come to that realisation, Oskar brings me into a big hug himself, one that mirrors theirs, welcoming me into his embrace with my head sitting perfectly on his shoulder. I begin crying a little again. I grasp his clothes, arms around him. I don't want to let go. *Please don't make me.*

"We ran into some people. They let us go," Luka responds softly in a soothing tone of voice. "We're okay."

"You better be." Zack clings onto him. I watch from the corner of my eye, twisting my head sideways to better gaze. But Oskar reminds me he's here for me too, so I close my eyes, relishing in the moment.

He looks over at Luka and Zack clinging onto each other, in complete silence. Luka peeks his eyes open over his shoulder. He smiles the best he can. Then mouths, "You can go." Oskar nods, suddenly tugging me away, through my untouched living room and into the kitchen. I drink in everything, all at once. The pictures on the walls. The cupboards of food, most gone off or out of date.

"It's been a while," I mutter.

"And somehow feels like no time at all." I stare at Oskar and he looks at me. "At least we have this place now. It's safer than a few tents."

"We still need to find Thena and Selene."

"Or we tell Jack about it, and let him deal with it." I frown, looking back at the knives on the side. Scattered. "I think that's the safer way here. Then we can focus on Jess."

"Jess." He nods again, and I soon follow suit. "We'll mention it." We stand in silence, drifting our eyes over everything. Oskar checks the food, plates, everything he can get his hands on it seems. "I'm gonna check my room." He flips his head over his shoulder.

"You sure?" *No.*

"Yes."

"Shout if you need anything." I nod. Of course. I turn, walking through my unsteady walls, Luka and Zack now talking on the sofa. They glance at me as I disappear upstairs on my own.

I forgot about most of the stuff in here.

I step in, goosebumps spreading over my arms and legs, feeling sick to the stomach.

Were my walls always a dull blue? Was my carpet always an old black, my desk a dirty white, my clothes everywhere, my laptop on a chest of draws? I have a picture frame on my chair, knocked over, but not quite shattered. Its silver embroidered white wood surrounding the broken picture has fallen, now lain on the ground.

I walk over, picking it up, two pictures side by side. One of my parents with little me, and a picture with my old friend group. I never got another frame for my current group of friends, but I did make a short scrapbook that's around a quarter full.

With a heavy heart, I rummage under my desk in a small cupboard, pulling it out. I open it up, holding my breath.

My favourite person. It reads.

With a picture of me and Piper below. I look away immediately, dropping it onto my desk as tears sting my eyes. I fling my palms to them as the door opens up again and then closes softly.

But there's only one person in the world who opens and closes the door so softly.

"Luka?"

"How did you know it was me?"

"Lucky guess?" I say, dropping my hands.

"Are you okay? What you doing over there?" He walks closer to me and I peer back at his gaze glued to the open scrapbook. "Oh."

"It's been a while since I've looked through it. I forgot the first picture was of her," I breathe heavily.

"Oh." He looks up at me. "Can I look?" I smile a little, nodding so I let him pick it up and I walk past. He starts flicking through it, and I realise my skin stings where I've wiped away tears so many times before.

"I haven't updated it in a while." I gaze up at my cabin bed, where I spent so many sleepless nights on Facetime with anyone and everyone I loved. I climb, falling onto an *actual* comfy mattress instead of a fake lumpy one. My dark ocean duvet below me, landing my head on top of one of my teddies I hugged close to help me sleep every night.

"Did you miss the bed by any chance?"

"Just a little." I sit up, grabbing my teddy bear, the one I got the day I was born. Petra. She's familiar in my arms, I lean on the wall with her.

"This is really sweet, Savannah," he says. I look over at him, emerging from below and beside my desk. "I had no idea you were making it." Piper knew. She said I was sappy and sentimental. She hugged me and said she loved me. "Why don't we keep this?" I flick my eyes to him, and he's finally looking back up at me. "For when you're ready to keep going through it all. Maybe even add to it or get a new one when we're out of this whole thing?"

"But we've changed." I don't know if I can.

"And I'm not denying that, I never did. It was just a thought. I'd like to keep it for memories at the very least." He puts it back on the desk as I turn, crawling onto my pillow, sitting up properly, leaning on the wall in silence as Luka comes back out.

"I think that part's a good idea," I say, almost under my breath. He looks up, and starts climbing onto my bed. "Are you okay?" I ask him. He edges closer to me, crosses his legs and sits in front.

"Erm," he hums for a short while, glancing everywhere but me. "I guess?"

"Is that a question?" I counter.

"I mean," he chuckles sarcastically. "We just watched *that*, and I just had Zack break down on me. No, I'm not okay." He wipes his eyes, shaking his head, then straightens his back. "I need to sleep for a hundred years, then maybe I'll be okay."

"I'm sorry, no can do. I don't know how to help with the sleep thing unless I put you in a coma repeatedly, and I don't even know how to do that either." He laughs a little more, looking at my duvet sheets, circling his palm against it. He leans closer to me.

He finds one of my hands, and the other reaches my arm. "Luka."

"Mmm?" He stares at me, feeling his breath hit my skin like fire meeting a flame.

"Can I help with anything?"

"No. Not really."

"Well." I lean back, gripping his hand tightly. "If there is ever a time I can help with anything, let me know?" His dimples are on show, nodding, flicking his hair back and out of his gaze. "Promise?" Because I know what he's like.

"Promise," he whispers and kisses, leaning into me. Then he wraps me up, pulling me to his chest. I fall into his arms. He presses his lips to my hair, and strokes strands between his fingertips. "Savannah."

"Yes?" I ask as I close my eyes.

I hear his heart beat.

"Don't go."

Savannah ✩

18th November

The silence is *almost* torturing downstairs, it would *actually* be torturing if anyone spoke what was truly on their mind. Thankfully, we're much more comfortable contemplating it all, staring at a wall, or the floor, or our hands. In complete and utter silence.

It's just the four of us in this one room and it feels empty. Even when we fill the sofa, nothing can fill the void this place has created.

"We should probably discuss where everyone's gonna sleep tonight." Zack leans forward on the single arm chair to our left.

It just became torturing. He turns his head to look at me.

"Don't look at me for answers, I don't live here anymore," I tell him.

"It was rightfully yours to begin with though."

"Not anymore."

"Can't we just sleep down here?" Oskar puts his hands behind his head. "It really doesn't need that much thought."

"I'm down for that," Luka murmurs to my left.

"Okay," I agree, and Zack merely sits back again.

"Glad we got it cleared up."

"I'm starving—" Oskar barely has time to finish his train of thought before the front door bursts open. My eyes widen, everyone turning their heads to watch Jack and Violet stumble through, slamming the door after them with their feet. Zack stands up, swiftly followed by Luka, but Oskar and I remain seated, watching from below. Jack scans the living room, and Violet looks at us, completely starstruck.

"Erm, Jack—"

"Where's Jess?" he asks immediately, so that's who he was looking for. Oskar stiffens beside me. I look at him, he looks at me.

"He stormed off, I thought you saw," I reply

"I thought he would come here after—" he stops abruptly. I look back over to Jack.

"Ambrosia went to make sure he didn't do anything stupid to Vincent," I say.

"You met Ambrosia and she didn't attack you?" Violet exclaims, jaw ajar. "This keeps getting more and more interesting."

"Savannah and I ran into Draven and Ambrosia," Luka says. "They didn't attack us. They didn't even try."

Violet lets out a breathless chuckle and her eyes are wide, shaking her head. "Wasn't expecting that."

"Ambrosia is nicer than you'd think, flower." Jack glances at her. "What doesn't make sense is why Jess isn't here—"

"Do we have to talk about him right this second?" Oskar blurts.

"Is there a problem?"

"Nope." He abruptly stands up, looks at me and then Zack. "But I don't want to deal with it, that's all. So if you'd excuse me." He walks past Zack, between Jack and Violet and upstairs to my room, all too quickly. I stand up next, wanting to follow him, but I freeze to the spot when I'm between Luka and Zack, restraining myself. Maybe he needs a moment.

"What the hell was that all about?" Zack questions, searching me for the answer.

"He's obviously overwhelmed," Luka tells him instead.

"I thought he'd be thrilled to know Jess is alive," Jack mutters under his breath.

"He is," all three of us leap down his throat. We glance between each other, but Zack's the one to step forward.

"I wouldn't have thought Jess would be ready to face us either," Zack explains. "His best fucking friend *died,"* his voice cracks at 'died', and Luka circles around me to be beside Zack, holding onto his arm with one hand.

"I believe Jess will come here when he's ready," Luka reasons, then looks at Jack. "He knows where you are, right?"

"I'm not even sure he knows you didn't leave," he mutters.

"Surely he'd think of that when Ambrosia and Draven randomly turn up at his side and—" Violet stops. "Where's Vincent? Is he gonna tell Achillea?"

"I don't think so, even he wouldn't fall so low as to admit he couldn't kill some humans in the middle of the night to Achillea," Jack smirks a little, staring at Violet.

"You have a point." She smiles back.

"Where would Jess be now?" Zack asks.

"He's hiding out at Oskar's house," I answer for him, staring at each other.

"Oskar's?" I nod.

"I think he wanted to be close to him, even when he thought he was dead," I assume. Zack's eyebrows knit together.

"That makes sense," he whispers softly.

"Is he physically okay?" Luka asks Jack, but Jack simply shrugs his shoulders.

"I hope so, just give him and your friend time. Give *yourself* time," he says softly. "Until then, you can all stay with us as long as you need," he offers. "Not that it's ever been *my* house." He stares directly at me. "We can help you—"

"Within reason," Violet interrupts.

"Within reason. Just keep out of the way, and out of sight. If someone like Vincent catches you again, it could be all of your death sentences." He glances between us, and I hold my breath, nodding.

"Understood," I mutter.

"It's a little weird how today is the day this new visitor returns *and* you all decide to choose today to come here too..." Violet trails off into a murmur, walking away and into the kitchen.

"Visitor?" Zack asks.

"Yes," Jack replies. "Someone was talking to Vincent all day. Clinging onto him practically." Shit. "This links to you?" If Selene and Thena really are here, does that mean they've been a part of their side all this time? That doesn't make any sense – Thena came to rescue us. She came and led us out, letting us stay in their camp. If she was against us, why did she do all that?

"We were following the camp leaders here," Luka tells him, glancing at me. "They said they'd go and never come back. Said they brought someone here with them. We wanted to know what this thing was about."

"I think we were all looking for an excuse to leave," Zack says quietly.

If we stayed, would Matthew still be alive?

Jack deepens his frown and says, "Hm, I thought only one woman was here, and she was with Vincent, but some creepy things are happening here too."

"Agreed!" Violet calls from the kitchen.

"What have they been saying?" Jack asks, crossing his arms over his chest, chin out. "To make you feel suspicious?" I shrink twice the size of

Jack, feeling so small. Because why *do* we think this? Because they've just been acting differently? Because they knew where we were?

"They're odd with how they act. Secretive. I've caught them spying on us, mainly Savannah," Luka speaks up.

"And they knew where we were. Thena came to find survivors, but as soon as she found us, she didn't go out to find anyone else. We've heard them talk about other people too, people not part of the camp." Jack watches Violet walk in, as she passes to walk up the stairs.

"I'm checking on the boy."

"Be nice," Jack calls back whilst he clings onto his chin. What's going through his mind?

"It's just— some things not adding up." Zack steps forward. "That's all. Maybe it's a superstition, but I don't know, they're just odd people."

"I think your leaders or whatever are working with mine," he considers. "Achillea's been more secretive than usual, rushing around, being quiet and spending time away from Ambrosia which is unlike her. She's left more things for Vincent to deal with, which back tracks down to me unfortunately. He's stressed, and it's not helping the rest of the clan and Jess—" He shakes his head. "He has the most leverage against him. Vincent might know he has a sister down in the prisons. If he's smart enough, and if Jess is stupid enough, Vincent could use it against him as blackmail."

"What do you mean, 'if Jess is stupid enough'?"

"If he does anything stupid, I mean. For example, harming him."

I widen my eyes. "Jess wouldn't—"

"He might have," Zack interrupts me, and we stare at each other. "Did you see the look in his eyes?" I purse my lips into a thin line. Because I did. Pure anger and pure hatred. "What do you know about your 'leaders' then? What are they trying to do?" Jack rolls his eyes, not at Zack, but in general. At what he *does* know.

"They're looking for a lost city," he says so simply, and sarcastically. "A fictional city. One that's impossible to be real, and if it was, there's no way down to it the way they're going about it."

"What do you mean?" I press.

"Achillea and Ambrosia believe their home is underground. Under this town to be exact." A city? Underneath our feet? Promptly, I look down at the ground, feet firm on the carpet, imagining I'm above a city with magnificent buildings, creepy old houses, everything in dark stones and beautiful wooden structures.

A lost city.

Is that how vampires were hiding all these years? And they got locked out? I don't understand. And judging by Jack's expression, he doesn't either.

"It's fake and they've officially lost their marbles if they genuinely and honestly believe they can find an entire city below our very own feet," Jack exclaims, gesturing dramatically.

"Why don't you just leave this place then?" Luka asks. I stare at Jack, watching his expression fade from anger to remorse in an instant.

"I'm planning to. Violet and I are leaving when it's most convenient. When we can slip out unnoticed. But," he takes a breath, sighs and releases the tension in his shoulders. "Then I met Jess," he says softly. "And he reminded me of myself when I was new here. I wanted him to have some sort of help navigating this place." Did he have a brother or sister worth fighting for too?

"I'm sure you *have* helped him," Zack tells him and walks closer.

"I second that," I say.

"And thank you for helping us all. You're probably what's kept Jess alive all this time," Jack says, and shakes his head smiling ever so slightly.

"No. You're the reason he's lasted so long. His friends and his sister. The thought of you all being alive has kept him going. Trust me, he'll come here soon enough to see you all again properly." Those words make me both crumble in place and warm my heart.

Alive?

"You must be tired," Jack says. "I'll leave the downstairs in your hands, and, of course, your room. Violet and I will stay upstairs." He nods, bidding his farewell to us. "Sleep well."

"Goodnight."

$\mathscr{Jack}$

21st November

"They seem lost," Violet says, whilst it's just the two of us in the living room. Her under my arm, both of us on the sofa, staring at an empty wall. "I feel bad for them."

"They need time."

"And when is that not enough anymore?"

"What do you mean?" I ask and stare at her. She backs away from me, standing up suddenly, breaking from my grip.

"What happens when they're tired of waiting?" She looks over her shoulder, down at me. "What if they've spent enough time alone, and Jess is still not here, and we still have no idea what Achillea and...these people from their camp are up to? What if they run out of time?" She spins around, gesturing furiously. "I just—" She sighs, rolls her eyes, crossing her arms over her chest, as she sits beside me on the very end of the cushions. I watch intently, her gaze on the carpet, hands raised to her chin. "I remember how we felt. How lonely and suffocating it was."

"They're not in the same position as we were, Violet, remember that." I place one of my hands on her back. "They're in a better place than we were."

"Not much better!" She shoots at me, staring into my soul. "They fucking watched their best friend die in front of them – I saw!"

"I didn't know you saw that much." She must've been hiding.

"Well, I did. What difference does it make now?" She looks away from me, huffing and I quickly take my hand back. "I wish." She holds her hands out in front of her. "We could help them. And I mean truly help them. Not just give them a place to stay. Like how Draven helped us."

"I think what we're doing is enough—"

"I know it's *enough* right now. But I don't know how long it'll stay like that."

"I'm not sure they're the type to get sick of what we're doing. We're giving them somewhere to hide whilst they figure out what to do next. Or until an opportunity confronts them." She purses her lips together, sitting up and lifting her gaze up again. "It's not like what we had to endure. They have us to protect them, and Vincent will never have to know they're here, and even Ambrosia is with us this time. Violet," she looks up, turning her head towards mine, "if they need anything else, they'd tell us. If they need our help in any other way, we'll provide it for them best we can, okay?" She hesitantly nods. "But for right now, there's nothing else we can do."

"Do we wait on Jess?"

"If he doesn't turn up soon, I'll go find him." I haven't seen him since witnessing his friend's death either. It's beginning to unnerve me.

"Sounds good," she says, facing me on the sofa, crossing her legs, frowning and finding my hands to hold onto. She's avoiding my gaze again. "I'm sorry, I don't mean to snap."

"It's okay. Understandable."

"I shouldn't be taking it out on you though."

"You're not. You're ranting to me. Not at me. That's one of my many jobs." She smiles, chuckling a little, meeting my eyes once again.

"Yeah? What are your other jobs then?" She creeps her fingers up my arm, electrifying my skin. I smirk, hiding my blush.

"Well, caring for you, keeping you safe, and as said before, letting you rant to me. I solve your problems if your head hurts, my love."

"Keeping me safe, huh?"

"Is that a problem?"

"I can protect myself."

"I never said you couldn't. I'm more of a 'backup to fall onto in case things turn south'." Or a, *being blackmailed to make sure they don't hurt you,* kind of keeping you safe.

"Good. Just making sure." I quickly kiss her lips, before being interrupted by a knocking at the front door. Meanwhile upstairs, Savannah's door opens immediately, and someone looms at the top of the stairs as I stand up, heart hammering fast in my chest, as I walk towards the front of the house. I glance up at Savannah waiting, who looks more panicked than I thought anyone could ever be. I check through the peephole. "It's only Draven and Ambrosia."

"Why?" Violet leaps to her feet and I watch Savannah back away a few steps, Luka appearing next to her, briefly, holding her hand and muttering something to her.

"You said you met them, right?" I ask and they look back at me, nodding silently. "I'm gonna let them in. And they won't attack. If Ambrosia advances, I'll simply stop her." Savannah's eyes widen.

"But you'd be in serious trouble—"

"I meant what I said." I turn back around, looking at Violet. "I think they'll be here scouting."

"Probably." I hear the upstairs door shut. And I open the one in front of me. I greet them, and they happily walk inside, as if it was always their house to invade. Ambrosia climbs the first step and Draven steps beside me.

"Violet! Long time no see!" Ambrosia exclaims, and I smirk as Violet merely waves back and smiles through bared teeth.

"Hello, Ambrosia."

"I'm sure you've heard," Draven starts. I stare at him, cutting straight to the point.

"Heard what?"

"The searches being made?"

"Searches?" Violet questions.

"For your human friends," he replies.

"We won't snitch, don't worry, babes. In fact, we're worried about them ourselves. We've seen Zayne sneaking around, asking Knights and even Nobles if they've seen any humans or suspicious people about. I'd avoid him if I were you.." I stare at Ambrosia as she talks, looking down on me with a crown still upon her newly braided hair. *Of course Zayne is searching.*

"You've had a change of heart then." She shrugs her shoulders.

"People can change..."

"I mean, once upon a time you killed plenty of humans yourself," Violet pushes a little far, but the Royal merely shakes her head.

"I know, but I've gone off human blood again." Again? "And besides, when I know their story, it makes me less reluctant to actually *do* anything to them."

"You *don't* know them though," I mutter.

"I think she more means how they link to Jess," Draven tells me.

"Exactly," she says, patting his shoulder aggressively. "Jess is one of us at the end of the day. And they're his friends. I don't want to hurt him anymore than we actually have."

"Rich coming from you." I smirk to make it appear like I'm only joking with her like an old friend. But from the bottom of my core, I mean it. Why has she suddenly changed her heart? She sighs, closing her eyes, flicking her hair out of her face.

"Look, I'm not one of those kinds that need blood to survive. And I actually haven't had blood for years now." I widen my eyes at her. Years? A royal not having blood for years is unheard of. "Achillea dislikes that about me. But she accepts it. I'm the one convincing her not to kill off these innocent humans and blah blah blah." She shoots her eyes back to me, stone cold, or is there a hint of warmth in them now? "I feel bad for them, babes."

"She was never like Vincent or Achillea," Draven comments, defending his best friend's side. "And neither have I been like them. If it was truly up to us, we'd probably go about everything else differently."

"I understand where Achillea is coming from. And Vincent in a weird way, but babes, we don't *need* to kill for sport. Sure it's fun...sometimes. But that's a completely different issue." Different from what exactly? A sacrifice?

"So you're not actually here to hunt these humans down? Like Zayne?" I ask. They both shake their heads.

"No, we're not here for that. Although, that's what Achillea thinks we're doing now, and Vincent," Ambrosia speaks.

"I swear, that little weasel is trying to get into her ranks," Draven mutters. I look at him with raised eyebrows, and he shakes his head again. "Vincent."

"That's to deal with for another day, hun." Ambrosia pats his head and he slaps her hand away. She merely laughs at it.

"I'm not a pet, Ambrosia."

"I know. It's hilarious to wind you up though." They smirk, hiding it by looking the other way.

"Moving on," he exclaims, crossing his arms over his chest.

"There's another reason as to why you're here?" Violet presses.

"Are the humans actually here? I can't think of where else they'd be," Ambrosia asks, genuinely curious.

"They're upstairs." We lock eyes. "Do. Not. Tell. Anyone." Her amber eyes spark.

"I wouldn't dare. That'd ruin the fun." She winks at me. "Keep them up there. Tomorrow night we're leaving anyway."

"What?!" I exclaim in sync with Violet, who steps beside me.

"That's the exact reaction I told you they'd have," Draven retorts.

"Tomorrow evening, we're *finally* leaving this desolate place to return home," she announces, clapping her hands together tightly, hope briming in her eyes as she sighs longly. "Finally."

"Short notice," Violet comments. She glances at me, her worry catching my attention.

"Technically," Draven jumps in, "it's only a small group going in the first pack. Achillea, Ambrosia, Vincent, you two, me, and three others." Could they be the leaders from the camp? Is Jade one of them?

"A very small group," I echo. "Why us?" I hold Violet's hand, fear piercing through my veins.

"Because you're Vincent's favourites," he mocks. I should have seen that coming. "We all know it." What about Savannah and her friends upstairs?

"Draven, we should probably go. I'm stargazing with Achillea for the final time and I do *not* want to be late," Ambrosia comments, looking around the house we'll be leaving behind. She nods along, as if impressed, and then finally looks back at Draven.

"Fine," they mutter, looking back at me as they open the front door. "Keep them safe, and I'll see you tomorrow night." I nod at them , holding the door as they leave, followed by a beaming waving Ambrosia. She whispers something to Draven about it being a clear night, just like the night she arrived here 4oo years ago. Or around there anyway.

I close the door, and the one upstairs opens immediately. I look up. Savannah's at the top.

"Are we staying here?" she asks. "*Can* we stay here? While you're gone, I mean." I thought they'd be earwigging. Thin walls and ceilings, I guess.

"Of course," I say calmly.

"Thank you."

"It's your house." She pushes her lips into a thin line, nods and returns to her room with her friends. I look at Violet, as starstruck as me.

As if we've both been sent to our own deaths.

"I'll have to find Jess for him to come stay with them. To protect them." Violet merely smiles at me, clearly amused.

"Jack..."

"What?" She opens her mouth to comment on something. Maybe my sudden protectiveness over these kids, but then she slams it shut and shakes her head.

"Nothing. Sort it tomorrow, until then, let's sleep." She yawns and stretches whilst I glance upstairs.

If they're left on their own, they won't last a week in this monster infested town, a new danger awaiting at every twist and turn. Whilst we're stuck down there, Zayne will be trapped up here. *Anything* could happen. *I hope Jess will help.*

Tonight, my flower's close to me. Laying on the couch, exhausted from everything, even the thought of tomorrow makes me more tired by the minute. So, with my arms wrapped around her, I count myself lucky that we have tonight, with the moonlight flickering through the curtains, and her cheek pressed against my chest, her breathing soft and slow.

I'm here to protect her always. And I dearly hope she knows this. Now, always and forever.

I press my lips to her hair, and she smiles softly in her sleep. This could be the last time we sleep comfortably for a while, in a safe and oddly familiar environment. With a twist of anxiety, something bubbles up inside in an instant. Words I've wanted to say, but never found the right way to say it. Found the right place to. The right voice.

"I love you."

It's the first time I've said such simple words in an order so specific. The first I've said 'I love you' *first*. Where I haven't just said 'love' either. Which should mean the same thing – which *has* meant the same thing. Which is why I haven't said those three words yet, but I've always wanted to say them. So I have now.

Maybe I thought it was pointless when we show this love in so many other ways, it never felt necessary. But it does now.

She suddenly looks up at me with a lazy smile and droopy eyes.

"About time you said it first."

"I've called you 'love' before, so I never thought it was much different."

"Does it feel different?" I nod with a small smile.

"Yes, it does." She smiles right back at me, gazing into my eyes, and I find myself in her dark pupils, reflecting my dishevelled appearance. I say it again, "I love you."

"I'm gutted I didn't say it first." Before I can respond, she boosts herself up and pecks me on the lips, before returning to be comfortable laying on my chest, embracing my warmth. I blush, relaxing and melting into her touch, anxiety and nausea drifting and fading away. "I love you too."

I don't want to lose her.

I *can't* lose her.

And if I do, then I lose myself. I could go feral. Maybe I'll go crazy. Or perhaps I'd finally give up, and let Vincent finish me off.

Jack

22nd November

Bright and early the next day, I make my way to Jess' base in the dawning sun. Admittedly, it's not as early as when he once barged into our room, but early enough to make him more cranky than usual, payback for when he interrupted my sleep so many times before.

I knock on his door. He opens it fairly quickly, deep bags under his eyes, bloodshot pupils, and his hair looks like it hasn't been washed for a week or more.

"Well, aren't you looking awake," I comment out of concern. He rolls his eyes, stepping aside for me to enter. I slowly step in, as he shuts the door, just watching me, with his arms crossed over his stomach like he's either starving or about to throw up.

"What do you want?" I glance into his living room, untouched still. Neat and tidy.

"I came to talk to you about tonight." When I look back at him, his eyes are wide, drowning in fear. "No, you're not joining us in this city."

"Then what have you come to discuss?" He seems as if he's given up completely. The defeated tone of voice. He's as pale as can be. As boney as ever, and as dishevelled as I've ever witnessed him. Maybe Oskar can help take care of him, because I'm not sure where to start. I wish I did though. But maybe my part is to push them together again.

"Regarding your friends." He freezes up, pursing his lips together tightly. "Both Violet and I are going tonight, against our will."

"What does this have to do with them?" He fidgets uncomfortably with his fingers.

"They're in our house. The one we were keeping safe for Savannah." He lifts his head up, instantly, a moment paused in time. "I'd like you to, at the very least, make sure no one goes snooping around. In a town full of monsters, people are gonna go through people's bases."

"You want me to protect them?" he asks hesitantly, looking at his feet.

"Is that a problem?" I swear my eyes deceive me when I see tears brim in his gaze.

"They won't want to see me. Get Draven, or whatever—" He flicks his wrist, marching past me in a huff and into his broken, tidy living room.

"Draven's coming with us. Vincent too. Ambrosia, Achillea, and three others who I don't know well enough. You're the only person who can help keep them from harm's way." I clench my fists into tight balls. "Don't you want to see them again?"

"They won't want to!" He stops, peering over his shoulder, glaring daggers, sharp enough to bruise. "Didn't you hear me the first time, Jack?"

"They need you," I mutter, shaking my head in almost disbelief. "They miss you, and they're waiting."

"Well, tell them they're gonna be waiting a heck of a long time then." His voice breaks, burning his mask to the ground.

"Jess." I step closer to him, as he looks away again, everywhere but me. "Why do you think that?"

"Because I couldn't stop him! You saw, didn't you?" he shouts at the top of his voice, a trembling one at that.

"They came all this way for you. They knew the risk, and they did it anyway."

"Doesn't mean they still think like that now. For all I know, they regret it!"

"They could have left then." He says nothing. But he shakes when he breathes. "But instead they're hiding out in Savannah's house. I don't know what else to say to make you see this!" He's crying ever so slightly, ever so slowly.

"I want to believe you. I really do—"

"If you still don't, go there yourself. They don't plan on leaving any time soon." I catch him itching his arm again. "Maybe they can help you, Jess."

"Are you done yet?"

"I came to tell you they need help being protected. You're known here, you can walk outside freely, but they can't, and you know that. They won't last a week without protection. And then, you'll not only have to save Sierra, but Oskar, Zack, Savannah, and Luka too," I tell him as he wipes his eyes harshly. "I probably won't see you again for a little while if this city is real." If. Only if. "So goodbye for now. And I hope you make the right decision." He remains emotionless as I leave his house with a slam of his door.

Jade is one of the three people who are joining today, along with a smaller woman with long black hair, with two knives constantly in her hands, and another small one, who introduced themselves as Annabeth. The other is a stranger who's constantly in between Jade and the woman.

Achillea and Ambrosia are leading, side by side with Vincent sucking up to Jade, whilst Draven tries to get to know the other two. Violet and I are hand in hand behind, as we leave our town's security. I desperately don't want to do this. But as the cyan sky overcasts above our heads, I realise I never had a choice to begin with. My fate always seemed out of my hands entirely.

They knew I wouldn't go without Violet. I think that's why she's here with me now. I can't think of any other reason or explanation. Guilt hangs heavy in my chest, looking over at Violet who holds her head high in any situation she's in, since I'm the reason she's here. And now that we are, the threat made days and weeks ago, seems so insignificant now. *If we had just ran away.*

At least this way I can guarantee her safety.

She looks at me, and gives me a confident, and stern smile.

"You alright there?" she asks. I watch her bow shift in her free hand, arrows on her back and knives sheathed around her waist. She hangs on tighter to my hand, circling my skin with her thumb, slowly but closely. "You're not worried, are you?"

"A little," I admit.

"It's gonna be just fine." I smile, and look away from her. I should be telling her that too. She seems more self assured than I, but that's how it's always been. I draw my sword in my right hand, gripping it tightly, an eye on anyone who could be a threat to my flower. I'm used to having my guard up, because of Achillea and Vincent, even Ambrosia but there's new people with us in this pack now. New people mean new threats. "Why us?" she suddenly asks beside me. I stare at her. But she's got her eyes on the new unnamed woman in front of us. "It always seems to be us."

"Always us," I echo and she glances my way briefly, before looking away again.

The closer we get, the deeper my stomach sinks. I don't know what we should prepare for, but Achillea and Ambrosia share a look to each other, Vincent stops messing around with fire upon his fingertips, and Jade disappears into the silence surrounding us. All as we approach the area I inspected all those days ago, before I met Oskar and reunited with Savannah.

"We stay close to each other, got it?" I whisper to Violet, head dipped lower, lips to her ear. She nods and that's final.

Everyone stops once we're beside the indent in the mountain I checked weeks ago. Achillea and Ambrosia look at each other, muttering amongst themselves. I'd love to know what the significance of this place is to them. It seems to mean a lot to them. A secret only they bare.

"Can we hurry this along?" Jade announces, tapping her foot on the ground, now in between the other woman and Annabeth, the stranger with a name. I ready my sword. I watch Violet let my hand go to grab an arrow for the ready. She glances at me, and warns me with cold eyes. Something isn't right.

Why is Jade trying to take control of our Royals? And why is everyone simply okay with it? Achillea looks back at Jade over her shoulder, stiffly nodding.

"Whatever you need to do," the cousins step out of the way, "please do."

"Thank you." Jade gives her best smile, a twist of genuine glass. "Annabeth, stand just..." a sudden cross splits on the ground. Did she just do that? Make the earth shake? "There." She looks at Annabeth who hesitates to do so. "Please."

"Okay," they mutter, stepping forward. And as soon as they're on the platform, a ring around their feet, they freeze. I look around at our people, everyone emotionless, Vincent watching intently and Draven in the dark like us.

"Thena," Jade simply says, and the woman beside her, spins her knives on her fingertips, grinning with sharpened fangs gleaming. Meanwhile, Jade flicks her head up to the clear, starry sky above, mutters a few words in a language I can't understand. *"Arma Vocare."* In a blink of my eyes, Jade whips her hand out beside her, and gradually, blood leaks out of her very own fingertips, to form a blood red sword. She glances at Achillea, offering a small smile and with the nod of the Royals head, Jade looks at Thena, smiles wickedly. They pull back their weapons, stepping forward swiftly and silently.

Before Annabeth can turn around to watch their friends betray her, Jade has dug her blood sword into their back. Thena leaps across and slices her head clean off, landing on all fours, blood spurting out from their neck, now splattered upon Thena's knives.

"It's been a while since I've done that!" she cackles, standing up straight, almost bowing in front of the Royals. My eyes are wide, stepping in front of Violet on instinct, watching Annabeth's body fall limp to the ground, their eyes still open, glazed over, turned cold. Draven's looking away, Vincent's grinning in silence, Ambrosia's staring up at the stars and Achillea's remaining poker-faced and neutral as can be.

As if this was her plan all along.

The sacrifice makes sense now. That order to find someone. Whilst I'm relieved I wasn't the one who sentenced someone to their death, I'm not exactly thrilled with having to witness it. My veins turn to ice, and my hands become numb.

The remaining blood of Annabeth's leaking body is absorbed by the ground itself. Where the blood has fallen and made pools is where the ground cracks into hundreds of pieces, before collapsing completely. Falling through to a cave of some sorts. I hold my breath at a hole in the ground, with jagged corners and a vast underground. So deep, it's pitch black.

"Well!" Vincent begins, clapping his hands together. "That was entertaining!"

"I'll take that as a compliment!" Thena laughs. The ground absorbed their body, and then collapsed all together? As if the weight of the blood was too heavy. Vincent looks at us, and then grins, tilting his head to one side.

"I was beginning to get peckish. I'm disappointed I couldn't try their blood—"

"Don't look at us, creep," Violet sneers. He grimaces, face falling as he raises his head, looking down on us through his nose.

"You might want to keep your mouth shut, little flower, or you might get someone killed with your attitude." He glares, sending daggers my way, and I stare right back at him. Violet stares at me, and as soon as he looks away.

"Come on," Jade beckons us closer to Thena who's about to jump down the gap in the earth. I assume hell's on the other side. "All of you."

"Leave Achillea and Ambrosia to be alone for a moment," Draven tells her, before looking at us. "This is a big thing for them." Vincent looks sorrowful for a moment which catches us all off guard, including Draven, who watches him walk to Thena and Jade. Draven's lips parted in shock. They mutter to us, "What was that look..."

"He looked almost upset," I point out under my breath. Like he was yearning for something. Or perhaps unpleasant memories are resurfacing.

Achillea and Ambrosia stand side by side, shoulder to shoulder, looking up at the galaxy above on this clear night.

"Do you remember the first time we saw them? How much work and effort we put into seeing them?" Achillea asks, as Ambrosia turns her head to stare. "It seems like it was only yesterday." "It sure as hell wasn't. Try about 4oo years ago, babes." Achillea chuckles a little, staring at her cousin. "It was the best night of our lives." "Will you miss this?" She looks around in the meadow, from the town lit up and then at the stars. "We'll come back for visits, Lea." "Will we?" "It's a promise." They both look up. At all the constellations. The burning memories. Each star tells a new story. "I love you. You know that, right?" Lea tells her best friend. "I do, and I love you too."

Jack

22nd November

This could've been avoided if me and Violet had already left. We wouldn't have met Jess or the humans or gotten attached. And yet here we are.

We can't turn back now.

Violet and I peer over the edge of the hole Jade created. Thena sprints past and into the void below, cheering with adrenaline, until she disappears from view. She abruptly shuts up, landing roughly on something I can't see which terrifies me even more. And there's no point in flying down, my wings still ache from the last trip here and back. All I can do is glide. Draven squirms uncomfortably, and surprisingly he looks at Vincent beside him, shaking his head.

"I can't—"

"Yes, you can! Close your eyes and hope Thena catches you!"

"No, wait, wait, wait, wait! Vincent!" He pushes Draven off, and follows down after him, laughing to himself, and they begin to fade. And then Vincent grabs Draven's wrist, stopping Draven from screaming as they look at each other with wide eyes.

"What are you waiting for?" Jade questions behind us. At least we won't die from the height. Thena's made it, and she's calling up for us to follow. Violet equips her bow back, and I sheathe my sword. I hold her hand tightly against me.

"We jump together," I tell her and she nods, convincing me it's all gonna be okay with the glance of her eyes. She counts down from three for lift off.

My stomach twists into a knot. Where will we land? Will it be safe? What will break our fall? But I guess there's only one way to find out.

"Three," I take a breath, "two," we look down at the abyss,"one."

I summon my wings in time with Violet, and we jump, plunging into the darkness below, my breath vanishing beneath me.

The night is suddenly endless. Violet has her own boney and featherless wings out as well, using them to glide, and I count myself lucky we didn't get any of Vincent's other attributes, reminding myself of what we avoided by luck.

Falling into a void has a...sensation to it. A surge of fear shoots through my veins because we don't know where we are anymore. We're in the unknown, somewhere we've avoided entering for years. We're in a dark cave of some sort, crafted by a collapsed sinkhole, caused by the ultimate sacrifice. We witnessed someone practically being absorbed by the ground itself, and out of all the supernatural things that have happened to me as of recently, that might be the weirdest, and scariest thing of all.

But I can't ignore the peace I hold whilst I'm freefalling through the air. The unknown could kill us, but it could also be someone's hopes and dreams coming to life. I'm beginning to consider that there is in fact a lost city down here. And if it truly is 'our kind's' kingdom, maybe it gives us a reason to slip away unnoticed. But now we have to find a way back up. But if they did that all those years ago, then I'm sure we can as well.

Maybe if I shut my eyes, let go of my wings, and allow myself to fall forever, I could be at peace with it. Because if this is what death feels like, I will happily welcome it with open arms.

I look down below, the landscape creeping up to meet us, thankful for once that Vincent is playing with his fire like usual, beside a shaking Draven and a fascinated Thena.

"Jack, my wings. I can't hold on much longer—" Violet cries, suddenly dropping, hanging onto my arm. We plummet into the tower with black and cracked stone at an alarming speed. Her wings have disappeared into mere specks of dust, and I do the same with mine because I can't keep both of us afloat. She doesn't use her wings often enough to be strong with them, which means she was struggling long before she said out loud.

I shriek, my chest dropping forward onto the floor of the tower. Violet still falls. "Jack!" she screams, echoing all around us. My heart leaps forward. I peer over the edge of the town to find Violet hanging there, holding her weapon in one hand and mine in the other. Fear plasters across her eyes, and she starts breathing incredibly heavily. I hold onto her arm with my free one hand.

"Vincent! I need light!" I yell and to my surprise, he hurries over and lights up our surroundings so I can just about make out the drop below. "I've got you, Violet." I begin to slowly lift her up, and she hangs on even tighter. Tears glisten on her cheeks, hanging helplessly, glancing down. "Eyes on me!" I exclaim, and she does so, flicking her hair out the way to stare at me with wide and bulging eyes.

I'm struggling. I'm not strong as it is, this is testing my limits. But I don't let go. I keep lifting, until two hands either side of me grab her arms, Ambrosia to my left and Draven to my right.

"Come on!" he mutters.

"We got you, hun!" she exclaims.

"Pull!" I yell, and we all heave her onto the tower's stone floor. She swings her legs over, crawling onto me, dropping her bow on the floor, wrapping her arms around me as quickly as she can. I hold her, sighing out of relief. Too close, that was *too close.*

"Thank you," she whispers, breathlessly as she leans back, looking at Ambrosia and Draven first. "Thank you." And then finally, she stares at Vincent, who's grinning with his light below his chin. "And you." He shrugs his shoulders. All he did was light it up, but it came in handy and helped our vision. He stares at me, and I nod in my gratitude.

"Yeah, thanks," I mutter, as I hold Violet's hands. We stare at each other and I give her a reassuring smile. "You're okay." She nods, sighing again, sitting back, nodding repeatedly.

"That was sort of terrifying," she mutters.

"Are you done yet?" Jade questions from behind us.

"Give them a moment, babes," Ambrosia defends us and I smile at that.

"We don't have time," Thena exclaims and I can practically hear her eyes roll. "Hurry up and let's go." I look back to watch Thena walk away with Jade trailing behind her. Thena laughs to herself, walking through an archway, lighting the way with an electrical torch, and Jade grins wickedly. And eagerly. Hungrily.

Ambrosia huffs, and turns to find Achillea looking at the city we've tumbled into. Violet stands, turns and watches too, and I quickly follow suit with Draven and Vincent. All of us standing in a line, looking out at the broken wreck of what *should* be a magnificent city.

Achillea begins to sob as silently as she can. Now that our eyes are adjusted to the darkness, outlines of broken towers, churches, buildings are everywhere. As if it's been attacked. I exhale sharply into the chilly air. It's real. *The lost city is real.*

But it's ruined.

I look over at Ambrosia gripping both Achillea and Draven's hands, holding her breath as a few tears roll down her cheeks. Vincent's grimacing, shaking his head a few times.

"Did *I* do this?" he mutters under his breath, cutting out his fire completely.

"No. It looks like it's been destroyed. Not just from fire," Draven cuts through. But his brother says nothing. *How are we meant to navigate this place now? Where are we going? And how far are we from the surface?* I gulp down a sudden gag of nausea as Violet stares at me.

"Are you okay?" I nod again, ignoring the pitch black to my vision.

"I don't...like the darkness," I murmur. She smiles softly, only slightly visible, taking my hand.

"Simple solution. Hold onto me."

"Okay, maybe it's not the darkness. It's whatever might be hiding in it. It's unfamiliar. And I hate it."

"You? Scared? About the monsters from kids' stories?" I smirk at her, rolling my eyes.

"Aren't *we* those monsters?"

"I guess." She soon laughs.

"I just want to keep you safe."

"It's gonna be fine. At the end of the day, as long as I'm here with you, there's nowhere else I'd rather be." My cheeks flush, as I lean towards her, kissing her lips.

"Since when did you become so sappy?"

"Don't get used to it." She pushes into me, and the cousins are already walking away. But Vincent and Draven simply stand side by side a few paces away from us.

"For what it's worth, I'm sorry. For how I treated you," Draven tells him, and to that, Vincent suddenly stares at him.

"Oh, yeah?" Draven looks at him and nods.

"Yes, I am."

"Huh." Vincent's gaze wanders.

"Surprised?"

"Never thought I'd hear you apologise for something that happened centuries ago."

"And I thought you've been holding it as a grudge ever since."

"Maybe I have, maybe I haven't." Vincent shrugs his shoulders and turns away, mind elsewhere.

"I thought you wanted my apology—"

"I never needed an apology, Draven! I overreacted – I can't believe we're talking about this now." He shakes his head and then faces his brother head on, locking onto his eyes, and he smiles sadly. "I needed a big brother. Not distance. And I thought you would pick up on that, since you claimed to know me so well. I..." he takes a breath, looks out into the darkness and releases the tension in his shoulders. "I needed you." And with that, he walks away, leaving Draven with wide eyes. He flicks them to me, in complete disbelief.

"I—" He's speechless. "I tried." It's like he's trying to reassure *me*.

Maybe because he had a chance to *be* a big brother, when I lost mine.

"You better go tell him that," I say. He runs after him. "We better catch up."

"What was that all about?" Violet asks. "Vincent and Draven are *brothers?*"

"I don't think they felt like hiding it anymore, I guess."

"Did you know?"

"Yes, but Draven made me promise I wouldn't tell anyone."

"Makes sense." She drops her shoulders, then tugs me towards the tower doors. "Come on. We better go before they leave us."

For some reason, everyone is heading up the spiral stairs instead of deeper into the castle.

"They built more," Ambrosia mutters to herself. "I remember when this was the tallest tower."

"They must have built more for protection," Achillea tells her.

"Why are we going up here? Shouldn't we be going the other way?" Thena exclaims impatiently. "I thought we were going to start setting up this mess of a place!" Achillea turns around and burns her eyes directly through her skull.

"We're doing things my way, and I say we go up for better light and to look out on *my* city."

"What light? Are you seeing things?"

"Shut your mouth, Thena. You don't want to see Achillea angry." Ambrosia rolls her eyes and they start walking up once more. But I've seen her angry before, and it's not as terrifying as she makes it out to be. I frown, holding onto Violet tighter.

"Oh? I would *love* to see you angry," Jade comments. Achillea glances back once again, but this time, she's smiling and raising an eye at her in a flirtatious manner.

I hope she hasn't fallen for a mere Jade jewel.

We make it up to the top of the tower, and Vincent keeps his lighter on again, everyone gathering around for both the small amount of heating emitting from it, and the light source when suddenly Achillea covers it with her hand and grins.

"We won't be needing that." She moves her hand up and flips it over, she stretches out her fingers to reveal a bright gleaming light emitting directly from her palm. *Her skin is alight.* It brightens up everyones shocked and surprised expressions whilst Achillea merely smiles.

"Oh my god—" I mutter under my breath.

"How long have you been able to do this?!" Violet exclaims, jaw dropped.

"I manipulated my abilities. The amount of starlight I've absorbed over the years, I assume, has made an impact on me. I trained in private." Achillea flashes her eyes at us. "You don't even know half of who I am."

"Mysterious as ever," Ambrosia comments, whilst Draven and Vincent remain silent, staring at each other from opposite ends. I'm still staring and mesmerised by the light coming directly from Achillea's fingertips.

"I'm sorry, we're not gonna address the elephant in the room?" Violet scoffs, holding on tighter. "Vampires have *fucking powers? That aren't wings and all the other shit we've heard of?*"

"No one told you?" Draven asks, as shocked as our tone. I shake my head.

"No, no one ever mentioned anything about it." He looks to Vincent next, opens his mouth to comment, but instead clamps his jaw shut, not risking a word.

"I suppose as clan leader, he should have been responsible," Ambrosia tells us. "But never mind, only specific and more mature vampires can wield 'magic' or 'powers' as you call it. I guess you're more humane than I had thought—"

"What's that supposed to mean?" I shoot at her. She stares at me and laughs.

"I meant nothing by it, babes. I forget you were humans once upon a time." I grit my teeth together. "Humans *always* refer to this kinda stuff as powers and magic and so forth." She flicks her wrist in dismissal.

"What are we meant to call it?"

"Abilities. It isn't magic, it's what's in our veins. We harness and control it," Achillea insists. It's still magical in my mind. And no one can change that.

"Whatever you wanna call it, it's something you've kept from us and—"

"We never kept it from you," Achillea informs Violet. "And we never had that intention. But only specific people can wield it. If you were not informed it was because no one thought you could handle it."

"But you don't know that." I take a step forward. "Either it truly did slip your mind, or you didn't want us knowing." I glare at Vincent who remains silent.

"Leave it, and let's get on with this," Jade announces, and turns to Achillea to beg. "Please?" When I flick my eyes to hers, emeralds gleaming, I take a mental note of what Savannah warned me. They couldn't be here for the greater good. Or whatever that might be. They must be here for something else. Unless they seemed suspicious because they were working with Achillea and Ambrosia to begin with.

There's too many possibilities. My head's spinning.

Jade and Achillea share a moment of silence, smiling at the other kindly, and whilst Achillea shows off her two dimples, Jade has none against her pale skin.

"Of course." Ambrosia glances at me, wiggling her eyebrows, as she nods towards the two. I cock my head to one side in confusion, and she simply smirks, and nods over and over again. "Let me show you why I *actually* came up here," Achillea continues, and walks past us to the edge of the tower's fencing. Violet and I swiftly follow. Once again, we're all staring out at the city the Royals and Nobles grew up in. Six of us, side by side.

Now that I'm here, staring out at the city they fought so hard to return to, I'm almost overwhelmed, considering this is exactly what I had expected. I imagined a place with magnificent stone, majestic buildings, and mesmerising people. I pictured the beauty this species could ignite to the rest of the world. I know not all of us are horrible things, but the ones I've met, most are monsters. But again, I've met many humans who are the same. Horrible, rude, despicable. Capable of monstrous things. But humans can be beautiful, forgiving creatures too. I must believe there's hope for vampires.

In my mind, they were always meant to be different. Perhaps I had enough of watching humans despise anyone who even *looked* different. I watched vampires be kicked to the floor and beaten if they were seen sneaking around. Even killed. Because they were *monsters*. But the problem here was that not all those vampires *were* monsters. Some never deserved any of it. If it were Vincent, perhaps I would think differently. Or if it were the people in my clan, or anyone close by, I'd think the same as well, but when it was just simple citizens who were just hiding because they were scared—

It breaks you when you see it in front of your own eyes. Especially when the victims are the ones who never deserved it.

So when I call the people around me monsters, I'm not referring to everyone in the world. I'm not referring to *just* vampires, and I'm not referring to *just* humans either. I'm referring to the people out there who are simply horrible. Who are horrible to others, who attack people, who hurt creatures for no real goddamn reason.

Achillea holds her hands out, and the light from her palm drifts outwards, and rises above the forgotten city. She clenches her hands into fists, before stretching them out with a flick of her wrist. The speck of light shatters into billions of stars, falling all over the city with one final bright star in the centre and highest point of the city.

But it is in ruins.

Everything is in ruins.

The buildings have crumbled to the ground, and all the lamp posts are broken, the pavement cracked and shattered, and it's a heartbreaking sight. What should be a glorious and beautiful city is in ruins.

Yet somehow, it's still breathtaking now, even without everything being perfect. There's beauty in ruins. Beauty in imperfection. Beauty in broken beings.

I look over to Achillea, who's even more distraught than before. Eyes wide, cheeks flushed, jaw ajar.

"Why... What happened?" she questions. "Who would do such a thing? How did anyone get down here? I don't understand—"

"Darling—"

"It doesn't make any sense!" Achillea exclaims, clenching her hands tightly, light emitting from everywhere all of a sudden. "How could I let this happen?" The ground shakes and I hold onto Violet's hands, steadying her.

"Achillea!" Jade speaks, laying her hands upon the Royal's shoulders. "I know a way to restore it." Achillea snaps her head back, eyes flickering between Jade's.

"How?"

"First, we need to make our way to the centre of the city, I will show you everything." *Why can't she tell us now?* I keep my grip tight around Violet when we're ushered back down the stairs, where Draven catches up to Vincent immediately and desperately.

"Vincent, listen to me! I always thought you never wanted me around, so I kept my distance!" he rushes through his words as the others already begin to walk away. Vincent's dismissing his brother with a single shake of his shoulder. "Vincent, please!" He stops, looks back and over his shoulder, and stares. Not menacingly, not grimly, not passionately.

He simply watches Draven begin to cry.

"Give me another chance," he begs through tear stained cheeks. "Please, I'll do anything—" Vincent suddenly cackles into the air.

"You can't do anything to rectify not being there anyway. There's no point."

"But I never knew you wanted me there! With the way you treated me, I always believed you hated me—"

"And for a short while I did! I hated your guts for years!" Silence falls onto their shoulders, as Draven follows Vincent down the spiral staircase once again.

"Then what changed?"

"I let go of a grudge, because it's meaningless and draining, Draven. Do we really have to talk now? It's exhausting walking downstairs whilst arguing—"

"Promise me we'll talk later."

"Really?" Vincent stops, and looks back up with raised eyebrows at him, but a brief and faint smile flickers across his lips. "A promise?"

"Pinky promise me? You always loved those." For a moment, I believe Vincent will just walk off, and leave it. But then he looks away and raises his hand, his pinky finger lifting and pointing at Draven. The older brother hooks his pinky finger around his younger brothers, solidifying the promise to talk again soon.

We make our way through the ruins of this beautiful city. Achillea and Ambrosia lead, hand in hand, smiling at fond memories.

"That's the library we spent all of our time in. That's the building we slept on looking up at the cave. This is—" They stop at one particular building, and Ambrosia chuckles half-heartedly.

"It's even more ruined than before," she whispers, whilst Achillea simply nods.

"It was hard to believe it could get any worse," she smirks. "I hope Jade can save it." A sudden jolt of guilt and pity spreads through my veins for them. I understand how desperate Achillea was to get her home back. Now that we're here, I feel terrible for never truly believing her.

All she wanted was her home back. I can't ignore that she went about it in the wrong way, creating an army all for this city. But again, if I had a plan, I would follow through no matter what.

She wanted her home back. Her childhood. Her innocence.

She never wanted to see her home become this. But it was simply never in her control. She's trying to keep it together as she stares at her childhood home. She notices I'm staring and turns her head to look at me.

"I'm sorry," I utter the words uncontrollably, and she smiles mournfully towards me, which is the first time she smiled at me all together. And at a time like this, I'm not sure I would have the strength if the roles were reversed.

Draven takes a step forward, wrapping an arm around her into a side hug, her head on his shoulder. He welcomes her into his embrace for a source of comfort, safety and familiarity. She digs her head into his clothes to hide, clinging onto him for dear life. And even when I shift my gaze to Vincent, he's looking solemn instead of his usual manic self. He's frowning, Vincent is frowning. And whether that be because of Draven or this city, I won't know.

Meanwhile, Selene and Thena begin walking down the street, showing no remorse whatsoever for anyone here. Violet holds my hand, and I look to where her eyes are leading – a building with what looks to be a bomb just sitting in the middle of an open roof. Through the windows, I see rubble lain across it, and it's huge. The size of its living room, and as tall as the first floor. Nothing has triggered it, and I hope no one has a burst of impulsiveness to touch it. For once, I don't think Vincent will be that person today.

"So it was attacked," she says beside me.

"Seems so."

"Who could make it down here, and how did they fit such big bombs in here?"

"I don't know." She looks up at me.

"If even *we* didn't believe this was down here, how did humans know?"

"Who said it was humans?" She widen her eyes.

"Who else would ruin this place? Clearly it's made for vampires, Jack, I don't get—" I grip her tighter.

"We don't know all vampires, love." She purses her lips together.

"I guess," she murmurs.

We start walking as a pack again, quickening our speed. The lamp posts surrounding have mythical creatures embedded in the metal, and the fountain is crumbling in the middle of this place. And the star Achillea created is above our heads, serving as our sun. Jade and Thena speak under their breaths, Thena nodding and makes her way around us and she smiles.

A forced smile. A fake smile. Something's not right.

Thena and Jade are behind and in front of us. They're cornering us. They're trapping us. Jade has a sword and Thena has her knives in her hands.

I hold Violet's hands tighter and closer to me. She looks, and slowly takes an arrow out of her pack, and grips it.

"Here should be fine." Jade looks up at the star, and then watches Achillea close as she steps forward and in front of her.

"How could I be of use?" she says. "I'll do anything. As long as it's to restore what was lost." She moves forward, and Jade raises one of her eyebrows.

"Anything?"

"Anything."

"Do you trust me?" Jade's wide eyes burn with determination and then she grins wickedly.

"Of course—" Her sword turns blood red. She steps forward. Past Achillea, and twists her body round to dig the weapon, swiftly into Achillea's neck.

Both she and Ambrosia *try to* shriek. Achillea doesn't have the voice to do so.

"Achillea!" Her cousin screams and leaps forward, but Draven quickly holds her because they don't have weapons, and Jade is flashing her eyes at them to hold back. "No, no, no, you monster! Draven, let me go—" Jade leans closer to Achillea's ear.

"Will you embrace death with open arms?" she whispers.

She groans, exhales, and falls to her knees, as Violet clings onto my arm, shock plastered on her face, same as I.

Achillea can't even talk. Instead, she chokes, struggling to breathe, bringing her hand up to grip the handle, around Jade's pale and cold hand.

"You think you're some big hero for getting your city back?" Jade makes direct eye contact with her, as Lea begins to weep, pulling the blade free from her neck. "You ruined my life. You turned me into one of *you*. And I'd be stupid not to take advantage of it." She extracts her sword, letting Achillea go, as her cousin screams, deafening us all. "You brought this on yourself. I'm Selene Jade. The new Queen to your little vampire army. And in order for this city to regain its former glory, you need to say goodbye to your world." And with those words lingering in the area, Selene Jade digs her blood sword through Achilleas chest, directly through her heart – the only way to kill a vampire. "Your home is no more."

A weapon of your choice, directly through the heart.

$\mathscr{S}$avannah

24th November

Knocking brings me out of my trance early morning. I'm sitting on the floor, back against the sofa, with Luka behind me, his hand in my hair. Oskar and Zack are sitting beside him, and we haven't even been awake for longer than 10 minutes, before a loud knock on the door jolts us out of place. I lunge for my knives on the coffee table, and I watch Zack stand first. And then Oskar. Then myself, and I pull Luka up too.

"Who would be knocking this early?" Luka mutters.

"And who would be knocking on supposedly Jack's door?" Oskar asks more importantly, but I merely shrug my shoulders, because the one person I *want* it to be probably won't be anywhere near us right now. But with Jack and Violet gone, it'll be someone dangerous. Someone poking their noses into other people's business.

"Only one way to find out—"

"It's me. It's Jess." My heart skips several beats. Zack stops walking towards the door, brows flinging up. Frozen. In. Time. "I-I'm not armed, or whatever, I mean I've got this sword, but only because I'm here to protect you, and I'm sorry." Oskar rushes past Zack, breathing heavily, almost stumbling over his own feet. "God, I hope I'm not talking to just a door. I'm sorry for everything—" He whips the door open, bearing the biggest smile I've seen in a long time. The door's wide, and before Jess has a moment to process anything, he's pulled into the living room, arms wrapped around his smaller frame. Oskar holds him as tightly, and as close to his body as he possibly can. *Never let him go.* Zack moves forward, quickly closing the door, as the two conjoined friends start rocking back and forth together in a mess of blurred tears.

Jess came back.

He buries his face into Oskar's clothes, gripping his jacket with shaking, trembling hands. Silently, he breaks down into a round of tears, his shoulders shudder. Oskar presses his cheek against Jess' head, holding his hair, holding him close, holding, holding, holding. They bask in each other's warmth, and for a few moments, I believe *they're never going to let go.*

The worry, the anxiety and the fear they felt for each other must've been like no other. Because when you love someone and you assume they're dead, and when you assume you cannot do anything to prevent it, must be the worst feeling in the world. That you're powerless to something so big and life threatening. But right now, they're reunited under these horrible circumstances.

But nevertheless, they're reunited. And I don't believe there's anything that can get between them again. They'll protect each other. With their lives. With all they've got.

Just Jess and Oskar.

Simply Oskar and Jess.

"How've you been?" Oskar mutters breathlessly, leaning away from him to grip onto Jess' arms instead, staring into each other's eyes and drinking it all in.

"Could be better." He nods, also in complete shock. "And you?"

"Could be a *lot* better." And then they're smiling ever so slightly again.

"I've missed you," Jess breaks down into another round of tears, shaking his head from side to side. "I've missed you all so much."

"I've missed you too," Oskar comments, chuckling a little, sweeping some of Jess' fringe away from his brows. "You have no idea."

"Don't hog him!" Zack makes his way to them, throwing his arms around Jess' shoulder, squeezing just as tightly from behind, smiling just as widely as Oskar.

"Don't leave us out of it!" Luka exclaims, and whilst holding my hand, he hurries over and swings his arms around, and I do the same, trapping Jess in the middle of a close group hug. A suffocating one at that, but one we all need at a time like this. With Luka and I on either side, and Jess in a sobbing mess, holding onto Zack's and Oskar's hands. I lean my head on his shoulder, laughing silently, a few tears of my own sliding down my cheeks.

"So, Jess, how's life treating ya? Nicely, I assume?" Zack suddenly asks and he starts chuckling, dryly.

"Very kind, as you can tell. Everything's going perfectly." My heart aches for him, because the sudden hurt in his broken voice is known to not only me in his room, but to all of his friends. I'm not the only one who can see.

"You're safe with us now," I say, and he turns his head to stare at me, with wide, bulging eyes. Perhaps even ones that show innocence buried deep within, exposed by those around him.

"I'm meant to be the one telling you that."

"We'll protect each other," Luka comments, trying not to let his voice shake too, glancing between us all. "And stick together now that we're all in the same place."

"I *never* want to be alone again," Jess says softly, shaking his head from side to side. "I thought you'd all hate me." He lets go of Zack and Oskar's hands, burying his face into his palms instead, itching his forehead. "I thought—"

"Hey, Jess." Oskar breaks through his thoughts, holding onto his wrists, lowering them so Jess can peer into his bright brown eyes over his hands. "We would never hate you. We've missed you so much. You're—" He takes a silent breath, refusing to cry again. "You're all I've thought about." Jess breaks into another brief smile, before breaking down once again.

"I'm sorry I couldn't save him," he whispers and Oskar immediately steps forward and hugs him again, around his shoulders and squeezing him as he sobs onto his shoulder. "I tried."

"It's not your fault," Zack murmurs softly. "We'll be okay." I purse my lips together, staring at Luka who stares right back at me.

"We'll be okay," he repeats. So as Jess sobs, we hold him close. And for the first time since we returned, I could call it a home, because the only family I have left are all in this house, in these walls, and under this roof. But I smile because Jess is with us again, and for that, I am grateful.

"I love you all more than words could ever tell," I say, and I know Matthew's watching.

My bedroom door opens suddenly to reveal Jess walking in. He nods in my direction, gives me a weak smile, and closes the door behind him, wandering towards me to climb onto my bed, and bobbing along to the melody of a song I've forgotten the name of.

"Everything okay?" I ask before he can.

"Mhmm," he hums. "It's odd to be around you all again. That's all." I catch him looking down at his hands, then lifting them to his lips. I've seen him do that a few times already. Like he's still getting used to 'what' he is.

"How's Oskar?" I change the subject. I smirk as his cheeks burn a bright red.

"He keeps staring at me as if he's making sure I'm still here." He shifts his gaze from his fiddling hands, and onto my eyes. "I can barely believe you're all okay with me being here. Jack visited me to let me know he's leaving for a little while and you'd all be on your own."

"Oh."

"And he told me you didn't hate me. I was scared to show my face." I frown as he looks away again. "But he said you were all missing me, and you were all waiting."

"I've missed you a heck of a lot, and that wasn't gonna change any time soon. Ask the others, I'm sure they'd agree." A smile lingers on his lips a moment more, perking up.

"So, do tell. What's with you and Luka?" I blush a bright red with wide eyes. "You two seem to have something going on now." Butterflies form in my stomach, as a grin creeps onto my face. "Wait, are you guys a thing now?"

"Perhaps," I chuckle. "I mean yeah, yeah we are now, I—"

"Oh my god!" he shrieks and grabs my hands excitedly. "You've liked him for forever and now you're finally doing something!"

"I could say the same with you and Oskar." He purses his lips together, hiding a smirk from me.

"No, we're different."

"How?"

"For one thing, even before this, I had less than accepting parents—"

"You could have hid it with ease like everything else you hid from them."

"I'm not even sure I had the time for a relationship!" I start laughing.

"Literally the oldest excuse in the book!" He shakes his head, clearly amused.

"Okay, well then, I'll ask you this. Can I really..." he lowers his voice, "risk it?" I tilt my head to one side.

"What do you mean?" He meets my eyes again and his expression softens.

"If *they* ever found out about us, then they'd use him against me or something! I'm not sure, I just know it's better this way. To protect him."

"Firstly, Oskar can protect himself, and secondly, don't you deserve this?" He raises his eyebrows and holds his breath.

"I want it," he sighs and releases the tension in his shoulders. "I really do. Every night here I've been thinking of how to do things differently, but it's too dangerous. I can't believe you came here to begin with and—"

"Doesn't us being here just prove how determined we are in being with you? How worth it you are?" He looks away from me. "How *he* wants to be with you no matter what?"

"No, no, that can't be it—" The door bursts open and we watch Oskar tumble in. Speaking of the devil.

"Sorry to interrupt, but I just thought of something." Jess glances at me with saddened eyes, as he swings his legs over to dangle down the ladder of my cabin bed, staring at Oskar.

"What is it?" I take a mental note of how intensely they stare at each other as soon as their eyes meet, with such care and concern. I don't quite know how they don't realise the other is so in love with them.

But the way they gaze at each other is like no other. I hope one day they're able to defy all odds and just take the jump. They deserve to find happiness, safety and comfort in each other. More than they realise – maybe one day they can see that too.

"Your cream!" Jess' cheeks blush bright red, looking at his dry skin. Even he'd forgotten about it. "Do you have it?"

"Erm." He covers his inner elbow with his palm and then looks up to Oskar who's edging closer to us. "No, no I don't. I didn't think about that before I came here."

"And I don't have any here either," I mutter when Oskar glances at me. "Sorry."

"It's okay. Did you get the special stuff from your house at the very least while you were staying at mine?"

"How did you know?" Jess perks up a bit, shifting uncomfortably as if his cover was blown.

"Jack told me," he speaks simply. "Jess, we gotta go back to get some!"

"No, no, no it's far too dangerous for you to go and I need you to stay here where it's safe."

"Jess." Oskar walks over and stands in front of him, and looks up into his eyes with a different level of sincerity I didn't know existed. "Either you're going, or I am." Jess clamps his mouth shut, furrowing his brow, and he half frowns and half glares at him. "Okay? So what's it gonna be?"

"Oskar, please don't make me leave again."

"I'm not saying it has to be you."

"I'd rather it be me than you."

"You need to take care of your skin."

"I'm sick of using steroids—"

"Okay, then where's your usual creams then? Lotions? Oils?" Oskar crosses his arms over his chest, watching Jess intently.

"I've almost run out," Jess heaves through a singular breath. "Look, I'll go when I have to, right now I'm okay."

"Don't make it sound like a chore, Jess. I'm only looking out for you, and I'm not gonna feel bad about it." Jess only nods in response.

"I'll go when I can and feel ready to." Ready to leave us alone? Just for half an hour or so doesn't seem that big but I suppose a lot can happen in thirty minutes.

"You okay?" Again, only a simple nod answers him. Jess begins to shift towards the end of the ladder and without looking where he's going, his foot slips from one of the wooden ladder pieces. He gasps suddenly, but regains himself while he's absorbed by his own mind. Jess props himself back onto the edge of the bed, breathing heavily. I watch as Oskar frowns, and curves his brow in concern. And then he suddenly smirks, pushes up and onto his tiptoes, wrapping his arms around Jess' waist who's still perched on the bed itself.

"Oskar, what—" He jumps back, carrying Jess off from the ladder, spins him 180-degrees and plants him on the floor.

"I'm not trying to be the bad guy here, but we can fend for ourselves as well. We've lasted this long for a reason and not by sheer luck, although it feels like it sometimes." Jess can't mask the smile creeping onto his lips.

"I'm sorry."

"Don't sweat it. But when you go, be quick, or else I'll come looking for you, alright?" He grins. And I watch him physically hesitate to do this, but in the end, he brushes some of Jess' hair back and behind his ear so he can better see his eyes. "And that, sir, is a threat."

Savannah

25th November

Jess and Oskar spend all of their time together. They're inseparable. And they need each other now more than ever.

Still no Jack, though.

"It's a beautiful night," Luka murmurs, staring at the night sky out my bedroom window.

"Yeah," I reply, following his eyes out to the faint stars above. "Clear," I comment. "It's been a while since I just looked up and saw the stars." He turns to look at me.

"Yeah?"

"Is that such a shock?"

"A little. You loved the stars."

"I still do."

"Is that so?" He smiles, leaning forward and he opens the windows wide, and looks down at the roof of the room below. The tiles are relatively flat for the most part, a little slanted the closer to the edge you are, but I've gone out to simply sit and think *so* many times. It wasn't when we're meant to be keeping it low, avoiding being spotted by anyone outside of this house currently. Luka looks back at me, then at the pile of blankets beside my desk.

He walks past, grabs them, turns the light off and lays the covers on the window sill.

And then a moment later, he's holding out a hand, offering it to me.

"Shall we?"

"It's freezing."

"Hence the blankets." He looks back at a few hoodies on my chest of draws. He leans back, pulls out two and passes a pastel purple one to me with a white stripe through the middle. "Please can I borrow one?" He flicks his hair out of his face, as I nod, smiling widely, wearing the one he passed me whilst he finds a plain baby blue shade. "Comfy."

"I only have the best hoodies, Luka," he chuckles at me.

"If you're ever missing this one, you'll know where to look."

"I'll make an exception." He smiles again, and offers his hand out like before.

"Thank you kindly." I lay my hand in his, and he wraps his fingers around my skin, a flood of warmth setting in. "Now, shall we stargaze?" I nod, and return his smile.

"Sounds like a wonderful idea."

"Then let's." He climbs onto the window sill, still holding my hand in his, as he steps over and jumps onto the tiles of the roof, our arms conjoined through the window gap.

Luka lays the blankets out on the roof for us, the moonlight floods my room. I may be worried about the vampires, but I can't let worry keep me from living. We step onto our blankets and take our seats, the cold air freezing my fingertips immediately. He lays down first whilst I watch the stars sparkle in his ocean eyes for a moment more.

He extends an arm out on the blanket. I lay my head down on his arm as he crosses his other arm over his body to hold my hand. He squeezes, his breath on my forehead as he rests his chin against my hair.

I smile briefly and turn my head to gaze up at the galaxy above.

The stars glow in the darkness, lighting up the sky above in a beautiful and breathtaking way. Because of obvious situations, I've forgotten a lot *about* myself. And the simplest things catch me by surprise. I've forgotten to admire the little things.

I forgot how less alone I feel with them. How tiny I am in comparison. To me, being such a small person who always fit in with the background, was the most comforting, calming and peaceful feeling I could ever experience. One of them anyway. I hadn't thought experiencing that *with* someone else would make such a big difference, but as I hold Luka's hand closer to me, I realise I was wrong about a lot of things. I was close minded, and maybe I am now. I have a long way to go.

I watch the brightest star burn, noticing a second one beside it and I smile sadly, as if they can see. *I think they're watching us.*

I release a stifled breath from my chest, "I miss you," I whisper to the two lone stars. *I love you more than words could tell.* Luka squeezes my hand.

"The moon is so pretty," he says, reverting my eyes onto the full moon above.

"It's beautiful." As I used to before, I begin to count as many stars as I can. 10, 27, 49, 52, 63... I lose count numerous times, before a separate question flings to mind. "Do you think they're watching?" I ask.

"Of course. What else do you think they'd be doing?" Silence settles around us but I know there's something in his mind. I twitch, and he takes a deeper breath. "How long do you think we all have?" I flip my head up to stare at him with wide eyes, as tingles spread all over my skin. He looks down at me and grimaces. "Sorry, that wasn't meant to sound as dark as it did." Before I'm able to form words, I lift my free hand to grip his, the one beside my head.

"Luka." But I'm left in slight shock and almost speechless. "We fight for another day, that's all we need to focus on."

"And if that's not enough?"

"Then future us can deal with it."

"And when future us becomes our present selves?"

"Then they can promise you one thing, we're not giving up. On anything. On each other." His eyes grow sympathetic, as if pitying me. "I mean it," I say desperately. "I'll fight for you. For me. For a better place for everyone."

"It's not certain that we'll make it, that's all. I was thinking...about seeing them." His forehead creases and his brows knit together.

"But the promise to fight *is* certain," my voice shakes. "I promise, I'll do my best and I'll protect you."

"And we'll be together?"

"Side by side." He smiles more, leaning his head down to lay a kiss on my lips. Sudden, but soft. Passionate, but slow. He lets my left hand go, lifting it to cup one half of my face, smoothing his fingers over my skin as I grip onto his sleeve.

"Thank you," he whispers in a low voice, barely a centimetre away. I flick my eyes from one of his to the other, seeing the stars shine in them, and I simply smile before pressing my lips to his again and shutting my eyes. My heart beats faster, my cheeks burn crimson, and my body is restless. He sits up, curving his arm so I move with him. He lightly pushes onto me with such care and gentleness it melts away anxiety. It's a kiss after another after another.

In this moment I'm his and he's mine and that's all that matters.

He leans over me, and I peek my eyes open a little to see the stars overhead. I let his clothes go, letting his other hand go to wrap my arms around his neck, bringing him closer to me. He lays one hand on the back of my head, nestling his fingers through my hair, and his other stays on my cheek, caressing me like a prized jewel.

He breaks away for a gulp of air, and we stare at each other, breathing a little heavier than I had anticipated. He smiles down at me.

"You have such gorgeous eyes," I say. Momentarily, shock engulfs his face.

"My eyes?"

"Like oceans."

"I think you've mentioned that before."

"They're so pretty. It's the first thing I noticed about you. I've never seen such deep blue eyes. So piercing."

"I used to hate them." Before I can object, he presses his lips to mine again. "*Used to.*"

I grin into his following kisses, with my heart hammering in my chest, I beg he doesn't hear it's a ticking time bomb. He lowers himself, and rests his head on my shoulder, half of his body on mine and the other on the blanket beside us. One of his legs over one of mine, and he interlocks one of our hands together, and the other he rests on the crook of my neck, sighing heavily, he closes his eyes, and takes deep breaths.

I gaze down at him and smile, collapsing my head onto the roof, my free hand running through his hair to calm his thoughts, like he's done to me so many times before.

"I'm scared," he murmurs quietly.

"And I'd be more worried if you weren't scared," I comment.

"Good point," he scoffs. "I'll protect you." My cheeks burn brighter. And shakes me to my core. My heart does a little jolt and my voice appears breathless when I say back,

"I'll protect you too." He squeezes my hand, and nuzzles his head into my clothes.

"We should do this more often."

"Yeah, that sounds like a good idea." I smirk, gazing at the small world around us, and the huge galaxy above. I hold him closer, praying he feels safe in my arms.

"I think we'll be okay," he whispers, more to himself than to me, but still I smile.

I'll make sure of it.

Savannah

26th November

"Crap," Jess curses under his breath, drawing the curtains together.

"What is it?" Oskar asks first, springing up from the sofa.

"A group of Nobles are headed towards the mansion where my sister is held."

"Surely they wouldn't do anything to hurt them. Not without the leaders here," Luka suggests helplessly, leaning forward on the cushions, eyes wide with desperation.

"Or it gives them the perfect opportunity to strike. Whilst they're out watching over people like a hawk, they could do what they like, what they please. Which means they could potentially be in danger!" he explains and then rushes to the front door and unlocks it.

"Jess, what are you doing—" Zack interrupts, lunging after him, but then Jess pierces his eyes through him whilst grabbing his sword lying against the wall.

"Stay here and stay quiet," he insists, before flying the door open and walking out to greet the Nobles. He shuts it after him, but Zack still walks towards it, and peers outside the peep hole. I notice Oskar biting his lip, shifting restlessly around the room.

"Oskar, he'll be okay," I say in a hushed voice. His eyes bore into my skull.

"It's still dangerous."

"Anything we do is considered dangerous right now. I've seen the way they treat Jess, and I know he'll be okay." He shakes his head back onto Zack, who's seemingly just as anxious, tapping his fingers lightly on his legs.

"They're talking," he announces to us quietly. "Looks civil."

"*Looks* civil and *is* civil are different," Luka murmurs.

"I know, but my point is, they're not attacking him, and he's not attacking them." There's a pause in suffocating silence. "They do seem to be talking down to him."

"But he's safe?" Oskar asks.

"I think?"

I look up to Luka in the armchair beside the sofa, and I lean forward, finding his hand to hold. It calms his bouncing leg as his eyes meet mine instantly.

The door flies open, and we watch Zack backing away and into Oskar as Jess steps in, closing it after him, leaning on the wood with a heaving chest. He flicks his eyes up to see us.

"I bought time," he mutters breathlessly. Oskar steps past a shocked Zack, a brief hand on his shoulder before approaching Jess. "I *almost* caught Zayne's eye—"

"Did they find us?" Zack questions, whilst Luka's legs bounce even quicker and even more uncontrollably. He squeezes my hand tighter, and I glance at his glazed over eyes staring at the carpet.

"No." He stares at Jess with wide eyes and I do too. "They don't suspect a thing. I left before Zayne could see." I don't even know if they're aware of who Zayne is, but if they do, they ignore it completely.

"Then what do you mean time?" Oskar asks urgently.

"I bought the *prisoners* more time. I lied, and said that orders by Vincent and Jack are that I'm checking the mansion instead of them."

"Oh," Zack murmurs.

"I'll go alone, of course—"

"No," Oskar insists, looking at Jess still beside the door.

"Oskar, remember who's hiding here and who's—"

"It's not safe."

"I'm 'one of them'." Oskar purses his lips together, surely he notices the way Jess' voice cracked, rising in anger.

"I'd feel more comfortable knowing you're with one of us."

"More numbers could complicate things."

"We could save your skin – if people are in the mansion who don't believe your orders then you need an alibi." The vampires *do* seem less likely to believe a newbie in their ranks. The fact that a few Nobles believed him just now was a long shot, but maybe they just wanted to get out of a job. Jess' eyes drop to the floor in calculation.

"If I go in with a human, they'll expect them to stay. There's people in the mansion anyway, and they might not take kindly to my abrupt demand of prisoner searching."

"There are people there?" I ask. He nods.

"Apparently there's a clan staying there. So they'll be guards outside, they'll be a Royal living there, and several Nobles. I have to go through an office in order to get under into the cave—" He rubs the bridge of his nose. "What have I done?"

"What if," Zack begins. "You bring—"

"I need to go alone," he exclaims, frustratedly.

"They'll be expecting someone else, Jess, bringing a supposedly human prisoner might be the safest bet," Luka mentions.

"As I was saying," Zack starts again, as Jess leans the back of his head on the wall. "What if you bring a 'prisoner' who wants to visit their 'sister'. To reassure the prisoner that their sibling is in fact alive, which will give them a reason to stay longer." That's a stretch, but it's possible, and he's more likely to make it that far with one of us instead of being on his own. The vampires should buy it, unless it's Zayne at the gates, but he shouldn't be. He's in Hillark. Not at the mansion.

"I'd much rather go alone," he repeats, bordering on being defeated.

"But that's not safe." Oskar steps in front of Jess, and holds his wrists up to let Jess stare right back at him, into his pleading eyes. "Let one of us go with you. That way you can go with Zack's story, and they can't question your authority, because you have a human." Jess' face suddenly lights up, and then stares directly at me.

"You've been seen here before." My cheeks burn red and my heart squeezes tighter. "If it had to be anyone, it could be you. Draven's already aware of you, and Ambrosia. If there's anyone close by who sees us and recognises you, they'll already know who you are, and won't question me." Oskar's breath flutters, and looks at me too. He smiles the tiniest bit, and nods repeatedly.

"There you go!" he exclaims, and I purse my lips together.

I look down to the sofa with Luka nudging me.

"Savannah?" Last time I went out with Jess in this place crawling with unfamiliar people of a different species, it didn't go exactly well. "You don't need to go if you don't want to."

"I'll go," I say. I don't want him alone. And with Zack's story, it makes sense if I'm the one. So I lift my head to look at Jess, and I nod. "I'll go with you."

"Thank you," he says quietly. "I truly appreciate it."

"Of course." He looks back at Oskar and they start mumbling to each other, and I watch Oskar's hand slip into his. I stand up, stretching my legs as Luka stands too, pulling me closer, engulfing me into his arms, squeezing tightly.

"Be safe," he says against my hair. "Please."

"Of course," I reply, wrapping my arms around his neck, kissing his cheek, quick and soft. He smiles, leaning back to kiss my lips instead.

"I'll be waiting for you," he says, and lets me go. I nod, smiling and the reflection of me in his pupils spark.

"I expect nothing less," I comment, turning around to catch Zack staring at me. He sighs dramatically, and then steps forward, holds onto either side of my shoulders, pulling a stern and serious face at me.

"Goodbye for now, my friend."

"Why are you acting as if I'll never return?" I smirk. He drops his jaw, and lays a hand on his chest.

"I'm offended you assume I meant such a thing. I'm merely concerned for your safety."

"Quit the dramatics," Luka laughs a little standing beside me. "She's not going to war."

"With the way you treated her, you'd think she was." Zack rolls his eyes with a smile, and returns staring into my soul. His fake expression fades away to reveal the glint in his eyes. Pure, raw and real. "But seriously, be careful."

"I will." I smile, relived by how much they worry about me. For years I thought no one ever did, and I feel like I'm only just getting used to it. He nods and returns my expression.

"You ready, Savannah?" Jess asks from the door, as I check my knives carefully sheathed on my belt. I nod. I'll grab a cloak or something on the way out to hide.

"Yeah, just coming."

"Come back in one piece."

"I will try, my friend," I respond to Zack, and we both nod at each other. I look at Luka's concerned expression, piercing my heart.

"Good luck," he says with a shaking breath, yet he still tries to smile. I lean forward and kiss him quickly, before rushing off to Jess and Oskar.

I haven't been outside for around a week. And with the sun shining so brightly above mine and Jess' heads, I feel a little jealous for everyone who's able to walk freely, without fearing for their lives. I take a breath, tugging the cloak tighter around me, hood over my head. The door shuts behind us, and Jess hooks his arm through mine, and with the other, he crosses his hand over to grip my shoulder. We lock onto each other's eyes. And he's frowning.

"I'm sorry."

"I forgive you." Even though there's nothing to forgive.

"We'll be quick." I nod. He begins leading us and I keep my head low. "Again, I'm sorry. I'll need to act snarky, and horrible just to be believable, and—"

"Jess." I bump my shoulder with his, keeping my eyes on my feet. "It's okay." He says nothing.

I want people to be passing the streets and muffled conversations to be voiced. But today, I can't hear anything except mine and Jess' heavy breathing, shaking the earth itself. We pass the fence towards the mansion in question, keeping our eyes low. Then Jess tugs me into a jog. We bound through the long grass, jumping over mounds of mud, almost tripping over sticky patches, but Jess still holds me as the outline of the mansion comes into view.

I try to focus my thoughts on how lovely it'll be to see Sierra again, but all I can focus on is the relief of the fact we avoided Zayne on the way out. After seeing what he could do the night of the attack, I'd take my chance with anyone else.

Jess slows down into a walk when we can see two guards either side of the huge double doors. A pattern on the outside of the doors engraved with black stone, looking magnificent and regal.

"You okay?" I mutter. He nods stiffly, tightening his grip on me.

"Let's just get this over and done with." Agreed.

We walk up to the door, and both of the guards stare at us.

"What're you doing here?" One of them mumbles under their breath.

"By orders of Noble Vincent," Jess holds his head higher and even deepens his voice. "I'm here to check on the prisoners, and this one," he nudges me, "wants to see her sister."

"Hmph, and she's allowed to? We don't usually—"

"By orders," Jess raises his voice even more, "of Noble Vincent and Royal Ambrosia, I have permission to let her see her sister. Would you like to question their word again?"

"Royal?"

"Yes, Royal." The guards share a look with each other.

"A Royal has given orders to this *kid*?"

"Well, we can't exactly turn them away."

"And if he's lying?"

"Can we please hurry this up?" Jess exclaims. "I have places to be!"

"Well, kid, we don't know if you're telling lies about where you come from."

"You were expecting people, were you not? We'll be in and out in ten minutes or less." They're not budging so I look up into one of the guards eyes, faking my plea as I clasp my hands together.

"Please, please let me see her! She's all alone and I—" I force my voice to break, willing tears to build up behind my eyes. "I want to know she's okay! She's only seven, sir, and," I breathe heavily, shaking my voice with each word. "I need to see her!" One guard rolls his eyes and pokes the other who starts walking over to us.

"Fine, we'll let you in. I'll escort you to the dungeon," Jess tenses beside me, and I do too, eyes going wide.

"Thank you, thank you so much! You have no idea what this means—"

"Shut it." The other guard spits, but Jess swiftly walks through the double doors opening.

The entrance hall is huge. There are two curved stairs at the very edges of the wall with a door in the middle, which I assume is an office. Two hallways stretch out either side of the main room and a massive chandelier's in the centre dangling from the ceiling with candles lighting it up. It's rustic, it's old, it's beautiful.

"Follow me," one of the guards walk past us in black clothing and chains hanging from them. His hair's gelled back and he bears flashing red eyes.

The guard opens the door between the stairs, revealing a person sitting at the desk who stares up at us through their eyelashes from scattered papers. Once they see Jess and I, they raise one of their brows in confusion.

"Visitors?"

"For a prisoner. Orders from Royal Ambrosia and Noble Vincent *apparently*." The guard informs, and my stomach sinks five feet below when the vampire at the desk tells the guard to leave, shutting the door behind him. They stand up to inspect us. Like a hawk.

They curve their face into a small smile.

"Noble Vincent, eh?" they say. "Well, a proper meeting is in order then—"

"We're only here for a visit," Jess interrupts, whilst the stranger flicks their short brunette box braids out of their face.

"Oh, I know. Don't worry, I'm not keeping you here." What's the catch? "A friend of Vincent is a friend of mine, I guess."

"You're a friend of Vincent?" Jess questions. The person switches their desk lamp on, and it illuminates their soft brown skin. I can't help but admire their beauty.

"Used to know him better than that."

"I didn't know Vincent knew anyone outside his clan, and the Royals."

"And Draven," they correct Jess, and he's starstruck beside me before shaking his head in disbelief.

"This isn't why I'm here."

"Oh." They cock their head to one side, still staring at them, finding all this very amusing. "You *weren't* sent by Vincent?"

"That is *not* what I meant." They erupt into a fit of laughter, before sticking out their hand over the desk, leaning forever closer. "Taylen, the name is. They and them Noble, the one and only." Jess hesitantly leans forward, and shakes their hand.

"Jess. He and him. Pathetic vampire." They glance at me, and I freeze completely, held under their gaze.

"And you are?" Jess tenses beside me again, gripping tightly. Protectively.

"My prisoner, Sa—"

"Oh, come on! Like I'm going to believe that! Those stupid guards might." They throw their hands around aimlessly, standing back up straight from leaning on the table, walking out from their desk. Then they crouch down beside a trap door. "I don't care what your business is, just make it quick. That's all I ask."

"Excuse me?" Jess' breathing quickens. They open it up, and then stands back up to stare between us.

"I'll make it simpler for you then." Rolling their eyes as they edge towards us, and Jess pulls me behind him. "Clearly, she is not your prisoner and I know because of how close you hold her and how tight your grip is. If you held any sort of power over her, you could just have her walk beside you, and she wouldn't be able to run away. She'd know you would have to brutally murder her. Prisoners should be too scared to risk escaping. Besides if it truly were her sister down there, then she'd be much more desperate, unless she's good at masking it." They glance at me while Jess trembles beside me slightly. "I don't care about your business, nor do I care about whatever cover story you have. You don't seem stupid enough to take a prisoner from under our supervision and escape anyway."

"Was that meant to be a compliment?" Jess asks.

"Sort of. If you want it, take it," they mutter, then directly look at me, leaning down to inspect my face. *Too close, too close, too close.* I lean back, and Jess steps in front of me and they back off immediately. "And a human?" A smirk plays on their lips. "My, my, this story is still unfolding it seems."

"Don't come any closer," Jess warns, and they hold up their hands in defence.

"Alright, alright! I'm not going to hurt you or anything, I'm just curious. I can assure you, your plot is safe with me." They lay one of their hands on their chest, right above their heart. "Now, go see your sister."

"I will," Jess says quietly.

"I thought it was going to be your sister, or is it brother? Were you lying about that too?"

"No," he sighs, defeated. "It's my sister. I was worried about her."

"Completely understandable. Although I don't have any siblings or blood family, I can sympathise with worry," they remark, stepping over the open trap door to be behind their desk again. "I haven't seen Vincent in around two or three years? Something like that. I still worry about that imbecile."

"You figured out my story, now what's yours with Vincent?" Jess asks, turning to face them. Taylen smiles, and sits back down.

"I used to know him. Isn't that enough?" Jess opens his mouth to ask more, but they hold their palm up again. "I suggest you see your sister sooner rather than later, we've already talked for too long. I won't say a word."

After a pause from Jess, he finally nods and says, "Thank you. I appreciate it."

"Don't mention it." Jess leads me to the trap door, and he enters first, but I stare at Taylen a moment more.

"I'm Savannah, she and her." They stare at me and smile.

"Nice to meet you. Stay safe, 'kay, human?" I nod, and swiftly follow Jess into the caves below.

Jess runs off, and I follow. He mutters to himself how many cells he's seen. At eight, he calls for Sierra in a rushed breath, kneeling down, gripping the bars. Whis sister runs out from the darkness, he sighs in relief.

"Jess!" She squeezes her hands through the bars to hug Jess' shoulders. He laughs a little, short and sweet, wrapping his own arms around her through the iron and steel bars separating them.

"I came to make sure you were okay."

"I'm cold," she shivers.

"I think that's the least of your worries." I smirk, lowering myself onto the ground to stare at her, as she looks at me too. Her smile reappears.

"Savannah!"

"That's me," I comment with a forced smile, ignoring the quaking anxiety in my stomach. This poor girl.

"I missed you!"

"I missed you too." She leans back from Jess and she holds his hands looking back at him with a confused expression, tilting her head ever so slightly.

"Where's Oskar?" I hold my breath, hoping she doesn't mention anyone else.

"He's safe, he's at Savannah's house. You'll see him soon, don't—" Her face falls completely. "What is it?"

"We're not going to be here much longer though!" My stomach drops ten feet below.

"What do you mean?"

"A monster told us we're going to be moving soon." Jess' eyes widen. *A monster?*

"Who?"

"I didn't see their faces!" Dread builds up inside me, swallowing again, glancing at the other cells.

So many hostages. So many humans.

"Do you know when?"

"Within the next few days, I think." Jess tightens his grip on the bars until they turn paper white. "Jess?" she says quietly, her lips trembling. "What's going to happen to me?" He shakes his head, slumping back, thinking of a reply, and I watch as his shoulders drop, his hands fall onto his lap and he gives up.

"I don't know," he whispers.

"Am I going to see you again?" The hesitation before Jess replies is heartbreaking.

"Yes, I promise. We'll get you out, okay? And until then, you need to stay safe and—" That's when a girl emerges from the darkest corner of the cell, and stands a few paces behind Sierra.

"I'll take care of her," she murmurs, crossing her arms over her chest.

"Weren't you in the cell beside her?" Jess asks, his voice shaking.

"Yeah. They moved me in here for more space." She walks next to Sierra, as the smaller Princeton stares at her. "I'll take care of her," she repeats. Jess nods and smiles his gratitude.

"I trust your word, thank you so much."

"Thank you," I echo, and she smiles at both of us next, forced and tight.

"Time is up," I hear Taylen yell from the other side of the cave, and I watch as Jess' eyes practically leak tears instantly, *time's up, time's up, time's up.*

"I'll see you soon, Sierra." He leans forward, and she does the same, pressing a kiss on her messy and frizzy hair. "I promise," he cries, "I swear. I love you."

"I love you too," she says, fear coating her voice.

"I'm sorry," he says next. "I'm sorry for everything."

"Was the reunion everything you were hoping for?" Taylen asks, as we climb up into their office again. They shut the door behind us.

"You swore you wouldn't tell anyone," Jess comments. I watch Taylen nod and smile softly. Like they have remorse for him.

"I intend to keep to my word."

"When are they planning to move the prisoners?" I ask the question Jess might be too afraid to ask.

"I believe tomorrow evening?" Jess flicks his eyes to theirs.

"Tomorrow?" he repeats, quickly wiping his eyes dry.

"Yes, they're due to take them down to the lost city."

"And I assume you're the one who's taking them."

"No," they say. "The Nobles from the town are. A horrible bunch under Achilleas leadership. You can tell who's under Ambrosia's umbrella," they perform a tiny bow for us. "Anyway, if that's all, have a safe trip home, and be careful." They clasp their hands together under their chin. "I hope Vincent's well." I hope not. He's a horrible being.

"He's in the city," Jess remarks, and then turns to me, yet avoids my eyes. "Let's go back," he says, and goes back to holding me beside his shoulder, looking at our feet. "Before anything else happens." I nod, and squeeze his arm which hitches his breath. He stares at me with tears in his eyes.

"We'll figure something out, Jess." He nods and wipes his cheeks again.

"Yeah, okay. We'll talk to them about it." Oskar, Luka, Zack. Our family.

The guards open our exit, and we're out for good, and we can go home.

But as soon as the doors close and the guards are either side of us, the one to my left, closest to me might I add, says loud enough for us to hear,

"I'm thirsty." I make the mistake of glancing back. He's licking his lips, lunging for my arm, and he grabs it, and with his free hand, he unsheathes one of his knives.

For a split second, I'm the girl being followed, told to hush and keep quiet with a glint of a blade in the light. For a split second, I'm powerless again.

I widen my eyes, staggering my breathing, as I grip Jess tighter. This time for safety. But he can't blow our cover, or else it could endanger us, it could ruin everything. But I can't feel my legs. And my chest is tight.

The guard pulls me towards him, and I flinch, almost tripping over my own feet.

"Just a sip—"

"No!" Jess exclaims and pulls me back, and free from the guards grip. I catch his eyes. Wide with anger. "She's mine!" The guards roll their eyes. And the one closest doesn't stop and heads towards me again.

With the knife in his hand. Pointed at me. Warning to keep quiet.

This has happened before. *A guy in black clothing. With a weapon. Heading towards me.* I grind my teeth together, eyes welling up with tears as Jess pulls me behind him with his hand closed around mine. No longer a hostage.

"Get away from her!" But then a hand from behind me clasps around my shoulder.

"Jess," I slip out, choking on tears, watching the other guard with his own knives as well. He's grinning.

"My friend wants—"

"I said, no!" Jess unsheathes his sword, swiping it across him and towards the other guard. Slicing his arm through his sleeves. "Stay back!" The guard lets go and backs away, glaring at me, crying out in pain. "How dare you touch her," he yells and points the blade at the second guard. "If you don't want me to report to Ambrosia what happened here, then I suggest you back off!"

"Is she really your prisoner?" My feet grow into the floor.

"Yes. If you question that again, I'll let your Noble know you attacked us before we could leave." They grimace, glancing at each other whilst the non injured guard starts sulking.

"Just a bite—"

"No!" Jess swipes his weapon again, but hits no one because that's not his idea. His plan was to make them back off. Now that they're walking backwards, he hooks his arm around mine and hurries off in one direction, breathing as heavily as I am. "I'm sorry," he whispers, and looks at me with saddened eyes. "I'm so sorry."

"It's okay." But I can barely whisper it. "It's not your fault." He gives me a sceptical look, and I point at my chest, "Catching my breath." He squints his eyes close for a moment, before turning his head to the grass again.

Breathing burns. I'm suffocating again.

Jess opens the door to my house, and I've never been more relieved to see it. Before I make it three paces into the warm, Luka attacks me from the side with his arms wrapped around my neck, squeezing tight. I immediately embrace him back whilst Jess ignores Oskar's urgent questions and heads straight upstairs.

"What the— Hey, everything okay?" he asks as Jess closes my bedroom door, and Oskar looks at me, but my eyes are glazed over with dried tears, directed at the sofa. "What the hell happened?"

"Everything alright in there?" Zack's cooking in the kitchen by the sounds of it.

"Sierra's okay," I mutter.

"Clearly Jess isn't," Oskar says.

"Did something happen?" Luka asks, muffled by the cloak.

"Some vampire guards tried to take me from Jess to... I don't even want to know," I murmur, closing my eyes tighter, whilst Oskar curses under his breath, and rushes upstairs whilst I bury my head into Luka's shoulder.

"But you're okay right?" he asks.

"I'm okay, a little shaken up, but that's all." I pause before adding, "They had knives." He holds me tighter.

"You're safe now," he whispers in my ear, spreading his hand to hold the back of my head closer to him. "I promise—"

"He hasn't done anything since you left. Just sat there," Zack exclaims from the kitchen.

"I was worried," Luka raises his voice, but I hear the smirk. He leans back from my hold on him to kiss me. He stares into my eyes, and sighs out of relief.

I give him the smallest smile.

I'm safe with him, with my best friends. My family.

Don't leave me alone.

Please.

Jack

22nd November

Selene pulls the sword free from Achillea's chest, letting her fall into a heap of mangled limbs against the beautiful stone path. Ambrosia screams another round of sobs, as Draven wraps his arms around her waist, hauling her back from kicking and punching the air.

Achillea lies lifeless in the home she fought so hard to see again. And it's what she's died for in the end.

Violet wraps her hands around my arm, staring at the corpse, barely breathing. I glance at Ambrosia, watching her escape Draven's grip to draw her knives. She crosses her arms in front of her, flipping her blades to be curved outwards around her body.

"You *monster,*" she exclaims through ragged breaths. "*Monster!*" She lunges forward, head low, pointed towards Jade as Thena sprints past us in a blur. Draven pulls his best friend back, as Thena runs across, laughing to herself, narrowly missing Ambrosia's head with her own weapons.

She was about to *slice* Ambrosia's head off.

The remaining Royal's eyes bulge, wide and tearful. Thena stands back beside Jade and smiles gleefully at her, even sticking her tongue out at the two of them.

"Stay in your place," she sneers, having the time of her life.

"You murdered my family, my favourite person!" She breaks down with red puffy eyes, only now dropping her knives, clinging onto Draven helplessly by his arms. "Achillea—"

"Ambs." Draven strokes the hair from her eyes, pulling her head to his shoulder. She holds on even tighter. "I'm so sorry." They cry with her, trying to conceal it best they can, when I notice Thena watching Violet and I. Vincent seems to have noticed too, who edges towards us from my left, yet this time, I don't feel threatened. Instead, it's almost reassuring that he's close. Even so, I pull Violet behind me more, so my body is in front of hers completely. Vincent glances at me, and I glance at him, and he's not smiling, not grinning, not smirking like his usual self. Just looking right back at me. No fire in his pupils, only pure calculations. And then he stares at Thena who's glaring at Violet with daggers in her eyes.

I hold my breath when Vincent proceeds to step in front of, not only me, but more so Violet. Like he's *defending* us. I widen my eyes when my mind clocks onto what he's doing. The way he stands, the way he presents himself, the way he's glaring right back at those devils.

He's protecting us.

Him. The tall guy with flaming ginger hair and blood red eyes. The menacing arsonist who ruined my life, is now *protecting* my life. The vampire who appears to only think about himself, his wishes and his needs, is thinking about *us* for a change.

He draws his sword. "It wasn't her fault, and it was never her fault. I thought I recognised your hair, your eyes but I never said a word, I thought I was wrong all this time!" He lifts his blade to point at Jade's neck. "Why did you kill her for something that she was never meant to be blamed for, huh? Something that was never. Her. Fault?" he shouts frantically.

"If it was anyone's fault it was—"

"Mine!" Vincent interrupts his brother's words as they stare at each other, longer than they should. More intense than before. But more longing than ever. "It was mine!" They look back at Jade. "I made you what you are. All she wanted – all she, Ambrosia and Draven wanted was to see the fucking stars! Was that too much to ask? And you killed her for it?"

"No, no, no, you have it wrong, *deliciae,*" Jade smiles, clearly amused with how things are playing out. "I didn't kill her *purely* for that reason, no. I thank you for the power I hold now." She summons a blood red dagger above her palm, and she spins, kicking high and sends it towards us. It narrowly misses Vincent's head. "She was the one to turn everyone I knew against me. She was the one who created this *awful* representation for us *monsters*. She was the one to have ruined everything." It seems to be an ongoing cycle. Wanting revenge on the people who ruined our lives. I suppose I'm no different. "Because of her, everyone feared me. I learnt to use that." She clenches her hand. "To my advantage."

"I regret it," Vincent spits. "I regret making you what you are. Achillea did nothing wrong. I deserved to die instead of her!"

"Vincent, no—" Draven objects, shaking his head in disbelief, almost pleading he didn't hear it right, but Jade speaks over him as the brothers stare at each other.

"Watch what you say. You may find you might regret it." Jade clicks her fingers, and Vincent stops breathing completely, dropping his sword to clench his chest in his hands, as if somethings squeezing him dry. He drops to one knee, shrieking in pain.

"Vincent!" Draven cries out, and with Ambrosia tightly in his grip, he rushes over to us. Violet gasps at the sight, leaning beside me. The remaining Royal circles around us to be on the other side of Vincent, whilst Draven drops down to the ground, his palm on Vincent's back.

Muffled dull green, blue and grey colours emerge from his palm and into Vincent's skin. Draven grimaces immediately, as Vincent inhales a deep breath, flicking his gaze up to Draven's. Wide and worried.

His brother's absorbing whatever is hurting him, so he doesn't feel anymore pain. Violet holds onto my hand tighter, and Draven breaks away, now the one who's struggling to breathe as Vincent watches them cough and splutter. Their younger brother snaps his head up at Jade, lunging for his sword and sprints towards her, head low like Ambrosia but there's no one to hold him back.

"Stop hurting my brother!"

"Oh my gosh," Violet whispers beside me in almost awe, as Jade steps out of the way of his first strike, but unable to avoid his speed, he slides his weapon down her shoulder blades. She yelps in pain, staggering back in a ruined dress whilst Thena steps forward with her daggers and throws one directly into his shoulder, piercing his clothes and skin.

"Vincent, stop—" Draven chokes and then looks up at me in pain. "Help him. Please, Jack."

As much as Vincent's used, abused, and been a horrible person to me, Draven has not. And tonight, I've seen a new kind of flame. A side I never knew existed in such a crude person. One that cares for his forgotten brother, and surprisingly, his clan members. Everything he's done to us hangs in the back of my head, but with Draven's plead echoing in my ears, I let go of Violet and draw my sword, as Vincent is smacked onto the ground repeatedly. I march forward.

"Jack, for the love of god, be careful," Violet says behind me as she bends down to comfort Draven, and as I step over our Queen's corpse. I fidget with the sword's grip in my hands, familiarity in its worst form. Jade and Thena watch Vincent squirm helplessly on the ground trying to reach for his sword, and the closer I edge, the clearer I can see tears staining his cheeks as he lies on the floor helplessly. Struggling to find any motivation to get back up.

So I step forward as Thena points a dagger at his back, about to pierce straight through.

Vincent may have killed before. But to the ones he's led and loved, he's stayed loyal to them. I still plan on leaving one day, but perhaps I don't need to teach him a lesson about how he treated Violet and I. Maybe he's already been taught it. And maybe he's already broken enough.

I bring my sword down, cutting Thena's hand clean off.

A blood curdling scream erupts, as I grab Vincent's wrist and haul him up to his feet in time for him to grab his own sword too.

"We need to run," I tell him, and for a moment, he's too starstruck to answer. But he comes to his senses when Thena shrieks.

"Wait a moment, my dear Jack," he smirks, as I turn around to stare at Thena holding her arm with her one and only hand left. Jade steps to her side, trying to calm her, then proceeds to glare blades at us. Vincent merely laughs to himself. "Good job, Jack." He looks down at me. "I'm proud." I wasn't trying to make him proud, but now is not the time to argue.

"Proud?" Jade barks and laughs, standing in front of her ally, and she rolls her eyes at us. "Proud of that? We're still in power here!" She holds her head up higher, looking down at us through her nose. "We still hold the higher ground."

"I wouldn't be so sure," Vincent says, coyly, and picks his lighter out from his pocket. "Poof," he laughs, drops it whilst it's alight and sparks light up the ground. The flames fly out everywhere, and he seems to be controlling it, hitting Jade's dress, burning patches in it as she flings her arms up to her face, crossing them to shield her eyes. Thena cries out, protecting her own skin, bending over to protect her newly engrossed wound on her non-existent wrist. "You have a lot to learn still."

"Run now?"

"Let's," he cackles.

I drag him along, as Jade starts to blow out the sizzling fire, tending to Thena's screams. We find Draven standing up with help from the two girls, grimacing, and I let go of Vincent to grab Violet's hand, now sprinting past, telling the others to move while we can.

"Keep up, love."

"Jack," Violet pants behind me. "Can we stop?"

"Hang on," I tell her, squeezing her hands. I tug her around a few more corners until we're in a dark alleyway, dimly lit by the dying star above.

"I'm scared," she breathes heavily, letting my hand go to lean on her knees, back against a ruined building with black stone bricks – the whole wall is beginning to crumble and deteriorate. She keeps her head low, her long raven hair falling either side of her face, shielding her beauty. The last time she seemed this way was the day we turned into these *things*. She didn't stop asking questions every other moment. She was shaking - like she is now. She could barely breathe. "I'm really fucking scared."

"Jack, what's going to happen to us now? What's going to happen to our friends? Will we ever see them again? What about our parents? Our dreams?" She begged me for answers I didn't have. I didn't have the right words to ease her anxiety. But I do now.

I watch as she drops her arrows and bows onto the floor, careful not to make a sound as she flips her head up, forehead slick with sweat from a mix of running and anxiety.

"Hey," I begin gently, stepping in front of her, and craning my head down. I bring my hand up to her chin, pressing my fingers to her skin softly, lifting her to meet my eyes. "We're going to be okay," I tell her simply. She purses her lips into a fine line, and speaks no words. So instead, I pull her closer, wrapping my arms around my flower, keeping her safe from physical harm, hoping I'm cancelling out any thoughts from swirling inside her mind. "I'm right here." I lift one of my palms to the back of her head, intertwining my fingers in her hair. "It's okay to be scared, my flower."

Her breathing shakes again, resting her head on my shoulder, embracing me in return, arms around my back.

"That night," she starts, "the one where we first met Vincent. It was the worst night of my life, and I'm feeling that *level* of fear again. Like everything we've done since then has been for nothing, because we're right back where we started. Alone. In an unknown place. And scared," she whispers the final couple of words, and yet she refuses to let herself cry.

"We're different. We're much stronger, and this time we have more of a reason to fight with others beside us." She says nothing, like she doesn't believe it. "My love, are we here together?"

"Of course."

"Then we're gonna be okay. I promise." I press a kiss to her forehead, and she sniffles on my clothes, and I realise it's beginning to dampen. So she *has* let herself cry. Her shoulders begin to shiver, and everything shatters into broken pieces, scattered around us.

"Okay." She nods, clinging onto me closer. "I trust you."

"I never break my promises. I'll love you beyond death." She leans back in my arms, pressing her fingers into my skin, and pressing her lips to mine in a hurry, rushed tears glistening down her cheeks.

"And I'll love you beyond whatever lies after our time is done, Jack," she whispers in a trembling voice, and I watch her stare into my eyes, struggling to maintain it with the amount of tears inside, blurring her vision. I sweep some of her hair across her face and behind her ear, hanging beautifully and framing her face perfectly.

"Whatever happens," I say, as I take her hands in mine warmly and I press them against our chests, connecting us together as one. "Whatever may come our way. As long as we stick together, and we don't separate, we'll be just fine." She breaks into a small and sad smile, the best she can give me, and lowers her eyes to our hands clenched and clasped together. "Okay?" I lift our hands and I kiss her skin, each knuckle carefully and slowly, catching her eyes again. "I won't let you out of my sight." She tilts her head ever so slightly, and weeps some more, breaking down and nodding repeatedly. I smile at her strength. "That's my Violet." My flower.

She takes a deep breath and wipes her eyes with one free hand, still nodding as if to reassure herself. "It'll all work out. I'm just overthinking."

But then, we're interrupted by a voice calling from close by, jolting both of us to widen our eyes.

"Oh, Jack, where are you and your pretty little girlfriend?" I flick my eyes between each of Violets', making sure she's okay, as she looks up at me, her brows arched and forehead wrinkled. She kicks her bow closer to the edge of the alleyway, the end of it all. No escape.

"In case we need weapons. If we escape," she tells me and I nod.

"I sometimes forget how smart you are, even in these messy situations. I'm sorry for getting you into this," I say in a hushed and quick voice, goosebumps spreading all over my skin.

"It's okay. I'd rather it be us in it together instead of apart anyway." I give her a small smirk, taking a breath and squeezing her shaking hands in mine once again.

"I heard you mumbling, darlings. Oh, do come out from your hiding spots, I want company! Your Queen demands it!"

Jack

22nd November

Violet shakes in my grip. Jade's behind us, pointing two blades at our backs as we walk into the square we were at not so long ago. It sends shivers down my spine. I glance at Violet and I'm not sure how she has the strength to, but she's holding her head up high beside me, like always. I squeeze her hand gently, and she takes a deep breath, puffing out her chest.

I hope the others escaped. Although with Draven seemingly still recovering from whatever Jade did, I'm not sure. But I know he'll be safe with Vincent and Ambrosia beside him. However, my heart plunges in my chest when we're seeing familiar silhouettes up ahead, lit up by a glow extracting from the body lain on the floor.

I see Thena, Draven, and Ambrosia.

No Vincent. A wave of relief washes over me to my complete surprise. Vincent made it out. Vincent escaped. How the hell did he manage that? But I suppose if anyone was escaping, it was gonna be that son of a bitch.

They stare at us as we approach. Draven's entire face drops in dismay.

"Right, now that we're all – where's Vincent?" Jade asks, as Violet and I walk to the lone Royal and Noble.

"He's disappeared. And if I go searching now, I'm going to be looking for hours in this maze. I'll find him later." Thena flicks her remaining wrist, a fresh bandage with blood seeping through on her other arm. She doesn't even look at me. But I stare right back at her anyway.

"Anyway then." Jade rolls her eyes, and doesn't wait to loom over Achillea's corpse. She bends down, and simply strokes her soft cheek, slowly but surely.

"Hands off my cousin," Ambrosia mutters under her breath, and behind gritted teeth.

"My, my, you are beautiful, even in death," Jade whispers in the corpse's ear. "Such a pity your corpse is more important for what I need." And suddenly, Jade digs her hand, clawed with sharp nails, into Achillea's hollow chest. Ambrosia flinches, and looks away.

"Finally, after centuries of planning!" Jade looks up at Thena with a wicked grin, her hand filling with blood. "This, Thena, is what we've been waiting for." Her face beams, as Jade pulls her hand out, clenched around something tightly, and I can't bear to imagine what it is, because that hand is coated with a thick and dark layer of blood.

"I'm so excited!" Thena's practically bouncing from one foot to the other, even with her one hand left. Jade is smiling as she stands, breathing heavily, as she clasps both of her hands together.

"You're about to witness a spectacle," Jade says softly in almost awe.

"Sure, and even if it were, we're *totally* going to enjoy it, after witnessing you murder Lea," Ambrosia spits. Jade's emerald eyes flashes at the *now* oldest vampire. Thena then walks over and punches her cheek, smashing Ambrosia's head with a shriek into Draven who catches her steadily.

"Let's not speak out of turn, please," Thena tells all of us and Violet takes another staggering breath beside me, shaking and trembling even more so as we stare at her. All four of us in quaking and quivering fear.

Meanwhile, Jade smiles as she spreads her hands out in front of her to reveal a blinding light, falling everywhere, and lights up Achillea's body on the floor. It glows. Jade glows. Everything *glows*.

Just like the stars.

"Long live the Queen," she whispers into the air, and the particles of light spread out into white specks of dust, like the galaxy. Ambrosia stares in awe whilst Draven turns to me. I look at him. The world lights his eyes up. I stare back at Jade who's smiling brightly. *Almost innocent-like. Full of childlike wonder.*

"Sidera Lucere," she whispers to the magic. They all, as one, fly high above us, and towards the ball of light posing as a star that Achillea once made. Was that the last of her abilities that made her whole? The dots of dust and particles which kept her stuck together?

Her soul?

As soon as the tiny specks of light join the star overhead, the ball of gas sets alight and explodes amongst the entire city. It sprinkles tiny rays of light everywhere, almost like confetti. As the dust hits the surface, the area surrounding that section glows for a moment before rebuilding itself. One star grows a tiny flower at mine and Violet's feet. Another creates a missing brick and mends a path. Then, the buildings are glowing – the foundations of what once was there before are faint, but when enough specks expand on one section, when enough stars combine together, the building practically mends itself.

The city is being brought back to its former beauty through both Achillea's lost stars and Jade's deceiving power, combined as one.

The tiny specs land all around us. The dark stoned street lamps light up our surroundings and the city returns to its former glory. But when our attention is shifted back to the one who made it possible, Achillea's nothing but a heap of ash on the pavement. I hope she knows how her magic helped her home return to its former beauty, because this place is truly breathtaking. I hope she can see it, wherever she is.

I turn my head to see Ambrosia gawking at the stars around her, and the magical aura filling the cave. She starts crying again silently and finds her way to Draven's shoulder for comfort. He rests his head on hers, only now do I notice his wrists tied behind his back.

Jade starts shaking her head in disappointment, clapping her hands together as if the job is finished.

"Thena, make a note. We're going to need a lot more greenery in this place," she says and Thena nods, smiling right back at her.

"Of course, my liege." Jade pinches her lips into a thin smile.

"*You* don't have to call me that, you know." She's lifting one of her hands higher to her chin to let her elegant green sleeves fall down into a glittering flow. She stares at me next. "Thena, escort our *guests* to confinement, by any means necessary." Violet's breath hitches beside me, and I squeeze her hand tightly. I want nothing more than to tell her it'll be fine. But two reasons stop me. One, I can't risk saying a word. And two, I don't know if that's completely true. Thena grins wickedly, and marches towards us, stopping in front of Jade.

"My pleasure!" She cracks her knuckles in front of us, and scans her eyes *through* us. "You," she says, eyes glued to Violet. I immediately step in front of her, shielding her with my body. "Ha, that won't stop a thing, sweetheart!" Shivers are sent down my spine.

"Don't touch her!" I shriek, but she clicks her fingers together. Draven edges closer to us and our shoulders touch. My heart drops when Violet suddenly grabs my arm with both hands and I whip my head back to see her eyelids fluttering close.

"Jack," she murmurs, before her legs give out, and I catch her as she falls into my arms.

"Violet," I say breathlessly, falling to the ground with her as she blacks out completely and lays limp in my arms. "Violet." I shake her shoulders, cupping her face with one hand, eyes wide and breathing shaking my world. "Love, please." Catching me off guard, tears spring to my eyes as I lean my head closer to her, resting my ear on her chest, relieved to find her heart beating, softly and slowly. "You're gonna be okay, I promise, just wake up." I start patting her cheek. I stare at her fallen expression.

"Jack, she'll be okay. She's alive, they wouldn't kill her," Draven says, from above me. I look up at him, fear glistening in my eyes.

"But what if, Draven?" I choke on my own words. I can barely do anything, but blink and look slowly at my world lying unconscious.

"You too," Thena cackles behind me. She clicks her fingers and a wave of dizziness overwhelms me and I wobble.

"Jack!" Draven calls as my head becomes unimaginably heavy, and I fall forward and onto Violet's chest, still clutching her. A slow, cold tear runs down my cheek. My vision goes dark.

My love, my flower. I'm so sorry. I'm not enough.

Jack

23rd November

Is she safe? Is she breathing? Is she beside me?

I twitch my hands and open my eyes wide, inhaling a gulp of air. I sit up, searching over my surroundings. A stone cold bricked cell. Steel bars cage me in, and we're *under* the *underground* city. Then I look behind me to a corner where Violet's lying on the floor.

"Violet!" I spring up, staggering over, falling to my knees at her feet, as she begins to stir. "Violet." I lay one of my shaking hands on her shoulder, and I nudge her gently when her eyes falter. "Please wake up." She's breathing at least, and I know I am too. We're alive. We're here. *We're breathing.*

And then she opens those eyes, and tears burn mine in complete surprise and relief.

"Oh god—" she mutters. I let her sit up, rub her head and fling her hair back behind her shoulders whilst I let the realisation that she's okay sink in. "Ow." She darts her eyes onto me. "Are you okay?" I release a shuddering breath, simply shaking my head, leaning forward to wrap my arms around her. She lets out a small stifled chuckle and embraces me back.

"I was terrified," I murmur.

"Of?"

"Losing you." She smiles a little.

"You soppy prick," she mutters, squeezing me tighter which sets my heart aflame.

"Shut up. I was going to cry for you." I smile back, relief washing over me.

"Aw, that just proves my point."

"That I'm sappy?"

"Yeah."

"You always knew that." I don't want to let go again. "You're okay?"

"I'm okay." She rubs her hand over my back. "Jack, you're breathing fast."

"I thought we established I'm shaken up," I point out. "I thought you died."

"I'm not gonna say it wasn't scary, but I'm perfectly fine now, so focus on that, my love," she says in my ear, her warm breath tickling my skin. "Sorry I gave you a scare."

"I suppose I'll forgive you." I move away, holding her arms as she holds my shoulders. Her emerald eyes flash at me, and her hair is a complete mess, but I don't care. She's beautiful no matter what. There's nothing that could change that. I lean forward, cupping one of her cheeks in my palm, stroking my thumb under her eye to kiss her lips, eager but slow. Savouring but messy. When she leans back, she has an amused smirk playing across her lips.

"You almost cried?" I roll my eyes, drying them with my hands.

"That's what comes to mind right now?" She laughs. And that's all I need for it all to be okay again.

I finally lean back, scanning over the area, catching my eyes on the opposite corner. Vincent's leaning on the bars, staring into nothing. Ambrosia's in the other corner, leaning on Draven's shoulder, asleep whilst he's watching me. He greets me with a nod. But no smile.

"I'm glad you're awake."

"Ambrosia?"

"She's a heavy sleeper." He looks down at her. "I'm not worried. As long as she's with me, I know she's safe."

"Did Thena do the same to you all?" He nods, and Vincent looks at me next. And he seems *remorseful*. Completely out of energy. Draven sighs heavily, and they stare at each other at the same time. Millions of unsaid words pass between the two. Millions of unsaid broken pieces of comfort.

"Thank you," Draven says in a small voice, before quickly looking away and at me. Or through me. I can't tell. *Is he thanking him for defending him?*

"I should be saying thanks to you, so don't say it again." Vincent shrugs it off, but continues to stare at him. "I mean it, Draven. I- erm." I can tell he's not used to talking to Draven let alone about his feelings, but he's trying and I applaud him for it. Violet sneaks her hand around mine, silently watching too. Vince clears his throat. "Thank you for helping that attack, or whatever it was—" Draven smiles and looks right back at him with sad eyes.

"I was trying to be a good brother. That's all. You were right earlier." The ginger leans closer into the bar, his eyes widening briefly. "I wasn't there for you. I was scared."

"Scared? Of me rejecting you?"

"Something like that," Draven mutters, looking at me. He seems exhausted. Bags under his eyes. Paler skin than usual, and his shoulders sag with an unimaginable amount of stress, "I'm sorry," he whispers. "I thought you hated me."

"I never hated you."

"That's hard to believe."

"No matter how hard, it's the truth, so do with that what you want." He shrugs his shoulders. But Draven's silently crying to himself, trying to hide it from Vincent. He wipes his cheeks, and Vincent looks back at him, rolling his eyes. "Oh my gosh, you big baby." He scooches closer, and it's an odd thing to watch him sit next to Draven instead of walking away from his sight. Clearly, his older brother notices this, his eyes wide in disbelief when Vincent bumps his shoulder with a smirk, and a cackle. "I said thanks, what more do you want?"

"A reset," he replies instantly. They stare at each other. Violet tugs on my arm and I watch her smile, crawl back and into the wall to lean on it and I follow her lead.

"Like a restart?"

"Yes," Draven says desperately, and I watch the two brothers. So different, yet so similar. The same nose, opposite hairs, the same species with different ways of living. Same shaped ears, different coloured eyes. Vincent glances at me, and shakes his head with an exasperated sigh.

"I'm too old for this."

"And we're not getting younger. Give me another chance. I didn't know you were waiting on me to say something all these years," Draven comments. "I thought you didn't want to talk to me at all, and—"

"Look, shut up. That's all in the past now, isn't it? Can we just focus on now? I understand you thought differently the past hundreds of years, but right now, we're talking again, so don't fuck it up." Draven breaks into a gleaming smile, and he nods like a little boy in a sweet shop.

"Okay," he replies softly and quickly looks at Ambrosia who seems to be stirring.

"I'm glad we got that caught up. Now if you'll excuse me, I'm going to sleep." Vincent punches Draven's shoulder and then lies down against the wall, closing his eyes.

"What was that for?" the raven head asks.

"Pay back," the ginger mutters, before kicking Draven's thigh and then falling asleep soundlessly. I smile and look at Violet who's dozing off.

"How are you tired?" I ask her, and she shrugs her shoulders.

"I don't know. This is me you're talking about."

"You could sleep for a year and still be tired."

"Maybe in a hundred years, the world will be better."

"And you'll still take a nap afterwards." She huffs out exasperated laughter, resting her head on my shoulder, as I put an arm around her.

"I love you."

"I love you too."

"Never scare me like that again please."

"No promises. That wasn't in my control."

"Try to prevent it then."

"Again, I'll try, but no promises. Now shush." She lifts a finger to my lips. "Let me get my beauty sleep."

Vincent's asleep. Ambrosia's awake, staring into oblivion, and Draven's holding her close to their shoulder.

"I can't believe she's the kid," Ambrosia mutters suddenly.

"We couldn't have known—"

"Pfft, she had white hair, Draven, we should've known." She buries her head into her hands, rubbing her temples. "How did we not realise?"

"What's done is done. What else were we meant to do?" they say helplessly.

"*Not* follow her down here."

"We followed Achillea down here."

Ambrosia snaps her head up to stare at him. "And now she's dead because we trusted her." What happened all those years ago?

"She trusted her too."

"Which is somehow even worse."

Draven grimaces, and leans his head on the wall behind him.

"What are you talking about?" I ask calmly. They both stare at me with softened and sincere expressions.

"You haven't heard the story?" Ambrosia asks curiously.

"I've heard rumours. Bits and pieces. But I don't know what happened." They glance at each other, reminiscing without sharing a word. Just a glance of their eyes are enough.

"When we lived down here, we were told myths, legends and stories about the 'Up Top' world, the *supra* world." She turns her head to look at me. "Achillea found books about those species from above. And she showed me these things called, *stellae,* which translated to stars. And my god, they were gorgeous."

Draven nods along. "And they were even prettier in real life," they comment.

"They really were." Ambrosia sits up to look at me again. "She said she wanted to see them. I said I'd help her achieve this dream."

"And you followed through," I say, and she smiles.

"Yes, we did," she says with a mix of confidence and regret, thinking it all over in her mind. "We found a way up, we saw the stars, and they were breathtaking. Vincent," she scoffs, "tagged along despite not being asked to." Draven grimaces again, but says nothing. "We admired the stars for a little bit, and then a family wandered towards us—"

"I was shouting at Vincent, because I was anxious, and in a bad mood. He took it out on the baby, not even a year old. He spat at her, and some of that blood trickled into her mouth, causing her to become one of us. The parents got help, and they imprisoned us for years. Decades. Centuries—" Centuries? Fear courses through my veins. Is that what will happen to us now?

"We were never meant to stay up there for so long. Sure, we hated our lives down here, but there was reasoning for everything. It was familiar. We were meant to visit. See what it was like and find a way back. It got slightly delayed, as you can tell. And apparently all this time, Jade has been plotting this! For all we know, she could be the reason this place is in ruins to begin with. Maybe she didn't *need* to kill Achillea. She wanted to out of spite for what we made her." Ambrosia's eyes have completely glazed over, whilst Draven shuts his own.

"Fucking hell," I mutter, leaning my head on the wall. "That's a lot."

"You say it like that, and I realise I could have spoken to Vincent a lot sooner. It doesn't seem as big, what happened. But I guess it still changed our lives."

"We were all kids, babes." Ambrosia taps his hand. "Don't beat yourself up over it."

"When did we come into the mix?" I ask, holding Violet close. A question I've pondered for years but always been too scared to ask. Draven inhales sharply, staring at me.

"Vincent went off on his own, having a little...episode. His instincts kicked in, and he raided a few houses of a town he found closest at the time. He was angry, upset and emotionally stunted," Draven tells me. "I think he regrets it." I tilt my head ever so slightly at him, his words sinking into my skin.

"What?" He nods, and soon enough Ambrosia does too. "He's been a bitch to Violet and I ever since we came here."

"Jack, babes, listen. He wasn't thinking straight when he found you two. As soon as he did it, he came back to us, and said he made a mistake, and that he'd take control over it. We had no idea what he meant, and then you two turned up at our doors a few days later," Ambrosia insists.

"Why is he horrible to us then? Threatens us? Hurts us sometimes?"

"When has he hurt you that wasn't for your blood?" I clamp my mouth shut, as she twists her lips into a smile. "And even then, when he's done that, it's usually to show people he has power over you, and not them. Plus, he *is* a psycho," she laughs a little and stares at him, shaking her head a little. "He can't help it through. He's a *Sanguis Potentia*. He gets his power from blood. He needs it to survive."

"I suppose." A nauseous amount of guilt twists in my stomach. "I'm struggling to believe it." I glance at the flaming red hair on the floor, tightening my grip on Violet. "He was threatening to hurt Violet if I didn't help him."

"Because he was around Achillea," Ambrosia points out. "Achillea was stricter and less merciful than you'd think." It's too late to find that out now though. I frown. "I-" Ambrosia rolls her eyes, and sighs. "Vincent's been the one protecting your life really. While everyone else in his clan, and in the Noble title were belittling him and saying he should kill you two, he refused! And instead, took you into his clan and, sure, he wasn't the nicest, but no Noble is! Draven's the nicest – and if they are, something is seriously wrong!" she exclaims, violently and passionately gesturing with her arms. "Believe me now?"

"No, I'm still sceptical."

"What about how Zayne treated you?" Draven asks me, and something pings in my head and twinges in my chest. I drop my head, eyes on the floor, shaking it. "When Zayne would tell him to kill you, Vincent never did. His intention was never to ruin your life, Jack," Draven tells me. "Maybe he did, but he tried to rectify it, and you know Vincent, he's not very good at that kinda stuff."

I spring my head up to stare at Draven, as my hands shake with some sort of anger. "You're telling me the only reason we're alive is because of him?"

"We've helped too, but people in your clan are less than forgiving and accepting of newbies," Ambrosia leaps down my throat. "You really had no idea?" I shake my head, jaw dropped at them.

"No!" I exclaim. "No, I didn't!" I've wished him dead sometimes. I sigh shakily, looking back down at the floor, eyes quickly drifting to Violet snoozing on my shoulder. "He never would have hurt her?"

"No intention of it," Draven says, and I close my eyes, pressing my lips to her hair.

"How did you get let out of the prison, or whatever?" I swiftly change the subject onto something I want to distract myself with.

"Humans forgot why we were in there, so they let us go. We hid our fangs and ran away. When people called us out for being weird and never fitting in, we went underground, found caves to hide in, and went from there." Ambrosia quickly finishes the tale. "The humans rejected us."

"But they let you out," I point out, and twist her words. "They're not all bad," I say, thinking of the humans I've met these past few weeks. She glares at me for the first time.

"But most of them. You know, we're not the only monsters," she spits.

"I'm aware of that." I roll my eyes. Am I a monster too? I don't want to be a human, nor a vampire. Neither of them sound pleasant. Neither of them seem like the good guys of this fairy tale. I don't want to be either. I just want to exist. I don't want to be a monster. But maybe that's too late.

My mind flips back to Vincent, and I glance at him, sigh and rest my head on Violet, closing my eyes, embracing her warmth.

My head is spinning again.

Vincent's *protected* us?

Savannah

27th November

"You need to stay, Oskar."

"There's no way I'm letting you risk your life on your own! What if something happened and we never found out about it?"

"Right now, all I want is for all of you to be safe! I don't want to be petrified that you're dead again."

"If we're right next to you, you'd know, and so you wouldn't *have* to wonder!"

"That's not—"

"Jess, come on! I don't—" Oskar takes a breath, smooths his hands out against his shirt and sighs, staring down at Jess. "I don't want to leave you for that long again, especially when there's a chance you could get hurt. We can help!" Jess' breathing stops completely when Oskar grabs a hold of his hands tightly, and then presses both of their hands to his chest. "Please," he says desperately, "I'm worried about you."

It's been like this for the past ten minutes or so. Jess arguing that we should all stay here, while he follows the prisoners and a group of vampires to the city.

"This could go on for quite some time." Zack leans in from my right side between Luka and I. "Should we step in or something? And y'know. Tell Jess we're coming either way? At *least* let him know?"

"Leave them for a few more minutes maybe," Luka suggests. "I mean look at them. They're having a moment. *Clearly* something is blooming. Perhaps they're finally realising the other one likes them," he jokes.

Through an argument? I think Oskar knew all along anyway, but then Jess' eyes falter, and he looks away.

"Do you realise how exhausting it is to constantly have to worry about the safety of your friends?" But then Oskar smiles in response.

"Yes, I do."

"Then you know if you come you'd only be making that anxiety worse."

"I don't think that's true." They stare right back at each other. "If we come, we'd be right by your side."

"And if something goes wrong?"

"Someone can stay behind then. If we're not back by a certain amount of days, then they can come get us, or get help, or—"

"That's not safe."

"Nothing is safe in this world, Jess. Please." Oskar leans closer to him, pressing their hands closer together. "I'm starting to think you've forgotten how stubborn I am."

"Oh my god." Jess rolls his eyes, and chuckles ever so slightly.

"In all seriousness, I don't know what I'd do if you suddenly disappeared on us and never came back. If you didn't come back...I don't know, maybe it'd tip me over the edge. This is something you have to do, and I understand that. But that doesn't mean you have to do it alone. I mean look at these idiots watching us. We're certainly not alone in this conversation." Jess looks over at us, and turns red at the cheeks and his ears.

"Rude." Zack crosses his arms over his chest with a smirk, while Luka hooks his pinky around mine, behind our backs.

"Don't expose us," Luka comments.

"We're going with you whether you like it or not," I add. "Or at least some of us. All of this arguing is exhausting when we already know what the outcome's gonna be." Besides, I don't want to be stuck in this house a moment longer anyway. I'm sick of it all. It feels as if it's caving in all the time. It's suffocating.

Memories resurface. A new one every moment. I don't want to come back to it. I'd much rather forget this place existed.

Jess closes his eyes, faces his head back towards the other and takes a silent breath as Oskar lowers his head to be at eye level with him. Their gaze meet. And everything stops.

"We're gonna be fine." He playfully pushes Jess' shoulders. "Okay? It's gonna be safer for you to be *with* people."

"Is someone staying behind? In case we're not back by...say, two days, they can get help or figure something out." Jess shakes his head and swallows hard.

"I will if you need someone." Zack steps forward. Jess looks at Oskar.

"You're looking down on me as if I'm a child," he comments. Oskar forces out laughter, lets his hands go, and steps away.

"Sorry, you're just so much shorter than me..."

"Stop making fun of my height!" Oskar merely laughs again. *Some things never change.*

"Whatever." He stands up straight again, and glances at us. And smiles.

"So I'll stay back?" Zack asks.

"As long as you hide in here, you should be fine," Jess says.

"Sounds okay to me."

"Do you mind being here alone?" Oskar asks him. "I don't want to leave Jess since this is my idea, and Luka and Savannah are practically inseparable." I blush bright red, and look away from everyone.

"I don't mind." Zack shrugs his shoulders. "I can handle myself, evidently." Both I and Luka stare at him. He edges closer to him, letting me go.

"What does that mean?" Jess asks, and I watch him look at Oskar and tug at his sleeve. "Did something happen?"

"Erm," Oskar murmurs, and Jess turns back to us, and wanders towards Zack who fidgets uncomfortably and shakes his head.

"Nothing, it's nothing—"

"Are you sure?"

"My point is, I can take care of myself," Zack takes a breath, forces a smile at Luka, and swiftly walks away and towards Oskar who starts talking to him in a low voice. Jess stares at me and Luka, and we stare back at him. His eyebrows curve and forehead wrinkles.

"The thing, the *attack*," he whispers. "Someone never returned. Florence, Zayne's twin, and he was distraught, and swore vengeance." His eyes flicker between us. "Is this relevant?" I purse my lips together, unsure of how to reply. His eyes widen when we don't respond. "Oh my god."

"I don't know what to say," I mutter, and Luka tenses and nods beside me.

"Yeah," he adds. Jess looks back with wide eyes at Zack and Oskar talking.

"I hope Zayne doesn't find out."

"Zack saved my life. If he hadn't then I'd be dead right now." Luka says, and I shiver at the thought.

"Again, let's hope he doesn't come for this house – maybe we should all go, but then if we did—" Jess starts rubbing the bridge of his nose, facing down. "If something happened to us then that person could come and help or even escape."

"Jess." I step forward and lay a hand on his shoulder. "Zack said he'd stay. Which means we're coming with you."

"Exactly," Luka sighs, and I glance at him. "We've got your back. I trust

Zack. He'll be okay alone." But Luka will still spend every waking moment worrying about him.

"Fine." Jess drops his hands and steps away from my hand, and proceeds to nod at us and walk to Zack in a light rush.

"We'll be leaving soon," I hear Jess say loudly for us all to hear. "Just, until then, prepare and relax I guess. We get Sierra, and we get back here. That's all."

That's all.

Luka and Zack engulf each other into their arms, holding tightly, safely and warmly.

"Stay safe, Luka."

"You too. Don't go outside and talk to strangers."

"Ah, yes, stranger danger," Oskar laughs as they step away, and he steps in to hug Zack this time. "Beware of them." Oskar clasps his palm against Zack's back, and he smiles a little more.

"Of course," he chuckles in response, before backing away, quickly wrapping his arms around Jess, and a sense of unease overwhelms me. My stomachs queasy.

"How long will you be?"

"I'm not sure," Jess replies, "but if we're not back in a week, then something's wrong." *Something's wrong?*

"Savannah," Zack says, and now he's in front of me. He lays his hands on either sides of my arm. "Be careful." I nod, and we smile best we can at each other.

"I'll try."

"No, you *will* be," he insists and quickly wraps his arms around me. "Okay?"

"Okay." I melt a little, fear paralysing me to cling onto him, hiding the tears that brim to my eyes. This feels too familiar. I don't want to be separated. Is this an awful idea? Should I stay or should he come with us? I shut my eyes tightly, twisting my hands around him, snaking my way onto his shoulder. "Wait for us."

"Of course. I pinky promise." I smile, leaning away from him and he lifts his pinky in front of us. I hook my end finger around his. We shake on it.

"Now you're bound to it," I say, and he laughs.

"Is that how it works now?"

"Yes," I add a more serious tone to my speech, but with a playful smirk, and I nod. "I'll haunt you if you leave."

"Good thing I wasn't planning on it." I take back my hand which lands naturally on one of my knives attached to my belt. Then the other. Check. I have my bow and arrows, check. I have everything. Now let's hope I don't have to use any of it.

"Right," Jess says, with a heavy breath as we glance at each other, all in a circle in my old living room. "Let's move then. If anyone questions anything, I'm bringing more prisoners down into the lost city. If we can break Sierra out sooner than that, we'll try, but for now, we follow them. We reach them. We break Sierra out, and we find a way back here. Understood?"

"Got it," Oskar says to my right.

"Best case scenario, we end up back here in an hour or two because we got her." I purse my lips together. We don't talk about the worst case scenario. Because there's nothing we can do to save ourselves past that point.

In the meadow behind town, Jess spots the group of prisoners and guards up ahead, headed towards the mountain face. We're far enough behind that we can't pick out anyone, but not so far we can't see the direction they're headed. I start fiddling with a bracelet on my wrist. I haven't felt this anxious since Piper passed. Or was it when I came to see Jess on my own? I can't remember. Everything's a blur.

"Hey, you okay?" Luka asks beside me, and I merely nod when he nudges my shoulder. "You sure?"

"Yeah, just anxious, that's all." Telling people when I'm anxious always seemed too daunting and scary oh so long ago. But with all we've been through, it's less scary. I'm not so worried about people brushing it off, people running, people ignoring it. Not that I'm asking for help, because I have my own coping mechanisms, sometimes it's nice to just let someone know. I look at him, and he takes my hand, breaking my other away from fiddling with the bracelet.

"We all are," he says softly. "But we'll make it. We haven't gotten this far just to fail. And hey, maybe my brothers are down there too and—" Luka abruptly tightens his grip around my hand and pulls back. "Hey—" I turn around, staggering towards him, and I widen my eyes at the sight of him being held captive by a woman in a cloak, dark gleaming red hair down her shoulders, a knife at Luka's neck, and her grip even tighter around his mouth, covering his screams.

My heart drops.

"By order of the Queen, you must *all* come with us," she orders and then smirks, glaring her eyes at me. "Or else pretty boy gets it."

"Luka!" Oskar exclaims from behind me. I don't dare take my eyes off his petrified expression, tears rolling down his cheeks, as he holds his breath, biting his lip and he scrunches his nose up.

"Queen? We don't have a queen. We have Achillea. Unhand him, and we'll come with you gladly—" Jess starts from behind before being interrupted by the woman's barking laughter.

"Achillea is no longer! Queen Jade has given me these orders, and I don't plan on disappointing her!" She grinds her teeth together, and presses harder into Luka, so much so he winces, and I immediately draw my knife with my free hand. I tug a little on Luka, He's stuck there for good, but his combined weight with her could be to my advantage. Out of the corner of my eye, Jess draws his sword and Oskar looks at me. I glance at him.

In fairy tales, the only way to kill a vampire is by a stake through the heart. But if I could injure her enough for her to release Luka because of the shock...

I tug again, and Luka stares at me with tears glistening in his eyes. I look at Oskar and he silently stares back at Luka and walks closer. I look at the two. *Gotta catch her off guard. Save Luka. He needs to live.*

"Well?"

"And what if we do come with you?" Oskar asks, and grabs her whole attention. "What do we get in return? A fancy hotel room to stay in? Safety?"

"Oskar, what—" Jess shakes his head as he interrupts.

"If you don't tell us what we get, how can we trust you? Who's this Jade person anyway?"

"Jade is our queen!" The woman steps towards the side, one foot beside Luka, the other behind. I watch. The next time she opens her mouth, I pull on Luka. The two of them stagger towards me, crying out as I jump, hooking my leg to the top of her shoulder, boosting myself up in one swift movement, using Luka's arm for help. I dig my blade into the crook of the woman's neck, and I press as deep as I can, her blood spurting onto my hand and knife, and her clothes and her hair and -

She screams, dropping her weapon which sets Luka free as she staggers away. Oskar sprints forward, pulls Luka's hand, and helps him away from the woman. I release her, pulling my blade free from her body. I land flat on my back. She tumbles away, crying out in pain, twisting and turning, holding her neck with her hands. *The grass is stained with her blood. Blood I caused. Pain I inflicted.*

With my breath hitched in my throat, staring at the wounded woman on the ground, I wonder when I let go of Luka's hand. And I wonder how long Jess has been behind me for, with his hands beneath my armpits, trying to haul me up to my feet.

"Savannah, come on!" I look up at him, snapping to my senses. I nod, wipe my knife on the grass to spread the blood off, then sheathe it, lifting myself to my feet, and Jess grabs my wrist and runs off with me, following Luka and Oskar. They start slowing down when they realise we're closer to the group than we had thought before. All of us catching our ragged breaths.

Jess lets me go, and looks back at the woman still on the floor, flailing, whilst I lock eyes onto Luka who rushes towards me instantly. I let him wrap his arms around me, twisting his hands around my back and over my shoulder, and with my clean right hand, I embrace him back, but I let my bloodied hand hang there. Refusing to dirty him.

"Thank you," he whispers breathlessly, "Thank you." I merely nod my head which is sat against his shoulder, still with wide and bulging eyes. "You saved me," he murmurs, holding me tighter, as I begin to shake and tremble.

"Did I kill her?" I ask.

"No, no you didn't," Jess tells me from somewhere close by. A sense of relief washes over me. I close my eyes, taking a breath.

"Okay," I say. "Okay." I sigh, as Luka rubs one of his hands over my back.

"Did I mention thanks?" he speaks softly and gently in my ear.

"Once or twice," I murmur, and he smiles a little. "Thanks Oskar."

"Oskar?" Jess asks.

"I rambled at her, didn't I? I thought Savannah was scheming, she pulled that face, so I did what I do best." I lean away to look at Oskar whilst Luka holds my sleeves. "Talk."

"Anyway." Jess shakes his head and peers past Oskar's shoulder and at the group stopped by the mountains. "We're close." I look back at Luka, and he takes my hand.

"I don't want to leave your side again," he says and shakes his head.

"We're almost even now. Just gotta save your life another few times." I chuckle nervously and he drops his expression entirely.

"Even? No, no, sweetheart, I've gotta save *your life* about...four dozen more times in order for it to be 'even'." My chest tightens, and my eyes widen.

"What do..." I trail off. But he smiles. *He smiles.*

"You've saved my life a lot more times than you realise." And then he tugs at me to start walking by his side. *He smiled whilst saying those words. So why are my eyes burning with tears, and my heart's so heavy with glass it could drop, and shatter in a moment's time?*

"Remember, you guys are here *with* me. Don't talk to them," Jess warns us as we close in on the back of the group. But no one marches up to him to intimidate, or question, or interrogate his intentions. Instead, we watch the madness unfold from afar.

"Jess," Oskar barely whispers, and I glance down to see him slowly wrap his hand around his fingers. "At the front." We all peer through to watch a vampire grab Sierra's small arm and yank her forward. She screams. Piercing our ears.

"Sierra," Jess chokes on his whisper. "What—"

"No!" The girl from the dungeons cries out, and she pulls Sierra back, and holds her close. Out of the corner of my eye, I watch Jess holding his breath. Oskar glances at him silently, and purses his lips together. So many unsaid words shared in one moment.

Instead of the girl being used, a boy steps out, and shields her with his body. Her eyes widen, and I can see the fear in her face, the tears in her eyes, the confusion before the dread. They talk amongst themselves, too quiet for me to hear from this far away. But the boy starts crying too, as he stands in a dent of the mountain, facing a vampire who towers over him whilst Sierra and the girl hold onto each other sobbing. The girl screams out another, 'no,' reaching her hand out as if that'll stop what happens afterwards.

The next thing I hear is the boy choking, and a bloodthirsty scream all caused by a *deadly kiss.*

Savannah

27th November

The boy's blood drips down from his clothes, his skin, his limbs, and seeps through the cracked mud on the ground. He crumbles to his knees, and I instantly feel sick to my stomach. He falls forward, smearing his face on the cliff stone as his being is falling *into* the ground itself. Like the boy is becoming part of the earth. Is it hollow beneath us? The vampire with blood on his hands turns to the group. And even glances at us.

"Right, that's done!" He slams his foot into the ground and the mud caves in on itself and falls into a cave. My brows fling up, jaw ajar at the now new hole beside the small mountain, an infinite amount of space below. "Let's go!" he yells, and simply looks down at the drop and *jumps,* as if no other logical thoughts need to go into this.

He just leaps. But he might be prepared. Us on the other hand, are not. Sierra looks back as other guards try to usher everyone along. And she meets her eyes with Jess and she goes to cry out. But the girl quickly swirls her into her arms, telling her to shush gently, so no one's suspicious. But Sierra never pulls her eyes from Jess, and Jess never leaves her gaze.

But she starts crying. And Jess looks away. First at the ground, and then at Oskar.

"I can't bear it," he says with tears in his own eyes. "I can't see her cry like this another time, Oskar—"

"I know, I know," he replies. Jess snaps his head back to his sister.

"I don't want to go! I don't, I don't, I don't!" she screams, kicking and punching the closest guard who tries to grab both the girl and her. "I just want my brother!" A millisecond passes and Jess is sprinting through the crowd, free from Oskar's grip. In a blink of an eye, we're all following him as fast as we can, escaping hands trying to grab us from all sides.

"Jess," Oskar calls.

"Jess!" Sierra's louder, and she makes a lunge for him. But the guard grabs her around her stomach and hauls her onto his shoulder. "Jess, no!" she screams.

"Sierra, I'm coming!" Jess yells, and reaches for her.

"Oh no, you don't!" The vampire shouts, then smirks as Jess draws his sword. "Say bye-bye to brother dearest!"

"Jess!" her screams fade when she and the enemy leaps into a black abyss.

"Sierra! No, no, no, no, no!" Jess shows no sign of stopping even when he's headed directly for the cliff face. A narrow guard stands beside said cliff, but misses Jess' body when he jumps into the cave below.

"Jess, wait!" Oskar gives us a fearful look, before he looks forward again, and jumps after him before the vampire steps forward. blocking Luka and I.

Luka grabs my hand so we're not separated. But even so, it doesn't stop the guy from grabbing my shoulder, dragging me towards him, and shoving me into the cliff face. Then with the other hand, he grips my neck, and lifts me into the air, legs dangling helplessly below me. My breath is whipped out from beneath me, an unsettling crack heard when he pushes my back harder against the cliff face, hands going limp, but Luka still keeps his hold on it.

Can't breathe. *Can't breathe.* Tears rush to my eyes as I blink furiously.

"Maybe this'll knock some sense into your stupid vampire friend," he mutters, and pushes harder, choking me.

My very own mind shocks me when I think to myself suddenly, *does this mean I can see Piper again? Matthew?* I don't want to die. *I really don't want to die.* I inhale as much as I can before I can't any longer, the energy completely drains from me, as I spot Luka draw his sword out of the corner of my eye. My capture hears, and he looks at Luka, and I take this opportunity to draw one of my own knives with my free hand.

"What do you think you're doing?" he demands and Luka smiles.

"Distracting you." And then Luka lifts his sword, and drags it down and across his shoulder. But it's not enough to let me go. He shrieks, and then laughs. "You won't be laughing for very long." The vampire immediately stares at me, as I dig my knife into his chest. He screams, and twitches, letting me go and I fall into a heap on the floor, coughing and spluttering up a mess. Gasping for air, Luka pulls me up to my feet, but I wobble, as I bend back down, grab my knife as the vampire lifts his own sword up, swiping at my head. Luka pulls me back, and I hold my breath as the blade lands on my cheek, which cuts a thin layer of skin off from my face. Like a paper cut. He almost beheaded me. He almost cut my head off.

I catch sight of all the prisoners trying to break free, which is why none of the other guards have come to help their fellow friend kill us, and I smile my thanks at a few before avoiding another swing from behind me.

I grit my teeth together, staggering back and turning around to look into the darkness below. I glance at Luka and he nods, holding onto my hand much tighter than before, and together we plummet into the darkness of the cave below.

I convince myself I'm falling into a void of simply nothingness.

I look up at the fading sunlight. Then I look down at tiny stary specs sparking up my vision. *Of a magnificent city.* The darkened streets from afar look beautiful in all their glory. Both ahead of its time, and far far behind. Odd how the styles we admire are the ways of hundreds of years ago.

I look directly below me– a small tower below us by the looks of it. Sierra, Jess and Oskar aren't on this tower though, so a surge of panic runs through my veins, jolting me awake. Luka lands on his feet, buckling below at the impact and then I land half on top of him, and half on the stone. I curse under my breath at the impact of my tiny cut on my cheek, and the cold stone. I sit up, letting him go, rubbing it, and when I take my hand back a light coating of blood is on my fingertips.

"Are you okay?" Luka breathes heavily. He sits up properly and leans closer to me. I barely nod, lips ajar.

"I guess." He lays a hand beside me, and edges closer to my face, eyes landing on my injury. "It's nothing." He digs his hand into one of his pockets and pulls out some tissue in a small packet, already open.

"I even brought some bandages in case of emergencies," he mumbles. He lifts the tissue up, and very gently dabs on the blood, and clears up the mess someone else made. I flinch, and he quickly finds my hands and holds them. "Sorry, I'm trying to be careful—"

"Thank you," I interrupt, "thank you for saving me." He continues to help clear my wound. I take a deep breath.

"Luka? Savannah?" Oskar? We look around as Luka folds the tissue up and I stand looking around for the voice. But he's not around the balcony, he's not at the door.

"Oskar?" I call.

"Down here!" I rush to the edge of the tower, looking over the stones protecting us from the fall. He's there, at the very bottom, looking at me, waving. "Where's Luka?" I look back at Luka running to me, brushing dust off, and he gazes down. "Okay, thank god. I can't find Jess!"

"He probably went off looking for her," I say back.

"Maybe he was following the vampires who took her," Luka shouts. "I'm pretty sure he'll be fine. Stay there, we'll find you." Oskar nods, and we start hurrying to the door which reveals a spiral staircase leading both up and down. We head downwards.

Oskar meets us at the bottom of the stone stairs and worry is written all over his face.

"Keep close, we need to find Jess, and quick." Ah, yes, because we have *no* time whatsoever to discuss the fact we have fallen into the earth itself, and below the surface into a magnificent and gorgeous city. A forgotten kingdom.

Luka walks forward, and I follow beside them, letting Oskar lead us in a small jog out of the steel engraved fences that guard the castle. I glance back at the towers, the stone bricks, the pavement, the lamps, the dark hallways found through the glass panes. It's like something from the past. A page torn out of a fairy tale. *A lyric from a myth.*

I look ahead and we pass street lamps with drawings on them. The houses are all unique in their different ways, nothing like the boxes I used to see everyday. Some here have balconies, others have lookouts, some have fountains and others have archways. I'm so tiny in comparison, it's reassuring. So instead of frowning at the dawning thought, I welcome it.

"Jess, where are you?" Oskar mutters under his breath as his shoulders rise and fall, peering into every alleyway we cross.

"He couldn't have gone far, Oskar, I'm sure he'll be okay," Luka says, and lays a hand on his shoulders, and Oskar stops completely in front of us.

"That's no guarantee," he whispers and looks back at us, with tears in his eyes as he draws his long sword. "But we lost him once, we're not losing him again."

"Exactly." I give him a strong smile, and Luka nods, taking back his hand and he glances at me. We all start walking off again, Oskar speeding up. We seem to be circling the castle.

But in a blink of an eye again, a vampire leaps out from a corner, jumping onto his back, his long sword clattering to the ground.

"Oskar!" I yell, stumbling forward to help him when a hand from behind grabs my wrist and covers my mouth with their hand. I widen my eyes immediately, thrashing my free arm around, and my knuckles come into contact with steel. I yelp, wiggling to get out of their grip when they twist my wrists together, wrapping a rope around my face, gaging my mouth and tying my hands together. They hold me around my stomach, arms either side of me but my legs are still free, my legs—

"Stop squirming!" The woman holding me exclaims, as if I'm the problem here, and *not* the person kidnapping me. A shriek rings out from in front, and Luka is being pushed away from the vampire holding Oskar. He's being pinned, and pressed to the ground, and I glance at Luka as someone grabs his neck from behind and he gasps, eyes wide and head held high to the cavern's landscape.

Is this it?

I've always pictured how it'd happen. How we'd end. How we'd die. And now that it's actually happening, it's much scarier than I thought. So I don't give in, I fight, and kick as much as I can, throwing myself around, gritting my teeth.

Heart hammering against my rib cage.

Is this it?

I look at Luka, holding my breath, as he elbows his captor's side, and draws his sword whilst the vampire's trying to get a grip on him. But to no avail, Luka twists his sword around and faces it directly at the capture's heart, until they freeze. But he doesn't stab them there, instead, he drags his blade down and digs it into the captures thigh, twisting and pulling it out. They cry out loud, and Luka doesn't wait to lunge towards me.

Why does it always come back here? To this?

Starstruck, the only thing I can do is shake my head. But the woman tightens my gags, and the rope on my wrists until it burns. I wince.

Luka circles her from behind while his captor's injured. I struggle some more. And then he digs his sword into the vampire's side, and through her stomach. She cries out, as I notice Luka's original captor getting up and spreading something over his thigh. He looks up, and directly at Luka.

"Lu—" But I can't talk with this gag. Blood spreads onto my back, the shock making me shriek, and freeze as the woman lets me go, the rope still tied and the gag still on my face. With wide eyes, I turn around onto my back, watching the woman fall onto the floor, spasming in pain and shock as Luka stands over her and stares at me, breathing heavily.

I look back at the vampire now sprinting directly for Luka, but I quickly rise to my feet, staggering in front of him, fear plastering my bones and as the enemy shows no sign of stopping.

And he lifts his knife at me. I hold my breath, and close my eyes the closer he gets but from behind, Luka pushes me roughly out of the way and onto the floor, slamming my shoulder into the ground. I open my eyes, flicking my hair out of the way to see Luka avoid the dagger as well and my heart flips in my chest. Instead, the captor grabs him by the shoulders again, disarms him with ease and lifts his blade to his knife. He starts dragging Luka away from me.

I gasp, widen my eyes, and I sit up. Luka simply stares at me, and shakes his head ever so slightly. But he's scared, I've gotta help. I've gotta—

Hands are lain on my wrists whilst I'm on the ground, and whoever it is unties the rope from my burning wrists. I look back with wide eyes. Oskar's free? I peer past him to see no one there, no vampire, no enemy, no Jess. He stuffs the rope into his pocket and loosens my gag, throwing it away, and I gasp for clear air, quickly shooting my eyes back to Luka—

To find him nowhere.

Tears spring to my eyes.

"Come on!" Oskar grasps my wrist, and I watch him, an expression too difficult to read.

"You got out?" I ask with a trembling breath.

"Jess got me out." He shakes. "Now come on, let's just go!" He masks his voice well, but I can still hear the break. The emotion. The crack. The falter. I let him lift me to my feet. His voice shows a gateway to what he's feeling, and as my eyes leak tiny tears, you can see it all. He keeps his grip on my wrist as he races down a few alleyways together, keeping as close to each other as we can and at some point along the way, I let loose on my emotions and I just end up crying most of the way to wherever we're going.

A void weighs my chest down.

"Oskar," I say when my lungs can't take any more. If I let him keep running, I think he'd never stop for air. "Breathe." He slows down, lets me go, and I lean on my weak and numb knees immediately.

He saved me. Again. *Luka saved me.* What will happen to him? And Jess! Goddamn it! Will he be with Luka as well? We were meant to all stick together.

We were meant to stick together.

A wave of dizziness overwhelms me, and my shoulder hits the wall. I sink down onto the ground, my legs collapsing entirely beneath me.

"Whoa." Oskar steps in front of me. "Hey, you alright there?" He kneels down, and in front of me. I clench my hands into fists, digging my nails into my skin, as I cry some more. They won't stop. The tears keep falling. But all I can remember is how sad he looked. He looked so scared. And he saved *me* instead of saving *himself*. I squint my eyes close.

"What now?" I croak.

"We'll find them," he replies softly to me, and I lift my head up to see him. "What else is there to do?"

"And if they're in separate places?"

"We find both of them, Savannah." He perches on the floor, and lays a hand on my shoulder. "We're not going to leave without them, okay?" I nod, lips trembling. "Savannah, hey. Listen, I'm scared too," he stutters and leans his head on the wall, eyes glazing over past my shoulder. The gloom in his pupils. The emptiness– it shakes my core. A shiver spreads through me. "I'm scared as well. You're not the only one." His expression softens completely. And I frown, almost breaking down into pieces again.

I sit on the ground more comfortably, back against the brick wall, rubbing at my sore eyes, trying to fathom how on earth we're going to get them back. We don't know where to start in this maze, they could be anywhere. And on top of all that, Jack is around here somewhere, which means Vincent. There are killers out there searching for us.

"What if we're too late?" I mumble to Oskar, as he moves to be right beside me. He stares, and I know he does, because he doesn't answer. Instead, he wraps one of his arms around my back, bringing me even closer to him, and I lay my head onto his shoulder, resting simply, as he rubs circles into my back with his hand.

"We'll be okay," he says, and then once again, he repeats, "we're not leaving them."

"And if we die down here, Zack's going to walk into his own death."

"We'll survive. I'm pretty sure they need Jess alive. And they wouldn't kill his friends, or else he'll go berserk, and you know he will. Like he did on Vincent." My heart burns and aches, and I close my eyes, grimacing. "We'll be okay, I swear. I've still got a kick in me. Don't you?"

I pause in thought for a moment.

"I don't know," I end up whispering. "I'm exhausted."

"So am I," he insists. "But Jess and Luka need us. And I don't want to leave Zack hanging up there. He'll go mad if he's left alone for more than a week or two max."

"I guess." I take a deep and silent breath. "Where do we even start?"

"Well, the castle seems like a good bet. We didn't find anyone out here, everyone must be in the castle. It's certainly big enough. And looks grand enough to hold prisoners."

"That's not a bad shout," I tell him. "We can start there then. But what if we're wrong?"

"Then we're utterly, utterly screwed, but we don't talk about that yet." I smirk.

"My lips are sealed." A beat of silence overcomes us in a single wave.

He wraps both of his arms around me tighter, and I hug him back as tightly as I can, sucking in deep breaths over and over again to calm my nerves.

Why does this feel like the end?

Savannah ⭐

28th November

The longer we wait, the more anxious I grow, but it means we have a better chance of the soldiers getting bored at trying to find us, and give up. So we wait a little longer. *And longer.*

"I'm starting to get restless," Oskar mutters, and shifts beside me.

"I can't say I'm the same." I yawn, and he pats my back, as he leans away from me and I take my head back from the perch on his shoulder.

"Surely they'll be gone now."

"I don't know." I shrug my shoulders, as he looks at me.

"Hey, perk up." He elbows my arm. "We're about to go save them." I lift my eyes to gaze into his, finding that he believes it. "Alright?"

"I'm just worried, that's all."

"As usual." I grimace. "I am too."

"You never seem it. I don't know how you do it."

"I'm good at hiding it."

"Good at acting." He forces out fond laughter at that comment. His goal's always been to be a musical theatre actor, starring in many musicals, plays and performances. It's been his passion. Always and forever. I'd still love to see his name in lights one day. *'... Starring Oskar Hay,'.* It has a ring to it, don't you agree?

"Yeah," he murmurs. "I miss acting."

"Acting is everywhere," I say, and he smiles at me.

"I more meant for a role, but yeah, I guess there's that."

"Will you still go down that route?" This is hardly the time for us to be discussing the possibility of an 'after' this, but right now, a distraction's needed, or at least something to look forward to. He leans on the wall, and looks around.

"I think so, it's just focusing on this right now that's complicating everything." I nod. "I'm not sure if it's possible or not, now that I can't continue it at sixth form, but I'll give it a try."

"I believe in you." He smiles brightly, reverting his eyes back on me.

"Thanks." He nods a few times. "Appreciate it. But until then, we gotta focus on this." He stands up, stretches his arms up high, and offers his hand out to me, and when I hesitate, he says, "We've come this far, Savannah. You're not giving up now. I won't let you fall." I smile a little bit, taking a deep breath before accepting his hand to help me up. I clear my cheeks and I nod his way.

"Let's do this," I say.

"That's more like it!"

We head out of the alleyway, and Oskar talks to fill the silence, which I don't object to. But all of a sudden he's talking about Jess. And death. And being told three months ago this was all going to happen. I'm getting sick of him acting oblivious to Jess and his own feelings.

"Oskar." I look at my feet. "If you knew we were going to die tomorrow. All of us. You and Jess, would you do anything different?" I see him hesitate in the corner of my eyes. "If you were told you didn't even have a year left with Jess." I look up at him again. "You're telling me *nothing* else would happen?" He purses his lips and his expression falls but he never looks into my eyes again. "We're running out of time, Oskar. You know we're borrowing it. Even if we get out of here, they'll hunt Jess and—"

"Don't you dare say anything more," he points at me, and grits his teeth.

"I'm not saying we're not going to make it. I'm saying you need to hurry it up." He blushes bright red again.

"Well, thank you for that enlightening information," he brushes it off immediately, and I take note of the shake in his voice. "What if we died when this all started?"

"Oh my god," I rub the bridge of my nose, shaking my head. "Oskar."

"And we're in this weird purgatory. Some sci-fi shit."

"Anything is possible at this point. I mean look at us – I wield a bow and a few knives, which I never thought I'd ever do and you now know how to whack someone with a long sword."

"Whack?" he snickers, staring down at me. "Really? I thought I was more intimidating than that."

"You're saying whacking someone with a longsword isn't intimidating enough?" I ask and look back up at him.

"It certainly doesn't sound it!" I laugh at him, looking forward again, noticing the castle perimeter gates closing in on me. "Right, let's just, go with the flow?" Oskar suggests, as he draws his long sword with both of his hands, blade pointing forward, and I nod, picking out my bow and an arrow at the ready.

"Sure," I say nervously, and we walk in, side by side.

"Most logical is down somewhere in dungeons," he says.

"I thought we'd go with the flow," I remark.

"This *is* going with the flow, because we have no plan going in," he replies. "We get Jess, Luka, Sierra and get out."

"And what about Jack?" He looks at me.

"You think he's gonna be a hostage as well?" I shrug my shoulders. "If we find him down there, we'll get him too." I nod as he looks away, and we head directly to a door slightly ajar, light breaking out. He puts a hand out in front of me, and he steps forward with his long sword and he peers into the hall and immediately looks away, sucking in a breath and mouths to me,

"Vampire." I purse my lips, air lodged in my throat.

"You open the door, and I'll shoot them."

"You sure?" he whispers back.

"Now before I hesitate." If I think about it too much, then I won't do it, and I'll back out. But we need Jess and Luka. It's up to us this time. And I don't intend to fail.

"Three, two, one." I step into the doorway, as Oskar opens it wide and the vampire looks at me.

They have their own life, they don't deserve this. But neither did we.

I just need to get them down.

I ready. I aim. And I release the arrow, and it pierces the side of their neck. Not enough to get them down so I panic, adrenaline surging through my veins, as I sprint in, and grab another arrow from my back. I knock them against the floor, with ease since they were still in shock from the previous attack.

Turns out, I didn't need the other arrow.

I lay them on the floor, knocked out cold, and I even press their clothes into the bloody wound to help, but I know it's not quite enough. So I stand, sigh and look back at Oskar walking in. He nods at me, and when he passes by, he lays a brief hand on my shoulder, before leading the way once again.

"Wait," I say. He looks back. "They'll need a gag, so when they wake up, they can't do anything." He raises one of his eyebrows, and then lifts one leg up, kicks off one of his shoes and pulls off one of his long socks. He throws it to me. "This stinks, Oskar, what the heck?"

"You needed a gag," he smirks, and I tie it around the vampire's mouth, guilt filling my chest immediately, and I cough back my own type of gag.

"That smells horrible. I feel sorry for the poor guy now." I look back at a shrugging Oskar and I shake my head at him. "Jesus, let's go." I walk past the unconscious vampire, and I follow Oskar down the hall. But for a moment he just simply stares at me for a moment. "What?"

"I wasn't expecting you to have this side to you."

"What do you mean?"

"A fighting side."

"I'm only doing what I have to do to get our friends back."

"Just unexpected from you. That's all." He walks through another door and finds a massive meeting room. "Well, this doesn't help."

"Look, the candles are still lit." I point out at the dark oak table in the middle of the room. I bring my eyes to drawings on the side of the wall. There's neat handwriting pointing everything out. "That's too easy to find surely."

"We're not meant to be here, Savannah, they never thought we'd get this far." I walk forward and further into the room, nearing the blue prints and drawings.

"The ink's faded," I say. "It's been here for years and years and years, and this is old paper, it's starting to crumble." It's more made up of lists than anything on the paper. Some in Latin, some in English, it switches between the two a lot. But one diagram I can clearly see: of round circles below planes of sorts breaking through rocks which I assume is the mountain above us. The circles are labelled *'bombus,'* which I assume translates to bombs. And arrows from those bombs are pointed at the city drawing of towers someone made. Then below it, there's a line separating that, and a picture of a woman who seems to have lines coming from her. Light? And underneath the figure are the words *Sidera Lucere*. Suddenly, Oskar shrieks.

I snap my head back, drawing my knives. Oskar's being dragged out of the room, punching his captures side, stubbing their toe and he kicks the air frantically. They've covered his mouth. And he's *taking him away from me.*

"Oskar!" I exclaim, and I lunge forward. *No room for doubt.*

I speed forward, readying my stance and blade. Once I'm close enough, and in the doorway, I pull back to throw my blade at the vampire manhandling Oskar, but a hand from behind grabs my wrist, and slams something hard into the side of my neck, shoving me against the wall and I scream at something cold being injected into my bloodstream. My vision darkens. Heavy eyelids take over, and I hit my head harshly on the ground, slumping to my side and they let me. Blood gushes down my face.

But that's the only thing I can register before complete darkness. In my mind, in my vision, in everything - before blacking out completely.

☆Jack☆

28th November

"Get off!" Jess? I shake myself awake from my dozing state, perking up from the wall. I adjust my eyes in time to watch Jess being thrown into the cell, onto the ground, at my feet.

"Jess!" I lean forward, as Violet sits up from my shoulder. I lift Jess up by his shoulders, but he springs up anyway. My eyes adjust to the dim lighting to watch another guard march down with Luka in his grip. Jess rushes forward to catch him as he falls. The smaller boy collapses onto his knees and grits his teeth as his fallen friend crumbles to the floor on top of him. Jess mutters something under his breath. He shoots his glare up at the guards slamming the cell door shut.

"Don't touch my friends again!" he shouts with a temper.

"Whatever. You'll be glad to know the pursuit for your other two *monsters* is *still* underway then." One of them snarls, and the two of them start cackling as they walk back down the hallway. Luka shoots his head up, and they both stare at each other with wide eyes.

"Savannah," Luka says breathlessly.

"Oskar," Jess whispers.

"What the fuck are you all doing down here?" Vincent yells, and the two boys flinch. Jess puts an arm out in front of Luka, resting his hand on his knee when he lays eyes on the vampire in the corner.

"I should be asking the same of you. You're in a cell," Jess points out and I smirk.

"He has a point," Draven yawns and I watch him patt Vincent's shoulder, leaning him against the wall again. "Calm down, Vincent, you're not seriously thinking about attacking them here." Vincent crosses his arms over his chest in a huff and rolls his eyes.

"No, but if I get peckish then you can't stop me."

"I sure as hell will!" Jess yells, and I flick my gaze to his as Violet holds my hand. I make my way back to her side.

"Jess," Luka says calmly and places a hand on his arm. They stare at each other. Luka seems hesitant to say it so I do,

"Calm down."

"Calm down? And how do I do that, Jack?" He looks back at me, and I only now notice how heavy his breathing has become. "We're trapped! Imprisoned! And Oskar and Savannah are out there being hunted, and I brought them in this – it's my fault!"

"Why did you come down here to begin with?" Violet asks gently.

"My sister's down here, and I came to save her from whatever would happen. But I've only made things worse, like always!" Jess throws his arms up, and looks back at Luka dropping his limbs, shaking his head at his friend. "I'm sorry." Luka swiftly wraps his arms around him. "I'm so sorry." But we can barely hear it.

"It's not your fault, Jess, we came voluntarily to help you. None of this is your fault." Luka closes his eyes and leans his head onto Jess'. "So don't apologise. *We're with you.*" I glance at Draven leaning on a sleeping Ambrosia, whilst Vincent minds his own business and stares into the darkness of the hallway. I then look at Violet who's watching the entire thing with curved brows and thinned lips.

"You okay?" I ask quietly, nudging her back into reality. She briefly nods, tightening her grip on my hand.

"It's just a sad world, isn't it?" She looks up at me. "The broken people keep getting stitched back together, only to be torn apart again," she says solemnly and looks back at the two boys holding each other closely, whispering in low breaths. "We didn't deserve what happened to us," she points at her chest, "they certainly didn't deserve it either." She points at the two boys. "Even they didn't," she nods towards the Royals and Nobles. "And yet we're the ones who get punished for something that's not in our control."

"What are we being punished for?" She shrugs her shoulders, and leans her head on the wall behind her.

"For something Selene's done I assume? Or maybe the wrong doings of mankind in general. I don't think anyone deserves anything that's happening right now. I mean, Jade has her own reasons, and I guess maybe even Thena does too. Vincent did, so what's the difference?"

"Jade's killed our queen, and she's taking this city for herself."

"It's like karma is deciding who gets to pay for whose actions." She drops her head to my shoulder and I snuggle into her. "It's a cruel world for broken people." She drops her voice into a whisper, and I feel her every word, cutting straight through my heart.

Suddenly, we hear several footsteps stomping back down towards us, and Jess and Luka sit up, leaning forward and they look out the cell.

"We bear gifts!" One of them laughs.

Jess gasps when Oskar comes into sight. Luka stops breathing entirely when he lays eyes on Savannah, both unconscious, both injured and both in the arms of guards. Jess and Luka leap to their feet, but one of the guards opens the cell door in both of their faces, forcing them to stagger back. First, Oskar's thrown in and Jess swiftly grabs his arm, glaring daggers at the guards.

"I said not to touch them, *demons*." But he doesn't do anything about his harsh choice of words, instead tears leak out of his eyes, as he lays Oskar down on the floor in the corner closest to us. "Oskar?" he weeps a little, checking his pulse first.

When Luka lunges to grab Savannah from the guard, the one without anyone in his arms slams him into the wall, and he cries out in pain. Jess looks up with wide eyes, but I'm quicker on my feet.

"Jack!" Violet hisses. I make my way over, pulling the guard harshly with his clothes, forcing him to let go of the shaken boy who falls to the floor in a trembling heap, eyes glued to Savannah. I suspect he's having a panic attack, so I throw the guard onto Vincent's side and past the door, hearing a slam of the iron bars.

"Stay down. Just breathe," I tell Luka, glancing at him, and then at Savannah, broken in the other guards arms. He merely grunts in amusement at the other grown man having a fit about being thrown around, and drops Savannah, and walks away.

Luka shrieks, "Sav!"

I catch her in my arms, and I pull her back up as if she's standing. I lift her into my arms, feeling a shock of blood on my neck from the side of her head. I widen my eyes, staring at her state, still breathing, flickering and heavy eyelids, and strands of hair stained red. Her lips tremble and her nose scrunches up. I quickly turn around to slowly lower her in front of Luka who takes her from my arms, and strokes her hair out from her hair. His panic only gets worse when seeing the dried blood.

"She'll be fine," I quickly say, and he looks up at me.

"In my back right pocket there's bandages. Could you get them for me please?" He shakes and I nod, kneeling down on the other side of Savannah, reaching for his pocket, because he doesn't want to let go of her. I pull out a roll of bandages. He weakly smiles at me. "Thank you." I nod back, and pass them to him.

"Do you need any help?" He shakes his head.

"No, thank you." I stand back up, looking over at Jess cradling Oskar, whispering something to him, and I walk back to Violet, minding my own business. She shakes her head.

"You do worry me sometimes."

"What did I do now?" I ask, amused.

"Jumping up to do something reckless again."

"You shouldn't be surprised at this point." She rolls her eyes and smiles.

"I suppose." She leans forward and kisses my lips, soft and slow.

Soon enough, both Savannah and Oskar wake up in the arms of their soulmates.

The two species are together here. vampire and human, and we're not ripping each other's throats out. That's gotta mean something, right? That perhaps not all vampires are monsters, and not all humans are savages? We started out in different stories, and we ended up here in the same cell, in the same place, at the same time. I can only hope Achillea's resting somewhere safe, Zack isn't working his mind into madness, and Sierra isn't crying over missing her big brother again.

Such different people are in this cell together. But somehow there's an understanding between us all, that perhaps we truly are in this together.

Time passes, and I'm not sure how long it's been, but I turn my head just in time to witness Oskar leaning forward to kiss Jess.

Ali Mitchell

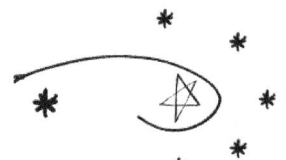

~Ultimo~

$\mathcal{J}ess$

28th November

I shouldn't have let them come.

I understand they have their own reasons for why they follow, but they should know how to be *without* a monster like me in their small group.

I shiver silently on the ground with Oskar close to me, snoozing to himself. I understand *he* has his reasons, but when he held my hand on the surface when I saw my sister in danger – I knew I had made a grave mistake. They were in that same danger Sierra was in. It's my fault if anything happens to them. *To him.*

Don't let him die.

I glance over at Luka waking Savannah up. She springs to life, and he wraps his arms around her as quickly as he can. Luka cries. Savannah shakes, and I look back at Oskar.

My lips tremble at his unconscious state. *What have I done?*

I move his head to be on my lap, running fingers through his thick, scruffy hair, caught in its tangles. He twitches and grimaces, and my heart jumps.

"Oskar?" I ask, as if he'd reply. "Please wake up. Wake up so you can tell me how to help you." He stirs and I hold him closer, head propped against my arm now, leaning my head on his, as I whisper into his ear, "*My love* – I need to know you're okay–" He stirs.

His eyes flutter open for a millisecond, and I lift my head from his. He finally focuses on me after a few blinks. My breath disappears from beneath me. His chest rises and falls in time with mine, and his lips part, glancing around us, realising we're not home. We're not safe.

And yet, when his pearly brown eyes meet mine once again, he somehow finds the strength to scoff. "Hello, darling," he says, amused by what's unfolding, and I shake my head, heart hammering in my chest at the sound of his voice.

"I'm glad you're awake," I murmur. I slump down, posture suffering for it as I close my eyes, sighing in relief. I loosen my grip on him but he seems fine for a moment more, staring up at the cave caging us. I find myself glancing over at Jack who's holding onto Violet, and then even Vincent in the corner, whose head lays on Draven's and when he notices me, he doesn't bother grinning like a lunatic. He frowns, and closes his eyes. I quickly look back at Oskar. "I was so worried," I murmur, like I'm only just realising he's actually *breathing* again.

He turns to look at me, and when he sits up, he's inches away from my face.

"Hey," he says, "I'm perfectly okay, Jess, I've still got some energy." And then he *smiles*. Even at a time like this. I melt into a slimy mess on the ground. I scoff, shaking my head in disbelief, and I look away. "What is it?"

"How on earth are you smiling?" I exclaim. He starts chuckling to himself, moving from my lap so the weight isn't all on my left knee. "How? I don't know how you do it." I gaze into his eyes, and I freeze into the ground itself, moulding myself back into a solid form again. He smirks even more, and looks back at Luka and Savannah, talking in low voices, still holding each other, I assume. He shifts to be sat in front of me, stretching his arms and my eyes glaze over, staring into the void.

What if they never came to help? Would things have played out differently? And would it have been worse?

Oskar catches me staring, but I don't look away. He looks back over to Savannah. "Is she okay?"

"I think so. She hasn't been awake long, and she's spent all of that time with Luka."

"I suppose we didn't get very far then."

"What do you mean?"

"Me and Savannah tried to come save you guys, but we got side tracked, clearly." He shrugs his shoulders, picking at something on his shoes. "It's fine. At least we're here with you guys."

"I'm not sure that's much better," I say, and when he looks back up to me, locking his eyes onto mine. I'm completely losing myself in the way he gazes at me. With such sincerity. The way he makes me feel safe in this fucked up world is...it should be impossible, shouldn't it? Safety is something I shouldn't allow myself to feel, because I'm never *truly* safe. And it's horrible. The sense of unease with every turn, every action. The doubt. The hesitation. And yet I've let myself feel at peace around Oskar, like he's always let me be. I suddenly lose him when he shifts his entire body to face mine, knees touching. His pupils dilate.

He's beautifully breathtaking.

"Jess, are you okay?" he asks softly, tilting his head at me, continuing to stare. I swallow a lump in my throat, and I hang my head low, blinking back several tears.

I remind myself who I'm talking to, *and then suddenly everything crashes down on me all at once.*

I have worn a mask since I was turned into one of these monsters. Or perhaps it was when I truly learnt what this world held. Secrets I only could've imagined in fantasies. I've refused to let my guard down since, not even when I was alone, because I never felt like I *was* alone. I was scared of not being lonely in those moments of solitude.

I have worn this mask for what feels like forever. And I haven't taken it off since. And it's beginning to suffocate me.

But today, I open my mouth to speak simple lies I've told a thousand times before, but I cannot bring myself to do so. I don't want to go another day with this facade.

"I'm tired," I say.

"Tired?" He purses his lips together, and he's finally not smiling. He finds my hands above our laps, and my heart flips inside my heavy chest. *Warm to the touch, and safe.* I let myself drop my stare to them, intertwined, his thumb circling my rough skin.

I bring both of my eyes back to meet his, and I shake when I exhale.

Tomorrow is not guaranteed, and I've learnt this in an incredibly difficult way. How one day I was in my living room with my parents, and the next I knew, I was chasing after my sister, screaming, taken from the safety of our home.

One day Oskar was there. Then he disappeared.

One day I had a best friend. And the next I didn't.

I've admired Oskar's every move, always too scared to take a step further. From when I first heard him sing, to him humming in his bedroom with the curtains drawn and his speaker blaring. When he first asked about my eczema. When my heart jumped because no one ever asks about it, to when he first brought me a batch of creams he believed could help. With him, the 'little' things everyday people would brush over, and think nothing of, would make my day, everyday.

He would smile at me when I couldn't see the sunlight, and I'd thank fate for his existence in those dark times, because he made me feel okay.

But in this moment, if you told me I would die in an hour, half an hour or even in five goddamned minutes, I'd tell you I had one regret. That I didn't try to do more with Oskar, my world, my everything. I'd cry on your shoulder, and beg for another day so I could tell him how everything he does lights up my eyes, and sets fire to my being.

I have lived everyday fearing for my life since my sister was stolen away. I have spent every night, questioning whether I would ever be able to see his face again, and now that I'm drinking in every part of him, imprinting his features in my mind so that's the last thing I'll see if I die in an hour's time. I'd be a fool not to take a risk.

Tomorrow is dangerous. The future is uncertain. And it's not guaranteed.

So I say, "Oskar," a knot in my stomach, my heart in my throat. I glance at his lips, then at the natural curls of his hair, then to his perfect blossoming brown eyes. His sweetest sincerest eyes. He tightens his grip on my hands. And he waits silently for my next question. "May I kiss you?" I can barely whisper it, but it's enough.

His face splits into a grin. He begins to edge his way closer to my face. Moments away.

Until his breaths on my skin, goosebumps spread all up my arms and legs. The hair on the back of my neck stands up, and with the rate my heart is going, I fear I really will die in five minutes from combustion.

He closes his eyes, and keeps on smiling brightly, as he presses his lips clumsily onto mine.

The tears I tried to push back resurface, slowly sliding down my cheeks, pressing into Oskar's skin as well. *And* he's a good kisser. This moment is perfect. And I finally smile. Because I'm kissing the boy of my dreams. I'm kissing the boy who's been there since the beginning.

I'm home.

Finally.

He takes a quick breath, breaking us apart, before laying one of his hands on my rosy cheeks, pulling me even closer. He flicks his eyes between both of mine, and says,

"Of course you may kiss me," he chuckles, and waits for me to do the same before kissing me again. He spreads his hand to the back of my nape, inviting me to bathe in not only my own warmth, but his as well. I don't want to be my own person. I want to be as close to him as possible.

And it feels- he feels- so *good.* So real. So perfect. We fit together effortlessly. I find myself thinking, *somehow* fighting to live another day when at moments I'd much rather have died – is all worth it just for right now. I have never in my life felt as loved by him as I do right now.

Oskar and I have lost countless battles, and I won't deny that. We've fallen down rabbit holes, tried to cross broken bridges, and fallen so far we couldn't see the light at the end of the tunnel. And even after all this time apart, even after all those painful moments, watching death take over, we've still ended up here, in the same place, at the same time. And I silently pray to never be apart from him for as long as we endured ever again, because to put it bluntly, I don't think I'd make it next time around.

Because it will always be him. The sun from the bottom of the ocean breaking through when I'm drowning. The light at the end of the tunnel. My final destination.

He always has been-- my home.

Deep kisses fill our mouths. I hold him, and he holds me.

Please don't let me go. I can't bear the cold.

"Jess! Move!" Jack shrieks, breaking the comfortable silence. We whip our eyes open, looking behind us at a guard walking into our cell, directly towards me. I gasp as they grab me by the scruff of the neck, and heave me to my feet, but Jack is already behind them, holding them in a headlock. I drop to the floor.

"No!" Oskar is breathless beside me, pulling me closer to him, but I'm trying to grasp my mind on reality. What's happening? The guard punches Jack's side, and Violet cries out as he folds to the floor, holding his stomach, grimacing in pain. The guard marches towards me again.

"Sorry to ruin your little reunion!" Thena? She pulls me up by the shoulder, and tears burn my eyes, paralysed in fear whilst Oskar pulls my arm, standing up, holding on so tightly it burns. "Queen Jade needs your audience." I shake my head over and over again.

"No, no, no, no, no! I'm not going back!" I scream, and start kicking in fury. Oskar doesn't let go. She starts dragging me away by my collar. "No!" I shriek. I begin to sob.

I'm pathetic again.

Luka stands abruptly, leaving Savannah on the floor, and hurries over, trying to loosen Thena's grip, whilst my free hand holds onto the cell bars. "Oskar!" I scream, and he shakes his head. Thena whips out her hand, and crashes it down straight for Luka's neck, and he crashes into the bars, falling onto the floor in a heap of dizziness. He shakes his head several times, but can't lift himself up again. Savannah rushes to his side.

"Luka—" She stares at me with wide eyes. "Jess!" And she tries to reach for me. I flick my eyes back to Oskar but I know Thena targets him next.

No, not my Oskar.

So I let go of Oskar, and pull myself from his grip. I elbow Thena's mouth to stay away from him which makes her stagger, unexpected, and so she's out of the cell. But she brings me with her, cackling, slamming the cell door shut. Cutting me off from my only friends in this world.

"Wait!" Oskar exclaims, cheeks drenched in tears, and I want nothing more to clear them away. I lunge forward, my final attempt to break free whilst he smashes into the cell bars. Thena tightens her grip on my collar, choking me and starts to walk down the hallway, talking about precious Selene Jade.

Oskar reaches for me.

He's right there. *He's right there*! So, I reach for him too.

I can't lose him. I can't be left alone again!

Our fingers touch, but it's not enough.

It's never enough.

The moments stolen from me. How can it be so easily swept away? The last thing I see of him is his tear stained cheeks. The last thing I hear escaping his lips is a scream. A shriek.

A cry for help.

It's my name.

"Jess!"

Jess ✦

28th November

I try staying level-headed, but the ghost of Oskar's lips on my own is still on my mind. I've given up shouting, and thrashing my hands around in a temper. I know that's not getting me anywhere. I make a note of my whereabouts, and it seems the other cells with humans encaged are next door to the cell I was previously in, down the hallway. I've created a mental map of how to get there, and how to get out for my next opportunity. Which I fear could be much longer than I had anticipated.

I wipe the tears from my cheeks.

I purse my lips, a door catching my knee as it closes, ripping my skin. I grit my teeth, the sting *almost* unbearable, and with one of my free hands, I bend down to itch it – just for a moment – but that's when Thena choses to climb up some stairs. I try walking backwards to help with the pain in my skin, but it hurts moving where I hit it, because I have no cream. And I haven't applied any in...days. It's sandpaper against my clothes.

I would ask for her to be kinder, but I know how that's going to go, so there's no point. I grin and bear it.

Thena drags me into a massive hall with dark, rustic red carpets leading in front of her. I turn my head to gaze at the dust covered shelves, candle sticks, paintings, lamps, chairs, tables, everything. This place hasn't been touched in years. Some of the candles attached to the walls are lit, the wax is melting away quickly, and the ceiling's high with a chandelier dangling down. This place would be beautiful if it were cleaned every so often. Then at the very top of the roof are wooden engraved of what I thought were mythical creatures – like what you see on the surface in old buildings. But the closer I look, I realise that those 'creatures' are in fact humans.

I look down at the dark faded rug leading to the front of the room. Golden lining at the very edge of the carpet. When this hall wasn't faded, I think it was beautiful.

But under the circumstances, that's all the admiration I can afford to give. Thena throws me in front of her feet before walking off and beside the doors, guarding my escape routes. I cough and splutter dust, and I hold my neck. My skin is burning where her grip was so tight. *Give me a break.*

Gasping for air, I lift my head up to see Selene Jade in a long, shimmering green dress reaching the floor, a thin piece of fabric above it like a protected layer. Her top half is skin tight, whilst below her waist is free falled, covering her heels, sitting on a glittering and majestic silver throne. She looks down on me, as if I'm her peasant, and she truly is a Queen. She holds the arms of her throne tightly, curling her lips, craning her head down all of a sudden. Her wavy long paper hair's tied into french braids, which fall either side of her ears, reaching past her breasts, and her earlobes glitter, pierced silver earrings attached with small silver hoops.

A silver crown encrusted with green metallic leaves sit on a table beside her seat.

Who does she think she is? I may not care for the vampires, but Achillea was the closest person they had to a Queen. And although I disagreed with her methods, she was an excellent leader. If Selene has taken over, and Ambrosia was the only one out of the two cousins in the cell, I can only assume Achillea is no longer with us, and I suspect Selene Jade's the reason for it.

"Jess, correct?" Her voice is like silk. Soft, slow and gentle.

"What's it to you?"

"You're the most recent vampire to join the ranks?" she begins. Matthew's face momentarily flashes inside my mind.

"No," I say with confidence, knowing he's a burning star like Piper now. "But the other perished."

"Oh, how unfortunate." She brushes it off. She doesn't care. I clench my hands into fists. *Watch your choice of words, I might not control my actions if you say a word against my best friend.* "Since you're the most recent, I assume you were human not so long ago?" She leans forward on her seat, a small but wicked grin playing on her lips. "I need your help." Oh god, this can't go well.

"Excuse me?"

"Come now." She leans back, and lifts her hands, as if it's obvious what she's implying. She thinks I'm still on her side? "If we're planning to take over a few human cities here and there, we need to know gritty details about them!"

"There are actual humans here that you have hostage. Why don't you ask them? I'm sure if you hold a dagger to their throat, they'd be more than willing to cooperate, or in fact, just ask me the questions! I'm right here, in your grip, I've got nowhere else to be!" Her expression sours as if she's bitten into a sweet she despises.

"Oh, no, no, no, no, no." She shakes her head, chuckling to herself. "They've been through enough." What? *Will she set them free?* "Besides. I need them for something much more important." My heart drops. "Well?" She stands up, her dress moving with her, walking down one of her tiny steps that make her seem higher than all. "Will you be my personal spy amongst them all?"

I could play along. It would make a good alibi to all vampires here against us. I could work on breaking everyone out. I could plot. I could plan. Or I go against her, and I risk being imprisoned on my own for eternity. I'm still ageing since I have yet to taste human blood. I might go insane. I might descend into madness.

There's an obvious choice here. And I hate it.

She floats down on light feet, and stands in front of me. She kneels down, smiles and grips my chin harshly, jerking my head up to meet her snake-like eyes. They pierce through my skull.

"Remember," she says, dropping her voice lower, cocking her head to one side. "I have all your friends under my power. One wrong move," she starts whispering, "and I could kill them." I swallow hard, fighting back violent shakes. She glares into my soul. "And I don't mind spilling more blood on my soul." She pushes me off from her, and I smack my palms onto the floor with a crash, gritting my teeth.

I find my mask again. And screw it in place.

"Well," she stands back up, and whilst I'm trying to find the strength to get up, she looms over me, and pushes one of her dark forest green heels into my back. I grimace. "Are you with me, or not?"

"With you." *Until I figure out a better option.*

"Good choice." She turns back around, lifting the weight from my body, but I don't find the strength to sit up. I know she's taken a seat at her throne. I know she's watching me like a hawk. And I know what I'm doing is wrong, and I need no one to tell me. "On the tower you fell from is a simple button. Somewhere below a crumbled amount of bricks. Should you find it, there's a way out. Go. And get more of the vampire army down here. Take a squad, and go to the nearest city. Hide your kind, and find out information about the human's weak spot. Where we can strike." What city does she think is close by? What does she think she's attacking?

"Apologies for the idiotic question." I finally lift myself up. "But what do you mean by weak spots? They're just cities. There's nothing interesting about them. No castles, no mansions. No nothing." That's when she smirks.

"Then attack, and cause a lockdown. And then we take it over. If there's a problem then there's always a solution."

"You have this kingdom. Is that not enough for you?"

"You're the closest thing to a human on our side down here." I'm not on *your* side. "You know how to act like them." *Not anymore.* "You'll fake being attacked by one. You'll make a scene. And then we take the city, because just down here is not enough for what they've done to us," she orders. "They'll pay for years of mistreatment. Humanity's not kind, it is not beautiful and it certainly is not the 'good' in this world. They need to be rid of the planet entirely."

"What about my—" *family.*

"Depending on your actions," she spits. "I may spare your humans, but only if you help." Humanity, or my family. "You'll return in three weeks. Or else your precious Oskar." She slowly runs a finger along her neck, and smiles, "Will pay for your mistakes." I widen my eyes, heart dropping in my stomach. "We deserve to be feared, and I've waited long enough for my revenge." She grins, cackling deep within her stomach. "And now!" Her eyes are wide, looking at Thena who's seemed to have emerged out of nowhere, "They're the ones who're going to be the outcasts, to make way for the *Nosferatu Age!*"

Vampire Age? She slowly turns her head to look at me, and flicks her wrist.

"Off you go," she smirks. "Thena, will you do me the honour?" Thena walks out, and past the table, directly towards me, grabbing my neck, baring her teeth, showing her tiny fangs.

"With pleasure, Your Highness."

Jess ✦

28th November

Three weeks.

She's tossed me out of her hall. She's left me to my own devices, *It's up to me now, she said.*

She's given me three weeks to cause a *lockdown* in the closest possible city. To create moral panic. I have three weeks to get the vampire army on my side.

I have less than twenty-one days to figure out how to save both the world and my family. Oskar's life is on the line. Savannah's. Luka's. Maybe even Jack and Violet, although she might have her own plan for them. I clench my fists, stopping before the exit of this castle and outside the perimeter.

I can't run. I can't hide. And I can't save the people I love. But I came for my sister, and guards are passing me with little less than a glance. Hope leaps onto my chest, and grabs my heart. I can save my sister. I can hug her. I can hold her. I can keep her from harm's way. I turn around, and march back, twisting and turning back to the dungeons. I could warn them about what I have to do. I can tell them to wait.

I speed up as I turn a sharp corner and down the familiar hallway to my friends' cells, and tears brim to my eyes, heart hammering in my chest when I near them.

"Jess?" Oskar's voice rises and falls. Hearing his breathing shakes my world. I grip the bars, pulling me to a stop as I peer into the cell of broken people. "Jess!" Oskar gasps, leaps to his feet and hurries over whilst Luka and Savannah stand from where they are, still in the corner. Oskar holds my hands around the bars, and his eyes glisten. "What's—"

"I have to be quick. Jade is sending me up to the surface to wreak havoc on cities close by. She's saying I need to create fear in the humans in three weeks, making a lockdown or whatever. If I don't, she'll—" I trail off shaking my head with my breathing hurrying. "I need to be quick," I repeat. "I'm not going to do what she says." Everyone's eyes widens.

323

"Jess, you'll be in danger if you don't—" Sav starts.

"No, *you* will be in danger." I stare at her, and her jaw drops ajar.

"Which is why I'm taking Sierra, and meeting Zack to think of a way out of this. More vampires will be making their way down here, so be wary. But," I look into Oskar's pearly brown eyes. "I'm not leaving you forever. I'm coming back. If I stay, we'll *all* die. If I go and - and think of something, we have a chance of getting out alive. *All of us.*" I glance at Luka who squeezes his hand through the bars, and lays it on my shoulder to calm my shaking, whilst Savannah slides her palm through to hold my hand. Both of them smile.

"We trust you," Luka says.

"If anyone can do it, it'd be you," Savannah says.

"What? Save humanity?" I joke breathlessly, but she doesn't laugh. No one does. Because that's what it feels like I'm doing. Saving it all. Or perhaps I'm being dramatic. I lock onto Oskar's eyes again.

He lays one of his hands on my cheek, brushing that tear away and he holds me.

"I don't—" I choke on my own words, squinting to keep back emotions. "I don't want to leave you all again." The anxiety of unsaid words between me and my Oskar melts away, because I finally have the courage to say it all. So it keeps spilling. "I really don't know how I can do it again, and what if I can't?" I lean my forehead on the bars, closing my eyes. *Don't let me go.* "What if I really don't make it this time around?"

"Hey, eyes up, mister!" he says so sternly it shocks me to my core and leaves me paralysed. "I won't have you talking that way about yourself!"

"Oskar—"

"You'll go up to the surface. You'll stay with Zack and Sierra. You'll find a way around this. And there's no immediate rush. Even if you're down here on the 21st day, I don't care. We will wait for you. *I* will wait for you." He brushes some of my hair behind my ear and somehow, even through all this, he smiles. "You will do it all because you simply can. I believe in you Jess, and now, quite literally, go save the world!" I let out a trembling breath. He takes back his hand, kisses his fingers, and then lays them on my lips. "And take care of yourself, okay?" He squeezes both of my hands again. "For me." *For Oskar.*

My heart breaks just a little more when I nod.

"Okay," I whisper, sniffing pathetically. I look at Luka who shakes my shoulders with a sad smile, giving me hope.

"We love you," he says, "you'll be okay." Savannah nods beside him and they both let go of me to hold each other.

"Exactly," she says quietly. "Good luck, and stay safe."

"You too," I say, then flick my eyes back onto Oskar, and he chuckles a little, shaking his head.

"I wish I could kiss you again." I blush bright red at his words. "But I suppose this way, you just owe me one, so you *have* to come back."

"I suppose so," I say. *I'm running out of time.* "I'll see you in three weeks."

"We'll see you in three weeks," he echos, and I let his hands go, eyes lingering on him a moment more, stepping back. I'd do anything for him to join me. But there's no way around it. I take a deep breath, nodding towards my family. All three of them standing in a line together.

"We'll miss you," Savannah barely whispers. Luka barely smiles.

"Say hi to Zack for me."

"Of course," I tell him, and I look at Oskar.

Say something, I think, but he's already told me everything he needs to. "I'll see you all soon." I begin to walk down the hallway, turning into a quick jog.

And I swear I heard Oskar whisper into the air around us, *"I love you more than words could tell,"* but I couldn't be sure. So I don't turn back.

I'm going to protect my sister from danger. Once and for all.

Selene Jade

28th November

When I was younger, I dreamt of home.

My hundreds of notebooks from over the years were full of drawings, scrawls of plans, ideas, and somehow, it led to a scene a little like this.

Sitting on a throne fit for a queen. And in this case, I'm the Queen in question.

For years before, I'd tell myself I deserved any awful thing that happened to me. If I was pushed into the mud, I'd say, 'I'm sorry for getting in the way'. If I was told no food for dinner, I apologised for being a nuisance. And the cycle went like that.

Did I mention? This was all because I had these fangs. And as the years went by, my ears began to point upwards. I was named the *freak* of the village. My parents were never the same after what *Vincent* did to me. But after I discovered this new power, I never resented him for it, I rejoiced.

I became the monster your parents told you about. The one hiding under your bed. The one hidden in the shadows – the monster that chases you when you turn your light off.

It passed down from generation to generation, adapting into many many different twists. Once came the story about Dracula. After, if people saw me, they'd call me his daughter.

But now, your kids, your grandchildren, your own blood will see that the real monsters in this world were humans all along. Telling those legends as mere bedtime stories? What was going through your minds when you had that smart idea, to scare your children when they should sleep peacefully in a deep slumber? Now, *that* is truly monstrous when really, the darkness and the shadows in corners, lurking where the light never sees, are your *friend*. You will learn this one way, or another. Whether through heartbreak, shattered pieces of your soul, or because of loneliness drowning your lungs. Don't resist. There's no point.

They were my best friends for centuries. Why can't they be yours?

I wanted to prove this idea that monsters were humans at age fourteen. At that point in my life, I was still ageing like I was normal. I had no idea what kind of side effects I would acquire.

I began showing demonic signs at age twenty-three. All the water in the world could not quench my abrupt thirst. I would drink from lakes, rivers, puddles, no matter how dirty, because I was so desperate, but I was never able to control my thirst. That's when I gave up on filing my teeth down. That's when my instincts took over.

I was twenty-four when I sipped my first drop of human blood. And, oh, it was addicting. I criticise myself upon why I had never tried it before.

I was thirty when I realised I wasn't ageing. And that I still looked twenty-four.

I found a job, posing as a mute so I never needed to show my teeth. I discovered where prisoners were held. I snuck, I hid and I checked the listing everyday to see if the demons who changed me were here. Little did I know, they were always there. They were always right under my nose. The names never changed. Decades past. A century.

I was 118 when I posed as a guard to explore the dungeons, trying to find the demons. I was 119 when I unintentionally used a power of mine that I never knew I had. I wipe someone's memory in the prison. An officer. Days later, he let the demons out of a high security cell, claiming he never knew nor remembered why they were in there to begin with. I wasn't strong enough to strike them then, so I held back. I watched like a hawk.

I changed my last name to match my identity. *Selene Jade. Green Moon. Time. That's all I need.*

That's all I ever needed.

I was in my 3rd century when I met Thena. I welcomed her into the small camp I created outside Hillark. Thena and I worked together to spy on the vampire army which was a few towns away. One clan hid in a small mansion in the forest. Thena talked them into being our inside voice. It took a hundred years to lure a solid amount of numbers I was comfortable with for this uprising. I wanted the power. I wanted the humans to suffer.

I yearned to be feared.

Approximately 400 years later, it all fell into place.

On the day I turned into a vampire, I watched one of Achillea's allies fall. I watched their blood strike the ground, and an entrance crumbled open. The entrance of the city opened up to me. I knew how to get in. But it seemed I was the only one who remembered.

Achillea didn't. Naturally, I took advantage of that. She never asked how I knew it all so well. She was too desperate to seek answers, after all. I knew what sacrifice needed to be made.

Since I was a little girl, I have dreamt of sitting upon my very own throne, in my own magnificent hall, with a crown glittering beside me at my fingertips.

Not so far out of reach now.

"When do you want to be crowned, my liege?" Thena smiles happily, bowing before me. I merely smirk, dancing along my lips.

"When the right audience has arrived."

Selene Jade

28th November

All those months ago, we believed that Jess would be the most problematic. He was taken from his family, his sister imprisoned, friends assumed dead in an infested town. I assumed the darkness inside him would take over sooner rather than later, and yet, when he was in front of us, I saw hope in his eyes for a brighter day. He's practically human still. I wonder what he truly thinks of himself buried behind the hope that flickered in his eyes.

I'm curious as to what I'm able to twist his mind into, to allow the darkness and shadows to fully engulf him, and take over. I always need more numbers. And he would be a powerful addition.

Thena slams the door behind Jess' back, and she quickly erupts into laughter, holding onto her stomach, as she faces me.

"Oh, he definitely hates me now, Selene, and I am *loving* it!" She drags out the 'o' in loving.

"He hated you before, Thena." I smirk, enjoying seeing her beam with joy. The spark in her voice has returned after quite some years. It's familiar. When I found her on the streets, she was on the edge. One more push, and she wouldn't have been here anymore. I'm just glad she held on long enough for me to be able to find her. It's for broken people like her that I want to destroy the world for.

"If he didn't before, then he definitely does now. I caught him kissing Oskar!" It was clear they had feelings for each other, I'm shocked she's even bringing it up. "And I dragged him away from him! They most likely wanted more time. I guess that would've been nice but oh well!"

She often talks about how *she* wanted more time decades ago. So I gave her immorality with a catch. She was more than thankful, and grateful, sworn to help me for as long as she lives until someone struck her down. She's been loyal ever since, and never anything else.

"Didn't you have a thing for someone?" she abruptly asks. I hesitate.

"I began developing feelings for someone, yes," I say, smiling a little more, leaning on the edge of my throne. "I mentioned it, didn't I?" She nods. "Well, they were very faint since vampires don't have great emotional regularity. Besides, it's easy to shut down romantic feelings for someone who's going to complicate things that have been planned for years in advance of meeting them." Her eyes flicker across the room.

"You never told me who."

"Achillea." Thena's jaw practically drops open, snapping her gaze back onto mine.

"No. Way. But you killed her – you *killed* the woman you—"

"As I said, it's easy to turn off romantic feelings for me, and before you say it, I didn't love her. I've waited over 400 years for this moment. I wasn't about to let my feelings get in the way of that." But even as I speak the truth out, my chest clenches. It's my dress. It mustn't be anything else. Not possible.

It meant nothing. Ignore it.

"Wow, you really are dedicated then. Strong." In this cruel world, you can't be anything *but* strong. Or else you get trodden on.

"I promised us a city. Don't we have it at our fingertips?" I lean forward, and she nods.

"Yeah, we have!" She marches over in front of me, and she leans over. She bows her head, almost hitting mine, so I lean back against my silvery throne. "Thank you for taking that sacrifice. For us! It'll be worth it, I promise." I smile a little.

"No need to be so dramatic, Thena," I say simply. "No need to bow, it's only me, and that'll never change. I'm a friend—"

"Best friend," she corrects, and stands up straight, laughing and pointing her finger at me. "Best friend."

"Best friend, then. To everyone else, I'm their Queen."

"And a glorious Queen you shall be!"

Selene Jade

The Beginning

The beginning
    The future starts today.
    The Jade reign begins.

If I truly were the villain of this story, like so many have told me, then why have I won? Because don't all *heroes* win at the end of a fairy tale? But I don't see a hero in sight. Only I sit on this throne. So surely this means, what I've done was for the good of the world?

    And don't worry, darling, there is always more to come.

~*Fin*~

Epilogue

Jess and Sierra had never seen the stars.

This wasn't because they were trapped in an underground city, not because they were imprisoned in an old village, and it certainly wasn't because they were the mistakes of the world. This was because they're lives were so hectic, so chaotic, so busy, that they never had the time to just stop. And look up.

But tonight, as Jess holds his little sister's hand in his own, and as they're shot back up onto the earth's surface, the first thing they lay their eyes on, are the breathtaking sea of stars in the deep night sky.

Now, they had not *never* seen the stars. But it felt like it when they saw them again after what felt like so long. With Sierra imprisoned for the past month and a half, and with Jess busying himself with whatever he could find. The night was far too dangerous, the stars felt so far. So lost upon their minds they had no need to look up. That is, until today.

Because as they step onto the grass, Jess' eyes brim with tears. Before his mind can take him some place else though, he quickly turns, picks Sierra up into his arms, and begins to sprint through the meadow. Skipping past holes and moulds, small dips and mounds, through the long grass reaching his torso. He doesn't let himself breathe, so Sierra clings onto him tighter, talking to him in a quiet, but incredibly distant voice trying to grab his attention. She wasn't getting very far, until he hears her weeping in his arms, fresh tears on his shoulder.

"I want Mummy, I want Daddy," she cries into the night.

Jess slows down, and simply holds her closer to his body, as he lets her silently cry her eyes out into his clothes. He falls to his knees. And weeps a story of his own.

He closes his eyes, hugging his sister tight in comfort and closure, and he sobs.

He cries for his mother and father. He cries for his dear Matthew, and he cries for his sweet, sweet considerate Oskar. He weeps for his family stuck in the cells below his very feet. He weeps for the town's innocence, the souls lost too soon, and the ones still trapped.

He sobs for the world. A world he can't save.

He had lost so much. His heart was struggling. His chest was crumbling. And his shoulders were being crushed by the weight the universe has placed upon him. All he wanted was his sister back. And now he has her back, he'll never let her go.

Eventually, Jess opens his eyes again, and finds himself gazing up into the beautiful night sky. At the mesmerising stars twinkling above. Evolving around them as if he never really mattered to begin with.

He spots the brightest star beside the moon and finds himself smiling at the memory of Oskar. He exhales shakily, silently praying that wasn't the last time he'd feel Oskar's lips upon his own. He silently prayed he would lay his eyes on him once again, and he'd hear his sweet melody of a voice another day.

But as he had discovered, tomorrow's not guaranteed, and with death threats freshly hung over, not only *his* head, but his *family's* as well, he couldn't afford to admire the little things like the stars, and yet he sat there still. Wasting away through time under the sky that made his insides shrink, and himself feel so small in an ever changing world.

No, tomorrow's not guaranteed. And no, he would not give up. There'll be a way around this, and Jess will find it. He'll see them again, because if there truly was no hope, then he wouldn't have left them to begin with. So with Sierra standing beside him, out of his arms, but still in his grip, he stands up straight, eyes glued to the stars prickling out of the darkness.

He's the one who got out. So, he's the one who'll save them this time.

He'll come back even stronger to fight for his family when they need him most. And they'll wait. Rotting away in a godforsaken cell in the underground lost city.

No matter what the price of getting them out alive will be, he'll do it. Without hesitation. Even if that means welcoming death with open arms.

He turns around, glancing at the mountain, the dent that appeared out of nowhere, the entrance to the city.

"I'll come back for you all," he whispers, gazing back up to the night sky's darkness, as a shooting star flies overhead. "I swear it."

And with one step in front of the other, he makes his way back to his hometown, to begin the battle of saving humanity from these monsters.

A monster he had become.

Acknowledgements

I made it.

Before I continue my little tangent on the most amazing people in the whole wide world - I want to thank *YOU* first! Whether you're a friend of mine, a family member or a complete stranger, whether you loved or hated this novel, I want to thank *you* for picking up this book, clicking on the cover thinking it looks pretty neat, ***and giving me and it a chance.*** I created Hillark and these characters and stories with the sole purpose of reaching out to those who feel a little alone - because that's how I found this passion of mine. I wanted to let someone seek some comfort through these broken words and soon familiar pages *because that's why I began writing.* I found a book at age eleven, and I fell in love with the stories and the characters this author wrote about. I'm very thankful for all the support the author has given me too. I count myself incredibly lucky. After finishing that series, I found myself wanting a world to call my own. So this was born.

So thank you, dearest reader, for giving Hillark a chance and learning these characters' tales. It means a lot to me since this is my debut novel, a start to a very long journey ahead. If you stick around, I hope to see you in the next book, Lost Ruins! You are all welcome home to Hillark *anytime* you need.

Anyhow! Onto the main event ~ *Acknowledgments.*

First and foremost, Jordan. Thank you. Without them, I would've given up already. And I would've been stuck trying to pursue something more... reasonable. A little less risky, let's say. I owe them the universe and more. So thank you. You are the light in my life.

Thank you Joe, my Matthew, my brother. I probably wouldn't be writing what I write today if it weren't for him hyping up my crappy romance pieces when I was 15. That was a heck of a time and he shall tell NO ONE what he read back then. But thank you for being there through all the messes that were thrown my way. You held me up.

Thank you to my rose, my sweet considerate Indigo. My cheerleader through the drafts and through the last two or three years. Thank you for joining my journey and being such a big part of it. She was there every step of the way. From being on call with me whilst I received my first draft of the cover, to being a beta reader, to being here with me whilst I read these words when they're finally in my hands. You are everything.

Jordan, Joe, and Indigo, you all deserve the world, the universe and all its stars and secrets.

So I dedicate mine to you. Always. Now. And forever.

Thank you mum and dad for all of your support over the decade of me writing! I didn't think I'd make it this far sometimes so I don't know how you felt, but here we are!

Thank you to my dearest sisters and I am so sorry for all the bookish rants and facts I've shared with you, most of which you never even asked for. I promise to dedicate a book especially to you.

Thank you to my wonderful editor who made incredibly useful and clever comments to help make this manuscript crisp and clean!

Thank you to my many beta readers who helped endlessly with constructive comments of the novel, characters and plot! It truly means a lot! So, thank you Indigo, Lark, Kaycee, Cate, Clay and Ophelia.

Thank you to my wonderful Arc readers, Indigo, Vic, Auggie, Mya and Cate for reviewing my novel!

And now onto the most amazing people ever - (a lot of thank yous, I know but these people deserve these mentions for being with me all these long years) - next, thank you *SO MUCH* Mirella and Annie for creating your own little pieces and planting them into the Hillark universe. These lovely folks helped create Thena and Ambrosia by helping me decide their names, aesthetics and their appearances. And little hidden pieces of their personalities reflect these two I know in real life. Thank you so much for being a supporter. I love you.

I swear, my speech will be finished soon. Hang in there.

Thank you to Ash, Chloe and Skye for seeing Lost City at its earliest and messiest and STILL believing in me to make it here. (Ash, I'm sorry, once again, for your favourite character's death...)

Thank you to my MANY writer friends, supporters and writergram accounts I love and adore who've known about Lost City even back in 2022, Indigo (again), Ruru, Vic, Auggie, Gab, Mya, Paige, Kaedynce, Zippy, Dallas, Alex, Tobei, Abi, Reba, Mere, Vivi, Brooke and Meredith.

(ALMOST THERE, I promise.)

Thank you to Donnell, who may not even noticed but inspired tiny little aspects of Oskar just by being him. I take inspiration from the people around me, and you were and are so much like him. Even before you knew who Oskar was. But thank you for being a cheerleader, a dear friend to me and my mini cheerleader!

A super extra small thank you to Fabio, I know as I'm writing this we haven't known each other ALL that long, but I feel it's right to just say, you celebrating Lost City with me and telling me all about your writing makes my day and makes me smile. So thank you, Fabiolo.

Thank you to a big old group of friends I had back in my secondary school years. Though we may not all talk with each other anymore, you all still have a place in my soul, and always a place in Hillark. The ones who were there when I first began writing seriously. And the first people to be there when Lost City began forming. Zoe, Amber, Isabel, Jordan (again), Shama, Niamh, Marta, Sammy, Mira (again), and Nadia. Thank you. So unbelievably much.

Last but never least, to Zoe. Thank you. For 14 years of friendship. For 14 years of fun. If, by some small chance, you pick up his book, and you read it or skip to the end and read this, I want you to know that you helped create Hillark in its own way too. When I began creating this home at age twelve, I took inspiration from the way it felt to be around you. It's evolved since, but you were an inspiration from the start. I truly felt like I could conquer the world with you.

So thank you.

I hope you all enjoyed my debut novel, Lost City.

Glossary

TIME
The prologue is set in 1662
To date present tense is set in 2037.

PRONUNCIATIONS OF NAMES
Achillea - A-cil-ee-I
Ambrosia - Amb-rose-ee-a
Thena - Th-ee-na
Sierra - See-air-ra

LATIN WORDS TRANSLATED
Supra ~ Above.
Supra terram ~ Land above.
Deorsum ~ Down below.
Hominies ~ Humans.
Nosferatu ~ Vampires.
Arma Vocare ~ Summon weapon.
Deliciae ~ Darling.
Sidera Lucere ~ Stars Alight

'TYPES' OF VAMPIRES
'Alatus' ~ These vampires have wings, summoned by an ability.
'Sanguis Potentia' ~ These vampires need blood to survive, as well as for power in general.
'Intelligentes' ~ These vampires can hold more information than others, and they're more observant, and can see further.
'Sol Sensitivo' ~ These vampires are sensitive to the sun, due to evolution adaptation of being hidden underground for so long. Some can stand it longer than others.

Printed in Great Britain
by Amazon

48458509R00188